London Detective Agency

by Stephanie R. Caffrey

LONDON DETECTIVE AGENCY BOOK ONE
MISTAKEN
IDENTITY
STEPHANIE R. CAFFREY

For Dawn.
Thank you for believing in me.

Acknowledgements

This book was born of a lot of hard work, and many drafts. And a lot of support from many, many people.

First, I would like to thank the amazing Dawn Dowdle. My first agent, and someone who read the first three chapters of this book, and immediately saw the potential in it. Thank you so much for believing in me and my writing. Thank you for being a great agent and friend, and I hope you're somewhere watching as this little book you believed in finally makes its way into the world. I miss you.

To Kelly, Shelly, and everyone at Rowan Prose Publishing, thank you for everything you've done to help *Mistaken Identity* make its way into the world. Everything from your support to the amazing covers, you all have been amazing, and I can't thank you enough.

Sydney, we've been friends for over a decade, and you have read and critiqued everything I've ever written. I appreciate your friendship so much, especially your enthusiasm for my books. I never could have gotten here without you, and I'm so thankful for fandom bringing us together all those years ago.

Louise, my wonderful Brit-Picker, thank you for being so patient with this American and not making fun of me too much when I gave Patrick and James baseball bats at one point. This book would be a whole lot less British without your help.

Sharon, Jamie, and Sarah, I never would have had the courage to put this book out in the world if it hadn't been for you three. Your friendship and encouragement mean more to me than you'll ever know. You're not only my best friends, you're family. And I love you ladies.

Alex, thank you for listening to all my woes while getting this out in the world.

To The Super Awesome Book Club for letting me bounce ideas off you. When you read this book, please be gentle.

To my parents, for always encouraging me to reach for my dreams. Your belief in me kept me going even if others said it could never happen.

My sisters, thank you for being the best, and inspiring a few characters in this book. I'm sure you can figure out who.

Arthur and Beatrice, this book started before you were in this world, but you both have been so patient with Mom while she worked on endless edits. And I thank you for the times you've let me work while I could have been playing with you.

And finally, to Matthew. Thanks for everything. For taking kid duty while I wrote, encouraging me to have this thing of my own outside of being a mom.

For being my romantic lead in this life we share together. Hopefully you can see yourself in my heroes, because the best parts of you are there in the best parts of them. I love you.

CHAPTER 1

EVELYN

Evelyn Stevenson briskly walked through the jetway into the terminal, and almost stopped. Heathrow was no Des Moines airport. The gray walls were all bare, and there was a distinct lack of signs directing her where to go. Crowds of people were bustling here and there, everyone trying to catch their flights, like her. She had never seen so many people in one place before. Toto, she wasn't in Iowa anymore.

Glancing around, she noticed most of the crowd was heading in one direction, so it was probably a safe bet to follow them. They probably knew better than she did. Besides, there should be signs that said where her connecting flight to Athens would be. Right?

Picking up her speed again, she began weaving in and out of the crowd. When Evelyn had booked the flight, with the help of the Iowa State University study abroad office, they had assured her the layover would be plenty long enough. However, they obviously didn't take circling the city for half an hour before landing into account. Nor the fact walking in the airport was akin to salmon swimming upstream.

She hitched her duffel bag up higher on her shoulder. The weight of it dragged her shoulder down, acting as an anchor, slowing her pace through the airport. It was almost enough to make her regret filling it so full of her research for her thesis. Maybe she should have kept some books in her checked bag. Did she honestly think there would be an opportunity to work on her paper before arriving to the dig site in Epidaurus?

As she got closer to her destination, at least Evelyn hoped it was, the denser the crowd became. Despite having to dodge people coming directly at her, she seemed to be making great time, and might actually make her connecting flight. As the optimism of not being stranded in London went through her mind, someone collided headlong into her, causing them both to crash to the hard tile.

"Oi, watch where yer going, mate!"

Evelyn looked up, trying to catch her breath after having the wind knocked out of her, and took in the woman she'd crashed into. Like herself, she had chin-length brown hair and brown eyes that were glaring at her.

Evelyn opened her mouth to apologize, but the woman quickly stood, grabbed her duffel bag, and began running in the direction she'd been heading.

Evelyn shook her head as the woman ran off and shrugged her shoulders before slowly pulling herself up from the ground.

She picked up her bag and began walking toward the transfer station. Shifting the bag on her shoulder, she frowned. That was odd. The bag didn't feel the same as it had before. It was lighter. Significantly lighter. Looking at it, her frown deepened. This wasn't her bag. It was the same brand and model, but Evelyn's was black with purple trim. The one currently in her hand was black with blue trim.

"Fuck," she muttered under her breath. Looking in the direction where she *should* go, and then in the direction the girl had rushed off with her bag, she began weighing her options. Thoughts of all those books and research currently in her bag, she hadn't checked it onto the plane for a reason. Evelyn needed what all was in there, and if that woman realized she had the wrong bag, she'd probably turn it in to this terminal.

She glanced at her watch. No matter how hard she tried, she would miss her connecting flight, so she might as well visit the ticketing counter in this terminal after she dealt with this bag-switch situation.

Frustrated, she headed in the opposite direction.

"Excuse me," she asked a random person. "Do you know if there's an information desk or a lost and found anywhere close by?"

"Yes. Keep heading in this direction, and the terminal will open up into an atrium. You'll find a security desk there. They'll be able to help you."

"Thank you." Evelyn smiled and began going to where the Good Samaritan had pointed.

Once reaching the atrium, the density of the crowds almost paralyzed her. It was so busy. She moved to a railing, bracing herself against it, and glanced down. From what she could determine, everything she needed was a level below her.

Bustling with people, various types of restaurants and shops lined the perimeter of the lower level. In the center, there was a circular counter area marked 'Information.' That must be where she needed to go. The only downside was it was on the other side of the security line.

She looked out toward the line for customs and bit her lip. Was it worth going through customs to get her bag back? On one hand, she really didn't want to wait in the really long line. On the other, she really needed her bag.

Sighing, she figured she needed to re-book her flight, anyway. It didn't matter if she was stuck on the other side of security. Besides, it would be fun to have an extra stamp in her passport. Optimism!

After waiting through what had to be the slowest line she had ever been in, Evelyn descended on the escalator and began weaving her way through the crowds of people toward the kiosk at a brisk pace. Once the counter came into view, she began slowing down, but not before she slammed into someone coming the opposite direction.

She gasped and held tight to the duffel bag, cursing herself for getting into the same situation *twice* in one trip. Maybe she should just re-book and go home. Was this all an omen?

"Sorry," the man she'd crashed into said with a thick British accent as he steadied her.

She looked up and was taken aback. He had to be one of the most handsome men she had ever seen. His features were very sharp, and his blue eyes stood out against his dark eyelashes. Dark hair was cut close to his scalp. He was lean, muscular, and looked like he spent his free time in the gym. She was struck speechless and couldn't help but stare. Handsome and British. Evelyn had one weakness, and he'd slammed into her.

She opened her mouth to respond to him, but he didn't give her a chance. He was pushing past her and moving through the airport. She watched him disappear into the crowd with slight regret. If only she had said something to him.

Evelyn continued to make her way through the crowd toward her destination, and just as the kiosk was within striking distance, a hand tightly gripped her upper arm, stopping her.

"Excuse me, Miss, but I think I can help you." The man's accent was thick. "If you'll just come with me."

She turned to look at the man. He was tall and, with her five-foot, three height, she had to look up to view his face as he stood at least a foot taller than her. She gasped. It was the man she had just run into. Mr. Handsome and British. Who she had immediately regretted not speaking to. Here he was, holding onto her arm, preventing her from moving.

She involuntarily took a step back. "What the—"

She was cut off by his large hand tightening its grip around her upper arm. She began to panic as he dragged her in the opposite direction of the kiosk.

Evelyn tried to get away, but he overpowered her. When she tried to drag her heels to stop them, he moved his arm so it wrapped around her upper body and brought his other hand up, holding onto her mouth so she couldn't scream. She tried harder to plant her feet to slow down her abductor, but it didn't matter. He was too strong.

Her gaze darted around, hoping someone would notice her abduction and put a stop to it, but everyone around them seemed so engrossed in their travels, no one even glanced their way. She brought her hands up in a feeble attempt to pry his away, but it, too, was fruitless.

Just as visions of being sent into the sex slave trade began to fly through her head, they stopped moving. She narrowed her eyes in confusion before they moved again, entering a room. Her abductor closed the door behind them, trapping her.

Her mind played different scenarios of things being done to her as full panic set in.

CHAPTER 2

PATRICK

The room was dark, smelled of antiseptics and other cleaning items. Patrick held back a sigh when he realized, in his haste to remove the girl from the airport atrium, he had put them in a cupboard full of janitorial supplies. In addition to the potent smell of chemicals wafting through the air, the room was dank and overly cooled. The girl shivered against him. Although, he wasn't sure if it was because she was cold or if she was terrified. His decision to force her into the closet probably wasn't the best idea he could have come up with. In fact, feeling her body close to his, and how small it was comparatively, really made him believe he hadn't thought his actions through enough.

The room was silent, save for the sound of their breathing—his even, hers rapid. Her chest rose and fell under his arm, increasing in speed with each breath. Patrick swallowed and decided to break the silence, put her at ease.

"You can relax." He cringed. *Smooth.* "I'm not here to hurt you. I'm here to take you to safety. The solicitor's office sent me after you called and said you were skipping town with everything you collected. I'm honestly surprised I even found you. I only had a grainy photograph to go on. And then, *boom*! You ran right into me. How about that?"

He frowned. Megan didn't seem to relax, even though he'd told her who he was. Then it dawned on him. Of course, she wouldn't be relaxed. She was being held against his body with his hand over her mouth.

"If I remove my hand, do you promise to not scream, to remain calm?"

She nodded vigorously. He removed it, and as soon as he loosened his grip, she hurried away from him. Probably about as far as she could get from him in the cramped space of the room.

"I don't know who you think I am, but I'm pretty sure you have the wrong girl."

He frowned. The voice coming through the dark room was wrong. It was all wrong.

"You're American."

"That's right, I am."

"Fuck," he muttered under his breath, storming across the space with surprising ease, despite the dark. Brushing against the woman as he made his way toward the door, he groped along the smooth wall until he finally found what he needed. With a flip of his finger, the switch on the wall moved, filling the room with a fluorescent light. He squinted at the sudden brightness, but soon his eyes adjusted and he could take in the sight of the woman he'd dragged, believing she was Megan.

Now that he'd had a full look at her, Patrick realized his mistake.

"You're not Megan."

"No, I'm not. Can I go now?"

"It's uncanny. You look almost exactly like her. Same height, same hair color and length, same eye color, same build, even the same bag."

The woman straightened. "Wait, you're looking for a girl who looks like me and was carrying the same bag as me?"

He narrowed his eyes. "Yes, I am."

"I saw her."

He took a step forward, forcing her to take a step back, causing her to bump into a mop bucket. "Where?"

"On my way to switch terminals. She was running in the opposite direction, and we crashed into each other."

"Which way did she go?"

"I'm actually not quite sure. The opposite way I was heading after I got off the plane. I tried to follow her, but I lost her in the crowd. When we collided, we accidentally switched bags. Before you grabbed me, I was about to turn this one in to security with the hope she had done the same with mine."

He glared at the woman before moving his gaze to the bag. "That's Megan's bag?"

She shrugged. "If it was indeed Megan I crashed into a little while ago, then yes, it is."

Patrick stared at the bag. "Bloody hell. What are the odds? I mean they have to be miniscule. I wonder if Colin will be satisfied with *only* the bag, but no Megan?"

he muttered to himself. He looked up and caught the eye of the woman. She had drawn her bottom lip between her teeth as she shifted from foot to foot.

"Um, since we can agree we have a case of mistaken identity, can I continue on my way? I really need to get going. I've already missed my connecting flight and really should re-book, so I can try to leave today."

Patrick looked up as the woman shouldered the bag and made her way to the door of the cupboard.

He moved to block the exit. "You're not leaving with that bag."

"What do you mean? I have to take it up to the information kiosk so I can try to get mine back."

"Yeah, I can't let that happen. I need that bag." He lunged at her, trying to grab it.

She jerked back. "I don't think so. I need my bag, and I think the only way this Megan girl will give me mine is if I give her this. So, forgive me if I don't give some random guy in a storage closet in the airport her property."

He glared at her. He thought this would be easy. Instead, this annoyingly attractive woman was giving him a headache as he tried to do his job.

He frowned and shook his head. This was no time to notice the woman in front of him was beautiful, especially with her eyes lit with the fire of annoyance as they were. He was on a job. And he needed to complete this job without losing his patience on a stranger in a broom cupboard. "I'll get your bag back when I find Megan. Right now, you can give me her bag and you can be on your way. You can even leave me your address and I'll post your bag back to you. How does that sound?"

The woman returned his glare. "How do I know you're really going to send me my bag? I have some important things in there. I need it."

Patrick couldn't help it. He laughed. "Important things? What could possibly be in there that's so important? Your extra makeup? Your hair dryer? Don't be so overly dramatic."

She narrowed her eyes into slits. "You know nothing about me, so I'd appreciate it if you'd withhold your judgment."

She was right. He didn't know her, but he would like to. In several different ways. But now wasn't the time.

"C'mon. Just give me the bag and write down your address, and I'll send you your beauty products." He held out his hand, smirking.

The American growled in frustration. "I'll give you this damn bag and the address of the Institute I'll be staying at in Greece, and you *will* send me my *research* materials. How does that sound?"

Fuck. Not only was she attractive, she was bloody smart as well? He was regretting the fact she was the wrong person. "Sure. That works."

The woman rolled her eyes and dropped the duffel on the ground. Shrugging out of her backpack, she pulled out a notebook. After scribbling some information on a piece of paper, she replaced the notebook and backpack to their rightful places. She pushed the bag toward him with her foot and shoved the piece of paper into his hand. He smiled as he opened the paper and took in what she'd written.

"Alright, Miss Evelyn Stevenson. I'll make sure you get your bag. Thank you for your cooperation. You may be on your way."

Evelyn raised her eyebrows, but said nothing. Instead, she moved around him and opened the door to the cupboard. The second she took one step out, it occurred to him that maybe letting her leave was a bad idea. Perhaps the worst idea he'd had all day. Moving quicker than he thought he could, he reached out and grabbed onto her backpack, dragging her back into the cupboard before slamming the door in her face.

CHAPTER 3

EVELYN

"What the hell?" Evelyn whipped around to face her abductor.

"Change of plans, sweetheart. You're going to have to stick with me. I'll take you to the solicitor's office, and we'll find a way for you to go on your merry way after that."

"Excuse me? I'm not going anywhere with you. I will not leave an airport with a stranger! Especially not to some 'solicitor's office.' You said I could leave if I gave you the bag. I gave you the bag. Now let me go."

The man sighed. "Look, I'd *love* to send you on your way right now and have you out of my hands. The last thing I want right now is to babysit some American bird. However, outside that door, somewhere in this airport, are members of the Fitzgerald family, looking for Megan, and now you. I can't, in good faith, let you walk out there and get taken by those men because they certainly won't be as nice as I am."

"Wait, I'm confused. Who is the Fitzgerald family, and why would they want me?"

"The Fitzgerald family is a notorious firm—" He pinched his lips together, stopping himself. He took a deep breath before continuing. "Look, you just need to know they're the bad guys, and they're outside the door."

"Firm?" she asked.

The man sighed. "Gang is what you'd call it in America. The mob, essentially."

She shook her head. "Wait. The mob wants *Megan*? I really don't understand what's going on here."

"Look, I don't have time to explain. I'm a private investigator, and the solicitor I work for sent me here to collect Megan. Instead, I found you. Now, I'm guessing, the firm thinks you know what Megan knows. The only solution is for me to take you to my connection at the solicitor's office, and we'll figure out where to go from there."

"No."

"No? What do you mean, no?" He threw his hands up before clenching them into fists, bringing one up to his mouth as if stopping himself from saying more.

"I mean no. I'm not going with you. I'm going to walk out of this room and go to ticketing to get on my flight to Athens. I have no intention of staying here any longer than necessary."

"Didn't you hear anything I've said? Those men are no good. They're not going to let you waltz on by."

"How do you even know they're here for me? You just said you're an investigator hired to pick up Megan. Maybe they're here for you?"

She didn't give the investigator any chance to respond. She turned on her heel, flung the door open, and walked out into the busy airport.

She looked around and found signs showing the counters for ticketing. She started walking toward them.

Hands grabbed both of her arms, squeezing tight, halting her right where she stood. She slowly turned her head, expecting it to be the investigator stopping her from continuing on her journey, but instead, two men glared at her.

The men were tall and wore black slacks, black shirts, and leather jackets. They were both bald, and their faces were expressionless. What made them look even more intimidating was the fact they wore sunglasses inside of the airport.

"Miss, we need you to come with us," one man stated.

"Well, I was just on my way to make my connecting flight..."

"We've been looking for you, sunshine, and you're going to come with us now."

The men tightened their grips on her arms and tried to drag her, but she planted her feet, attempting to stay put.

"Listen, guys, you both seem pretty reasonable. I'm not who you're looking for. Seriously. Look, I'm not even British. So, can you just let me go on my way?"

The man on her right let go of her arm and reached under his leather jacket with his right hand. His left hand carefully pulled the jacket back from his chest, revealing his hand holding a gun.

"We can do this the easy way or the hard way. And the hard way can get really messy," the man not holding the gun replied. "Where's the bag?"

She couldn't take her gaze off the gun pointed discretely at her. Her heart was pounding. "Wh-what bag?"

"Stop being cheeky. You know exactly what bag we're talking about. Where is it?"

"I-I-I lost it." She didn't know what to say. No way to know how to act in this situation. She was regretting leaving the safety of the janitorial closet and the investigator. At least *he* didn't have a gun. At least she didn't think he did. If he did, he hadn't pointed it at her.

"You're being cheeky again. It looks like we're going to have to do this the hard way."

The man holding the gun let go of his jacket and formed his left hand into a fist.

She tried to move away, but the other man still had an extremely tight grip on her arm. She watched in slow motion as the man's fist came toward her. She closed her eyes, braced herself, and waited for the hit.

However, it never made impact. She opened her eyes in time to watch him go crashing to the ground. What apparently was a trashcan fell to the floor beside him. She looked to where the man had been previously standing and there stood the PI. He'd come after her. She tried, and failed, to not swoon at the fact he was rescuing her from the bad guys.

The man holding her arm loosened his grip and made to take a step toward the investigator. However, a fist made contact with his face instead. The force of the blow caused him to let go of Evelyn's arm completely. She moved herself out of the way as the PI landed another blow to the gang member's face, causing him to fall to the ground next to his partner.

The man didn't waste any time. He closed the distance between himself and Evelyn, taking hold of her hand. He had the duffel bag slung across his chest.

"Alright, time to make our great escape." The PI tightened his grip on her hand and dragged her through the busy terminal.

He seemed to know where he was going. Glancing up, her gaze caught on a sign pointing toward baggage claim and the exit. She opened her mouth to protest, to tell him she had absolutely no intention of leaving this airport, especially with a strange man whom she'd just met, but she never had a chance. They ran right through the doorway and then, before she could even process what was going on, they were outside, the sun blinding her momentarily.

The investigator didn't slow down. She tried to keep up as he pulled her through the parking lot, his grip tight on her hand. He led her to a No Parking zone, where a blue MINI Cooper was parked. He stopped in front of the car, opened a door, and shoved her unceremoniously inside, backpack still on her back, closing the door behind her. Before she processed what was going on, he climbed in the opposite side, threw the bag into the backseat, started the car, and peeled away from the curb.

All Evelyn could do was stare at the man sitting beside her, as Heathrow Airport faded into the distance.

The scenery outside the window quickly turned from various businesses and hotels to rolling hills and trees as they sped away from the airport. Her mind raced, trying to process the encounter at the airport, while also trying to reassure herself they were *not* driving on the wrong side of the road.

"I would at least put your seatbelt on," he spoke up from beside her, without taking his gaze off the road.

She said nothing. Instead, she slipped her backpack off, settling it by her feet, and pulled the seatbelt around her. "Where are you taking me?"

"To my contact at the solicitor's office. I figure we need to let him know what's going on. He'll probably know what we should do next."

She was quiet for a second. "I'm going to die," she muttered, mostly to herself.

"What are you on about?"

"I'm going to die! My mother with her endless viewings of *Unsolved Mysteries* and all of her worries about me getting sold into sex slavery are coming true. And I've made the gravest error of all. I'm in a car with a stranger, heading to a second location. You're never supposed to go to a second location. And regardless of whether you're going to murder me or sell me, what about my luggage? Did my luggage go to Greece without me, or did it stay here? What—"

"Oh, bloody hell. Will you shut your trap for one bloody minute?" He growled. "You're not going to die. I have no intention of killing you. Well, if you keep prattling on like you are, you may drive me to contemplate it, albeit briefly. But I'm not a killer. If you had let those other men take you to a second location, well, that would be another kettle of fish entirely. The solicitor is a lawyer. He's not going to sell you. Everything else you don't need to worry about at this moment, so can we just drive for a few minutes in peace?"

"Well, excuse me for being concerned about my situation. I'm not exactly used to fleeing from airports in foreign countries with strange men."

The man barked out a laugh before quickly stifling it. He glanced over at her, his eyes bulging as he held in his mirth.

She shook her head. "Oh, fuck off. It's not that funny."

"I mean, it is a bit. 'Fleeing airports with strange men.' You make it sound very Hollywood."

"It doesn't feel very Hollywood to the person who it is affecting."

"I imagine you do little fleeing in your real life. More like sitting with your nose in a book, shirking from sunlight like a vampire."

"Fuck off. You don't even know me. For all you know, I could run half marathons."

He laughed. "I'm an investigator. I'm pretty good at telling someone's character from a glance."

"Oh, really? And what have you deduced about my character in the five minutes you've known me, Sherlock?"

The investigator glanced at her quickly before returning his gaze to the road. "Well, you're in your early twenties, and a student at University. You prefer books to sports. You care a great deal about your appearance, judging that you've just flown across an ocean and you don't look like you spent eight hours on an airplane. You carry yourself with an air of confidence, are very intelligent, and yet you can't defend yourself or think logically when you're presented with a crisis."

Her cheeks heated before she glanced at her loose-fitting jeans and the plain blue tunic she was wearing. She quickly took in her appearance in the side mirror. She looked like hell. "In what world does my current appearance give off that I haven't been traveling for eight hours on a plane?"

"It just does."

She took a deep breath, her face warming at the implication of his statement. "Well, you want to know what impression I get from you?"

"Not particularly."

She ignored him. "You're a pretentious ass who thinks he's better than everyone else. You think you're so important because you're this private investigator. And I'm guessing by the way you look, your name is Nigel."

The PI's hands gripped and re-gripped the steering wheel as his gaze grew stormy. "Patrick. My name is Patrick. Nigel? What the fuck is that?"

"Not so great being on the other side of the judgment, is it?" She laughed and turned her attention back to the changing scenery as they approached what she deduced to be the Thames River, with the London Eye looming in the distance.

CHAPTER 4

PATRICK

Patrick said nothing for the rest of the drive. He kept his gaze on the road as he maneuvered the narrow streets of the neighborhood. He couldn't believe how completely fucked up this case was, and one day into it. One job. He had one job. Get the girl, get the bag, bring them to the solicitor, and get paid. That was it.

Oh, if only it were that easy. Instead, he'd grabbed the wrong woman but the right bag, and now he was stuck with an American who wouldn't stop shooting him dirty looks as he drove. When she wasn't looking out the window, that was. He was usually pretty good at his job, considered one of the top private investigators in the city. So, it was pretty damn frustrating when he did something wrong.

He glanced over at the woman, relieved she was looking out the window. He didn't want her to catch him looking. She seemed like a nice enough person, and his stomach turned when he thought about what he was putting her through. He ran his gaze down her body for the first time since they left the airport before moving his gaze back to the road. Fuck, she was fit. Very fit. He wouldn't mind taking her back to the flat and—

He shook his head. He couldn't afford to be having thoughts like that. She was a client, sort of. Plus, she probably hated him right now. Any ideas of wooing her he'd held when he first ran into her at the airport were now irrelevant.

He groaned as he pulled in front of the posh building. He sat behind the wheel for a second, gathering his patience before he needed to enter the building.

He never enjoyed visiting here on a good day. Now he was expected to go upstairs and tell his contact, his *father*, Colin, he'd failed at the first assignment he was given in the case. He could just hear the derision in his voice now.

"Where are we?" Evelyn spoke from beside him, interrupting his thoughts. "I thought you said we were going to the solicitor's office?"

Patrick rolled his eyes as he turned the car off and opened the door. "It's Sunday." He stepped out of the car, carrying the duffel bag.

He didn't even pause to see if she was following. He took the stairs to the entrance two at a time. When he heard her footsteps behind him, he opened the door to the building.

"It's Sunday? I don't even know what that means." She was practically jogging in order to match his steps as he walked to his destination.

"You're a smart woman. What do you think it means?" He stopped in front of a door, raising his hand to knock.

"Has anyone ever told you how much of an ass you are?"

"Several."

The door to the flat opened before either one could say anything more.

Colin was middle-aged with hair that was grayer than brown, and stood in the doorway. "Patrick."

"Colin."

"Your...errand took much longer than I had expected. I expected you here thirty minutes ago."

"I ran into some complications."

Colin looked toward Evelyn. "Who's that?"

"The complication."

"I see. Why don't the two of you come inside? We shouldn't be discussing business in the hallway." He stood aside, letting Patrick and Evelyn enter the flat.

The flat was still as sparsely decorated as it had been the last time he'd visited. The living area housed only a leather couch and a coffee table. Off to the side, where one would normally keep a dining room table, sat a large wooden desk, piled high with paperwork, the screen of a computer monitor, barely visible. There was a small kitchen that was rarely used and then a full-sized bed against a wall. He wasn't surprised.

Patrick moved immediately in the couch's direction, setting the duffel bag on the coffee table before plopping himself down. Evelyn stood near the entrance, arms folded across her chest, her gaze shifting between Colin and Patrick.

"Don't be shy, love. Have a seat." Patrick patted the spot next to him.

She walked over to the couch and perched as far away as she could from him.

"This isn't Megan." Colin pointed at Evelyn. "I specifically told you to go to the airport and stop Megan from fleeing the country."

"Well, if you'd provided me with an actual picture of Megan, rather than one that was so blurry I could only make out vague features, I may have been able to get her. The picture showed she was short, had brown hair to her shoulders, and was carrying this duffel. Evelyn here fit that description, so I stopped her."

Colin sighed, pinching the bridge of his nose, closing his eyes. "And why didn't you let her go on her way once you realized your mistake?"

"Two Fitzgerald goons were waiting for her. They apparently realized she had the bag. I couldn't let them take her."

"I still don't understand *why* she's here. Why did you bring her *here*? Why is she not at Heathrow, waiting to go wherever it is she is planning on traveling?"

It was Patrick's turn to sigh and pinch his nose in frustration. He gestured to the duffel bag on the coffee table. "She was carrying that bag. The Fitzgerald arseholes were about to fucking shoot her. What was I supposed to do? Grab the bag and let them kill her?"

"You keep gesturing to her bag. Mentioning her bag. What's so special about her bag? We were after *Megan's* bag."

"That's Megan's bag!" Patrick shouted. "That bag right there. They somehow swapped them at the airport, and now she has it. I was going to keep the bag and let her on her way, but the Fitzgerald goons grabbed her not five seconds after I let her leave. And I'm not in the business of letting innocent girls get murdered, so here she is. Do you understand now, you senile old man?"

"That's Megan's bag?" He gestured to the bag in question.

She sighed. "Yes, that's Megan's bag. She and I crashed into each other and switched bags accidentally. I wanted to turn the bag into security, hoping Megan had done the same with mine. However, this jackass grabbed and stopped me before I could. I'm pretty sure he's the reason I was put on the radar of those goons in the first place. Now, can we please figure out what to do about getting me where I need to go? I really want to go to Greece."

"What on earth is she talking about?"

"He dragged me out of the airport! I'm not supposed to be here. I need to have this figured out so I can get back into the airport and continue on to my program. Patrick said you'd be able to take care of everything."

Colin closed his eyes and massaged his temples. "You've made a right mess of this whole situation. When I suggested to my office we hire outside help to gather evidence against the Fitzgeralds, I assured them you and James were the right way to go. I said you were mature and professional and would get the job done. And now, one step into the endeavor, and you've made a bloody mess of the whole damn thing."

"This isn't my fault! If you had just—"

"I don't want to hear it. This is spiraling out of control. Maybe you aren't the right person to be on this job."

"You know I'm the right person for this job. You know why I need to do this. I didn't fuck anything up. If anything, I did a damn good job with the information you gave me. We have the duffel bag, and that's the most important piece, right? We'll find Megan. I fail to see where I've fouled this up." Patrick's face was burning with rage.

"You've upset this poor girl, for one thing. You've literally kidnapped her. You've let Megan slip away to God knows where. And you're letting your emotions get the best of you. You've created quite the mess for me to clean up already. I can't imagine what will happen if I let you continue to work on this case."

Patrick opened his mouth to retort, but was cut off.

"You need to go cool down. When you're ready to act your age, we'll continue this conversation."

Patrick cursed and stormed out of the living area, kicking the desk chair on his way to the farthest corner of the flat. He was far enough away to be alone, but close enough to still hear and see what was going on.

Colin turned toward Evelyn. "Now, dear, why don't you tell me about what is going on and where you need to go. I'll make some calls tomorrow, and we'll get you on your way."

"Well, you see, sir—"

The doorbell rang, interrupting her.

"Hold that thought." Colin excused himself to go answer the door.

Patrick took a few more deep calming breaths before he walked back into the living area and took a seat next to Evelyn. "I'm sorry about that."

She looked at him. "It's alright. I would have been frustrated, too. I mean, how many ways did you really need to explain the bag isn't mine?"

He smiled. "I know, right? I swear, the older that man gets, the denser he is. Bloody annoying, that."

She gave him a tight smile. "Do you work with him a lot? You guys seem close."

He shrugged. "This is the first time we're working together professionally. But he's my dad. Even though I would never describe my father and me as being 'close.'"

She stared at him. "Your father? But you referred to him by his first name."

He shrugged again. "Like I said, close isn't a word I'd use to describe my relationship with him."

She looked like she wanted to ask more questions, but was interrupted by Colin walking back into the room.

He was carrying a plain cardboard box. He didn't speak as he carried the box over to his dining room table to set it down.

Patrick followed him to the table, gesturing for Evelyn to follow him. They joined him around the box. The three stood there staring at it until Colin pulled out his pocketknife and sliced open the top, his hand shaking. He peeled open the lid and peeked in. Then he slammed the top of the box closed and moved away, covering his mouth.

Curious, Patrick and Evelyn looked at each other before she nodded at Patrick.

He moved forward and opened the box. She peeked over his shoulder. She covered her mouth and stifled a scream.

"Jesus Christ," Patrick breathed at the sight.

Inside the box, nestled next to Evelyn's duffel bag, Megan's head sat staring up at him.

Chapter 5

PATRICK

"Shit, shit, shit." Patrick ran his hand through his hair. He couldn't tear his gaze away from the box on his dad's table. He'd never seen a dead body before. It wasn't as cool as he'd imagined. In fact, it was downright terrifying.

He stole a glance at Evelyn. She didn't look well. She was also still staring at the box, but she looked a little green around the gills and was swaying. Before he could react, Colin came up behind her, wrapping an arm around her shoulders.

"Come on, my dear. Let's walk away and take a seat, shall we?"

He led her to the couch and sat her down. As soon as she made contact with the sofa, it was like flipping a switch, and she began to sob. Colin tried to comfort her, but she shrugged him away, laying down on her side, curling into herself.

Colin walked back over to where Patrick stood at the table. "That's it. You're officially off the case."

"Fuck off! You can't sack me without giving me a compelling and reasonable reason why."

Colin pointed at the box. "That's why. This is no laughing matter. And there's no way I'm letting you continue on this case when I'm getting heads delivered to my place of residence. This has grown too dangerous. I'm not willing to risk your life for this. I'll talk to my partners tomorrow, and we'll figure something else out."

Patrick shook his head. "No way, Colin. No way am I letting you take me off this case now. If anything, you need me to stay. We have leverage. We have the bag.

We have the evidence we need against the group. All I need to do is find someone willing to place Mickey Fitzgerald under arrest, and we're good. Can't you see we have the advantage here?"

Colin shook his head. "And what about her?" He pointed at Evelyn. "We've already put her in too much danger as it is. I refuse to put her in anymore."

"She's not in any danger. They just want the bloody bag. They don't even know who she is. I'll take her back to the airport tomorrow morning and get her on a plane to wherever it is she is going, and then she'll be as far out of harm's way as possible."

Colin ignored his outburst. Instead, he reached inside the box.

"What are you doing?"

Colin pulled out the bag that had been nestled next to the severed head and placed it on the table.

"Evelyn, dear, will you please come over here? I want to determine if there's anything missing from your bag."

She got up from the couch and wiped her eyes. She inched toward the table, avoiding looking at the box.

"Should we even be touching any of this? Isn't it evidence?" she asked, hesitating.

"Technically, yes. In any other case, we wouldn't be touching it, but it really doesn't matter. Any investigation is going to be just for show. Nothing ever happens to The Fitzgeralds. We'll call the police, and within twenty-four hours, all the evidence will disappear. You might as well have your things before I call it in," Colin explained. "Go ahead and open the bag."

She carefully unzipped the bag and reached inside.

Patrick looked on. Instead of what he considered typical items he thought a girl would have in her bag, Evelyn was pulling out book after book. He shifted closer and looked at some titles. They were all regarding Ancient Greek history, and some city named Epidaurus. There were about seven books on the table, along with several composition notebooks, before the bag was empty.

He let out a long, slow whistle. "Blimey, that's a lot of books. It's like you're a grad student or something." He brought his gaze up to meet hers and smirked, giving a wink.

She narrowed her eyes. "Hmm, imagine that. I was telling the truth."

"Is there anything missing?" Colin asked, bringing everyone back to the situation in the room.

She nodded. "The first draft of my thesis."

Patrick frowned. "Why would they want to keep a copy of your thesis? I can't imagine they're interested in," he picked up a book off the table, "*Sleeping Rituals at the Temple of Asclepius.*"

She shook her head. "Well, inside that draft, I had slipped my itinerary for this trip. It has my name, the location of the dig, the address of my accommodations, and every single excursion planned for my stay."

"Well, there you have it." Colin slammed his hand on the table, causing everyone to jump. "There's no way you can take her to the airport now and put her on a plane."

"I'm still not following. Why not?" Patrick asked.

"They know who she is. They know what she looks like, her name, and where she's going. It's not safe for her any longer. She's no longer anonymous."

She frowned. "I don't understand why they have an interest in me. I didn't even know who they were until today."

"You have the duffel bag, my dear. They probably feel you know too much."

"But I don't even know what's inside the bag. I know nothing. At this point, I want to go home. I don't even want to go to Greece anymore. I just want to go home." Tears welled in her eyes.

Colin looked at Patrick and gestured at him.

Patrick looked at the crying woman beside him and panicked. He knew nothing about comforting women. He knew nothing about women. There was a reason he was still single at nearly thirty.

"Look, Evelyn, you heard Colin. You're going to be stuck in London for a while, so you should get used to the idea." The minute the words were out, he knew he'd said the wrong thing.

Her mouth dropped open. She sputtered for a moment before words finally formed. "How is this helpful? Have you ever comforted anyone? It's like you've never interacted with humans. Are you a robot?"

"I'm not a robot! I'm not saying anything that isn't true. You're stuck here. You should just get over it. There's no point in crying," Patrick shouted.

"Patrick!" Colin chastised. "That's quite enough. I didn't bring you up to be so rude to women."

"You didn't bring me up at all, old man," Patrick spit out.

"That's enough. I won't sit here and listen to you be so insensitive to this poor woman or take your anger out on me. You're nearly thirty, and I expect you to have a little more respect."

"Fuck you, Colin. You don't have any right to—"

"I said, that's enough! If you wish to continue on this case, you're going to have to set aside your personal feelings and grudges, and act like the professional you are."

Patrick let out a growl. "Fine."

"Apologize," Colin demanded.

Patrick turned toward Evelyn, who was standing with her arms crossed, staring at the floor. "I'm sorry I've been such an arse to you. I don't know why I'm being a tosser, and I'll endeavor to try to be more civilized from this point forward."

She looked up from the floor and met his gaze. She narrowed her eyes at him. "I accept your weak apology and I hope I get to see this more civilized version of yourself."

He opened his mouth to retort, but Colin spoke instead.

"Great. Now that that's settled, let's move on, yes?"

Evelyn and Patrick reluctantly nodded.

"Now, Evelyn, as much as you want to go home right now, you have to accept you're where you're safest. If we let you go now, we'll most likely be receiving your head in a box next. Patrick, you need to let go of any personal feelings tying you to this case. Emotions cloud your judgment. If you want to remain involved, you need to become neutral. It's too dangerous to lose focus. The second your focus shifts, it's over. This isn't a cheating spouse case, son. This is a different kettle of fish altogether."

Patrick nodded. "I understand. I'll be better, I promise. No more emotions until Fitzgerald and his compatriots are locked behind bars."

"Excellent." Colin sounded weary. "Now, there's not much we can accomplish this afternoon, as it's Sunday, and I'm sure Evelyn is feeling the effects of traveling. I'll call you tomorrow once I meet with my partners. You take the bag. It'll be safer with you, and you'll be able to use whatever's in it to move the case along."

"Yeah, that works." Patrick moved around the table and into the living room, grabbing the bag and moving toward the door.

"Ahem." Colin cleared his throat. "Aren't you forgetting something?"

Patrick looked around the flat and shrugged. "I didn't come in with anything else. Just the duffel. I've got everything I need."

"The girl, Patrick. You're forgetting the girl." Colin appeared to be running out of patience for him.

"Wait, what?" She sputtered. "You expect me to go with him? I thought I'd be staying here with you."

Colin shook his head. "You're not safe here. The Fitzgeralds obviously know where I live, and they probably already expect you'll be here, as evidenced by your bag being delivered with the head. You'll be much safer going with Patrick. His residence isn't as well-known as mine, and he and his partner, James, are better equipped to protect you than I am."

Patrick sighed and moved back into the room. He went over to the table and threw all the books and notebooks back into Evelyn's bag, and slung it over his shoulder. He walked to the couch and picked up her backpack, where she'd left it. He then moved to the entryway before stopping and turning around to glance at Evelyn, who was still standing by the table.

"Well, are you coming or not?"

Behind him, she huffed, and her hurried footsteps tapped behind him. His stride was longer than hers, and it would be with their height difference. It was petty of him to not slow down. He was frustrated with his dad, not with her, per se.

He opened the driver's side of his car, throwing the bags and backpack into the backseat before climbing in.

Seconds after he shut the door, the passenger door opened, and she climbed in. She'd barely closed the door before he peeled away from the curb.

CHAPTER 6

EVELYN

They drove the twenty minutes to his flat in complete silence. Evelyn spent the entire drive staring out the window, trying to take in what little she could see of the city. Which were mostly tall, stone buildings that surrounded either side of the narrow road they were driving down.

They pulled up to a building, and Patrick turned to her after shutting off the engine.

"As my dad told you, I live with my best mate, James. He's also my business partner. I don't want you to panic if you run into him in our modest flat. Good news. Unlike Colin's, the flat is a two bedroom, so I'll bunk you in mine. Follow me."

Before waiting for a response, he reached into the backseat, grabbed all the bags, and exited the vehicle.

She sighed and opened her door. She had to run to catch up to Patrick as he unlocked the door to the building. She followed him up a flight of stairs and then down a hallway to the first door on the left. Once the door was open, he entered and began flipping on lights as he moved through the flat.

She followed him inside and into a small, crowded living room. There was a worn couch along one wall and desks piled high with papers lining the other two.

Patrick moved to a door on the left, throwing it open. The sparsely decorated room housed a full-sized bed whose rumpled solid green bedding made it obvious it was rarely, if not ever, made. He dropped her duffel and backpack on the floor at the foot of the bed. She wrinkled her nose at the thought of sleeping in the clearly unwashed bed.

"This is my room. You can use it for the duration of your stay. I'll take the couch." He turned, left the room, and headed toward the desk under the window. He placed Megan's duffel on the floor beside the chair and booted up his computer. His desk was a mess, covered in papers and empty energy drink cans. In fact, the entire flat was a mess. It truly held up to the stereotypical 'bachelor pad' environment.

Evelyn looked around at the empty cans and beer bottles that lined the surface of most of the furniture and the counters in the kitchen, which was open to the living room. She counted at least three pairs of socks strewn about the floor. She looked down the hallway, which she assumed led to the bathroom and the second bedroom. There was a wet towel lying in the middle of the floor, as if the two feet into the bedroom were just too much to handle to travel. The floor of Patrick's bedroom was littered with clothing. Whether they were clean or dirty, she wasn't sure.

"You can have a seat." Patrick didn't look up from his computer screen.

She looked toward the couch and wrinkled her nose in disgust. The couch looked like something they'd found on the side of the street. The brown upholstery was worn and stained and the cushions sagging.

"I'm actually kind of hungry. I haven't eaten since this morning on the airplane," she said.

Patrick, still glued to his computer, gestured toward the kitchen. "Help yourself to anything you want."

She glared at the back of his head and moved into the kitchen. She opened the refrigerator and narrowed her eyes. The only things inside were beer, energy drinks, and half-eaten takeaway containers. She closed the fridge and began opening cupboards.

Empty. Empty. Empty.

"Um, Patrick?" She was trying to control her temper.

"Yeah?"

"You are aware you have absolutely nothing edible in your kitchen, right?"

"Not true. I'm fairly certain we have some takeaway in there. You're more than welcome to it. And I know for certain we have tea. We always have tea. We would be terrible British men if we didn't. In fact, I'll make some in a minute, since you Americans are rubbish at making tea. Care for a cuppa?"

"Hate to break it to you, but I couldn't find any tea. Your cupboards are literally bare. Also, how old is that takeaway?"

"Honestly, I have no idea. I can't actually remember the last time we've eaten a meal here. Which would also explain the lack of tea in the flat. Been picking that up from the corner shop lately."

She couldn't control herself any longer. She picked up an empty beer can from the counter and chucked it at him, nailing him in the head.

"Oi! What was that for?" He rubbed his head.

"I'm hungry. I'm supposed to stay here with you for who knows how long, and you and your roommate live like pigs. Oh, and did I mention I'm *hungry?*"

"Order takeaway, then. Bloody hell, are you useless."

"How? From where? Patrick, I'm not *from* here. You need to help me with these things."

"There's a curry place three doors down. Just walk down there and get something."

"Fine." She started for the door, patting her pockets to make sure she still had her money. It was a good thing she'd had the mind to get money in the right currency before leaving on her trip. She had just placed her hand on the doorknob to leave when a hand on her arm stopped her.

"Never mind," Patrick said. "I don't know what I was thinking. It's Sunday, the curry place is closed on Sunday."

"What about a grocery store? I can walk to a grocery store and get *something.*"

He shook his head. "I can't just let you go out there alone. Have you already forgotten? You're wanted by an infamous crime syndicate. I think the jet lag is getting to you. You should go have a lie down. We can get you food later. Perhaps I can text James to bring something home with him."

"When will he be home?"

"Who knows? It depends if he's doing something for a case or if he's just out."

"Argh!" She growled in frustration. "You know, I think I've solved the mystery."

"What mystery?"

"Why you're so rude. There's no food here. You're hangry."

"Hangry?!" Patrick laughed. "I am not hangry. I am just concerned about your safety. Once the shops and restaurants are open, I will feed you. It is Sunday, remember?"

"Oh, that's right. It's Sunday. How could I have possibly forgotten?" she threw back at him, her words positively dripping with sarcasm.

"Who's the hangry one now?" he asked, not quite under his breath.

She let out a screech in frustration before grabbing her backpack and storming into Patrick's room, slamming the door behind her.

CHAPTER 7

EVELYN

Evelyn gasped, sitting straight upright in the bed. The room was dark and unfamiliar. She threw the covers off and jumped out of bed before remembering where she was.

She glanced around, taking in the dirty clothes on the floor and the bare walls. "That's right," she muttered, "I'm in Patrick's room, somewhere in London." She sat back down on the bed, placing her head in her hands, breathing slowly. Oddly, the familiar rich, woodsy smell of his cologne that permeated the air calmed her. As she exhaled, her heart rate slowed to a normal level. A few more deep breaths in and out, and she became calm.

She removed her hands and laid back on the bed. A strange dream had awoken her. In it she was back at the airport, and she was running. Only this time, Patrick wasn't with her. She was alone. And this time, she didn't get away from those men. They'd caught her and dragged her out of the airport, kicking and screaming. The next thing she knew, she was in some nondescript room, tied to a chair. A man with a scarred face came in and, with a thick New Jersey accent, began telling her all the things he was going to do to her now he had her. He pulled out a hammer and began slapping it against his hand and walking slowly toward her, laughing maniacally. She'd started screaming, and that was when she woke up.

Evelyn let out a small, quiet laugh. "No more gangster movies when I get out of this mess."

She was about to settle herself back in the bed to get more sleep when her bladder chose that moment to remind her it needed attention. She sighed and thought about the location of the bathroom in relation to the room she was currently sleeping in and of all the crap on the floor between here and there and let out a groan. After getting off the bed, she went to where Patrick had dropped her backpack. It only took her a second to find the tiny flashlight she'd packed with her for emergencies, and finding her way to the bathroom without sticking her bare foot in an old slice of pizza was definitely an emergency.

Not sure of the time, she quietly opened the door and peeked her head out into the main living space. The room was lit with the glow of a computer screen. She glanced toward where she knew Patrick's desk was located. He was slumped over with his head on his desk, obviously asleep. In his sleep, he looked relaxed and peaceful. More handsome than he had appeared all day without the stress tightening up his features. He didn't look very comfortable, but Evelyn didn't want to be the one to wake him. She wasn't sure which Patrick would appear. Joking, sarcastic Patrick, or snarky, rude and hangry Patrick, and she wasn't in the mood to deal with either if she was being honest. Besides, sleep might actually make him more pleasant to deal with later. She clicked on her flashlight, taking care to make sure she pointed it at the floor, and started her journey to the bathroom. As she made her way down the hallway, she noted the towel that had been in the middle of the floor earlier had made its way out of the hallway.

She turned into the bathroom, closed the door, flipped the light on, and had to stifle a groan of disgust. The sink was covered in whiskers and dried toothpaste. The toilet lid was up and looked as if it had been a while since someone last scrubbed it. She closed her eyes and counted to ten before opening them and walking over and flipping the seat down and lining it with toilet paper. After doing her business, and trying her hardest to wash her hands, even though the action made her feel dirtier for the effort, she decided that if she were going to be stuck in this apartment for an indefinite amount of time, when it came time to purchase food for the apartment, she'd demand cleaning supplies too, and she would clean the damn apartment herself.

The thought of buying food reminded her it had been a very long time since she'd last eaten, and she was starving. Which, of course, reminded her that these men kept no food in the apartment, and she was going to be hungry until the morning when they could venture out in search of food. She flung open the door and stepped into the hallway. She began walking toward the bedroom, only to run into a solid wall of man.

She looked up, expecting it to be Patrick, but instead was greeted by someone who she had never seen before. He had longish, dark, rusty-red hair and green eyes. He was wearing a Pink Floyd shirt and jeans, and was barefoot. And he was smiling at her with a big wide grin that showed off white, slightly crooked teeth.

"Oi." He laughed. "Is it my birthday? To what do I owe the pleasure of having a gorgeous bird run into me after exiting my bathroom?"

Her cheeks heated. "I'm sorry. I wasn't watching where I was going."

The man tilted his head to the side, still smiling. "An American bird. How odd. When I came home, I noticed Patrick asleep at his desk, but no one else. Did he bring you home and shag you and then leave you alone in bed so he could work? *Tsk tsk*. What bad manners he has. You'll find I have much better manners than he has."

She shook her head. "No, no shagging. He brought me home, but we didn't do anything, believe me."

"Oh? Then what are you doing in our home?"

"It's a long story. A very long story. One that I would probably be better at telling you in the morning, after I've had something to eat. I think the hunger has moved on from eating my stomach lining to eating my brain cells. I'm having a hard time focusing on things. Like who are you?"

The man let out a laugh, taking a step back from her. "I'm James, Patrick's flat mate and fellow investigator." He stuck out his hand.

She grasped his hand and shook it. "I'm Evelyn, Patrick's client, or hostage. I haven't quite figured out what I am exactly."

James threw his head back and laughed. "You're funny. I like you. Now, what was this you were saying about hunger? Didn't Patrick feed you?"

She shook her head. "I have had nothing to eat since breakfast on the airplane. What, yesterday morning now?"

He clicked his tongue, shaking his head. "Remind me to take Patrick to task for not properly entertaining a lady." He reached into his pocket, pulled out a chocolate bar, and handed it over to her. "It may be a bit melted, but it's something, right?"

She took the chocolate bar and smiled. "It is. Thank you very much."

"You're very welcome, milady. Now, if you'll excuse me, I'm knackered and was about to head to bed. But we'll have a chance to chat more in the morning, yeah?"

She smiled and nodded. "Yeah."

"Brilliant. Goodnight, Evelyn. It was a pleasure meeting you." And before she could respond, he walked the few feet into his bedroom and closed the door.

She stood in the hallway for a few minutes and tried to figure out what had just happened. Was he flirting with her? He'd thought she was there with Patrick, but that didn't stop him from flirting and trying to pick her up. Did the two of them share women? She shook her head, trying not to think about the sex lives of the men she was staying with, and began walking to Patrick's room.

She took a quick peek at Patrick as she walked past. Still slumped over, sleeping on his desk. He hadn't moved a muscle. Unbelievable. She wondered if he was always such a heavy sleeper or if he was faking it so he wouldn't have to talk to her. She shrugged and moved to open the door to his room.

When she got back into the room and closed the door, she looked at the candy bar. It was a Flake Bar. She had never had one of these before. She ripped off the wrapper and took a big bite and moaned. The thin chocolate flakes melted the second they hit her tongue. It was probably because she was starving, but she was pretty sure it was the best chocolate she had ever tasted. She ate the rest in two bites before climbing back into bed. She pulled the covers up and was asleep as soon as her head hit the pillow.

CHAPTER 8

PATRICK

The sun came in the window, causing Patrick to flinch as it reached his eyes. Odd. He had blackout curtains on his window. The sun shouldn't be shining in his face. He moved to sit up and then immediately regretted that decision. His neck had a crick in it, and his back was stiff. He opened his eyes and was greeted by his computer screen.

"Fuuuck," he groaned, stretching his back.

"You fell asleep at your computer again."

He turned. James was leaning against the kitchen island, holding a steaming cup of coffee.

"Where the hell did you get coffee? I thought we ran out last week." Patrick's voice was still rough from sleep.

"Well, Sleeping Beauty, while you were snoring away on your keyboard, I ran up the road to the shop and picked up a few things to get us through breakfast. It's come to my attention we have no food in this flat, and if you're going to be entertaining gorgeous birds, you're going to have to feed them." James smirked.

Patrick ran his hands through his hair and down his face. "I'm not enter—wait, how do you know about Evelyn? You didn't come in until late, and she's been in bed for ages."

"I ran into her in the hallway in the middle of the night. Chatted her up and gave her my Flake Bar. What were you doing sleeping at your computer when you had *that* waiting for you in your bed?"

"It's not like that. It's a long story."

"That's what she said, too. I think it's time you fill me in on this so-called long story. Because, now, I've gone beyond curious and am moving slightly into dead-cat territory."

Patrick rolled his eyes, standing. "I think I need some of that coffee first, and then I'll start filling you in."

James reached behind him and produced an already filled cup of coffee. "I'm one step ahead of you. Start talking."

Patrick sighed, taking the coffee from James. "Fine. You know the Fitzgerald case we're working for Colin?"

James nodded. "Yeah, you were supposed to be at Heathrow to stop Fitzgerald's ex from fleeing the country with a bunch of evidence."

"Yeah, I was there, at Heathrow, and Colin didn't tell me much, just that I was supposed to be meeting a girl with brown hair carrying a certain duffel bag. So, I'm at Heathrow, and I grab the girl with the bag that looked like the one he described. Only, it's not the one I was supposed to nab. It's this American, and she somehow has the bag we need. I keep the bag and I let her go. Only Fitzgerald's lackeys have already honed in on her and are waiting. I'm not about to let her get hurt, so I help her, and I may have technically kidnapped her."

James took a sip of his coffee. "Did you ever find the girl you were supposed to find?"

"Yeah, they delivered her head to Colin's yesterday."

"Fuck!" James almost dropped his coffee mug. "Her head was delivered to your father's home?"

Patrick nodded. "In a cardboard box. Colin wanted me to drop the case, but I refused. He sent me home with the bag and Evelyn, and when Evelyn went to bed, I went through the bag and shit got worse."

"How can things get worse than your contact's severed head being sent to your father like some kind of fucking message?"

Patrick walked over to the duffel bag and opened it. He reached in and pulled out one picture and handed it to James.

"Is that Superintendent McGovern and Mickey Fitzgerald?" James asked.

"Yep."

"And Fitzgerald's handing him loads of pounds?"

"Yep."

"Fucking shit."

"Yep."

"What the fuck are we going to do?" James asked. "I thought the plan was to get the bag and the girl and get her to testify against Fitzgerald. And then *turn everything over* to the police so they could actually arrest the fuckers."

"Yeah, that was the plan. I wasn't expecting to find out the plan was doomed to fail from the start. We can't get anyone to arrest the arsehole. He's virtually untouchable. I can't even think of one officer in Tower Hamlets who probably is *not* being paid off by the Fitzgeralds."

"C'mon, there has to be one. I seem to remember not everyone was willing to become a corrupt arse while we were there."

Patrick shook his head. "We're going to have to do some digging. There are hundreds of officers in the borough. We're going to have to be thorough, but we might be able to come up with at least one. But don't get your hopes up."

"That's the spirit! Now, what are you doing about Evelyn? Is she stuck here?"

He shrugged. "Colin seems to think the Fitzgeralds are gunning for her because they assume she knows what's in the bag. Which she doesn't, by the way. She can't know what's in the bag. She can't know anything, really. If she knows nothing, she'll be able to leave and not have to stay for the trial. Also, if she were to get captured, she'll have plausible deniability."

"But we'll not let it come to that, yeah? We're going to make sure the Fitzgeralds don't get to her."

Patrick said nothing.

"We're going to protect her, right? That's our job. That's why Colin sent her here rather than keeping her at his fortress, where they sent a fucking head, right?"

"Well, we need to lure the Fitzgeralds out into the open and become vulnerable so we can get our loyal officer to arrest them, yeah? And they want the bag and the girl, yeah? So..." Patrick motioned with his hands, as if the rest of the sentence was obvious.

James swung his arm around to gesture toward the door which Evelyn was behind, forgetting he was holding a mug of coffee as it sloshed out and onto the floor. "We're not using that girl as bait, Patrick! Jesus Christ. What's going on with you? I know this case is personal, but my best mate would never suggest using an innocent girl to lure crazed criminals into the open."

"Oi! There's nothing wrong with me. And I said nothing about using the *girl* as bait, did I?" Patrick shouted.

"The words never came out of your mouth, but you heavily implied them. Look, I'm upset about what happened to your mum, too, but that doesn't mean we need to sacrifice an innocent woman to get your vengeance. Think about what you're saying, mate!" James' expression softened with the mention of Patrick's mum, but neither wanted to ruminate on the subject.

"I know what I'm saying, and I am not saying we sacrifice that part of our bounty. I'm talking about the other part. Because when it all comes down to it, does it matter what we sacrifice if Mickey Fitzgerald is sitting behind bars, paying for all the crimes he's committed? The only person who would be upset at the loss would be my dad. What's wrong with a little collateral damage?" Patrick gestured at the floor next to his computer.

James opened his mouth to respond, but the slamming of a door interrupted him. The two men whipped around to see Evelyn, disheveled from sleep, standing in the room, tears in her eyes.

"Collateral damage?" she whispered through tears.

"Evelyn, I—" Guilt ate away at Patrick.

She shook her head. "Don't. I was able to hear everything. These walls aren't exactly soundproof, just so you know." She closed her eyes as tears made their way down her cheeks. "I need some air." She ran to the apartment door, opened it, and ran into the hallway, leaving two shocked men staring after her.

CHAPTER 9

EVELYN

Evelyn burst through the doorway to the street. She stopped and stared at the road for a minute before choosing a direction. She didn't know where she was going, but she knew she had to get away from that apartment and, more importantly, Patrick.

She wiped tears off her face, but they kept coming. After doing really well holding herself together over the last twenty-four hours, she'd found the proverbial straw that broke the camel's back.

Patrick was an ass. A handsome ass, but still an ass. They'd been at odds ever since they met, but sacrificing her to the Fitzgeralds? Not caring if she lived or died as long as he got what he needed in the end? That was low. And she didn't want to spend a second longer in the same room as him. She wanted to get as far away from him as possible.

She had absolutely no idea where she was or where she was going, but that was an insignificant detail she could eventually deal with. Everyone here spoke English, and she'd watched enough movies and documentaries to know London was all connected to a subway system, so she was bound to find an entry to get on eventually. Right?

"Evelyn! Wait!"

She paused and looked over her shoulder. "Fuck."

Patrick was running up the sidewalk toward her.

She turned back around and continued. "Go away, Patrick." She didn't pause.

It didn't take long until Patrick had caught up and was matching her strides. Even though he had basically sprinted to catch up with her, he wasn't even remotely out of breath. That made her resent him even more.

"Where are you going?" he asked.

"I don't know. Away from you. But apparently, that's not going to work."

He sighed. "Look, I'm sorry. I didn't mean for you to hear anything I said back there."

She scoffed. "Yeah, I gathered that. Most people who want to sacrifice their hostage for the 'greater good' rarely tell their grand scheme to said hostage before offering them up to the bad guy."

"I'm not..." He paused. "I'm not going to sacrifice you to the greater good. I never even said I wanted to sacrifice you."

"No, but you did say I would be collateral damage."

He sighed. "No, I didn't. You heard wrong, or interpreted it wrong, or whatever. I was telling James we would sacrifice the *bag*, not you. I'm not a monster."

She stopped walking and turned to look at him. "The bag? You were talking about the bag?"

He shrugged. "I was. I don't know why you and James jumped to the conclusion I was willing to sacrifice you to Fitzgerald. I wasn't that bad yesterday, was I?"

"You were rude. You yelled at me. You starved me," Evelyn enumerated on her fingers. "I'm pretty sure you may actually hate me."

He had the decency to look embarrassed. "Okay, so yesterday may not have been my finest moment. But I don't hate you. Am I annoyed by you? Yes, very much so, but I don't hate you. I don't think I hate anyone, other than, you know, the Fitzgeralds. I'm sorry I came across that way, but I have a one-track mind, and when something doesn't go the way I want it to, I overreact."

"And put women in your room to slowly starve to death?"

"Bloody hell, you were not going to starve to death, but you're right, I've been an utter bastard."

"Well, I wouldn't classify you as an *utter* bastard. Just bastard will do."

Patrick looked at her like he was seeing her for the first time before he started laughing. Really laughing. She had barely seen the man smile in the last twenty-four hours, let alone laugh.

She looked at him like he'd grown three heads. "What's so funny?"

"You. In fact, this entire fucking situation we're in."

She grew more confused. "Situation we're in? How is our situation at all funny?"

"I can't explain it. It's just that I admit, I *have* been a complete arse to you the last twenty-four hours, and you *still* stopped and talked to me after running out of my flat after you had thought I'd said I'd gladly sacrifice you for my cause. You're an anomaly, Evelyn... I'm sorry, but I don't really recall your last name."

"Stevenson," she answered automatically, still trying to process what the hell was going on in front of her.

"Let's start over a bit, eh? Patrick Miller." He offered his hand.

She looked at the hand in front of her suspiciously. This was a complete one eighty from the day before. He barely gave his name before dragging her all over London. And he wasn't exactly warm toward her the entire day. What was his game? Was he trying to gain her trust so he could turn around and betray her later by giving her up to the Fitzgeralds, despite saying she had misheard him? Should she even trust this man?

On the one hand, her gut was screaming at her *hell no*, telling her she should run in the opposite direction, and keep running until she found her way out of the country and onto the first plane to Greece. On the other, her head was telling her she did not know where she was or how to navigate London. For all she knew, she was being watched by the Fitzgeralds right this very second, the man in front of her could very well be telling the truth, and be the only person able to protect her. Besides, even through all the times he was being an ass to her, Patrick had some moments where he seemed like a decent enough guy. There was potential for something, she didn't know what yet, but something.

"It's not going to bite you, is it?" Patrick gestured to his hand.

Making a split-second decision, she grabbed his hand, shaking it. "Evelyn Stevenson."

He broke out into a wide grin. "Nice to meet you, Evelyn. Now, James is back at the flat doing his best Mr. Muscle impression and making it much more hospitable for guests. How about we continue down this road to the small café and get a bite to eat, and we can try to be honest with each other for a change, yeah?"

She nodded and began following him down the road, hoping with every step she took she hadn't made the world's biggest mistake and just signed her own death sentence.

CHAPTER 10

PATRICK

Silverware scraped against plates, and soft music filled in the background of Little Rock Café. Patrick looked on as Evelyn sipped her cup of coffee while they awaited their food. She kept looking at him over the rim of her coffee mug and narrowing her eyes. He hid his smile behind his own mug. It wouldn't do to have her see his amusement at her suspicion.

Since their confrontation in the middle of the sidewalk, she hadn't said a word to him. She quietly followed him to the café and then only spoke to give the waitress her order before falling silent again and observing him. She didn't trust him. And he didn't blame her. He hadn't been very kind to her in the last twenty-four hours. He wouldn't trust him either.

What had happened to him in the last year? When did he become this utter bastard who Evelyn met yesterday? There was a time when he would have seen a girl like Evelyn and turned on the charm, flirting with her. Gaining her trust and getting her to think her actions were her own idea rather than his.

He looked back at the girl, who sat across from him, and again had to admit she was very attractive, even for being in the same clothes she'd obviously been wearing for two days and not having had a shower in just as many. Her brown hair was mussed, and she had bags under her chocolate eyes, but there was something about her simplicity that was attractive.

He shook his head. He couldn't risk seeing her as anything more than a client. That was what she was. His client and his responsibility. She was in trouble, and he needed to do everything in his power to protect her. Even if it was forgetting about how well her T-shirt accentuated her curves. Patrick closed his eyes and counted to ten. If James wanted to shag her, he could shag her. Patrick was going to keep things completely one-hundred percent professional between them. He neither wanted nor needed the complications of a woman right now. He needed to focus on protecting her and getting that fucker Fitzgerald behind bars.

"Are you okay?" Evelyn asked.

He opened his eyes and looked at her. She'd gone from eying him suspiciously to looking over at him with concern.

"Yeah, yeah. I'm good. Sorry. I didn't sleep well last night."

She smiled. "Yeah, I saw you asleep in front of your computer. It didn't look very comfortable."

"It wasn't. I've got a wicked cramp in my neck that won't let up, and there's a pain between my shoulders. It's quite the reminder I'm not as young as I used to be."

"Your dad said you were almost thirty. That's not old."

He smiled. "Thirty is ancient. Thirty is the new fifty, don't you know? It's quite a bit older than you. You're in Uni, yeah? So, you're what, nineteen, twenty?"

She laughed. "Yeah, I'm attending university, but I'm a grad student, not an undergrad. I'm actually twenty-three. But thanks for thinking I was nineteen. That made me feel good."

"Well, I'm not much older than you. I'm the ripe old age of twenty-seven."

"Have you always been a private investigator? How does one even go about getting a job like that?"

He shook his head, swallowing the bite of his newly arrived eggs. "No. Actually, after I completed my A-levels, I joined the Metropolitan Police Service, and I was an officer for about seven years. I've only been a private investigator for the last two years."

"Why did you stop being a police officer?" She cut through her Spanish omelet.

She was obviously starved as he took in the several plates of food surrounding her. He smiled. It seemed pretty on brand she wasn't coy or timid when it came to food. He dated too many women who were afraid to eat around him. She closed her eyes as she took a bite of omelet and smiled. She was beautiful when she smiled. Patrick made a vow to make sure she did more smiling in his presence than crying from now on. She opened her eyes and looked at him quizzically. Probably wondering why he was staring at her while she ate like some nutter.

He cleared his throat and returned to the conversation. "Corruption. I don't know what you've been able to pick up on between what Colin, James, and myself have been saying around you, but the force has become very corrupt in the last five years, coinciding with the meteoric rise of the Fitzgerald Family here in Tower Hamlets."

"Tower Hamlets? I thought we were in London."

Patrick swallowed. "London is a fairly large city, so they divided it up into thirty-two boroughs. We're in Tower Hamlets, one of the poorer parts of the city."

"So, is London's entire police force corrupt? If it's as large as you say, you'd think that would take a lot of work."

He shook his head. "Only ours, it seems. Mickey Fitzgerald is a smart bloke. He keeps most of his business dealings and crimes centralized here. That way, anything he does occurs in the jurisdiction of the local police and then he can get away with it a lot easier. Consequently, since the Fitzgeralds have moved into town, the crime rate has increased and the safety of the area has gone down. Try to remember that before you go running off by yourself again. You're not exactly in the safest part of London. Five years ago, maybe, but now," he shook his head, "the borough is becoming almost unrecognizable."

She gave him a sympathetic smile. "I'm sorry. If you didn't like the corruption here, why didn't you transfer to another borough? Didn't you like being an officer?"

He shook his head. "After all the pressure to cave to Fitzgerald's demands, and watching all of my former colleagues in the force cave, I became very disillusioned with wearing the badge. If our small little borough could become corrupt, what was going on in the other boroughs? I didn't want to find out. I put in my resignation and set up my investigation agency with James. And we've been doing pretty well, if I say so myself."

"And James was also an officer?"

He nodded. "He was. He and I were partners at the end. When he also became disillusioned with the force, we came up with the idea to start the agency together. We found the flat we're living in, moved in, and set up our office, since we couldn't afford to rent a separate place. London is bloody expensive."

"Do you solve a lot of murders? I keep picturing you as Sherlock Holmes."

Patrick laughed. "No, definitely not Sherlock Holmes. We do a lot of cheating spouses. You wouldn't believe the number of men and women who'll pay exorbitant amounts of money to get at least one picture of their significant other shagging someone else. We make a very good living on just staking out and following someone for a couple of days and getting the money shot."

"Wow. I had no idea that that was a thing."

"Yeah, and if we're not doing a cheating spouse, we're finding a missing dog or missing money from a till. It's usually all quite boring."

"Then how did you pick up a case that involved taking down the major crime syndicate in your borough?"

He quickly took a bite of his food. "Colin, actually," he said after swallowing. "His solicitor's office is desperate to build a case against Fitzgerald, and they're trying to do whatever they can to have it ready in the event he actually gets arrested."

"And they need someone outside of your borough's police to help out."

He pointed his fork at her. "Exactly. And a few days ago, this girl, Megan, fell into their lap. She'd been sleeping with Fitzgerald, but then had a change of heart a few months ago and began putting together loads of evidence against the bastard."

She stopped her fork halfway to her mouth. "Wait, if she called your dad wanting to turn in evidence and be a witness, what were you doing at the airport?"

He smiled, wryly. "Well, the bitch got cold feet, apparently, and called from Heathrow saying she was going to hop the first plane out of the country. Colin called me and begged me to run to Heathrow and pick her up. And I did, and that's how I met you and fucked up the entire case."

They sat quietly for a few minutes, both eating, before she spoke.

"I'm sorry for messing up your first big case. If I wasn't in a such a hurry and not looking where I was going, I never would have crashed into Megan, switching bags, and you never would have mistaken me for her. And she would probably still be alive."

He shook his head. "It's not your fault, so please don't think it is. I'm the one who fucked up. I was so focused on finding the bag, I didn't pay attention to anything else. All I wanted to do was prove to Colin I could handle this case."

"Why do you call your dad by his first name? Is that something they do here in London?"

"I don't want to talk about it," he said gruffly, focusing more on his plate.

"Earlier you and James were arguing about how this case was personal to you, same with you and Colin. Something about your mom?"

He coughed. "Look, why don't you finish your breakfast and we can go back to the flat and check in with James, yeah?"

Her face fell, and she concentrated on eating her breakfast.

They finished their meal without either one of them saying anything else.

CHAPTER 11

EVELYN

Upon returning to the flat, Evelyn was floored. She couldn't believe this was the same place she'd stayed the night before. The floor no longer looked like the substitute for the trash can. The couch, while still the ugliest thing she had ever seen, no longer had food and empty bottles surrounding it. She was pretty sure she could see the kitchen counters sparkling from the front door.

"Wow." She resisted the urge to pinch herself to make sure she wasn't still laying in the bedroom sleeping.

James emerged from the back of the flat, yellow rubber gloves on, an apron around his waist, and a mask across his mouth, brandishing a scrub brush.

When he caught sight of Evelyn, he reached up and pulled the mask off his face to hang around his neck. "You like?" He gestured around the flat.

"I do. It's amazing. How did you manage all of this in the short time we were gone?"

"Let me tell you, it was no easy feat. And don't go into the bathroom yet. That's not ready for a lady. Patrick, mate, how the fuck did we ever let that room get so bad? I'm half expecting to find a nest of rats or cockroaches or something in there."

She glanced back at Patrick as he walked into the flat and shut the door.

"I don't know. Maybe it's because we're rarely here anymore. We're always coming and going and sleeping in the car on a stakeout."

"Touché," James answered. "Oh, Evelyn, before I forget, I went to the girl two doors down and gave her a sob story about my sister being in town and how the plane lost her luggage. She lent me about a week's worth of clothes for you to borrow. She seems to be about your size, so I hope that will help you."

She looked at the man in front of her in awe. This man barely knew her. She had a brief conversation with him in the hallway in the middle of the night, and he had not only found her clothes for her stay, he had cleaned the entire flat for her. "Thank you. I don't know what to say."

James flashed her a smile that made her weak in the knees. "When you realize this one is not as bad as he seems, remember I'm the one who got you clothes and shag me, not him."

Before she could react, Patrick brushed past her and headed into his room. "I'm going to change." He didn't bother to turn around to speak to them before slamming the door.

"What's his problem?" She turned back to James.

James shrugged. "Fuck if I know. He's been very touchy lately."

"I've noticed. What's up with that? I asked him at breakfast, and he completely ignored me and shut down."

The smile fell off his face. "Well, if he doesn't want to tell you, then it's not my place. But if you wait, I'm sure once he gets to know you better, Patrick will tell you anything you want to know."

She sighed and looked back toward the shut door. For every answer she was getting, she had even more questions. And now he was locked in that room with her stuff and if she was going to be out here, alone, while James finished the bathroom and Patrick did, whatever Patrick was doing, she could at least work on some research for her thesis and—

"Fuck a duck!" She exclaimed.

"What's wrong?" he asked.

"My parents! My professor in charge of my program! The director of the dig! They're all expecting me to be in Greece right now! I was supposed to email or call my parents. What if the director has already called and told them I never showed up? What if they think I'm dead? Fuck, fuck, fuck!"

"Whoa. Calm down. Why don't you use your mobile and call them?"

"I didn't want to pay for international service. My cell phone is a glorified alarm clock right now."

"Why don't you go over to Patrick's computer and send an email, making up an excuse about why you aren't there? It'll probably be easier through text, anyway."

She glanced over at the computer and began breathing easy again. Why didn't she think of that? This jet lag business was definitely playing with her head.

"Thanks. Don't let me keep you from...whatever it is you were doing."

She smiled at her. "I'm tackling the shower. Give me thirty, and then I'll show you the clothes I dug up for you and allow you to clean up." He flashed her one more cheeky grin before pulling the mask back up to cover his face and retreating to the bathroom.

Evelyn shook her head before turning toward the computer. She walked over, sitting in Patrick's desk chair. No wonder he had a sore back and neck. This chair wasn't exactly the most comfortable on the planet. She minimized all the windows Patrick had open before pulling up the internet browser and logging into her email. After staring at a blinking cursor for ten minutes, she finally composed an email that had just enough truth in it that it would be believable.

Hey Everyone,

I'm sorry I didn't get in contact sooner, but this is the first time I've been able to sit down and compose an email. Remember how I was worried about my connecting flight in London? Well, I was right to worry. I missed my connection to Athens! I've been at the airport all night trying to re-book, and they're having difficulty accommodating all of my travel arrangements.

Unfortunately, I'm stuck in London for a little while. As soon as I know more, I'll let everyone know. Please don't worry about me. The airline has set me up in some nice accommodations. If I had to be stuck somewhere, it seems London is a good place to be stuck. Maybe I'll get some sightseeing in.

Evie

"What are you doing?" Patrick's voice right behind her caused her to jump.

Holding her hand to her chest, she turned to face him. "I'm emailing my parents and program directors so they don't worry about me."

Patrick nodded. "Good idea. I don't know why we didn't do that earlier."

She shrugged. "Probably because we were too busy shouting at each other."

"Quite right. I couldn't help but notice you signed your email 'Evie'. Is that what you're called?"

She nodded. "Yeah, almost everyone I know calls me that."

He seemed to think about that new information and file it back for later. "Duly noted."

She quirked her eyebrows at him and was about to say something when James shouted from down the hall. "Evelyn, the bathroom is safe now. The clothes I borrowed are in a canvas bag which I have set inside the bathroom door. And since I know your toiletries are more than likely somewhere between here and Greece, you may use whatever you find inside the shower. Feel free to commence the cleansing."

"Well, don't let me keep you from tidying up. After all, James worked hard to make our loo worthy of your use, *Evelyn.*"

She looked at him, and tilted her head, puzzled at this emphasis on her full name, especially after she told him everyone called her Evie.

He met her gaze, holding it.

Her heart rate increased as seconds stretched between them as they held each other's gaze before he broke it with a smirk and turned to walk back into his room, closing the door behind him.

As she watched the door close, she willed her heart rate to slow down back to normal. She had no idea what had just happened between them. Nor did she want to think too much about it. The first hot shower and clean clothes she would experience in almost three days awaited her just down the hall. She could analyze whatever it was happening between her and her investigator after she washed away the grime of traveling and didn't smell of blah.

She quickly hit send on her email and headed down the hall, the puzzle of Patrick sitting in the back of her mind the entire way.

CHAPTER 12

PATRICK

Patrick laid on his bed and listened to the water running in the bathroom. He closed his eyes and tried to make sense of the way he was acting. No matter how many times he ran it through his head, he still didn't understand why he had this sudden rage every time James spoke to Evelyn. He had no interest in her as anything other than a client, so why did it matter if James flirted with her?

Because I saw her first, the little voice at the back of his head muttered.

He pressed his hands firmly against his eyes, willing the little voice to shut up. He needed to focus on the case, not on whether Evelyn and James were going to sleep together. He needed to figure out what to do about getting the evidence to the police.

He began running over the names of everyone he knew from the force who were still in Tower Hamlets. Then he started eliminating the ones he knew for sure took bribes from the family to look the other way. And then he eliminated the ones who were on the fence about taking bribes. And finally, he eliminated the bloody chief superintendent because who the fuck saw that coming? That left him with one name. One name, he was certain, would still be clean.

He was about to stand up and go fill James in on what he had figured out when the door to his bedroom flung open, revealing Evelyn, whose hair was still wet from the shower, wearing clothes about two sizes too small.

"Oh, I'm sorry. I didn't know you were still in here. I was going to grab my hairbrush." She gestured at her bag on the floor.

Patrick waved off her apology and gestured to her bags. "Don't worry about it. More importantly, what the bloody hell are you wearing?"

She bent down to retrieve her bag and set it on the bed. "Well, apparently, James is terrible at discerning when women are even remotely the same size." She pulled out her hairbrush and began combing through her unruly hair, the T-shirt pulling even tighter against her chest and riding up a little, revealing a sliver of her stomach. "I hope you guys solve this case sooner rather than later, because I don't know how long I want to walk around London looking like this."

He gave her a once-over and then resumed his position of lying back on the bed and staring at the ceiling. "It's not so bad. If you're going for the Julia Roberts in *Pretty Woman* look."

She scoffed and then something soft crashed into his face. He brought his hand up and lifted a pile of his T-shirts, looking at her. "What was that for?"

"Consider that me helping make this room match the rest of your flat." She smiled.

He waited until she was zipping her bag back up and depositing it on the ground before throwing the shirts back at her, nailing her right in the head.

She sprung back up and tried to glare at him, attempting to not smile and failing.

He went to lay back down, humming Roy Orbison's 'Pretty Woman' when the clothes came sailing back at him. He ducked out of the way this time, letting out a laugh as he dodged his dirty laundry.

She half growled, half laughed in frustration, causing Patrick to look up at her. He had to admire the way her nose scrunched up so nicely when she narrowed her eyes and pursed her lips in frustration. He wanted to lean over and—

"So," he said, a little louder than he intended, "if you're done in here, we should go out and find James. I just thought of a solution that will get us on the path to getting you wherever it is you want to go. Whether it's on to Greece or on your way back to the States."

Her face lit up with that bit of news, and he had to pretend he didn't notice her eyes were the most expressive part of her, and it made his heart skip a beat.

"Really? What did you figure out?"

He shook his head. "I'll tell you out in the living room with James. That way, I only have to tell it once."

She nodded and walked into the living room.

He closed his eyes, counted to ten, and then followed her out.

In true James fashion, he was already in the living room, perched on the side of the couch where Evelyn was sitting, chatting her up, in the ten seconds Patrick stalled in his room. He moved to his desk, pulling out the chair, and turned it to face them, before sitting down.

"Evie was just telling me you have a solution to our little corruption problem."

Patrick tried not to cringe when James addressed her in such an informal way. "Yes, I did. After mentally going over every officer I know in Tower Hamlets and trying to figure out who wouldn't be in the Fitzgeralds' pockets, I came up with one name."

James leaned forward on the arm of the couch. "Really? I've spent all morning going over the names, and I couldn't think of one. Who was I missing?"

"Well, maybe you know something I don't, but I came up with Harry."

James was silent for a minute. "Harry. I completely forgot about the bugger. He's been chief inspector for so long he slipped my mind. However, if the chief superintendent has fallen to Fitzgerald, how can we be sure Harry hasn't?"

Patrick shook his head. "I'm sure he hasn't. You don't know Harry like I do. He wouldn't do that. He's one to uphold the law above all else."

James sat back for a few minutes. "If you're sure, then he's the only chance we have of catching these bastards."

Evelyn chose that moment to speak up. "I'm sorry, but I'm feeling a little left out here. Who's Harry?"

"Harry was my mentor when I joined the force," Patrick replied. "He showed me the ropes, and he was the senior officer they partnered me with. He became the father I always wished I had. He's a great guy, and it disappointed him when I left the force, but he also understood why I needed to."

"Are you sure you're not allowing your sentiments for this guy get in the way of your judgment? Don't get me wrong. I trust your judgment, but I want to make sure you're absolutely, positively sure this guy isn't going to sell us out to the Fitzgeralds before you bring him in on whatever it is we're doing. I'm not even sure what it is we're doing, and I want to be filled in on that, by the way." Evelyn pointed her finger moving it between the two men.

Patrick didn't hesitate. "I trust him. I don't know what it is, but my gut is saying this is our one shot. He's the only person in the police office here who's honorable enough to stick with his beliefs and not accept bribes from the Fitzgeralds. He wouldn't do that."

Patrick waited as Evelyn looked at James for confirmation. He gave her a subtle nod, and she turned back to Patrick.

"If you feel this strongly, and you along with James, both trust him, then I say we go for it. Like I said, I trust you both. It's crazy because I don't even know you, and really, I don't have much of a choice anyway, but I trust you."

Patrick gave her a small smile. "Great. Believe me, this will be what we need, and he'll be our ticket to blowing this case wide open."

He reached over to his desk and found his mobile. He scrolled through the list of names until he found Harry's. Hitting the send button, he listened while it rang.

"Hello?" Harry answered.

He smiled, hearing the voice of his old mentor and father figure. "Harry? It's Patrick."

Harry chuckled. "Patrick, how are you, mate?"

"I'm doing well, Harry. How are you?"

"Not bad, not bad. And to what do I owe the pleasure of this phone call?"

Patrick swallowed. "I'm calling you about a case I'm working on. I was wondering if you'd be able to help me out."

"Anything, anything. What can I do for you?"

"Well, the case has a layer of confidentiality surrounding it, so I don't want to disclose too much over the phone. Is there any way we can meet and discuss this?"

Harry was quiet for a few minutes. "Of course, of course. But can you give me any kind of hint as to what the case entails, so maybe I can prepare a little before we meet? My brain isn't what it used to be. Help an old man out."

Patrick didn't respond right away. He needed to think about this. And maybe get James's opinion. He reached over and grabbed a pad and pen and scribbled a note on a page, holding it up for James to read.

"Fitzgeralds?"

James nodded.

He scribbled again. "*Megan?*"

James shook his head in the negative.

"It's about the Fitzgeralds," Patrick told Harry.

Harry got really quiet for a really long time. Patrick almost thought he'd lost the call.

"What about the Fitzgeralds?"

"I can't tell you right now, but I can when we meet in person. I will tell you this could change everything."

"Uh-huh. Well, then, I'll meet with you and see if I can help you. How about later tonight? Say, around eleven? And we should meet somewhere public. That way we know the walls won't have ears."

"Er, okay." Patrick was confused. "Where is it you want to meet?"

"How about The Southbank, on the promenade?"

"Yeah, yeah. We'll meet you there around eleven."

"We?" Harry asked. "Who else is coming with you? I was under the impression it would be just the two of us."

"Nah. I'm bringing a couple people with me. People who need to be there."

"Who?" Harry sounded a little harsher, but Patrick shrugged it off.

"James Moore. You remember him when we were all officers, yeah? He's my partner. And my client, Ev—"

He broke off when James began slashing his hand next to his throat. "And my client will be there as well."

"Okay, well, I guess it would be okay to bring them. I'll see you at The Southbank at eleven."

Before Patrick had a chance to respond, Harry disconnected the call.

Patrick stared at his mobile for a few minutes before setting it back on the desk.

"Well, what did he say?" James asked.

"We're to meet him at The Southbank on the promenade at eleven tonight."

James quirked his eyebrow. "Did he say why we were meeting at such a public place?"

"He said it would be better to meet in public. That way, the walls wouldn't have ears."

James laughed. "You're fucking kidding, right?"

Patrick shook his head. "Nope, that's what he said."

James shook his head. "I don't bloody believe it."

Evelyn looked back and forth between the two men, confusion etched on her face. "I don't understand? What's so funny?"

James and Patrick exchanged a look, and James gestured for Patrick to go ahead and explain.

"Here in London, we have CCTV: Closed-Circuit Television. Basically, we have cameras all over the bloody city, showing what everyone is doing. Every move someone makes is being recorded when they're out on the streets of London. So, when Harry said he wanted to meet us at the Southbank Promenade so the 'walls wouldn't have ears,' that's ironic because we're going to be meeting somewhere that literally has eyes and will leave a record," Patrick stated.

"Then why are we meeting there?"

"Fuck if I know." Patrick shrugged. "Look, let's not read too much into this. He's agreed to meet, and he's agreed to help. We'll have an ally in the police department, and we'll bring down Mickey Fitzgerald."

James stood. "Listen, mate, you need to slow down and gain some perspective. Just because we have an ally in the department doesn't mean we'll be bringing the Fitzgeralds down immediately. It may take some time. You can't expect justice overnight."

"And why the bloody hell not? We have the evidence! We have quite literally a bloody head in a box. We have an officer to arrest him and press charges, and a solicitor to prosecute him. Why shouldn't I expect things to move quickly and for us to get rid of the fucking Fitzgeralds once and for all?"

"Because life doesn't work like that. Just because, on paper, it looks like we have an open-and-shut case, it doesn't mean we really have an open-and-shut case. There are so many factors that could work against us. We need to slow down and figure out if we're really doing everything, we can to make sure we don't get screwed over in the end." James gave Patrick an intense look.

Patrick stood. "I don't need the negativity. If you don't think we can accomplish this, then I need you to stay out of my way. This is the first chance we've had to make any progress, and I won't have you buggering it up."

The two men stood in the middle of the living room, staring at each other. You could cut the tension in the room with a knife.

James was the first to speak. "Listen, mate, I'm not going to get in your way, not intentionally anyway, but I'm not going to stand back and watch you get hurt. I'm going to be the voice of reason. I'm going to tell you when you're doing something stupid. I'm going to slow us down when I think we're going to do something rash. You're my best friend, and I'm not going to lose you to the Fitzgerald family or to your obsession. Do you understand?"

Patrick narrowed his eyes and breathed heavily through his nose. "Yeah, I understand."

"Great. So, what do we need to do to prepare for tonight?"

Patrick relaxed when James changed the subject. "We need to get Evelyn something appropriate to wear first, I think." He gestured to her.

She had been previously ignored during their spat.

James looked at her, giving her body a once-over. "I don't see anything wrong with what she's wearing right now."

She stood, placing her hands on her hips. "Well, I'm voting with Patrick that I need new clothes. So, it looks like you're outvoted."

"You'd think a bloke would get a little more thanks for going out of his way and finding you a perfectly good wardrobe for your stay in London, but I guess being a gentleman is a thankless job these days," James said dramatically.

"These clothes are two sizes too small."

"Her clothes are obscenely tight."

Patrick and Evelyn spoke over one another.

James held his hands up in defeat. "Alright, alright, I get the hint. We'll go out and get you some new clothes. Maybe on the way back we should take Evie to get some fish and chips at the place you love. Then come back here and talk strategy. How does that sound?"

Patrick shrugged. "Sounds good to me."

Evelyn nodded. "Sure, as long as during that strategizing meeting, you two fill me in on everything, and I mean *everything,* going on. If I'm going to be involved,

I want to have an equal say in things. And in order to have an equal say, I have to have equal knowledge."

The two men exchanged looks. After a few more seconds, they both shrugged and turned to Evelyn.

"Fine. We'll tell you what's going on and will answer any questions you have. Within reason," Patrick conceded.

"But—" Evelyn started.

Patrick held up a hand and shook his head. "Within reason or nothing at all."

She sighed, crossing her arms across her chest, and Patrick's eyes were immediately drawn to how the shirt pulled tight against her breasts, accentuating them.

Apparently noticing where Patrick's gaze had landed, she let out a huff of frustration and lowered her arms, placing her hands on her hips. "Fine, within reason. Now can we go get me some clothes so I can breathe again? I'm afraid if I take anything more than shallow breaths, the button on these jeans is going to pop off and kill someone."

Patrick's gaze snapped back up to hers at the comment, and he couldn't help but start laughing. Soon, Evelyn and James joined in, the tension in the room dissipating. As soon as the three caught their breath, James gestured to the door, and they all exited, still smiling at her comment.

CHAPTER 13

EVELYN

The three of them returned to the apartment with full bellies and several shopping bags of clothes.

"I'm pretty sure I just spent my first month's food budget on a new wardrobe." Evelyn set the bags on the couch.

"Well, we'll feed you. Don't worry." Patrick walked to the fridge and put some food inside they had purchased at the supermarket on their walk back. "I think this is the most food James and I have had in our flat in months."

"Well, I'm probably not going to be here for a month, so it may end up being a problem for me if I end up going to Greece rather than back home."

Patrick froze, his back stiffening.

She cocked her head to the side, but before she could question his strange behavior, Patrick shook his head and turned around.

"Well, we can send some of this food with you when you leave, yeah? That way you won't starve." Patrick walked back into the living room.

"Thanks. That's really sweet of you." She paused and narrowed her eyes. "Who are you, and what did you do with Patrick?"

He looked stricken, but when she laughed, he joined in with her.

"Haha. I know I've been a complete arse, but I can be nice when I want to be."

She shook her head. "Nah, I don't believe it. James, I think we have a case of an invasion of the body snatchers here."

He took two steps back to the kitchen island, picked up the dish towel, and chucked it at her, who caught it as it got close.

"Children, children," James said with mock authority, "we need to focus on what it is we're going to do tonight."

The reminder of their situation sobered the group instantly. It was becoming easy to forget circumstance forced them together, and they were not just getting to know each other like normal young adults.

Evelyn sank onto the couch as Patrick took his spot in his desk chair. James took a seat on the floor, sitting cross-legged.

"So, where do we start?" Evelyn asked.

"Let's discuss tonight first, and then we'll answer any questions you have," James replied.

"Within reason," Patrick added, pointedly.

"Within reason," Evelyn parroted back.

"Tonight, we're going to meet at the Southbank Promenade at eleven. How much should we disclose to Harry?" James asked.

"I say we tell him everything," Patrick stated. "We know we can trust him, and we'll need him in the loop so we can get an arrest."

Evelyn shook her head. "I disagree. Shouldn't we keep some knowledge to ourselves? What if he turns out to *not* be trustworthy? Do you want to reveal all your aces so early in the game?"

Patrick frowned. "We've already been over this. Harry is like my father. He won't betray us. He's the most loyal and upstanding man I know."

"That's great, and I'm sure he is, but what harm is it if we keep some stuff to ourselves? Like the chief superintendent being in the pockets of the Fitzgeralds? Or Megan's head being delivered to your father? Or whatever else you found in that bag? I'm just saying maybe we should be a little more cautious." Evelyn rambled off key points.

Patrick opened his mouth to respond, but James interrupted him. "The lady has a point, and I'm wanting to agree with her. I say we only reveal what's absolutely necessary to get him to agree to be our man on the inside. Once we know for sure he's on our side, we can let him in on the things we've left out, little by little."

Patrick sighed. "Fine. Since I'm outvoted, I guess we'll do it your way. But what *do* we reveal at the meeting tonight?"

"We reveal that you're working with a solicitor's office to bring down the Fitzgeralds. We have the required evidence. We just need someone inside the Municipal Police Service to make the arrest and file charges. The solicitor's office will do the rest."

"How do we explain Evelyn?" Patrick gestured to her.

"We don't. We just say Evie's identity is on a need-to-know basis. That we're bringing her along because she's essential to the case, but we can't reveal how just yet."

Patrick turned to Evelyn. "Are you okay with that?"

She nodded. "Yeah. You know, I'm starting to think it would be fine if you left me behind. I mean, this will probably turn out to be pretty dangerous, right?"

Patrick furrowed his eyebrows. "How so?"

"Like, what if he has a gun? Doesn't this have the potential to become a shootout?"

Patrick shook his head. "Not likely. We have very strict gun laws here, and most police officers don't even carry a gun. More than likely, we'll be fine. Plus, we'll be meeting in clear view of the CCTV cameras. No one would be stupid enough to do anything like that on camera."

"But those guys at the airport yesterday, they had guns," Evelyn argued.

"Love, they're career criminals working for a major crime syndicate. Do you think they care about our strict gun laws?" James asked.

"Yeah, I guess you're right," Evelyn sighed. "Even knowing all of this, I'm going to be nervous the whole time. I'm not used to being in the middle of a criminal investigation."

"What are you used to?" Patrick leaned forward.

"Sitting in the library with my laptop and a pile of books, researching."

"I knew it!"

"No one likes someone who gloats."

"What do you like to do for fun?" Patrick asked. "Because that does not sound like fun."

Evelyn shrugged. "It's actually a lot of fun for me. I don't get out much. Since going to grad school, I've sort of distanced myself from my friends and become really engrossed in my research. The one thing I've been looking forward to was going to Greece and working on that dig. This trip is the first time I've ventured outside of my comfort zone and outside of the country. Actually, really traveled on my own. My mom was *so* worried that something would go wrong before I left. I kept reassuring her I'd be fine. How ironic that I find myself wanted by the mob."

"Don't worry," Patrick whispered to her, "we'll make sure you get to where you're supposed to in one piece."

She smiled. "I really appreciate the thought, but don't promise something that you may not be able to deliver. If these people are as dangerous as your dad, you, and James are implying, it seems the odds may be stacked against us. But let's not ponder on that. Tell me about this mysterious event that has you and James yelling at each other."

Instantly Patrick lost any humor in his face and put on a blank mask, hiding all of his emotions. "I don't want to talk about it."

James sighed. "C'mon, mate. She has the right to know."

Patrick whipped his head around to look at James. "No, she doesn't. I'm drawing the line here. I'll answer anything else, just not this."

She huffed. "Fine. Can you at least tell me what Mickey Fitzgerald looks like? Do you have a picture I can see?"

"Ye—" James started.

"No," Patrick interrupted.

"Patrick!" James shouted. "C'mon. She should at least know what she's up against."

Patrick shook his head. "No, she doesn't. I want her to know as little as possible because, if for some reason the Fitzgeralds outsmart us and capture her, if she knows nothing, maybe, just maybe, they won't kill her."

"So, I'm supposed to not know anything? Then what's the point of even coming tonight if you want to keep me in the dark?"

"I can't risk leaving you alone in the flat. What if the building is being watched? If you're with us, we at least have a chance to prevent anyone from taking you. Leaving you behind would leave you vulnerable," Patrick explained.

"I'm not some damsel in distress, you know. I can take care of myself."

"No, you can't," Patrick pronounced each word harshly. "Not against these people. Trust me. I would feel much better if you were to never leave my sight."

She growled in frustration. "And here we are, back to being an ass. I really thought we had moved past this. That we made some sort of progress in the last few hours."

"If caring about whether you live or die makes me an arse, then I'm the biggest arse in Great Britain and proud of it."

"You're infuriating!" Evelyn shouted.

"You're impossible!" Patrick shouted back.

"Oh my God, just sleep together already!"

That shut the two bickering adults up as they turned in shock at what James had said.

He shrugged his shoulders. "Seriously. If the two of you have it off and get it out of your system, maybe we could move past this mutual attraction and be productive."

"What?" she screeched. "You think that, I, that he, that we..." She shook her head.

Patrick turned to James. "Thanks a lot, mate. I need some air." He stood and walked out the door, slamming it behind him.

Taking her cue from Patrick's quick exit, Evelyn gathered up her shopping bags and bolted to Patrick's room.

***

When Evelyn emerged from Patrick's room, changed into appropriate clothing and ready to head out, Patrick had already returned to the flat. She had no idea how long he'd been there, but he was sitting and working at his computer. She had holed herself in the room, on the bed, with her laptop and research and was plugging away on her thesis. Just because she was stranded in London didn't mean her professors would excuse her if she didn't meet any of her deadlines. She wouldn't have a lot of the firsthand knowledge and research she was hoping to have by participating in the dig.

He had looked up when she walked into the room and gave her a small smile. She returned it and could feel a weight lift off her shoulders. They were good again. Sometime between breakfast this morning, and the teasing over the clothes in the bedroom, they had fallen into a rapport. To then dissolve into a shouting match was a little disheartening. However, the smile was a good start. Hopefully, they could continue to get along as the evening progressed. Or else it would be a long, long night.

They decided parking at their destination would be too difficult, so they opted for the Tube, which allowed Evelyn to tuck the experience away as a typical tourist thing to do in London that she could report later to her parents.

The Southbank promenade was bustling with people, and it was hard for the trio to find a place to stand where they wouldn't get run over by passersby. Evelyn looked out at the river as the moon reflected over the water. Behind her, the London Eye turned, and the multicolored lights of the County Hall shone. She didn't know there could be something so beautiful in the middle of such a busy city.

After what seemed like an hour, they finally found a spot near one of the old-fashioned-looking lamp posts that allowed them to get out of the crowd and hopefully allow Harry to notice them. The promenade was long and, even this late at night, was full of tourists.

"How is he ever going to find us here?" Evelyn had to shout so they could hear her over the crowd.

Patrick shrugged. "I have no bloody idea. I'm more concerned about how many people will overhear us here."

"Having second thoughts, mate?" James shouted.

Patrick shook his head. "No, not at all. I trust there's a reason Harry wanted to meet us here."

They waited in silence for a while.

"Favorite superhero." James broke the silence that had fallen around the group as they waited.

"What?" Evelyn asked.

"I'm pretty partial to Superman, myself. Indestructible he is. Plus, he has the Fortress of Solitude. You can't beat that."

"Spider-Man," Patrick smiled. "Fucking badass scientist who also kicks major ass. But is also human and can be defeated, unlike your choice, who can only ever be defeated by some rock only billionaires can buy."

James scoffed. "Exactly. That's why he's, as I said, indestructible."

"That takes all the fun out of superheroes if you can't fear for their safety. You read or watch something with Spider-Man, and you're on the edge of your seat hoping the villain won't defeat him. With Superman, as long as there's no kryptonite, there's no tension."

Evelyn smiled, watching the two men banter back and forth. You could tell they had this particular debate often, and that James started it in order to work as a distraction. It was working.

"You both are wrong," Evelyn spoke up. "The superior superhero is obviously Iron Man. He's a billionaire, not unlike Batman, however, he's also a badass scientist like Spider-Man, and he has the added bonus of the shrapnel floating in his chest which, if his arc reactor ever stops working, not only is his suit useless, the shrapnel will enter his heart and kill him."

The two men stared at her, and James started laughing. "I knew I liked you from the moment we crashed into each other in the middle of the night. But Evie, my sweet, sweet Evie, how very wrong you are. Let me tell you all the ways in which you are and why you should change your answer to Superman."

"Not a chance." Evelyn laughed. "We all know nothing you're going to say is going to change my mind. Iron Man is better than Superman for the crucial fact he is Marvel. Marvel beats DC any day of the week."

"Fuck yeah it does," Patrick agreed, holding his hand up for a high five, which Evelyn gladly slapped, "two against one, mate."

James shook his head. "I don't know how two very smart people can be so very wrong about something like this. DC is obviously better. We have Superman *and* Batman. Plus, the most recognizable villains."

"Marvel has recognizable villains," Evelyn retorted.

"Yeah? Name some."

"Doc Oc."

"Green Goblin."

"Loki."

Evelyn and Patrick looked at each other and smiled. They were on a roll. Completely in sync. Something fluttered inside Evelyn's chest as she held his gaze. She tried to push it aside and focus back on the conversation. She didn't have time to focus on whatever this feeling was inside. But for the first time since the airport, she thought of Patrick as attractive. Probably because below all the snarky, broody exterior, he was just as much of a nerd as she was. And that was definitely something she wanted to focus on later. Much later.

"Loki isn't exactly a villain, though. More like an anti-hero," James retorted, bringing her back fully to the conversation.

"I'm sure I could say the same about DC villains," Patrick volleyed.

And so, the three of them stood in the middle of the promenade and loudly debated all the merits of each and every superhero and their respective universe. Every once in a while, Evelyn caught Patrick glancing at his watch, frowning, as the time continued to creep past the agreed upon meeting time. Around eleven forty-five, the crowd had thinned out a bit and the noise level reduced. The trio, who had grown tired of standing, sat on a bench overlooking the Thames. Evelyn, still not on the right time zone, was struggling to keep her eyes open as their conversation slowed down.

"Mate, I don't think he's going to show." James leaned around Evelyn to talk to Patrick. "We've given him forty-five minutes. Evie here is going to fall asleep on this bench, and we still have the ride on the underground back to the flat. Let's go, and you can call him in the morning to find out why he didn't show."

Patrick vehemently shook his head. "No. Let's give it a little more time."

James sighed and leaned back.

Evelyn decided that if they were going to sit and wait, it wouldn't hurt to rest her eyes for a few minutes. She closed her eyes and relaxed for the first time all day. She thought about all the stuff she'd experienced since landing in London and couldn't believe she'd only been in town for a little over twenty-four hours. The rapport between them making it feel as if she'd been in town and known the boys for weeks. The boys. When did she start thinking about them as 'the boys'? Probably sometime between shopping and them all meeting back up about an hour before they were supposed to meet Harry.

She involuntarily started leaning to her right and, before she could catch herself, something warm and soft stopped her. Smiling, she burrowed herself into the warm, soft wall and relaxed even more. Whatever this wall was, it was comforting and smelled really nice. She tried to figure out what it was she was leaning on, but soon her mind decided to enjoy the warmth and not question it.

CHAPTER 14

PATRICK

Patrick looked at the sleeping girl on his shoulder and then looked up at James, who shrugged.

"I told you she was tired."

Patrick sighed and looked at her again. He almost shook her awake, but decided he would wait until she needed to be up. She was only here because he insisted, she had to be here. If he hadn't, she would be back at the flat, sleeping soundly in his bed. He shifted his arm, trying not to wake her as he wrapped it around her shoulders. He moved his body a couple of inches to the left until their sides were touching. He pulled her toward him until her head rested in the crook of his neck, and she relaxed again. He looked up to see James looking at him, eyebrows raised.

"You're telling me you're not attracted to her at all?" James gestured at their intimate positioning.

Patrick glared at him. "There's no attraction. We've been friendly. This is what a friend would do when their other friend just happens to fall asleep on their shoulder."

"So, if I were to fall asleep on your shoulder, you'd put your arm around me and let me snuggle into your neck?"

Patrick scoffed. "Of course."

James smirked. "Good. I'm glad, we've cleared this up because I've decided I'm going to shag her before she leaves."

Patrick couldn't help the rage that boiled up in him, his face forming a scowl. His arm tightened around Evelyn, pulling her toward him, almost possessively. He opened his mouth but stopped himself short before declaring his claim on her. What the fuck?

James laughed and pointed at him. "No attraction, my arse. You want her. Admit it. You've fancied her since the moment you grabbed her at the airport. Don't try to deny it. You're my best friend. I know you better than you know yourself."

Patrick sighed. "I'm not admitting to anything. Besides, I don't have the time for anything right now, and she's going to leave in a few days, hopefully, so there's no point in starting anything."

"I never said you had to be in a relationship with the girl. Just a one-off. It's been a long time since you've had a shag, and you're way overdue. And what better than a girl who's only in the country for a little bit? It can be a little wham bam thank you ma'am, and then she's on her way and you'll never have to see her again."

Patrick shook his head. "For someone who claims to know me better than myself, you really don't know me. I could never do that to someone I know. Some girl I pick up at a club? Sure. One night, never call her again. But by the time I'd get to the point where I'd be able to sleep with her and have her gone, I'll have known Evelyn for days. She would be an acquaintance, possibly a friend, and I could never do that. It will be much simpler if we remain not intimately involved. Too many emotions I don't want to deal with."

"You know, you're allowed to be happy."

"I know."

"Okay. Just making sure you're aware, since you seem so fucking set against doing something for yourself."

"I'm not set against doing something for myself. I just said, in any other circumstance, I would take the leap. See if anything would come of this. But, I can't. Not during this case."

"*Sooo*, why can't I shag her, if you're going to let her leave thinking you're just friends?"

Patrick smirked. "Because, mate, I saw her first."

They both started laughing, Patrick trying to not move his body so he wouldn't wake Evelyn.

As their laughter died, James wiped at his eyes and grew serious again. "How much longer are we going to wait? It's been over an hour. I don't think he's going to show. I know how much you hate to admit it, but maybe we should leave. Evie has already checked out. She has the right idea."

Patrick closed his eyes. "Maybe you're right. Maybe we should—"

"Holy shit."

Patrick opened his eyes and looked over his shoulder to where James was looking. Walking up the sidewalk toward them was Harry. It was well after midnight, and the Southbank Promenade was, while not deserted, certainly less crowded. Patrick gently shook Evelyn, and she lifted her head off his shoulder. She opened her eyes and looked at him, blushing, before pulling away.

A pit in Patrick's stomach grew at the sight of the man walking in their direction. While he was confident, they had made the right choice coming here tonight, there was a nagging feeling that maybe his confidence was a wee bit misplaced. And that feeling, the one that lingered in the back of his consciousness, made him realize he should be ready for any scenario tonight.

Because nothing was off the table.

CHAPTER 15

EVELYN

Evelyn opened her eyes as her soft wall moved. Looking up, she realized she wasn't leaning against a wall at all. She was actually leaning against Patrick, who was looking at her. Her face warmed, and she looked away before moving down the bench from him, leaving some space between them. She rubbed the sleep out of her eyes and turned her head in the direction the boys were looking.

An older man, with graying hair and wearing a dress shirt with slacks, was walking toward them. She looked around. The Southbank had emptied quite a bit since she'd fallen asleep. It was almost deserted. James and Patrick stood, the latter offering his hand to help her get to her feet. She accepted it and tried to hide the heat that filled her face as their hands touched. As soon as she was on her feet, she dropped his hand and busied herself with dusting off her pants as they waited for the man to finish his approach.

The man stopped in front of them. "Patrick, mate." He smiled. "It has been too long."

Patrick returned his smile. "Harry, it's good to see you."

The two men closed the gap between them and embraced.

"I wish we could have got together under better circumstances," Harry said as they pulled apart.

"Yes, but I do thank you for taking the time to meet with us. I had no idea who else to call."

"Nonsense. You know I'd do anything for you." Harry turned toward Evelyn and James and smiled. "James, it's good to see you as well." He extended his hand, which James accepted. "And you, I don't think I've had the pleasure."

Before Evelyn could respond, Patrick spoke. "This is my client, and she wishes to stay anonymous, if you don't mind."

Harry's hand dropped back to his side. "I don't mind at all. It's a pleasure to meet your acquaintance, Miss."

Evelyn opened her mouth to speak, but was, again, interrupted by Patrick.

"She's happy to meet you, too. We didn't think you were going to make it. We were just about to leave."

Harry coughed. "Well, I got here at eleven, like we agreed upon, but I had such a shit time trying to find you through the crowd. I went and got a cuppa and waited until the crowd thinned out."

Something wasn't right. Evelyn couldn't put her finger on it, but her gut was saying Harry was full of bullshit. She didn't know him, so maybe he was always squirrely like this. Plus, Patrick didn't seem to want her talking, so she'd just keep her mouth shut. James nudged her. She looked at him and he subtly shook his head and returned his gaze to Harry. She got the message loud and clear. There was something off. It wasn't just her imagination. James noticed it too. But unfortunately, Patrick wouldn't want to hear it, so they couldn't question Harry in front of him. He'd become defensive of his mentor. He would have to put together the pieces himself. This man wasn't who Patrick wanted him to be.

For his part, Patrick was looking confused as well. "So, you left us waiting here for over an hour? Why have us meet in such a public place if you didn't want people around?"

"I have my reasons," Harry barked. "Now, enough with the questions. I'm here, aren't I? It's late. I have work in the morning. Tell me about this case."

Patrick closed his eyes for a second and then opened them, looking a little wearier than before. "Well, a few days ago, a case was brought to me from the solicitor's office—"

"Colin?" Harry interrupted.

"Yes," Patrick replied slowly. "Anyway, the solicitor's office gave me this case, dealing with the Fitzgeralds—"

"Why didn't they bring it to the police? Aren't we more equipped to handle a crime syndicate than two young, inexperienced private investigators?"

Patrick narrowed his eyes at that, and Evelyn could see him visibly tensing up. He looked like he was going to yell or say something he might regret, and they had all agreed earlier that evening they would remain levelheaded and calm, in order to maintain the upper hand. She reached out and gently laid a hand on his arm.

He jumped, but then relaxed. He looked over his shoulder and gave her a brief smile before turning back to Harry.

"You know why he came to us instead of the police. I don't have to waste my breath spelling it out. Do you want to hear about the case or not? You're right, it's late, and we would all rather be in bed right now."

"Please, continue. I promise to not interrupt anymore."

Patrick took a deep breath and slowly exhaled.

Evelyn moved to remove her hand, but he stopped her, taking her hand.

"As I was saying, the solicitor's office brought this case to me a few days ago. A former lover of Mickey Fitzgerald's came forward, saying she had sufficient evidence that would put Fitzgerald behind bars for a long time. Well, when they went to meet her, she lost her nerve and decided to flee the country, taking the evidence with her. I met her at the airport and retrieved the evidence. All we need is someone to make the arrest and press charges."

"And that's where I come in?" Harry asked.

"Yes. We'll need you to arrest Fitzgerald and make sure there are charges brought up against him, and Colin and his team will do the rest."

Harry brought his hand to his chin and began rubbing it. "What kind of evidence do you have, exactly?"

"Photographic evidence," Patrick responded.

"I don't know, Patrick. This seems awfully risky, what with circumstantial evidence. Why would I risk my career, and my life, by arresting Mickey Fitzgerald, only to have him back on the street within twenty-four hours?"

"He won't be out on the street in twenty-four hours. We have some pretty solid evidence, and he's going away for a long, long time." Patrick's grip on Evelyn's hand tightened as he struggled to maintain his cool.

She gave him a reassuring squeeze as James took a step closer to them, closing her in between the two. He was obviously getting uncomfortable with the current situation and suspected something was going to go wrong, and soon. And, to be honest, the bad feeling Evelyn had at the beginning of the meeting had only intensified as it continued. The tension between the four of them had only begun to grow. And if she was feeling off about the situation, the boys, being investigators, were more than likely also feeling it. Which was probably why she was currently sandwiched tightly between them.

"Let me see it then," Harry responded. "Let me see this hardcore evidence you have. Convince me you have a case."

"I won't be showing you anything until I can be assured, you're with us."

"So secretive. C'mon, Patrick. You're like a son to me. I was there for you when your father wasn't. You can trust me. You know I have your back."

"I'd still like your word you're on our side. That we can trust you."

"You can trust me. I don't know where all this mistrust is coming from, but I'm guessing it's from James and your American tart. I promise, I'm on your side."

All three immediately tensed at his words. Patrick's grip on Evelyn's hand tightened as James moved in even closer. Evelyn couldn't help but start shaking in fear.

"We never told you she was American," Patrick stated.

Harry sighed. "Oh, bugger. You're right. I suppose you didn't. My mistake. I guess the cat is out of the bag now." He reached behind his back and pulled out a gun, pointing it at the trio. "You'll hand over the evidence and the girl, and I'll let you go."

Patrick looked like he'd been slapped in the face. "What the fuck! I thought you were clean."

Harry chuckled. "Poor naïve Patrick. I was never clean. I'm just an excellent actor. Anyone who is clean on the force is a fool and won't last long. You're lucky you got out when you did, or else your poor father would have been planning two funerals."

"I trusted you." Patrick's voice trembled.

"Yes, and you were a fool. Now, hand over the girl and the bag."

"Do you think we'd be stupid enough to carry that much evidence around with us?"

"No, I guess you wouldn't. I'll just take the girl then."

As he took a step toward Evelyn, Patrick moved in front of her, and James grabbed her, pulling her back. It was as if they'd rehearsed the move as it went so smoothly.

Patrick took a swing at Harry, which Harry easily blocked. He made a lunge for Harry's gun hand.

Evelyn watched the two men struggle for control of the weapon. She couldn't tell who had the upper hand, which made her nervous.

Suddenly, a blast rang through the quiet of the night.

Evelyn screamed, her hands coming up to her ears, startled by the sound.

She watched helplessly as Patrick fell to the ground and Harry ran from the scene.

CHAPTER 16

EVELYN

James let go of Evelyn, and she rushed over to Patrick's side. He was lying on the ground, but he was still conscious. She inspected his body, trying to find where he had been hit.

"Oh, my God," she cried.

Patrick moaned on the ground. He moved his head back and forth.

She gasped.

The left side of Patrick's head was gushing blood. She couldn't even see where the wound was, there was so much blood.

"Fuck, fuck, fuck." Tears raced down Evelyn's cheeks. "What do I do?"

James knelt next to her. "Fucker runs fast. I couldn't catch him. What do we have?"

"Harry shot him in his head. He's losing a lot of blood." Evelyn never took her gaze off of Patrick, who was growing pale and sweating, but he was still mostly conscious.

James ripped his shirt over his head and tossed it at Evelyn. "Use this to apply pressure to the wound. Don't stop, don't ease up. It's important you use as much pressure as you can to stop that blood. I'm going to run and get a cab."

James moved to run into the road, but Evelyn called out to him. "Wait! Why aren't we calling an ambulance to take him to the hospital? Wouldn't that be faster?"

"We're not taking him to hospital!" James shouted, running toward the road.

She turned her attention back to Patrick. She wadded up James's T-shirt and pressed it to the wound as hard as she could.

He hissed.

"I'm sorry," Evelyn whispered.

"It's okay." He closed his eyes. "Bloody hell, this hurts. I always thought getting shot would be heroic, but nope, just hurts like hell."

"I'm so sorry. If it weren't for me, you wouldn't have gotten shot."

He opened his eyes and gave her a half-smile. "What? You think I'd let him take you? Did you think I was going to let you be collateral damage or something?"

She laughed, wiping her cheeks with her shoulders. "Haha. I knew when the time came, you wouldn't let me get hurt. You're a better man than I thought you were, Patrick, Patrick?" She looked down, and his eyes were closed. He no longer seemed conscious. "Patrick?!" she shouted, jostling him. "Wake up!"

He moaned, but didn't wake.

"James! Where are you? You need to hurry!"

James came running back to her. "The cab's waiting at the corner. We need to move him there and keep pressure on the wound at the same time. I can't carry him by myself. Do you have anything that we can use as a tourniquet?"

Evelyn moved her hands to her pants and undid the belt buckle before ripping the belt out of the loops. She handed it to James. They worked together to wrap the shirt around Patrick's head before using the belt to hold it in place. Once the belt was tightened, James moved so Patrick's arm was around his shoulder, and he was supporting most of his weight.

"Love, I need you to get under his other arm and help me move him. We need to do this quickly. I've paid the cab way too much money to get us to where we're going as quickly as possible."

She moved into place as quickly as she physically could. With James supporting most of Patrick's weight, it was easy for her to keep up and help support Patrick. The cab wasn't as far off as she'd thought it would be, and they arrived at it almost instantaneously. The cabbie jumped out of the driver's side and opened up the rear door for them. The three of them managed to get Patrick into the back seat, lying down. Evelyn didn't hesitate before climbing in after him.

"Are you sure you want to ride back there with him? I don't mind."

She shook her head. "I'm smaller. I fit better. Stop wasting time. Let's go. I don't like the shade of white he's turning right now."

James didn't say another word as he shut the back door and ran around the car to get into the passenger seat. As soon as James was in, the cabbie didn't hesitate before peeling away from the curb, speeding down the street.

Evelyn sat back and moved Patrick's head to rest in her lap. He was burning up and sweating profusely. She started running her hands through his dark hair, wanting to show him some comfort but stopped herself short. She didn't want to hurt him anymore than he already was.

Up in the front seat, she could hear James talking on his cell phone, but she couldn't make out what he was saying or who he was talking to. She instead focused on the man lying on the seat next to her.

They weren't in the cab for long before they pulled up in front of a building. James was out of the cab before it had even come to a complete stop. He ran around and threw open the door. She climbed out as the door to the building flew open and an older woman came running out, pushing a metal gurney. Evelyn jumped out of the way so she wouldn't get run over by the cart. James and the woman easily transferred Patrick to the gurney and ran inside. Evelyn quickly followed.

Evelyn found herself in a waiting room. There were nondescript chairs lining the walls, a counter, and several potted plants. She looked around. She couldn't see James, the woman, or Patrick anywhere. She looked toward the doorway to the right and surmised they probably went that way, but the hallway was dark, and she really didn't want to go exploring. She'd had enough adventure for the night. James would come out and find her and explain what was going on. Wouldn't he?

She moved to one of the chairs and took a seat. As she sat down, she started shaking. It took her a minute to realize she was sobbing uncontrollably. The events of the last thirty minutes hit her all at once, and every emotion she had been holding in overwhelmed her. She was on their radar. They knew who she was. The mob wanted her, and they sent a police officer to kidnap her. In public. In front of those closed-circuit television things Patrick had told her about. And with a gun! Patrick got shot making sure the mob didn't kidnap her.

What the fuck had she gotten into? All she wanted to do was go home. Fuck Greece! Who needed to go to *another* foreign country, into more unfamiliar lands, with even more strangers? All she wanted to do right now was curl up in bed with her mom and cry and never leave. Tell her mom she was right she should have never left. It's a dangerous world out here, and she found herself in the middle of it.

She moved to bury her face in her hands and noticed they were covered in blood. Patrick's blood. She cried even harder. She wrapped her arms around her body and slipped to the floor. She curled up on the cold, hard linoleum and listened to the quiet of the strange building she was in. Yet another situation she had no control over since arriving in London.

Somewhere in the back of the building, she could hear a man scream. And scream and scream. She recognized it as Patrick. He sounded almost inhuman and in so much pain. The screaming was relentless and growing more and more frantic. Evelyn moved her hands to her ears and closed her eyes. She started rocking back and forth, humming the tune of her favorite Beatles song, as the tears continued to roll unchecked down her face.

***

"Evelyn," a voice called as a hand gently nudged her. "Evie, wake up."

She blinked open her eyes and noticed the sun was peeking through the windows of the lobby. She sat up and grimaced as her back popped.

She looked at James from her place on the floor. "What's going on? What time is it? How's Patrick?"

James lowered himself to sit next to her on the floor. He rubbed his face, which was showing a past five-o'clock shadow. "It's late, or early, I guess. I would guess it's around five. Patrick's doing okay. He's resting, but he's out of commission for a while. The good news is, he wasn't hit. The bullet just grazed him. He was fucking lucky. The bad news is, the wound was deep, and he lost quite a bit of blood, but my mum was able to stitch him back together. And my mum says he probably has a concussion from hitting the ground. We're waiting for him to wake up so she can make sure he's coherent enough to send home. Where we will be tasked to make sure he doesn't move for a few days, while his body recuperates from the blood loss and recovers from the concussion."

She blinked, trying to process everything. "Wait, your mom? She's a doctor?"

"Veterinarian. This is her clinic. I didn't know where else to take him, and she lives in a flat above the clinic. Which, I want to apologize, we should have let you up there, and you could have slept in the guest room rather than on the floor."

"It's okay. You had more important things to deal with than my sleeping arrangements."

"Do you want to go up there and take a shower and freshen up, or something?"

She shook her head. "I'm okay. I'd like to see Patrick, if that's okay?"

James nodded. "Of course."

He stood and offered his hand, which Evelyn gladly accepted. As she stood, the full effects of having slept on the floor for hours hit her. James took her by the hand and led her through the doorway and into the back of the clinic, where all the exam rooms were. He took her into the first room on the right, and there was Patrick, lying on the exam table, sleeping.

Since the clinic was a veterinary clinic, it wasn't a normal exam table. It was completely metal, with metal legs and wheels. In order to make it more comfortable, they had placed lots of blankets on the surface, and there was a pillow placed under his head. He wasn't wearing a shirt, and his head had a large white bandage wrapped around it. He wasn't as pale as he had been the night before right after he was shot, but his breathing was still shallow.

She brought her hands to her mouth to stifle a sob.

James wrapped his arm around her shoulder and pulled her to him. "He's going to be fine, Evie. He's fucking lucky the bullet just grazed his head, right around his left temple. The wound really looked much worse than it was. Head wounds bleed a lot, making them look more urgent than they really are. If he were actually shot, it would have been worse. Much, much worse."

She filled in the blank that James wasn't going to say. Dead. He would have been dead. She would have lost one of her only friends in this country. Someone who drove her crazy but also who was someone she really wanted to get to know better.

"There's a chair right over here. I can't promise how comfortable it is, but it's probably loads more comfortable than the floor you slept on."

She nodded, still not trusting her voice. She moved out from under James's arm and pulled the chair up right next to the table Patrick was lying on. She sat and stared at him.

"Since you're back here with him, I'm going to run upstairs and take a shower and try to freshen up a little. Then maybe you should, too, considering..." he trailed off, gesturing at her.

She looked at her hands. Patrick's dried blood still covered them. She'd totally forgotten about that. She nodded. "Okay. That's a good idea."

"That phone in the corner is connected to a phone in my mum's kitchen. It's leftover from when I was little and she needed to check on me while she was down here working. If you need anything, or if something happens, pick it up, and the other end will ring."

She nodded again.

He placed a hand on her shoulder. "I promise, everything is going to be okay. Try to relax. After we're both cleaned up and refreshed, we'll sit down and talk about what happened."

"Yeah, and we need to figure out what to do next. Because I don't think we had a backup plan if this one went pear-shaped."

"We didn't. Patrick didn't want to make one. He was so sure—" James broke off, shaking his head, "we'll talk when I get back. I promise. try to relax, and definitely try not to worry."

He turned and walked out of the room, leaving her alone with Patrick and her thoughts. Everything they had planned relied one-hundred percent on Harry not being a back-stabbing bastard. They weren't counting on him betraying them. Patrick had been so sure of his loyalty; they didn't even try to research and find someone else. Patrick's father was counting on them to find someone to arrest Fitzgerald, and they failed. For now, at least.

Patrick's father. Someone needed to tell him Patrick got hurt. Right? Her parents would want to know if she'd been shot and was being patched up by a veterinarian. But would Patrick's father? Patrick and Harry both had alluded to a strained relationship between the two men, and two days ago, when they were in his flat, their relationship didn't scream warm and fuzzy. Patrick called him by his first name, for Pete's sake.

She wouldn't be telling any of the events of the past twenty-four hours to her parents any time soon. As far as they were concerned, her trip to London involved sightseeing and eating lots of fish and chips, alone, in the solitary space of a hotel room. When this was all over, when they figured out what they were doing, she was going to have to have the boys take her to a few places to take some pictures and get brochures and then have them help her alter the time and date stamps on them, to make her lies more believable. She hated lying to her parents, but telling them she was almost kidnapped twice, would not go over well. She could guarantee that. They would never let her leave the house again. Which, at this point, wouldn't necessarily be a bad thing, but she knew eventually she'd get over the trauma of this trip and want to venture out again. She might be eighty, but she had to think it could happen.

She looked back at the man lying on the table, and her heart ached. He jumped in front of a man with a gun for her. He wrestled a man with a gun for her. He got shot for *her*. They didn't know each other well, only been acquainted for forty-eight hours, and yet it was beginning to feel like there wasn't a time when she didn't know him. Yes, their personalities didn't mesh well and their stubbornness clashed with the others, but she had to admit, it had become kind of fun to verbally spar with him. He looked kind of cute when he was being frustrated and furious with her. Working him up had become quite the pastime.

Looking at him now, she wished he'd wake up and spar with her. She didn't even care if he woke up and resented her for getting him hurt. She wanted him to wake up so she knew he was okay.

She reached out and took his hand. It was cold, which made sense. James said he had lost a lot of blood. She wondered how long it would take for him to recuperate from an injury like this. Especially since he wasn't in a hospital, and she was pretty sure he didn't get a blood transfusion. She was ninety-nine percent sure animal blood wasn't compatible with human blood. But she was a historian, not a scientist. She hoped James hurried back. She had so many questions. And he was the only one with answers. Well, and his mom, who she still hadn't met. She'd seen her briefly last night when she and James wheeled Patrick in from the cab. And then she was gone.

Evelyn sighed and held Patrick's hand between the two of hers. She rubbed her hands over his. "C'mon, Patrick. You need to wake up. Please. Wake up and let me know you're okay."

She moved her chair closer to the table and rested her head against his body. He didn't smell right. Gone was the rich, woodsy smell that had become comforting the last few days. A clinical, antiseptic smell had replaced it. She closed her eyes, taking comfort in the rising and falling of his chest with every shallow breath he took. She allowed that feeling to lull her to sleep.

CHAPTER 17

PATRICK

There was a weight on his chest, making it difficult to breathe. He was cold. Freezing. Except in the spot where the weight was. That was warm. And his entire body ached. His head was full of a fog, and he couldn't quite clear it out and think properly. He tried to remember what had happened, but the fog wasn't allowing any thoughts through. He focused and then remembered. Meeting Harry at The Southbank and Harry betraying them. Harry trying to kidnap Evelyn. Getting shot. And then nothing else after that.

Fuck. Am I dead? He started to evaluate and take an inventory of everything. He was breathing. Yes, he could definitely tell he was breathing. That was a clear sign he wasn't dead. But he couldn't wake up. His eyelids were heavy and glued to his cheeks. He needed to wake up. He needed to open his eyes. What if Harry had ambushed James and Evelyn after he got shot and the Fitzgeralds had captured Evelyn and they were torturing her right now while he lay on the pavement?

Wake up, Patrick, he urged himself. *Wake the fuck up!*

His eyes flew open, and first thing he noticed was he was no longer on the pavement near the Thames. He was in a room somewhere. His eyes adjusted to the dimly lit room, which was when he noticed the reason, he was having trouble breathing was because someone was sleeping on him. Their hands were on his, and their head was on his chest. He turned his head slightly toward the person and breathed a sigh of relief. Evelyn. She was fine and keeping vigil over his sickbed. He wondered where they were and how long he had been out. They weren't in hospital because there would be more machines and more people. Definitely more people. He turned his head to the other side. On the wall there was a giant poster of a dog running through a field of grass. He knew that poster. They were in James's mum's veterinary clinic.

He closed his eyes against the headache forming. He had been so confident everything would go their way. He didn't even know where to even start with coming up with a new plan. And James and Evelyn were going to look to him to lead, and he was fucking useless.

He pounded his free hand on the metal cart, causing the whole thing to shake. Jostled by the movement, Evelyn sprung up from where she was sleeping on him with a gasp.

Her head whipped over to look at him, and she immediately started crying. "Oh, my God, you're awake!"

Patrick winced, but nodded. "Yeah, I'm awake," he whispered, struggling to even do that. He tried to sit up, but she stopped him, placing a hand on his chest. Her warm touch on his cold skin made him keenly aware of the fact he was shirtless.

"Stop," she said, softly. "You need your rest, and trying to get up right now doesn't constitute resting."

"I need to bloody well get up, is what I need to do. We don't have time to rest. I need to get started on a new plan. We need to figure out what we're going to do about getting you home. We need—"

"Patrick, you were shot in the head. Well, technically, the bullet grazed you, but fuck it, for all intents and purposes, we're going to say Harry shot you. The important part is you've lost a lot of blood, and you have a concussion. What you need to do is rest and do what James's mom says. When we get back to your flat, we can start planning what James and I can do next while you get better."

Patrick shook his head. "You can't—"

"I don't want to hear about what I can or can't do. You were shot. You. Were. Shot. You lose your vote about what's going to happen. Your new job is to relax and heal and not strain yourself. I don't want you to kill yourself over this. It's not worth your life. Mickey Fitzgerald is going to go to prison, eventually. You don't need to be the one to personally do it."

"Yes, I fucking do," he yelled, sitting up and immediately regretting it. He brought his hand up to his head, wincing. "I need to be the one to bring him down. It has to be me. No one else."

"Why?" She brought her hand up to lay on his shoulder. "Why does it have to be you?"

"Because he fucking killed my mum!"

Silence fell over the small room. The only sound was his heavy breathing and the ticking of the clock on the wall.

"What? Is that why Harry said last night your father would have had to plan two funerals?"

Patrick closed his eyes and got as comfortable as he could on the metal gurney. "Yes."

"When?"

"A little over a year ago."

"I'm sorry, Patrick. I'm so sorry. I've made a complete mess of this for you. You were hoping to use Megan to get Fitzgerald, and I was a complete klutz and fucked the whole thing up."

"Don't blame yourself for this mess. We don't know for certain anything would have been better if you weren't here right now. If anyone is to blame, it's Harry."

She nodded and wiped away her tears. "God, I'm so tired of crying. I don't usually cry this much, so please don't think I'm always this emotional."

"Considering you were almost snatched last night and watched someone get shot, I think you're holding up pretty fucking well."

"You didn't see me last night in the waiting room."

Patrick reached out, taking her hand. "You're holding up pretty fucking well. I'm standing by that statement."

"If you don't mind me asking, why did Fitzgerald kill your mom? Was it because you and your dad were working against him?"

"It was a case of mistaken identity. He had a hit out on a female solicitor who had something against him. His asshole goons saw my mum leaving my father's office late one night and thought she was the solicitor. Gunned her down right there on the street."

"Oh, my God."

Patrick closed his eyes, tightening his grip on Evelyn's hand. "Dad came running out of the office when he heard the shots, but by the time he made it to her, she was already dead. No time to even call for an ambulance. It was shortly after that Colin and I began working harder to bring the Fitzgeralds down. We want our city to be safer."

Evelyn rose, and standing on her tiptoes, wrapped her arms around him in a hug. He winced when she brushed his head but ignored the pain and brought an arm around her to return the hug.

"Ah, um." Someone cleared their throat behind them, and they leapt apart, turning toward the door. James stood there, still in the clothes he wore the night before, but looking freshly shaved and showered. "Sorry to interrupt this touching moment, but Evelyn, you should head upstairs and wash up."

Patrick looked at her and noticed, for the first time, the blood on her hands and how disheveled she looked.

"Yeah, okay." She took a hesitant step toward the door.

"Out the door, take a left, first door on your right leads up to the flat. My mum will show you where everything is."

She nodded, looking once more at Patrick, before exiting the room, leaving the two men behind.

"How are you feeling?" James asked.

"Like utter shit, but I'll get over it. Good thinking bringing me here rather than the hospital."

"It was pure instinct and adrenaline. I didn't even start thinking coherent thoughts until this morning. Poor Evie slept on the floor in the waiting room all night because I didn't even think about making her get up and go sleep in my mum's flat. All I could think about was getting you here and making sure you didn't fucking die on us."

"Well, thanks, mate. I don't even know how to thank you for saving me."

"Don't thank me. Thank my mum. She was amazing. She stitched you up. There was so much blood, I didn't think that—" He choked up.

Patrick closed his eyes. "I'm sorry for scaring you."

"Only you would apologize for someone shooting you."

Patrick opened his eyes. "I can't believe Harry fucking shot me."

James looked at him, concerned. "How are you feeling? Emotionally, I mean. The man was basically your father."

"I'm trying not to think about it right now. At the moment, I don't think I can handle the situation. I think once we get back to the flat and I have time to process what the hell went down last night, the full weight of the betrayal will hit me. But right now, my head fucking hurts and all I want to do is go home and lie down in my comfy bed and make a plan for where we go from here. Because we've fucked up, James. We don't have anyone else to arrest Fitzgerald. We don't have a backup plan. And we've screwed over Evelyn. She's stuck here and can't go home or to Greece, and that's on us."

James nodded. "Yeah, I've been thinking about Evie and her situation, and it makes me feel worse than anything else. We promised her we'd meet with Harry last night and then she'd be on a plane in a couple of days. And now..."

"And now we don't even have a timeline. When can we get out of here?"

"As soon as mum convinces Evie she needs a long hot shower, rather than just scrubbing your blood off her hands, she'll be down here to discharge you, on the grounds you will go home, relax, and *not* go chasing after criminals."

Patrick smiled. "Your mum knows me too well."

"That she does. And you will go home and relax. I'm going to see to that." He grew serious. "You're lucky that bullet just grazed you. There was so much blood, I thought for sure the bullet had actually entered your body. I've never been more scared in my life. My mum didn't have any anesthesia she could use on you, only animal grade, so she had to work on you without any painkillers. It's something I never want to experience again."

Patrick looked at his friend, and his chest tightened. He really didn't know how serious everything had been last night. But looking at all the dried blood on Evelyn's hands, and listening to James describe how his mum had fixed him up, it was sobering, to say the least. He could have died last night. He could have died, and his dad wouldn't know he really did love him. He would have died, and his dad would have had to bury him next to his mum, thinking he wished he had any other man as a father than him. How fucking selfish was he?

"Hey, don't you dare start feeling fucking guilty about anything that happened. It's not your fault. You thought we could trust Harry. I trusted your judgment. We were all responsible for deciding to go last night. You weren't solely responsible for the events that transpired. Harry betrayed us. You didn't."

Before Patrick could respond, the door to the room opened, and James's mum walked in. "So, let's see about getting you home."

CHAPTER 18

EVELYN

James opened the door to the flat and let Evelyn through. She rushed into Patrick's room, picked up the bag of clothes she'd bought the day before, and rushed into the bathroom to change. While she had showered at the clinic, she could still feel the dried blood on her skin. Patrick's blood. She would never be able to associate the outfit she had been wearing with anything other than Patrick getting shot, so she might as well throw it in the garbage. She threw on her new outfit quickly and walked back to the bedroom as James was settling into a chair and Patrick was settling back against his pillows under his comforter.

She looked around the room and was about to settle herself on the floor when Patrick spoke up.

"Here, why don't you sit next to me? You've sat on the floor enough the last twenty-four hours."

She eyed the small spot on the bed next to him. They would have to be awfully close in order to both fit there. They had spent a lot of time in close quarters lately, and Evelyn really wanted to sit down and analyze her feelings about everything, but there wasn't time. She decided, for once, to just enjoy the moment.

She moved toward the bed, sitting on his right side. Their legs were touching and, to make matters even more intimate, he moved his arm around her shoulders, pulling her close to him.

"Do you mind?" he asked quietly, nearly whispering in her ear. "I've found your presence comforting, and I've come to enjoy having you close like this."

She shook her head. "I don't mind." If a hot guy wanted to flirt with her, then she was going to go along with it. She could over analyze every little thing after her life was no longer in danger.

"Oi," James called out, "best mate still in the room. Please don't forget that."

"Noted."

She leaned closer to Patrick, and he began running his hand up and down her arm.

"So," James spoke up, "where do we go from here? What's our next step?"

Patrick sighed. "We need to find a new police officer to arrest the Fitzgeralds, but I don't even know where to start. Are there any officers who are clean anymore? Or are they all in Fitzgerald's pockets?"

"There has to be," James replied. "I refuse to believe every officer in Tower Hamlet is crooked."

"But last night, Harry implied every cop was crooked. He said either you're crooked or you're dead. At least that's what I took out of his ranting," Evelyn commented.

"Yeah, that's what I understood, too," Patrick agreed.

James shook his head. "What if Fitzgerald and his friends just *think* all the police are in his pocket? What if there's someone who's a double agent, so to speak?"

"But how will we know? How will we determine who's worth trusting? We thought we could trust Harry, and look how that turned out," Evelyn questioned.

"I can do some research, and hack into computers with personnel files and start weeding through every officer in the borough until we find one who's trustworthy. Unfortunately, doing that will take some time. In fact, it could take weeks," James replied.

"Don't worry about the time frame. Just focus on being thorough and finding someone. How certain will you be once you find someone that they're clean?" asked Evelyn.

"Ninety percent. I don't think I can be any more certain. We will have to hope they don't show up to a meeting with a gun and take us all out."

Patrick sighed. "What if we don't find someone? If you go through everyone in there and every single cop is in that man's pocket, what then? We need a backup plan for our backup plan. We need to plan for the unthinkable."

The three were quiet.

"What if we draw him out and make him commit a crime in a different borough? Use jurisdiction in our favor. Then we'll have the other borough's officers arrest him. He doesn't have all of London under his thumb. Someone will have to arrest him," James piped up.

Patrick's face lit up like a Christmas tree. "James, you're bloody brilliant. But how do we draw him out? Get him out of his comfort zone, so to speak?"

"Me," Evelyn spoke up.

"What?"

"No bloody way!" James and Patrick shouted over each other.

"They want me. What if we use me as bait to draw him out? And his crime is attempted kidnapping, or even kidnapping. You guys can have the local police on notice, and they can swoop in and arrest him before he even has a chance to take me."

Patrick was vehemently shaking his head next to her. "No. We're not using you as bait. It's too dangerous and too risky. What if the officers don't believe us? What if they don't get there in time? I'm not going to sit back as Fitzgerald takes you and fucking murders you."

"I agree with Patrick, sweetheart. It's too risky."

"It's only a backup plan, right? We're counting on the fact you guys will find someone here who isn't dirty, so if you do, we won't ever have to use this plan. If you don't, won't we be desperate? And don't desperate times call for desperate measures or whatever?"

Patrick shook his head. "I'm still not liking it. At all. We'll find another way. We'll draw him out in a different way, if it comes down to it."

"Yeah, there are always more ways that involve not sacrificing a life."

She sighed. "Fine, but if you can't think of anything, my offer stands."

"We won't be using it," Patrick stated firmly. "We'll figure something out."

James nodded. "We'll think of something when the time comes. But you're right. Hopefully, we'll not have to use it. We'll find an officer who isn't crooked. We'll find someone who will help us. In fact, I'm going to go start the search now. If you need me, I'll be on my computer." He stood and walked out of the room, taking the chair with him.

Evelyn and Patrick were left alone, sitting on the bed, his arm around her.

He turned to her. "Hey, I know I've said it before, but I'm sorry for being an arse the last few days."

She turned toward him. "It's okay. I get it now. This case is personal, and you were frustrated it wasn't going the way you hoped. And you took it out on the person you thought caused the problems, me."

"You amaze me. The way you can understand a situation. Mind-boggling."

"I would have figured out the reason sooner if you had been open and honest with me when I was asking questions yesterday, rather than filing it under things I didn't need to know."

"I'm sorry. It's all so incredibly personal and painful for me to talk about."

"What changed?"

"What do you mean?"

"What changed between yesterday and today? What made you finally open up to me?"

"I don't know. Maybe my near-death experience? Mortality really puts things into perspective. I don't want to be an ass to you anymore. You helped save my life. And for that, I'll be forever grateful."

She shook her head. "I didn't do much. I held a T-shirt to your wound."

"Which helped slow down my bleeding. I don't care what you say, or how serious, or not, my injury turned out to be. You helped save my life. And I don't know how I'll ever repay you for that."

"You don't need to. I'm glad I did it."

"Me, too. Because it's given me a chance to do this."

Patrick leaned in and closed the small gap between them. Their lips met, lightly at first, but Patrick applied a little pressure, and Evelyn returned the kiss. Patrick brought his good arm up to the back of her head, cupping it, allowing the kiss to deepen. Evelyn's heart raced. She'd been kissed before, but there was something about this one that made it unlike her other first kisses. It was almost as if she were sharing it with a close friend, but she barely knew Patrick, so that was impossible. Right?

The two drew apart, short of breath, resting their foreheads against one another, eyes closed.

"Wow." Evelyn breathed.

"Yeah. Took the words right out of my mouth. I don't know why I was so reluctant. I should have done that day one."

Evelyn opened her eyes, pulling away from him slightly. "You've wanted to kiss me since day one? You seemed so annoyed and put out by me even existing."

"Yeah, I wanted to kiss you. You're fucking gorgeous. But I have a one-track mind. I've been so obsessed with nailing Fitzgerald and getting my revenge for my mum's death, I kind of decided I had no time for a relationship. But then you come into my life and you're gorgeous and sweet, and all I can think about is what it would be like to kiss you and hold you, and I can't have that in my life right now. Plus, you were supposed to leave in a few days, and it wouldn't have been fair to either of us if I started something we would have to end so quickly."

"So, you were an ass to try to drive me away."

"Right in one. Plus, I learned *very* quickly you're even more attractive when you're riled up."

"I'm guessing your near-death experience last night also changed your mind about kissing me?"

"Of course. That, and the fact your time table has been moved back a bit. You're now stuck in the country for a little while longer. I might as well take advantage of it. Unless you have any objections."

"I have absolutely no objections. I have been kind of attracted to you as well, but you've been such an ass. I never wanted to act upon it."

"Well, I'm glad we have a mutual attraction." He yawned. "I'm sorry, but I think I'm starting to hit my limits here. I think I'm going to have a lie down."

She brushed a kiss on his forehead. "Okay. I'll leave you to rest for a bit then."

"Lie down with me?"

She shook her head. "Maybe later. Right now, I really need to work on my thesis. I still have deadlines I need to make. Rain check? I mean, you're kind of taking over the space you gave me to sleep on."

He laughed at that. "I'll hold you to it."

"Deal." She stood. "Get some rest. You need it. Mrs. Moore said you need to rest a lot so you can replenish all the blood you lost last night."

"Alright. I'm not going to argue with you. See you soon."

"See you soon." She scooped up her backpack and duffel bag and walked toward the doorway. She turned around to look back and Patrick had already slid down so his head was on his pillow, lightly snoring. She smiled and closed his door so they wouldn't disturb him and he could get a good sleep, something he hadn't had since she arrived.

"Is he sleeping?" James asked from over in the corner on his computer.

"Yeah. He was out the second his head hit the pillow. Any luck yet?"

"I've only been able to look at a handful of officers so far, corrupt as fuck."

"Of course. Well, I'm going to go sit in your room and work on my thesis so I won't bother you. Oh, and James?"

"Yeah?"

"For the record, even if Patrick wasn't interested in me, I wouldn't have shagged you."

As her words struck him, James' mouth popped open, and he struggled for a comeback for the first time since they'd met.

A wide smile spread across her face as she turned. She smiled all the way down the hall to his room to work.

CHAPTER 19

EVELYN

Evelyn stared at the blinking cursor on her laptop. It had been three days since they returned from their ill-fated meeting with Harry, and she should be writing more of her thesis, but her brain wasn't cooperating. How could she focus on ancient sleeping rituals when her, whatever you wanted to call it, was recuperating in his room? No matter what she tried, she couldn't get him to open up to her. She had a feeling this whole completely shutting down thing had to do with a lot more than just with the betrayal of a beloved mentor. If only he would *talk* to her, then she might be able to find a way to help him. However, despite everything that had happened, she was still virtually a stranger, so she really didn't blame him for not opening up.

She minimized her writing program and opened her internet browser. Obviously, writing about healing treatments at the Asclepeion, and how they related to healing treatments of modern medicine, wasn't going to happen right now. Instead, she opened her email. Once she waded through all the junk mail that clogged her inbox, she smiled. There was a new email chain from her sisters. She clicked on it and didn't even have to read a complete sentence before she began laughing hysterically.

"I didn't know Ancient Greece was so funny."

She jumped, turning toward the corner of the living room.

James sat at his computer, turned around in his chair, looking at where she sat on the couch, smirking at her. She had forgotten he was even in the room. He was so quiet sometimes.

"I've quit writing for now. I'm checking my email. My sisters and I have this really long email chain going right now."

James fully turned his chair to face her and leaned back. "Yeah? Is it jokes? Please tell me your email chain is just sending puns and dad jokes back and forth to one another."

She laughed. "No, it's not jokes. Most of the time it's mundane things, like what we are eating or what book we're reading right now. But right now, we're speculating on the love life of a very popular, and hunky, Hollywood celebrity."

"Celebrity gossip via email. Seems slow."

She shrugged. "I didn't want to pay the exorbitant international cellular fees, or else it would be text messages. Email works. Besides, it's a great distraction right now."

He nodded sagely. "Yes. From the stress of watching your new boyfriend get shot in the fucking head."

"He's not my boyfriend." She focused her gaze on her laptop. "At least, I don't think so. I don't know what we are."

She looked at the blinking cursor on the screen after she hit reply. She wanted to make a witty comeback to her sisters, but nothing was coming to mind. What she really wanted to talk about, she couldn't. She considered her sisters her very best friends, and all she wanted to do was tell them she was starting a new relationship with a man who jumped in front of a gun for her like he was a fucking superhero. But she couldn't.

"Don't look so glum, Evie," James said, pulling her out of her thoughts. "It's only been a couple days, there's plenty of time to define whatever this is."

She sighed, shutting her laptop, she would reply later. "I know. It's just, this is all unfamiliar territory for me. And it doesn't help that whenever I go into the room to check on Patrick, he's asleep."

"Well, he *was* shot in the head and received a concussion for his efforts."

"I know. And I'm not mad about him sleeping so much. I'm *glad* he's sleeping. He should be resting as much as possible. But sometimes I feel like he's maybe faking his sleep, in order to get out of talking to me."

He laughed. "Love, he's not that great of an actor. I think you're just building the situation up in your head because everything is so unknown. Just give it time."

She leaned her head back on the couch she was quickly beginning to love and understand why the guys kept it around, despite its sad and disgusting façade. "You're right. All of this is probably stemming from the fact that I'm stuck in this apartment with just the two of you, and the last few days I've been mostly on my own."

He grimaced. "Yeah, my fault, really. Since the computer can run the algorithms, I need it to on its own, I don't really need to be here, and we really need the money…"

"You don't need to explain yourself," she interrupted. "I understand."

"Hey! Why don't you come out with me tonight?"

"Another stakeout?"

Since they had been back, James had been out every night on a job. She wasn't sure if he was actively seeking jobs or if they really had all these jobs lined up before.

"Yeah, it'll be fun! We can stock up on crisps and biscuits. Enough tea and coffee to keep us awake, but not too much where we're going to need to take a piss every half hour. I'll even let you have a turn using the binoculars."

She laughed, shaking her head. "You know, I'm lonely, but I don't think I'm sitting in a MINI Cooper for hours waiting for the money shot lonely quite yet. But thank you for the invite."

He rose from his chair, picking up his backpack as he went. "You're welcome. Is there anything I can get you before I leave?"

She shook her head. "I'm good. I might make myself some cup noodles later and see if Patrick will actually eat any of it."

"If you need anything, you know how to reach me." He began moving toward the door, but stopped. "Oh, I called Patrick's dad earlier to fill him in on everything. He said he might stop by at some point. But he was very vague on the when. I thought I should make you aware if he comes while I'm gone."

"Thanks for the heads up. I'll make sure I let him in."

"Have a good night, Evie." James opened the door and left, the apartment immediately feeling quieter in his absence.

She picked her computer back up and opened it. She quickly typed a response to her sisters. It was vague and focused on the topic at hand. Despite their protestations, she was pretty sure that the two stars were, in fact, dating. She sent the email and minimized her browser.

She tried to force herself to open her document, but instead found herself staring at the closed door of Patrick's room. She stared at it, as if she could will him to wake up and want to spend time with her. Which was ridiculous. James was right. Patrick was doing exactly what he was supposed to be doing. But why did it make her feel so helpless?

This whole "being in a relationship," or whatever you wanted to call what she and Patrick were doing, was completely foreign to her. While she dated a bit in college, there was no one she was ever really serious about. She had definitely never slept with a man before this trip, literally or figuratively, and now she found herself sharing a bed with someone she barely knew, and it didn't feel weird, in fact, it seemed almost natural. It was as if she were Alice having fallen through the rabbit hole. She landed in London and became an almost completely different person. Evelyn in Iowa would never have been comfortable sparring with a man one day and then sharing his bed the next.

She was still debating whether she should try to wake Patrick or actually work on what she needed to work on when there was a knock on the door.

She froze.

No one ever knocked on the door unless they ordered takeaway, and she was pretty sure Patrick wasn't in his room ordering food.

James had reassured her their address was unlisted for everyone's safety, so it couldn't be a client. And she was pretty sure Patrick wasn't in his room ordering secret takeaway.

Her heart raced with all the possibilities of who could be behind that door. Visions of a Fitzgerald goon, led there by Harry, busting down the door and kidnapping her while Patrick slept in the other room began playing through her imagination.

"Hello?" a male called through the door. "It's Colin. Anyone home?"

She breathed as she realized it was Patrick's dad. She stood and opened the door. Standing in the hallway was Colin. His hair that was styled impeccably when she met him on her first day in London was mussed, and he was wearing his dress shirt untucked from his slacks. In his hand, he held a bag of takeout.

"Evelyn," he greeted. "James called me and filled me in. I brought some curry and the hope my son will allow me to see him."

"Yes, he told me he had called you before he left. Please, come in." Evelyn stepped aside to allow Colin entry into the flat. She shut the door behind him and turned around.

The two of them stood awkwardly just inside the doorway.

"So," Colin said, "where's Patrick?"

Evelyn gestured to the closed bedroom door. "Laying in his room. Where he has been since we've come home."

"And he's..."

"He's okay. He's pretty upset about everything. He seems to be in pain, but I honestly don't know. He won't talk to either of us."

"Yes, that seems on par with my son. When his mother died, he threw himself into work, and he didn't talk to me for months, which wasn't unusual for him. I was never the best father, but at least, when my wife was around, I got to see him in passing. But Patrick tends to close in on himself when the going gets tough."

"Patrick told me about his mother. I can't believe it's so similar to my situation. Mistaken identity. The Fitzgerald lackeys must be completely face blind."

"Yes, well, that's not completely true with what happened to his mother. I told him it was a case of mistaken identity for him to not have to worry about anything. The truth of the matter is, his mother was specifically targeted. I'd been working on trying to take down Mickey Fitzgerald and his firm for quite some time. At one point, I was getting fairly close to closing in on him. He must have decided it would be prudent to send me a message I could never forget, so he had my wife murdered. After that, I moved and backed down on the case. Then Megan fell into my lap, and I couldn't pass over this opportunity. And as you can see, this second attempt is going just as well as the first. That's why I'm here. I need to tell Patrick we're backing off the case. I can't lose my son the way I lost my wife."

"Fuck you."

Evelyn and Colin both turned to look in the direction the voice came. Standing in his doorway, well, more leaning on the doorjamb, was Patrick. He was shirtless and his sweats hung low on his hips. The bandage on his head stood out starkly against his skin, and his face looked haggard. His eyes were filled with tears.

"Patrick," Colin started.

"I heard the door open and then voices. I was worried Harry had come to finish the job. But no, it's my own father come to twist a knife into my gaping wounds."

"Patrick," Colin tried again, taking a step toward his son.

Patrick shook his head and moved back into his room, shutting the door behind him.

Evelyn moved to go speak with him, but Colin held up a hand, stopping her.

"No, I must go." He handed Evelyn the bag of food. "I bought enough for everyone. Please help yourself. I'm going to go try to fix things with my son."

Evelyn took the bag of curry from Colin and watched as he didn't even bother knocking on Patrick's door before letting himself in. She took the food to the kitchen, plated herself up a serving, and went back to the couch. Once settled, she reopened her laptop and pulled up her thesis. She could at least try to get some work done and pretend she wouldn't be hearing every word Patrick and Colin had to say to each other in the bedroom.

CHAPTER 20

PATRICK

Patrick had just made it to the side of his bed when his door flew open, allowing his dad entry.

"I don't recall inviting you in," he bit out.

"I wasn't about to ask permission. I knew you wouldn't let me in, and I need to talk to you."

"So, you can lie to me more?"

"I lied to protect you. I knew you'd run into the situation half-cocked, hellbent on some sort of revenge if you knew the Fitzgeralds had targeted your mum. I knew if I told you they killed your mum because of me, you'd hate me. Know that I lied out of a place of love."

"You're right." Patrick's eyes burned with his unshed tears. "I would have hated you if I'd known. And lying to me didn't stop me from wanting revenge against Mickey Fucking Fitzgerald. The bastard killed my mum. Doesn't matter the circumstances."

"I should have realized you would have wanted revenge regardless. If I'd admitted that to myself, I would have never hired you to help with this case."

"Of course, I want revenge! I'm pretty sure I've even mentioned it to you, but you wouldn't have realized it because you were too busy with work, which has always been more important than your family."

"And if you're not careful, you're going to turn out exactly like me."

Patrick scoffed, rolling his eyes.

"It's true. I've seen it. Your dedication to this job is no different from mine to my own."

"Only I don't have a wife and son to neglect."

"Because you haven't taken the time to look for someone. When's the last time you went on a date?"

"Fuck you. I'm nothing like you. And I think that's what bothers you the most."

"You're everything like me, and I think that's what bothers *you* the most."

Patrick didn't have anything to respond with. Maybe his dad was wrong. Maybe he was right. Either way, he was distracting him from the situation.

"That girl out there," Colin pointed at the door, "is counting on you to get her home. In fact, I distinctly remember telling you to drop this case after I had a head delivered to my door, and, as expected, you ignored me and continued on. You're letting her down, and you're putting yourself in danger. They could have killed you, Patrick, and you can't even begin to imagine how much that would have destroyed me. Drop the case. Take the girl on a tour of London. Get her home safely."

"You expect me to not do anything now that I know Fitzgerald had mum killed? If anything, I want to take the whole bloody firm down even more. I'm not letting Evelyn down. I'm saving her life. Harry was going to take her to the Fitzgeralds. I stopped that. Sure, she's not on an airplane home, but you said it wasn't safe to send her anywhere. We don't even know if the Fitzgeralds have any connections in America or not. You told me to keep her here and keep her safe. I'm living up to my end of that bargain. She's still here. She's safe."

"You need to drop the case."

"Fuck that. I'm in too deep now, Colin. I'm seeing this to the end."

Patrick watched as his father's shoulders drooped in defeat. He knew he'd won at that point. Colin wasn't going to say anything else about it. Patrick sat on the edge of the bed before bringing his legs up, allowing himself to sit with his back against the headboard. Just the small amount of energy he exerted to move about the room and argue with his father had completely drained him of energy. He was exhausted.

"I left some takeaway with Evelyn. Please make sure you eat. You need your strength in order to heal." He moved to the door, but as soon as his hand was on the handle, he turned his head to look back at Patrick. "I love you, son." Not waiting for a response, he turned the knob and exited the room.

Patrick closed his eyes and listened to the muted sounds of Evelyn and Colin saying goodbye to one another. His head was pounding, and his chest was heavy with emotion. He swallowed down the lump in his throat. He wasn't going to cry.

The door to his room opened, and without opening his eyes, he knew it was Evelyn.

"Do you want any food? I can bring you in a plate."

He didn't know if it was the fact, she didn't need to ask him how he was feeling or the fact her voice was so kind. The sob he'd been holding in broke through. He could feel her before he even knew she'd crossed the room as she eased herself onto the other side of the bed and wrapped her arms gingerly around his torso.

She laid her head against his shoulder and placed her other hand gently on his cheek. "Shh, it's alright," she whispered into his ear.

"They killed my mum," he sobbed.

"I know."

The two sat in silence in each other's embrace as Patrick let his emotions wash over him. Once he finally stopped crying and had himself under control, he shifted them so they were lying so he could wrap himself around her body, pulling her against his chest. Lying in bed, arms wrapped around Evelyn, the tension left his body. He leaned his head forward and buried his nose in her hair. She smelled of his shampoo and that stirred something inside of him. Not only did it comfort him, but it also awakened something inside of him, causing him to feel slightly possessive.

His dad was right. It was his job to protect her, to make sure she got home safe. And he needed to do everything in his power to make sure the Fitzgeralds didn't do to her what they did to his mum. There was no way he was going to let the firm use her as a means to get him to drop the case. He was in this for the long haul. The Fitzgeralds were going to be taken down and brought to justice. No more collateral damage. Those days were done.

"I'm not going to let them kill you," he whispered against her head.

She hummed sleepily in agreement, and that was all the acknowledgment he needed in order to relax the rest of the way and drift off into a dreamless sleep.

CHAPTER 21

EVELYN

Evelyn opened the door to Patrick's room. It was dark inside, even though it was midday. It took a few seconds for her eyes to adjust to the dim light after being in the brighter living room.

Her gaze immediately found the bed in the center of the room. Patrick was on his side, covers pulled up completely over his head.

"Patrick?" she called out tentatively.

No response.

She sighed. She took a step back and closed the door behind her. She walked back to the couch and picked up her laptop, settling it in her lap.

"Is he sleeping again?" James asked from his spot in front of his computer.

Evelyn looked up from her own computer. "Yeah, he is."

He sighed. "Has he even moved from his bed at all since his dad left the other day? Because I'm wracking my brain, and I don't think he's ever even emerged from his room."

"He uses the restroom, otherwise he just sits up in bed and eats whatever I put in front of him. Either he's not a picky eater or he's not even really paying attention to what's in front of him."

"Has he showered?"

She hesitated before answering, wrinkling her nose. "I don't think so."

He let out a disgusted groan. "How do you share a bed with him if he hasn't showered in nearly a week?"

"Believe me, it's becoming difficult. I think he's taking this 'take it easy' thing a little too seriously."

"Has he started talking about it to you yet?"

She shook her head. "No, in fact, he's taken great lengths to ignore me even more ever since his father talked to him. James, the things they said to each other…" She trailed off, remembering the two men yelling at each other. "It's pretty obvious the two have problems they need to work out. Didn't he say Harry was more like a father to him?"

"Yeah, he was closer to him than anyone else in his life."

"So, essentially, his father betrayed him and then shot him."

"It's a fucking mess. Almost Shakespearean. He should really open up about it and talk with someone. I keep hoping it will be you. What do you guys talk about in there?"

"Nothing really, not since the night his dad left, actually. He just kind of lies there and sleeps on and off. When I try to engage him, he clams up and refuses to say anything. He just stares at the wall. The only time he talks is to occasionally ask if you've found anything yet."

"What a great relationship you have. Are you sure you don't want to upgrade to the non-broody Brit?" He smiled and gestured to himself.

She picked up one of her pencils and threw it in James' general direction, laughing. "I'm sure. I'm really, really sure. It's just," she paused, all the glee she was feeling just seconds ago draining out. "I'm just starting to get worried about Patrick."

"You need to get him to talk. You need to force the issue and convince him he needs to get everything he's feeling off of his chest. And then make him take a fucking shower. And hopefully, after steps one and two, he'll decide to join the land of the living because we're getting really close to having to take the next step."

She set her computer on the coffee table and leaned forward. "You found someone?"

"Maybe. I don't know. Someone I've found seems promising. I need to run a few more checks on him. He seems clean right now, but I've been at this stage with a few other blokes and they failed out at the next step."

"But this is the first *actual* progress we've had all week." She found herself growing antsy.

"It is. Maybe when Colin calls next, we'll have something to tell him for once." He rubbed his eyes with the palms of his hands.

"Have you slept?"

"Yeah. I've gotten a few winks here and there."

"I hope this all pans out because if it doesn't, your lack of sleep will have been for nothing."

"At least there's been nothing from the Fitzgeralds since Harry's betrayal. It's been rather convenient for both our research and Patrick's recovery," James pointed out.

"Yes, but is it a good thing or a bad thing they're being quiet?"

He shrugged. "I don't know, and at this point, honestly it doesn't even matter. We're doing our best, and I'm feeling great about our plan and what we've accomplished so far. Besides, if Plan A doesn't work out, we have the backup plan."

"Do you want to be the person to tell Patrick we're implementing the backup plan? Because I sure don't."

"Good point. We'll make this plan work before we have to tell him we're sending you out as bait to catch Fitzgerald in the act."

They each went back to working on their computers. In the past few days, she had finally been able to get a lot of work done on her thesis, and she was actually ahead on some deadlines. It helped she was basically under house arrest. She hadn't left the flat in a week, not since *that night*. With Patrick healing and moping in his bed and James either attached to the computer or doing jobs, it left no one available to assist her with going out and making sure she didn't get kidnapped. Not that she was totally eager to get out and do anything. Even so, cabin fever was a real thing.

"I called my program yesterday," she stated, breaking the silence without looking up from her computer. "I told them I wouldn't be able to make it."

James stopped his typing. The creak of his chair indicating he had turned it toward her. "Oh, Evie. I'm sorry. I can't even begin to explain how terrible Patrick and I feel about you missing out on your program."

She shook her head. "It's fine, really. I gave them a story about being stuck in London for a family emergency, and they moved me to the next session at the end of July."

"Brilliant!" James exclaimed. "Well, brilliant that you get to still do your program, not that you have a set leaving date. I don't want you to get the wrong idea. I enjoy your company."

"And I enjoy yours as well. I'll be sad to leave, but I've been looking forward to this trip for so long, I really want to make sure I get to go on it."

"Have you talked to your parents yet?"

She shook her head. "Not yet. I was going to video call them, and then I was going to just call, but I've chickened out. I think I'm going to shoot them an email and call it good. I never lie to them. I just know if I try to verbalize it, they'll be able to tell I'm not telling the truth."

He pointed at the computer in her lap. "You should email them right now. Get it over with. Like ripping off a plaster."

She sighed and opened her email. She typed up a story about being stuck in London because of some error, and how the airline is making it right. She was staying in a hotel funded by them and getting lots of sightseeing done before she needed to leave for the next session. Before she could second guess herself, she hit Send.

"There. I did it."

"Good job. Shall I reward you with a sweet?"

She laughed. "No, but after we wrap up the case you and Patrick can take me around the city so I can build up enough evidence to support the massive lie I just told my parents."

"Deal."

With lying to her parents out of the way, Evelyn reopened her thesis document. At least with being trapped in the apartment with nowhere to go for the next month she'll at least be traveling to her program with a mostly finished thesis, if the last week was any sign of how much work she would get done.

She sighed and stared at the document open on her computer screen and the books spread out on the coffee table before her. She needed a break, and honestly, to get out of the apartment for some fresh air.

She stood to stretch, and looked over at James, who was engaged fully in whatever it was he had to do on the computer to make sure this man was the one they'd been looking for. She didn't want to bother him any more than she already had. He was their only hope for getting this thing moving.

She looked at the closed door to Patrick's room. Her only hope for getting the hell out of the flat for an hour was behind that door, and she was going to make it her mission to pull him out of his funk and get him to take her anywhere but here.

CHAPTER 22

PATRICK

Poor Evelyn. His father's words echoed through his brain. *You're letting her down.*

He knew he was, yet he couldn't get himself to act on anything. He hadn't even asked her how she was handling everything. Watching him get shot. Being stuck here without an end date in sight. He'd promised her he'd have her on a plane in a couple days, but here they were, over a week since she'd been stranded, and she was still here. What did she tell her parents? Had she even told her parents? These were things he was sure she'd told him at one point, but the last week was such a blur. He wasn't even sure of anything anymore. And all of this wasn't even taking into consideration his newfound intense feelings of keeping her safe at all costs.

The door to his room opened, and the object of his thoughts walked in, giving him a small smile.

"You're awake."

"Yeah, I am. I have been for a while now."

"Why didn't you come out and join us? Mrs. Moore said you were done with bed rest. There's no reason to stay cooped up in here. It would probably make you feel better if you got up and moved."

"I wasn't in the mood to be social."

Evelyn sat on the edge of the bed. "Want to talk about whatever's been bothering you?"

"I'm fine."

"You're not fine. You've been in here moping for a week. I think you'll feel better if you talk about what's bothering you."

"I don't want to talk about it. I'm tired." He wrapped the covers up around him. "I'd like to be left alone."

She ripped the covers from him.

"Oi, what the fuck!"

"You're not tired. You're using that as a defense mechanism and as a way to get rid of me. I'm tired of you avoiding me, Patrick. I'm tired of you pushing James and me away. You need to talk about what's bothering you or you're going to fall deeper into this depression."

He sat up, glaring at her. "I'm not going to talk to you about my feelings. We're not going to sit in here and plait each other's hair and have heart-to-hearts. If that's the kind of person you think I am, I'm sorry to disappoint you, sweetheart. I'm not touchy-feely. And even if I were, you'd be the last person I'd open up to. I don't even know you that well."

He waited for her to get angry and storm off, hurt, but he was surprised when she stayed on the side of the bed, looking at him with a sympathetic gaze.

"Bullshit."

"What?"

"Bullshit. Don't try to pull this crap on me, Patrick. You can't push me away like that. I'm onto you, remember?"

He sighed and lay back on the bed. "Can't you just leave me alone? You've done enough, allowing Colin to come in here last week and go off on me. Just let it go and allow me to have this time to feel sorry for myself, yeah?"

"No. I'm done letting you feel sorry for yourself. You smell."

"What?"

"You haven't showered in a week. You're starting to smell, and if you don't do something about it, I'm going to sleep on the couch."

"You can't be serious?"

"Completely serious. You've stopped taking care of yourself. I know we said you needed to take it easy, but this is fucking ridiculous."

He winced at the profanity. She'd rarely used such language since she arrived, so he knew she was serious if she was pulling out all the major swear words.

"Please," she begged. "Please talk to me. Your mentor, your *father figure*, betrayed you. He shot you. Yell about it, scream about it. Throw something against the wall. Break something. Just do *something*. Keeping these emotions bottled inside isn't healthy."

"I don't want to talk about it," he gritted. "I don't want to yell or scream or anything. I just want to lie here, in my bed, and do nothing else."

"Seriously? Seriously? That's it? You're just going to lie there and give up? What happened to the Patrick who was out for revenge? Where's the fire? Where's the passion? You're going to let one minor setback get you down and let your mother's killer walk the streets?"

"Minor setback? I was fucking shot! Do you think I want to give up? Harry was the only family I had. I trusted him with my life, and he tried to take that away from me. Getting shot did nothing but remind me what dangerous work I'm doing and showed me I'm—"

"Human?" Evelyn supplied.

"Yes! And I don't like how vulnerable this injury has made me. I don't like I wasn't able to protect you or stop Harry from leaving the promenade."

"Good. These are all valid feelings. Thank you for finally opening up. I've been waiting all week for you to talk to me. Everything sucks. And your father figure shot you. Remember that conversation we had before we met up with Harry? The one about superheroes?"

He nodded.

"You're not a superhero, Patrick. You're not Superman or Spider-Man. You're Patrick, a regular human man who has feelings and vulnerabilities. I am here for you. I hope you know that. To listen to you, and comfort you and be whatever you need during this time. However, that all being said, you need to get the hell out of this bed and continue living your life. Start thinking about what you can do next. We still have a shot to bring Harry down with the rest of the Fitzgeralds. James is pretty damn sure he has a lead. He's finishing up as we speak. Please get out of bed and join us. Help us bring them down."

He sat on the bed, deep in thought. "You make some valid points, but I don't think I can. I'm not ready to trust anyone outside of this flat. Can you please leave me alone? I'll understand when you don't come back in for bed tonight."

He lay down, pulling the covers up and over his head, summarily ending the discussion. The bed shifted as She stood, and he listened as she moved to the door.

"You know, the reason I started having feelings for you was because of how strong and assertive you were. I'm having trouble melding the you from a week ago with the you I see right now. The Patrick who saved me from the airport wouldn't let Harry defeat him. He'd go out there and take him down. By lying here in this dark room, you're letting the Fitzgeralds win. You're allowing them to get away with all of the horrible things they're doing in your city. Think about it. I hope I see you out there soon."

She opened the door and left the room, allowing him to close his eyes and reflect on all of the things she'd said during her visit.

CHAPTER 23

EVELYN

Evelyn sighed and leaned against the bedroom door. She didn't know how else to get through to him. And she was no closer to leaving the damn flat than when she went into the room.

She pushed away from the door and reached into her pocket. There was still some money left over from what she took out the day she was supposed to only have a layover in London, since James insisted, they pay for all of her food while she was here. She was confident she could remember the way to the restaurant where they stopped for fish and chips the week before. She could easily walk down there, get supper for the group, and return. It would be easy, and she'd be quick. James and Patrick wouldn't have to worry about her.

"I'll be back in twenty minutes." She slipped her shoes on.

"What?" James looked up from his computer. "Where are you going?"

"I'm going to pick up some supper."

James stood. "I'll go. Why don't you stay here and keep working on your paper?"

"James, I've been stuck in this apartment for a week. I need to get out and get some fresh air. I need to see something other than these walls."

"Then I'll go with you."

"Stay here and finish up whatever you're doing. I'll be fine. I'm only going to the fish and chips place we went to when I first got here. I'll be there and back before you know I'm gone."

James stood in the living room, looking unsure. After a minute, he finally sighed. "Fine, but take my mobile. If you run into any trouble, call Patrick, and we'll come find you, okay?" He handed her his phone.

She took his cell and put it in her pocket. "Deal. Now, get back to work. I'll be back in a jiffy."

She opened the front door and walked out. She practically ran down the hall, down the stairs, and out into the street. Once her feet touched the sidewalk outside the apartment building, she stood there and lifted her face to the sky.

She closed her eyes and took a deep breath. Fresh air. The sun was getting a little low in the sky, and there was a soft breeze, making the summer evening feel absolutely wonderful.

"Gorgeous night for a walk, isn't it?" a male voice said from beside her.

She jumped and opened her eyes. Standing next to her was a middle-aged man dressed in a dark black pinstriped suit. His jet-black hair was slicked back, accentuating his graying sideburns. He looked at her with emotionless gray eyes, although his mouth was turned up in an attempt at a smile.

"Yeah, it's beautiful."

"Ah, an American. What brings you to London?"

"Visiting my boyfriend." She really was getting good at this lying thing. She should look into acting or something when she got back to the States.

"Really? How does an American lass end up dating a British lad?"

"Internet. We met in an online group, really hit it off, and started dating. This is the first time we've been able to meet in person."

"And you're out here without him? If I'd flown thousands of miles and across an ocean to be with my online paramour, I wouldn't want to waste one second without him."

"I got hungry, and he needed to catch up on some work he's neglected."

"Ah, so you're out here all alone?"

She stopped smiling. There was something about the way he asked the question. It didn't seem like a question a stranger on the street being nosy would ask. It was something else.

"I, um, need to get going. I promised I wouldn't be long." She moved around him, making sure she seemed confident about where she was planning to go.

The man moved and blocked her path. "What's the hurry, Evelyn? I thought we were having a delightful conversation."

She froze. "How do you know my name?" She started backing away, looking around for a way out of the situation.

"I know everything about you, Evelyn Stevenson. And I think you know all about me, which, I have to say, is a bit of a problem. Which is why you're going to have to come with me."

"I know nothing about you! I don't know who you are!"

"You're a terrible liar. Did you know that?" The man took a step toward her. "But it's okay. It won't take long for me to get what I need from you."

She turned to run, but he grabbed her and pulled her toward him. She struggled, kicking her legs and wiggling, trying to get free. She opened her mouth to scream, but he held a cloth up to her face, covering her mouth and nose. She smelled something sweet, like almonds, before everything went black.

CHAPTER 24

PATRICK

Patrick lay in his bed, staring at the ceiling.

Evelyn had been right. Of course, she was.

He was too busy lying in bed feeling sorry for himself to take any sort of action. All the fight had left him when he started really thinking about what his dad had said. He was becoming his father. Obsessed with the job, and it was becoming detrimental to his personal life.

However, his solution to the problem, lying in bed, staring at the ceiling, feeling sorry for himself, was ruining everything just as much. He was in danger of destroying the budding relationship he had with Evelyn before it even started, just by the power of doing nothing. He needed to change. He needed to get out of bed and finish this damn case. The sooner the case was over, the sooner everyone he cared about would be safe. And the sooner he could shift his focus back to smaller jobs and make room in his life for other things.

Like Evelyn.

He sat up, rubbing his face. The skin was greasy, a byproduct of not washing since his injury. If his face felt this bad, he knew the rest of his body was just as disgusting. He probably smelt terrible. Another fact Evelyn had gotten right. He needed to take a shower before he apologized to her. Or groveled at her feet for forgiveness. Whatever it took to get her to never look at him the way she had before storming out of his room.

Just as he moved to get out of bed, the door to his room swung open and a distraught James came storming into the room, as if he was searching for something.

"What's wrong?"

"I need your mobile." James held out his hand.

"What? Why?"

"Just give it to me."

Patrick shook his head and reached over to the nightstand, grabbing his phone and tossing it to James.

James immediately opened it and dialed a number. He listened to it ring and ring and ring.

"Fuck." He immediately dialed it again.

"Who are you calling? More importantly, why aren't you using your own phone to do it?"

"I'm calling Evie. She has my phone."

Patrick froze in bed. "Why would you need to be calling Evelyn? Shouldn't she be here, safe in the flat?"

"She wanted to get some fresh air, so I let her go pick up dinner from the chippy down the way. I thought it would be fine. She'd be back in ten minutes, twenty tops. That was over an hour ago." He hung up and dialed a third time.

Patrick stood. "Why the hell would you think letting her leave the flat on her own was a good idea? The Fitzgeralds want her. They tried to take her when we were *right there*. They wouldn't hesitate taking her when she's alone! What were you thinking?"

"I don't know. Maybe that the poor girl had been cooped up in this flat for a week straight and deserved to go out? She was so confident everything would be fine, I let her go."

Patrick went at him, his anger fighting with the growing panic. "Why didn't you go with her?"

"I was busy looking into the officer who I'm pretty sure is our guy. And I thought she could handle going down to the corner alone. She is an adult."

Patrick grabbed James by the collar and pushed him against the wall. "I trusted you to take care of her!"

"And I did! I'm sorry. I thought—"

"Well, hello there, Detective Miller," a voice came through the phone, interrupting their argument.

Patrick grabbed the phone out of James's hand and put it on speaker. "Who is this? Where's Evelyn?"

"Evelyn can't come to the phone right now. She's a bit, detained, at the moment."

"Put her on. I want to talk to her."

"*Tsk, tsk, tsk.* So demanding. So hotheaded. Harry warned me you'd be hard to negotiate with. Just too damn stubborn."

Patrick winced at the name of his former mentor. "Put her on the phone."

"I'd love to, but unfortunately, my associates are busy having a conversation with her right now. But never you mind. You'll have your precious Evelyn back before the night is through. And when she returns, she'll have a message for you, and I expect you to take the message *extremely* serious."

The line disconnected, and Patrick and James were left staring at the phone. Patrick pulled his arm back to throw the phone against the wall, but James caught his arm and stopped it.

"Don't do that. What if they drop Evie off somewhere and she needs to call us?"

Patrick relaxed his arm. "You're right." He threw the phone on the bed instead. "This is all my fault." He ran his hands through his hair. "If I'd gotten out of the fucking bed like she asked, repeatedly, or talked to her, she never would have felt the need to go out alone, and Mickey *Fucking* Fitzgerald wouldn't have her right now."

"You don't know that. He's obviously been watching the building if he managed to get her the second she walked outside. If you were with her, nothing would have been stopping him from taking the both of you or killing you and taking her. This isn't your fault."

"It's completely my fault. I did this. I was too busy feeling sorry for myself. We need to do something. We need to find her."

"We don't even know where to start looking. Look, I'm almost done running algorithms on this officer who I think is our ticket to getting the bastard behind bars. You need to go take a shower and start smelling human again. I need to finish up my research. And wash your sheets while you're at it. It stinks in here. Let's regroup in an hour. We will figure this out."

"An hour? She could be dead in an hour!"

"He's not going to kill her. Didn't you hear him? He's sending her back with a message for you. Shower, and we'll regroup in an hour."

James left the room, presumably to return to his computer.

Patrick watched him walk away before sliding to the ground, pressing his fists to his eyes. First, his mother, then Harry, and now Evelyn. Was he destined to lose everyone he cared about to Mickey Fitzgerald?

His chest tightened. It was becoming harder to breathe. Gasping, he looked frantically around the room. He stood, moving around his bed to the lamp on his side table. He picked it up, ripping the cord from the wall, and threw it against the wall. It made a rewarding crash. It was satisfying and made him feel slightly better, so he looked around again, picking up the nearest object, and throwing it, too, against the wall.

And another, and another, and another, until he curled up in a ball on the floor and wept.

CHAPTER 25

EVELYN

Evelyn woke up in a seemingly empty room. Her head was fuzzy, and there was a terrible taste in her mouth. She blinked as she looked around the dimly lit room. It was small, with bare concrete walls and a small metal door directly across from her. It was sparsely furnished with only a table and a few chairs against one wall and the chair she currently sat in.

She closed her eyes as she struggled to catch her breath, her heart hammering inside her chest. Someone had kidnapped her. She had barely stepped outside the building for a minute before she'd been kidnapped by who she could only assume was Mickey Fitzgerald. She would never hear the end of this from Patrick.

She tried to move her hands, but they were bound behind her back. She looked at her feet. They were tied to the legs of the chair. It was like she was a character in a Nancy Drew novel, and not the Nancy Drew heroine, more like one of her hapless friends who always ended up needing to be saved.

The door across from her opened and two men entered, briefly letting in a bright light. One was the man who'd abducted her. The other was one of the men from the airport. They shut the door behind them and stood in front of her.

"Ms. Stevenson, so glad you have finally decided to join us. We have some questions." The man who'd abducted her walked over to a corner and dragged a chair from the table to in front of her and sat. "There are two ways this can go down. You can answer all the questions I ask, truthfully, and then I'll return you to your detective unharmed. Or you can be difficult and we'll be forced to pull the answers from you in any way necessary. What will it be? Are you going to cooperate?"

She nodded slowly. She thanked every god in existence that Patrick had kept her in the dark about anything having to do with the Fitzgeralds. She'd be able to cooperate, tell the man what he wanted to know, without compromising the case in any way, and be back home in one piece.

"Great. I'm glad. Now, where's the bag?"

"I don't know."

"See, this is what I was talking about. This is the perfect example of you being difficult." He made a hand signal to the other man in the room, who pulled out a pair of pliers from his back pocket and took a step toward her.

"No, I am. I am cooperating. I really don't know. I gave the bag to Patrick when I first met him, and I haven't seen it since. I don't know what he's done with it. I swear," she screamed.

Fitzgerald held up his hand, halting his associate. "Now we're getting somewhere. The fact you don't know its exact location is disappointing, but we can work with this. What did that *slut* put in the bag you don't know the location of?"

"I don't know. Patrick wouldn't let me see anything in it."

"So, I'm to believe that when you switched bags in the airport you didn't look into it? Weren't you curious?"

"I just wanted my bag back and to get on my airplane. I didn't care what was in the bag."

"And in the last week, the detectives haven't told you anything about what was in it or even looked inside yourself?"

"Patrick has made it abundantly clear anything having to do with the bag is on a need-to-know basis, and I'm not on the list of people who need to know. He's done a great job at isolating me from the case he's trying to build against you. In fact, I didn't even know what you looked like until now."

He brought his hand up and started stroking his chin. "Hmm, smart man, keeping his cards close to his chest."

For a minute, Fitzgerald sat there, staring at her. She couldn't read what his eyes were saying, but it seemed as if he were trying to work out a difficult puzzle.

"I cannot believe it," he murmured, almost to himself, as he continued to stare at her.

"What?"

"The resemblance is uncanny. You and Megan could be siblings." He stood and moved closer to her as he spoke. "Except, you would be easily labeled the more attractive sister, by far." He leaned in, his face close to hers.

His expensive cologne smelled bitter and had been applied liberally.

"Maybe," his accented voice was low so only she could hear it, "we don't use you to send a message to those lads. Instead, I keep you here to warm my bed at night." He ran a finger down her cheek, and her heart sped up.

But, as quickly as he'd leaned in, he was gone, moving away from her. "Except, a promise *is* a promise. Jimmy, rough her up a bit, pin this note to her, and drop her off on our good detective's front step."

He turned to leave the room.

"Wait! I answered your questions. I did what you asked! I thought that meant I wouldn't get hurt."

"I said you wouldn't get tortured. I never said anything about you leaving here unscathed."

As he walked to the door, the phone she had forgotten about rang in her pocket, causing him to stop. He turned around slowly and walked back to her. He reached into her pocket and pulled out the cell, smiling when he saw who was calling.

"Now, this will be fun. Make sure you do a good job. Really send those boys a message. I'll take care of the investigator."

He walked out of the room, carrying James's phone.

The door closed behind Fitzgerald, and she looked at the man in the room with her. He was smiling at her as he moved closer.

She closed her eyes and waited for the pain to come.

CHAPTER 26

PATRICK

Patrick walked out of the bathroom feeling slightly better after showering and shaving for the first time in a week, but he was still on edge. He'd be much better when they found Evelyn and had her back with them.

"Have you finished your research yet?" He moved into the living room.

"I have. This guy is completely clean, on paper and digitally. If he's being paid off by the Fitzgeralds, then they've covered it up really well. Which I highly doubt, since the chief didn't even come clean when I ran my thorough search on him. I think we've found our arresting officer."

Patrick allowed himself a small smile. "Excellent. Now what? We can't just call the bloke and beg him to arrest Fitzgerald right now."

"No. I'm sure he'll take some convincing. We need to pull what evidence we're willing to share from the bag and set up a meeting, somewhere private, and start working on convincing him to help us."

"What about Evelyn? We need to get her back. This is going to take too long—"

"I know, but what else can we do? Neither of us owns a gun. We can't start looking for the Fitzgeralds. That's not going to work in our favor. We can't defend ourselves against an arsenal. We need to follow the plan and trust we'll find her in time."

Patrick opened his mouth to argue, but a loud bang against their front door interrupted him.

They looked at each other before moving slowly toward the door. James signaled for Patrick to get behind him and cautiously turned the door handle. He opened it, and they both gasped at the sight before them.

Lying in a bloody heap on their doorstep was Evelyn.

"Evelyn!" Patrick moved forward and knelt next to her.

He moved his hand up to her neck. There was a strong pulse. She was alive. She was just unconscious. He slipped one arm under her knees and the other under her shoulders, lifting her, and brought her into the flat. He went into his room and set her on the bed.

"Is she—" James asked from the doorway.

"She's alive. I just need to see her wounds."

He moved her hair, and his heart ached to see bruises already developing and causing her face to become discolored. As if being used as a punching bag wasn't enough, she had tiny cuts up and down her arms, which were the source of the blood.

"Get me the first-aid kit and whatever we have that's frozen." Patrick didn't take his gaze off of her.

He ran his hand down the side of her face, softly and slowly caressing her. She was here. She was safe. And whoever hit her was going to pay. He was going to make sure of that.

James was back in the room before Patrick even realized he'd left. The two of them began working on dressing all of Evelyn's wounds and stopping the bleeding.

"Patrick, have you seen this?"

He looked up. Pinned to her shirt was a piece of paper. He shook his head.

James took the paper off her shirt and opened it. He read what it said and then handed it to Patrick.

Drop the case, or next time, we'll be delivering her corpse.

Patrick crumpled the note and held it, closing his eyes.

"What are we going to do?"

James began cleaning and bandaging the wounds on Evelyn's arms while Patrick began applying the frozen vegetables to the worst of her bruises.

"Every fiber of my being is saying we ignore it and keep pushing, but then there's the part of me—"

"That says it's just a case and we need to drop it so we don't lose Evie."

"Exactly. Maybe we should take her to the hospital. What if she's hurt internally? Maybe we should have her checked out."

"No, no hospital," came a soft voice from the bed.

They looked at Evelyn, who was slowly waking up. "And you can't drop the case because of me."

"Evelyn." Patrick brought his hand to her forehead. "How are you feeling?"

"Like I've been hit by a truck which, judging from the size of the man who did this to me, isn't that much of an exaggeration."

He smiled. "No offense, but you look like you've been hit by a truck. Does anywhere hurt worse than other areas? Do you think anything is broken?"

She shook her head. "No. Everything hurts equally. He kept saying he was going easy on me. Which, if this is going easy, I don't want to know what would have happened if I hadn't cooperated with them."

"Are you sure you don't want us to take you to the hospital? We can get some x-rays done to make sure you're really okay."

"No. I'm fine, really. And if you take me to the hospital, they're going to call my parents since they're my emergency contacts, and then our whole tourist ruse is up."

"I'm so sorry, Evie," James said from her other side. "I shouldn't have let you go off alone."

"Don't be. I was quite insistent you let me. I can't believe I had barely taken one step outside before they kidnapped me. I'm looking forward to hearing you guys telling me 'I told you so' for the next forever."

Patrick smiled weakly. "I'm glad to see they didn't take away your sense of humor during your abduction."

"I have to laugh about it or else I'll break down, and if I breakdown, I don't think I'll be able to stop."

He sobered. "You terrified me, Evelyn."

She looked at him, tears pooling in her eyes. "I'm so sorry. That wasn't my intention. I wanted to go out, bring back food, and hope maybe it would help get you out of your funk." She looked at him more closely and smiled. "You showered."

"Yeah, I had to. I couldn't go on a rescue mission looking and smelling like a homeless person."

She smiled. "If I'd known all I had to do was get kidnapped to get you out of bed, I would have gone out for food a week ago."

He shook his head. "You're ridiculous." He gazed into her eyes.

"I know." She returned his intense gaze.

James cleared his throat. "I'm going to go out there and leave you two kids alone."

He left the room, closing the door behind him.

She shifted over in the bed, and Patrick took it as an invitation to settle in next to her. He lifted his arm, and she tucked herself against his side, laying her head on his bare chest.

"I was so scared," she whispered. "He said he was going to let me go, but he's a hardened criminal. I didn't think I could believe him."

"I was scared, too," Patrick whispered back. "I thought Fitzgerald had succeeded in taking another person I cared about away from me, permanently." He tightened his arm around her and planted a kiss on her head. "Please don't go out alone again."

"Done. I never want to leave this flat again. Maybe even this bed. I think you had the right idea. Let's just hide away here, forever."

He chuckled. "I don't think I had the right idea. I think you were right to make me get out of bed. I was being foolish and cowardly, hiding away in here. You and James were busy working on the case while I wallowed."

"Well, to be fair, James made progress on the case. I made progress on my thesis. Let's give credit where it's due. Tell me more about how you're feeling."

"Hurt. Betrayed. Not depressed about it anymore, necessarily. Sad, maybe, would be a better word. Like it'll take a long time for me to trust new people again."

She gave him a small smile. "All of which are perfectly normal and okay feelings to be having. I don't know why you were hiding out in here. We could have helped you work through them, you know."

"I know, but I wasn't feeling very logical, you know? I guess I wanted to wallow. I've never really done that before. After mum was killed, I threw myself into my work. I never mourned. And I guess Harry betraying me and getting shot kind of piled on top of the suppressed emotions, and I guess I kind of imploded."

She leaned up, giving him a peck on his lips. "I get it, and I'm sorry I wasn't more sensitive to your needs."

He shifted them so they were both lying on their sides, facing each other in the bed. He ran his hand up and down her arm and her side, careful to avoid her injuries. "Don't apologize. I was a mess, and you were right to point that out to me. I wish I'd had the sense to get out of my funk on my own and not because my, um, female companion had gotten kidnapped by my arch nemesis."

She laughed. "Female companion?"

He shrugged. "We've never really defined what we are to each other, and I don't want to say we're in a relationship, especially since in the last week I've been nothing but an arse to you."

"You've been hurting, both physically and emotionally. I'll give you a pass for this one. How's your head?"

"It hurts still, but nothing like it was before. It's nothing I can't handle."

She gently touched his forehead, leaning forward. She placed a soft kiss near where his injury was. She pressed another kiss on his cheek, and then another on his jawline. She looked at him, meeting his intense gaze before bringing his head down so she could give him a proper kiss.

Their lips touched, and he eased them into a gentle kiss, mindful of the injuries on her face. She opened her mouth, and he took advantage, deepening the kiss.

Reluctantly, he pulled away as things were becoming more heated.

He pressed his forehead against hers, closing his eyes. He ran his hand softly through her hair and cupped her cheek. "We should stop before this goes any further."

"But—"

"You're hurt. We have plenty of time to go further later, when you're better. You're here indefinitely, remember?"

She let out a soft puff of breath as she silently chuckled. "You're right."

He pulled away, and he moved her until he was on her other side and he was spooned behind her, his arm around her waist, holding her tightly against his body. Her warmth reassured him she was okay.

"Why do you call me Evelyn?"

"Well, last I checked, it was your name."

"I know that, but, well, I mean, I told you everyone calls me Evie, and James even calls me Evie, but you always make it a point to call me Evelyn. I was wondering why."

"Well, it's like you said. Everyone calls you Evie. I don't want to be just anyone."

"Wow, excellent answer."

He planted a kiss on the top of her head. "I'm glad that you think so."

They fell quiet again and enjoyed lying in the bed together.

"Don't give up the case," she said finally.

"What?"

"Don't give it up. You guys have worked so hard, and you finally have leads and evidence to bring the man who killed your mom to justice. Don't give it up because of me."

"I'm not going to put your life in danger. I can't sit back and ignore a very credible threat to your life in order to get someone arrested. My dad ignored the warnings, and it got my mum killed. I don't want to take the chance the same will happen to you. There'll be other chances to catch Mickey Fitzgerald. Believe me. I'll just let some other fool do it."

"But you guys are so close! You need to do it. Meet with the police officer James found. Find out what he can do for you. You have to do at least that. James spent a week finding him."

"Fine. We can meet with whoever James found, and then we clean our hands of this whole thing. I don't think you've had a chance to look in a mirror, but, no offense, you look terrible. And I don't want to take a chance you could end up looking worse, or even dead, because I was selfish and wanted to see out my vendetta personally."

She turned so she was facing him. "I don't need to see a mirror, thank you. I was there. I can imagine what I look like. Let's take the case one step at a time. I don't want you making any final decisions right now. We've all had a very emotionally trying week. Between the head, the betrayal, and my abduction, we've all been on high alert on an almost constant basis. Just promise me you won't give up because of me."

He brushed her hair off her face. "I promise."

She burrowed deeper into the covers. She moved slightly so her head came to rest on his pillow. He moved so she was nestled into his body, her head tucked into his neck, his chin resting on her head.

"I'm so tired. I may never leave this room again. You guys are on your own. Come and get me when it's time for my plane to leave in three weeks."

"What? You've booked a plane?"

She looked at him. "Yeah. I'm pretty sure I told you sometime in the last few days. My program rescheduled me for the end of July. I fly to Athens from here in about three weeks."

"Oh."

"Hey, you knew I'd have to leave eventually."

"Yeah, I know," he said flatly. "I've never really thought about you actually leaving, though."

"Well, I don't leave for almost a month. Let's make the most of the time we have together. As...companions."

"Yes, companions," Patrick agreed absentmindedly.

"For the record, I'm starting to wish I didn't have to go," she whispered.

He wrapped his arms around her, pulling her closer to him until her head was in the crook of his neck. "I wish you didn't have to leave, either."

CHAPTER 27

EVELYN

When the two finally emerged from Patrick's room, James was sitting on the couch reading the paper, barely able to contain the grin on his face.

"What are you grinning about?"

James folded the paper and set it aside. "It's my job as the best friend to be a bit cheeky, so I'm going to perform that duty with gusto."

Patrick sighed as he pulled a chair out for Evelyn. "I'm too tired for riddles, James. What on earth are you talking about?"

James looked absolutely giddy, clapping his hands, wearing a goofy grin on his face. "Bow chicka wow-wow." He waggled his eyebrows.

Patrick sighed and opened his mouth to respond to him, but James continued on.

"Oh, I'm not done. You two were so adamant you weren't going to shag. You were all, 'No, James, I'm not interested in her like that,'" he raised the pitch of his voice in a mocking tone, "but I should have put money on it, because you two totally shagged."

It was Evelyn's turn to bury her face in her hands. Her face burned in embarrassment. She was about to protest, but, again, James interrupted to continue on his tirade.

"Now, seriously, I'm happy for you two. I could sense the attraction and the sexual tension from day one. I'm glad you guys finally acted on it. Are you going to do a long-distance thing when she leaves in a few weeks?"

Patrick and Evelyn glanced at each other.

"Well, first off, we didn't shag. Who do you take me for, James? The girl was just abducted and abused just a few hours ago."

"You didn't shag?" James's face fell, seemingly more disappointed about their lack of sex than he really should be.

"We didn't shag," she confirmed, "and we haven't really discussed what's going to happen when I leave."

"We're going to focus on the now and then figure out where we stand in a few weeks."

"Well, now I'm disappointed with my skills as an investigator because I can't believe I was so wrong. Let's move on before I embarrass myself further. Where do we stand on the whole Fitzgerald thing? Because, as I'm looking at you, Evie, I'm really thinking we need to drop the whole bloody thing."

She brought her hands up to her face, touching the bruises. Her face hurt, but her eyes weren't swelling shut, so she knew she wasn't too bad. She still didn't want to look in a mirror. The way Patrick and James were reacting to her, she wasn't sure she wanted to see the extent of her injuries. She looked at her bandaged arms. Yeah, she didn't want to know the full extent of her injuries.

"We've decided to stay the course," Patrick said.

James's eyes widened. "You're fucking kidding."

He shook his head. "Evelyn insisted."

James's head whipped over to look at her. "Evie, you need to rethink this. They've threatened your life. They've already captured you once, and even though you look like hell, no offense, they were fairly easy on you. I don't even want to imagine what they'll do if they get you again."

"But they're not going to get me again. Like I told Patrick, you guys are so close to bringing them down, to arresting Fitzgerald, it would be stupid to give up now."

James looked at Patrick, who shook his head.

"She's got a point. We're very close to breaking this wide open. If we can get this done now, we can put this behind us. If we drop it, how many more innocent people are going to get hurt before someone else gets to the point we are now?"

"There are many private investigators in the greater London area, Patrick. We can go and anonymously drop off the bag of evidence and all the research we've done on their doorstep. We would move ourselves out of the danger zone, and the Fitzgeralds would still be on the brink of getting taken down. Or have you forgotten what they did to poor Megan?"

Patrick looked like he was going to consider it, but before he could agree, Evelyn spoke.

"You guys, don't. You can't give the case to someone else. This is personal. You have to see it through to the end."

"Not if your life's in danger. James has a point. We can give this case to someone else. We don't have to be the ones to actually follow through on it. We can sit on the sidelines, taking you sightseeing, while someone else is in the line of fire for Fitzgerald. Wouldn't you rather enjoy your last few weeks here, seeing the Tower instead of being cooped up in this flat, worrying if you step out the door, you'll get snatched?"

"How is sightseeing out in *public* any safer than continuing on with the investigation?"

"Because we won't actively be trying to destroy the Fitzgeralds. We'll be dropping the case, just like they want."

"But, your vendetta—"

"Fuck my vendetta. Look where it's gotten us so far. My father had a severed head shipped to him, my father figure fucking betrayed us, and then fucking shot me, and you got kidnapped and injured. Nothing good has come from me seeking vengeance for my mother's murder. Nothing. I'm not going to sit back and watch another tragedy occur while I attempt to take down the largest crime syndicate in London. I'm sorry, but I can't watch anyone else I care for get hurt, or worse. I can't take the chance I'll open that door and find your head in a box next."

The room fell quiet after Patrick's rant. He was breathing hard, trying to rein himself in.

James turned and looked at her, raising his eyebrows, but said nothing. He was leaving it up to her. He was on Patrick's side. She knew that. She seemed to be outnumbered. But how could she make the boys see they were making a mistake? That they were going to regret dropping the case? She took a deep breath and exhaled slowly.

She had her work cut out for her. "I didn't take you for cowards."

Both men's head whipped over to her, their eyes narrowing. Jackpot.

"We're not cowards," James replied.

"No? You're giving up at the first sign of trouble. You guys have worked tirelessly on bringing down the Fitzgeralds, and they send you a note telling you to give up or else, and you're going to listen to them? What the hell is wrong with you? You can't let them win."

"We're not letting them win, and you keep forgetting they *murder* people. We're not giving up," Patrick stated.

"You are doing exactly what they want you to do. And when you do, Fitzgerald is going to spread it all over town how easy you two gave up, and no one will want to hire you. You'll be known as the detectives who quit when it gets hard."

Both men scowled. It seemed to be working.

"Think about your business."

Patrick shook his head. "Fuck my business. We can rebuild our business. You could die. Do you understand that? They've threatened your life. Why don't you understand?"

"I understand. Believe me, I understand. I was with them, remember? I was there. They had me. They're really fucking scary. But you know why I'm not worried? Because I have you guys. I know you two won't let anything happen to me."

"Have you forgotten you got kidnapped on my watch?" James pointed out.

"Only because I was insistent to go out on my own. It was all on me, not on you two at all. I wish you'd stop blaming yourselves."

"We blame ourselves because it was on us to protect you, to make sure you were safe. We dropped the ball."

"And now you know how stubborn I am, and you'll now no longer drop the ball. You know what the stakes are, and you know the risks, and what to expect. You won't let anything happen again. The situation we're in is not a joke. And we've all learned it the hard way. But with everything that's happened with Harry and me, wouldn't you rather see it through? Why would you give this to someone else after everything we've gone through?" And then she remembered the conversation they had way back that night at the promenade. "Would Superman or Spider-Man give up?"

The boys were silent and then looked at each other. Evelyn could tell they were having a silent conversation. The way they looked at each other, the expressions in their eyes changing, their eyebrows moving up and down, at the way they could communicate with each other without saying anything impressed her. It was truly a testament as to how close they were.

"Fine, but you're going to listen to us this time and do what we say. No more venturing out on your own, no more being stubborn, and no arguing if we tell you to do something you don't like. If we're going to defy the Fitzgeralds, we're going to do it in a way that keeps you safe."

"I'll do whatever you say. I learned my lesson the hard way." She touched her face.

"I don't want to make it sound like we're ordering you about. We're doing this for your own good. We care about you, and we want you to live and make it to your program," Patrick explained.

"Yeah. I get it."

"Good." He turned toward James. "What did you find out during your scan of all the local officers?"

James smiled. "I thought you'd never ask." He walked over to his computer desk and picked up a stack of papers. He handed the stack to Patrick. "Joseph McCleary."

Patrick began rifling through the papers.

"He's been a member of the force for less than a year. He's a total rookie. He's young and itching to prove himself. He's stayed out of the Fitzgeralds' pockets because they don't think he's going to last. Which means they don't see him as a threat, either. He's currently the only officer in Tower Hamlets who isn't being paid off by the family."

"Do you think he'll meet with us? Do you think he'll help?"

"This case is something he'll jump at. I guarantee it. He's so desperate to prove himself, he'd love to be the officer who arrested Mickey Fitzgerald. The press alone would make him giddy. An early promotion to sergeant would be the icing on the cake."

"How do we contact him without raising red flags everywhere?"

"Easy. We send him an encrypted email asking him if he's willing to meet. Then we send another with a location and time."

"Do we tell him why we want to meet?" Evelyn asked.

James shook his head. "We don't tell him anything other than we have something for him that will make his career. He's so obsessed with his career that he'll bite."

"How sure are you this will work?" Patrick asked.

"Ninety percent."

"The other ten percent?"

"That he'll think we're taking the piss and not meet with us. Also, if he does meet with us, he won't want anything to do with the case because of the dangers associated with it. If the solicitors can't get Fitzgerald behind bars and bring down the entire family with him, then this whole thing will paint targets on not only our backs, but his since he's the one who will arrest him."

"So, you're certain he's not going to meet with us and betray us?"

"I get why you're concerned. And I can't guarantee with one hundred percent certainty, but I've done the research. I've run my algorithm twice on him. He's come back clean both times. He's so new to the force, he hasn't had time to become corrupt. He's mostly been on patrols and follow-ups on suspicious activity. Unless Fitzgerald has decided in the last five hours to get him on their payroll, and he accepted, we're golden."

"Send the email then."

"Are you sure?" Evelyn questioned.

"Yeah. I mean, at least this time we've done some research. We're prepared. We're not going to go into this blindly like we did last time. We're going to learn from our mistakes, remember?"

"Yes. We'll learn from our mistakes, and everything will be fine."

James walked back to his computer. "Constable McCleary," he read aloud as he typed. "We are a pair of local investigators. We have a case we think you will want to see. It's a career-making opportunity. In fact, if you don't agree to meet with us, you might find it to be a career-ending mistake. Once we hear from you that you're willing to meet, we'll send you another message with a time and place. We look forward to hearing your reply."

"Sounds good," Patrick said.

"Excellent. And send."

"Now what?" Evelyn asked.

"Now we wait."

CHAPTER 28

PATRICK

"Bloody hell, this is the stupidest thing I have ever seen," James exclaimed.

"It is not. It's awesome."

"This would never happen in real life."

"That's because it's not real life," Evelyn said.

"But why aren't they questioning what's going on? I mean, aren't they a little suspicious that they walk down into a basement and there are all these weird trinkets lying around?"

"James, shut up. You'd think you'd never watched a movie before in your life," Patrick said.

James huffed. "Of course, I've seen a bloody movie before, but I can't stand movies when they're full of idiots. I mean, why can't horror movies have some intelligent people for once? The characters never use their brains. And these people don't even understand they're walking into a trap."

"You understand this movie is a parody, right? The filmmakers are making fun of the horror genre." Evelyn leaned against Patrick on the couch.

"I don't fucking care. If you're going to parody something, at least add an element they're all missing. And every movie in the genre is missing the smart person."

"Just shut your trap and watch the movie." Patrick turned his attention back to the film.

James narrowed his eyes, but watched the film.

It had been a few hours since they'd emailed Constable McCleary, and he still hadn't responded. They were becoming anxious, and rather than risking their lives by leaving the flat, they ordered takeaway and put on a movie to distract them from checking the email for a response every two minutes.

Patrick was enjoying the brief moment of relaxation. They were simply three friends, sitting in their living room, watching a terrible movie. He glanced at the woman in his arms, and couldn't stop the smile that spread across his face. She was right. If they solved the case now, and arrested Fitzgerald, they'd be able to enjoy her last three weeks here. If they'd given the case away, they wouldn't have been able to enjoy anything. He would have been wondering what-ifs, and they would still have to look over their shoulders because the Fitzgeralds would still be out there. And even though they'd said they'd leave them alone if they dropped the case, they were hardened criminals, and how much could they actually keep them to their word?

He tightened his hold on Evelyn, drew her in closer to his side. She sighed and cuddled with him, laying her head on his shoulder. He was in trouble. What he was feeling for her was more intense than he was ready for. He didn't know how he was going to ever let her go in three weeks. It would be one thing if he knew she'd be coming back, but she wouldn't be. She'd go to Greece for her six-week program, and then fly back to the States. They'd be reduced to keeping in contact via email or video chat. And he'd read about long-distance relationships. They never lasted. They had these three weeks together, and that was it. And he wasn't sure if he was ready for that to be it. He didn't want their *whatever* to end.

Why couldn't he admit they were in a relationship? If he couldn't even admit it in his head, how could he be expected to admit it aloud? It probably had something to do with the fact he'd never been in a relationship before. He was a lone wolf. Loved the one-night stand, love-them-and-leave-them thing. He'd never had a desire for a serious relationship. Until now. This woman, who he never would have met if he wasn't on this case, was the first to come into his life who could even make him consider giving up his bachelor ways. And that wasn't only scary, it also made him sad. Because, of *course,* it was a woman he had no future with. One who was going to leave him in a few short weeks and he'd never see again.

Fate was a fickle bitch.

"Mate, you okay?" James asked. "You're looking pretty pissed off over there."

Patrick shook himself out of his thoughts. "Yeah, I'm fine. Just thinking about what I'm going to do to Fitzgerald when I'm finally able to confront him."

"You're not going to do anything to him." Evelyn moved away from him slightly. "You're going to allow the police to arrest him, and then we'll sit back and watch his trial like normal citizens of the world."

"You think I'm going to let the police arrest him on their own? I'm going to be there. And when I'm finally face-to-face with him for the first time, I'm going to take out all of my anger and frustration on his face."

She pulled out of his embrace completely. "Wait. Has this always been the plan? You being there with the police?"

"Well, yeah, James and I are going to be right there with PC McCleary when he arrests him. The man needs backup. You didn't think we were going to send him in there alone, did you? That would be sending the poor bloke to his death."

She turned to James. "Is this true?"

"Well, yeah. I thought you knew. I mean, I thought it was a pretty obvious step in our plan. I didn't think we needed to actually spell that part out for you."

She shook her head. "What's stopping the Fitzgeralds from killing all of you the second you step into their...whatever you call their location. Their hideout?"

"Their lair," James replied. "I like to think they have an evil lair where they do all of their evil planning."

Patrick and Evelyn looked at him and shook their heads.

"What? Mickey Fitzgerald is obviously an evil super villain. He has to have a lair. I'm sticking with the lair and ignoring your judgmental looks."

"Well, answer me this. Even with three of you, you're outnumbered. You have to know that."

"It's a chance we're willing to take. We can't let PC McCleary walk into the headquarters—"

"Lair," James interrupted.

Patrick glared at him. "—alone. Three men are better than one, no matter how you look at it."

"But—"

"They're less likely to kill three blokes who walk into their lair than one bloke who walks into the lion's den alone," James stated.

She shook her head. "You know that's bullshit. There's nothing that will stop them. They're murderers. When were you planning to tell me this?"

"I didn't think you needed to be told. I thought you had deduced it on your own. You're a smart woman. I didn't think we needed to spell it out for you," Patrick replied.

"Well, obviously, you needed to. And where am I going to be when you guys storm the castle, so to speak?"

"Colin's," Patrick spoke without hesitation.

"You're going to drop me off at your dad's and have him babysit me while I worry about you as you deliberately put yourselves in danger?"

"Well, we're not taking you with us, if that's where you're going with this."

"Why not? Why can't I be there? Wouldn't four people be better than three?"

"Because it's too bloody dangerous! You would be a distraction, which would be the reason the mission would go wrong."

She moved completely away from him and stood. "Fine. I'll remove myself starting now. I would hate to be a *distraction*." She turned around and walked to Patrick's room.

"Where are you going?"

"To go pack my stuff. You should take me to your dad's now. I would hate to be the reason you blow the case."

"You're being ridiculous and completely overreacting." Patrick followed her. "You know you can't be there with us. I don't know why you're acting this way."

"Because I'm tired of you seeing me as someone who isn't part of the team. After everything, I'm still not good enough to be in the know."

"I didn't keep you in the dark on purpose. You know that. I honestly thought you knew this was the plan. You didn't honestly think we were going to send the poor bloke in alone, did you?"

"No. I thought he'd have his own team to bring in."

"What team? Right now, he's the only one who might be willing to arrest Fitzgerald. He's it. He doesn't have a team. We're his team. James and me. We're it. So, I need you to calm down and start thinking rationally."

"Why can't I go with you? I'll be going crazy sitting in your dad's apartment waiting for you to get back. I want to be there to make sure you're going to be okay."

He stopped in front of her, bringing his hand up to cup her face. "Because if the mission does go wrong, if we're ambushed, if the family lives up to expectations and opens fire on us, I want to make sure you're not there. That you're safe."

She closed her eyes. A tear escaped down her cheek. "Please don't think like that."

He shrugged. "We have to take everything into consideration. Mickey Fitzgerald and his gang are hardened criminals. They may decide to take us out rather than going quietly. We need to be prepared."

"So, you guys could be walking to your deaths?"

"It's a real possibility," he whispered.

She shook her head as another tear made a trail down her cheek. "I don't like it. I don't want you to go."

"We have to."

She moved forward, closing the gap between them, embracing him, burying her face in his chest as she sobbed.

He wrapped his arms around her tightly, rubbing his hands up and down her back.

"Hey, guys," James's voice arose from the background.

They moved away from each other and turned to look at him.

"I'm sorry to interrupt your Hallmark moment, but our elusive PC McCleary has emailed us back."

Patrick took her hand and walked back into the living room. "And?"

"And he's agreed to meet. We've piqued his interest. He wants to meet as soon as possible."

Patrick sat, rubbing his mouth with his hands. "We should meet tonight."

"Are you sure? So soon? It's already late. I think we should meet tomorrow. Fresh minds and all that. Give him more time to read the email and prepare."

"I agree with James. We rushed into the meeting last time, and we all know how that turned out. I think we should meet tomorrow night. Give him twenty-four hours to prepare and give us time to really hammer out a plan. We need to make sure we're the ones in control this time. One hundred percent in control. We don't want to be surprised again."

Patrick sighed. "You're right. Tell him we'll meet him tomorrow night at ten."

"Where? I don't think we should have him come here, and I don't think we should meet in public again. We can't risk getting caught on CCTV and having someone on the Fitzgeralds' pay roll see us. That would blow everything."

Patrick steepled his fingers and brought them up to rest in front of his mouth. "We should meet at the office."

"I forgot about the office," James stated.

"The office?" she asked.

"It's this abandoned building about two miles from here. When we first went into this business together, we joked about setting up our agency there. We visited it and we even talked to an estate agent about buying the building. But holy shit, even as an abandoned building, it was fucking expensive. So, we ditched that thought and decided to use our flat as our office as well," James explained.

"We haven't visited the office in forever, and I don't think anyone will even associate the building with us," Patrick added. "It's the perfect place for a clandestine meeting."

James began typing on the computer. "Alright. I pulled the exact address of the office out of trusty Google and made a nice map. I'll copy and paste it into the message, like so. Voila! We have a response. We have a meeting with PC McCleary at ten tomorrow night at the office. And that's all the message says. And it's sent."

"This feels like a cheesy spy movie," she stated.

"That's what makes it so fun." James chuckled.

"Now that we have to wait until tomorrow night for this meeting, how are we going to keep busy?" Patrick asked.

"Well, let's finish this shitty movie, then the two of you can fuck like bunnies. Tomorrow, we can watch even more shitty movies until it's time to go, if you two can stop shagging long enough to grace me with your presence, that is." James wore a cheeky grin.

Patrick picked up the pillow from the couch and threw it at his head.

James caught it and sent it back, and the three started laughing.

The tension left the room. They settled in to finish their movie.

CHAPTER 29

PATRICK

After the movie ended, Patrick picked up his phone.

"Bloody hell, I'm starving. Takeaway?"

Evelyn sat up and stretched. "Yes, please."

"None for me, thanks," James said, standing from the couch. "I'm off to my mum's for dinner. She wants to spend some time with me while not in an emergency setting. You two lovebirds have fun, yeah?" He gave a wink before exiting the flat, leaving Patrick and Evelyn alone.

Alone.

He couldn't think of a time they had the flat to themselves. Well, not a time when he wasn't wallowing in his bed rather than spending time with her.

"Curry?" he asked, unable to keep the excitement from bleeding through his voice.

"Sure. What's got you so happy?"

He quickly tapped in a delivery order from the curry place down the street into the app on his phone before setting it aside. He turned so he was facing her. "We're alone."

She laughed. "Yes, I watched James leave."

"We have the flat to ourselves. We just ordered in takeaway." He paused, waiting for her to pick up on the significance of the moment.

"Yes." She tilted her head, eyebrows down. "Why are you just stating obvious things? Does your head hurt? Are you having delayed symptoms from the concussion?" She reached out to touch the plaster on his head that covered his wound.

He shook his head, a wide grin spreading on his face. "Oh, sweet Evelyn. Don't you realize? It's our first date!"

She brought her hand back to her lap. "Our first date? We are in your flat."

"Who cares? We can't exactly leave because of being wanted by The Fitzgeralds. And really, we don't need much more than each other and some good food for it to be counted as a date, yeah?"

He could practically see the wheels turning in her head as she came to this realization.

"Best date ever," she declared.

He chuckled. "You're having a laugh."

"I'm serious. I don't need to leave the house or put on makeup. Best. Date. Ever."

"Well, then." He rearranged himself on the couch, tucking one leg under his body before resting his elbow on the top of the cushion, leaning his head against his hand. "Tell me more about your life in Iowa."

She also rearranged herself, mirroring his position. "Shit, I feel like I'm being interviewed on a talk show."

"C'mon. We've done things all wrong. We've skipped so many basic things. I want to know about your life. Outside of," he gestured with his free hand, "all of this."

"Okay, well, what do you want to know?"

"Everything."

"I'm the oldest of three sisters. My sisters, Elizabeth and Michelle, are easily my best friends. In fact, my entire family is very close. Elizabeth and I chose to go to Iowa State because of its proximity to our home. Going far away really wasn't something we desired to do."

"And yet you decided to travel halfway around the world."

She smiled. "I did. This was me getting out of my comfort zone. And boy is the universe flashing all the signs about how I probably should have stayed home. In my rut."

"But then you wouldn't have met me."

Her gaze met his. She smiled softly. "You're right. I guess there's been *something* decent about this whole debacle."

"If you're so close to your family, it must really be killing you lying to them about everything."

"You don't even know. It's why I haven't called them or video chatted. I'll just cave like a house of cards the second I look into my mom's eyes."

He could feel jealousy start to creep up. "You're very lucky to have the family you do."

She readjusted her position on the couch so she could move closer to him. She took his free hand into her own. She said nothing, just took his hand in hers. That one small action meant the world to Patrick in this moment.

He cleared his throat. "What are some things you do for fun in Iowa? I looked it up in a quick web search shortly after you came, because honestly, it's a place I was never aware of. And all I got were pictures of corn. Is your entire state made of nothing but corn fields? Do you live on a farm?"

She laughed. "No. I don't live on a farm, and our entire state isn't made of corn fields. We have some large cities, but the population of our entire state is equivalent to the population of Los Angeles."

"The weather must be pretty mild if you have vast amounts of farms."

"Wow, already talking about the weather. This date must be fizzling out."

"Evelyn, I'm British. There's nothing more we like to do than talk about the weather."

"Well, in that case, our weather is not mild. We have brutally cold winters, with several days below zero Fahrenheit. And our summers are hot and muggy, which helps our corn grow."

"And you spend all summer inside with all your glorious air conditioning I've seen in films."

"No, we spend our summer catching lightning bugs in jars, wading through creeks, and going to the State Fair to eat cotton candy the size of your head."

He scoffed. "You're having me on. It's not really the size of your head."

"It really is. So much sugar."

There was a knock on the door, interrupting them. Patrick reluctantly let go of her hand and stood. He opened the door to retrieve the takeaway and returned to the couch.

He and Evelyn moved in tandem spreading out the food on the coffee table. They were so in sync, it was as if they had done this several times. It was so fucking domestic, he couldn't help but imagine that this was what life could be like if she could just stay.

He shook his head and brought himself to the present. No use imagining things that couldn't happen. It only led to heartbreak.

"So, I've talked about myself, what about you? What was it like growing up in London?"

"Well, no creek stomping and catching lightning bugs, for one thing."

She laughed as she took a bite of her dinner. "Well," she said after she swallowed, "I imagine growing up in the city would be quite different than growing up in rural Iowa. Have you always lived in Tower Hamlets?"

"No, I grew up in a more posh neighborhood, but not too posh, more middle class. It was all quite boring. I went to school, and I obeyed my parents, until about secondary school when I really realized my dad was never around and I began to resent him."

"Yeah, I gathered he wasn't around much from everything you and he have said since I've known you. Were you and your mom close?"

"Yes, but probably not as close as you are with your parents. But we were close enough. She was my only parent most of the time."

"What made you want to become a police officer?"

"Rebellion. My dad wanted me to be a lawyer like him, and my A-levels were okay, but not great. I didn't think University was my thing, so I signed up to be in the police. Went through training and was placed here, in Tower Hamlets."

"Where you met James."

He smiled. "Where I met James, and we became the only two fucking sods with morals in the whole borough."

"And the rest is history?"

"The rest is history." He set his fork aside having finished his meal. "You know, starting this business with James was like having a dream come true. I finally had something I could call my own. Something I could control. And I don't even care that I have to spend night after night in a fucking MINI Cooper waiting to get a picture of some asshole cheating on their spouse. I don't answer to anyone, and it's fucking amazing."

She moved closer to him, having finished her meal. She reached over and placed her hand on his cheek, gently caressing it.

He moved his head so he could place a kiss on her palm.

Her gaze immediately flew up to his. Her eyes were so soft and full of emotion.

He leaned forward and closed the gap between them, capturing her lips with his.

She returned the kiss, moving the hand she had placed on his cheek until it was on his shoulder, pulling them closer together.

He brought his arms around, settling his hands on her waist, before running his tongue across her lips. She opened to him, deepening the kiss.

She moved her hands, dragging them up the back of his neck until she tangled them in his hair, all the while being careful of his left side, which was still tender to the touch even a week later.

He moaned as her fingers massaged his scalp. He brought his hands down to the hem of her shirt, inching it up. His hand met with the bare skin of her back. It was warm and soft. He started moving it up her back. When he met the strap of her bra, she froze.

He pulled back, letting his eyes focus, and frowned.

Her eyes were wide.

"What's wrong?"

"Um, I think we left something very important out of our 'getting to know you' session."

"What's that?"

She pulled her lower lip between her teeth and looked down. She was quiet for a long time.

"Evelyn, whatever it is, you can tell me." He worried he did something wrong, or she was going to tell him she was dying of cancer, or she was a prophet and the world was going to end in the next five minutes.

"I don't have a lot of...experience," she finally said, almost haltingly.

He breathed a sigh of relief. Not dying of cancer. "That's fine, love. It's not a big deal."

"Except it is," she insisted, "because when I say I don't have a lot of experience, I mean..." She paused, taking a deep breath, still keeping her gaze on her lap. "I mean, I'm a virgin. And I don't think I'm ready to have sex. At least, not right now. At this moment."

He looked at the beautiful woman in front of him, who just opened up to him about something so deeply personal, something she was clearly embarrassed to admit, and was completely in awe of her. He didn't think he could like her any more, and this happened. She was so fucking brave.

She must have read into his silence something he didn't intend, because she began to move away from him. "If this is a deal-breaker for you, it's fine. I can just sleep on the couch—"

He placed his hand on her arm, stopping her. "It's not a deal breaker. Not at all." He pulled her closer to him, cupping her face between his hands. "I like you, and I enjoy getting to know you. Do I want to have sex with you? Fuck yes. Am I willing to wait and move at the pace you're comfortable with? Also, fuck yes."

She gave him a tentative smile. "Are you sure? You're not going to yell at me and call me a prude?"

Fire burned behind his eyes. He knew immediately with the specificity of the statement someone had said that very thing to her in the past. "Who the fuck would even do that? Whoever did that to you was wrong and an arsehole." He took a breath, composing himself. "Yes, Evelyn, I'm sure. Intimacy doesn't just mean shagging. It can also be sharing your deepest thoughts and fears. And we've been doing that. I can wait until you're ready to move to becoming physically intimate."

She leaned forward and placed a soft kiss on his lips. She pulled away almost as quickly as she began. "Thank you."

"No thanks needed. Truly." He brushed her hair out of her eyes. "Shall we move to the bed? To sleep?"

She nodded, and the two of them worked together to clean up their dinner.

As they moved through their nighttime routine, which had become synchronized like clockwork over the last week, Patrick could feel the same thoughts from earlier creeping back into his mind.

What if this could be forever?

They settled into bed, and he turned off the light.

She moved until she was settled with her head on his chest.

"If you had made it to your program, what would you be doing right now?" He ran his hands through her hair.

"At this exact moment? I would probably be sleeping."

He laughed. "No, just in general."

"Well, I would be working at the ancient site of Epidaurus, helping excavate and rebuild the Temple of Asclepius."

"So, you would be like Indiana Jones?"

"Not quite. More research, less exploring. Only Greeks may do the actual digging, so I would be doing a lot of dirt sorting. And research."

"What's special about the Temple of Asclepius?"

She smiled. "Oh, so much. When people got sick, they traveled to Epidaurus to visit the Temple. You see, Asclepius was the god of healing. And they believed he visited in your dreams and healed you. So, people came and slept in his temple in order to be healed."

"Wow, how fascinating. Did it work?"

"I mean, it's pretty widely agreed the priests and doctors basically dosed the people with hallucinogens so they all said Asclepius visited them in their sleep."

He laughed. "Is that all Epidaurus is known for? Drugging people into believing a god was visiting them in their sleep to heal them?"

"No. They're also known for their amazing theater. I've read if you sit all the way at the top, you can perfectly hear whatever is being said on the stage. And the person doing the talking at the bottom doesn't even need to raise their voice. Trying it out was something I was really looking forward to."

"You'll still have a chance. You're going there at the end of summer, yeah?"

"Yeah."

He noticed a change in her. Thinking about her trip had seemed to bring her down a little. "Tell me about your research. Is it all about Asclepius?"

"No, actually. It's about healing myths in Ancient Greece in general."

And then she was describing her research and everything she had done so far. Her foul mood quickly dissipated, bleeding into excitement as she talked about her work. He enjoyed listening to her talk about something she was obviously passionate about, even though he didn't fully understand everything she was saying.

Eventually they both grew tired, so they rolled over, and he wrapped his arms around her body, pulling her in close.

He pressed a kiss against the shell of her ear before whispering, "I think I've caught feelings for you."

"I think I've caught feelings for you as well," she whispered back.

Smiling at her answer, he closed his eyes and drifted off into a peaceful sleep.

CHAPTER 30

EVELYN

"You guys thought this would make a good office?" Evelyn stared at the dilapidated building they stood in front of.

The single-story building looked as if all it would take was a strong wind, and it would fall over, if it hadn't been made of pure, undecorated concrete. The door was held closed with a chain, but it seemed it was only there as a formality, since the two large windows on either side of it were missing their glass. The roof also seemed like a formality, as it was missing several parts and looked as if, at one point, there were tarps draped over them, but they were long gone.

"It has character," Patrick defended.

"See why we were confused about it being so bloody expensive? We thought they'd be happy to get rid of it, but the fuckers were greedy and wanted loads of money for it. Way more than we offered," James said.

"The estate agent actually laughed at our offer. She thought we weren't being serious. She thought we were having a laugh."

"What did you offer?"

"Twenty pounds," they said in unison.

Evelyn laughed. "You know what? This building looks like it's worth twenty pounds. I don't know why she wasn't taking you seriously. How much did they want for this pile of concrete?"

"Half a mil," Patrick said.

"You're joking." She couldn't believe it!

"One hundred percent serious."

"Ridiculous. So, are we having our meeting out here?"

James shook his head. "No. We're having it inside. Not in public, remember?"

She turned back to look at the building. "You want me to go in there? There are probably mice."

Patrick smiled. "Oh, there are loads of mice and rats. But don't worry, they aren't spies."

"I'm not going in there. I'll wait out here for you to finish."

James shook his head. "We can't let you do that. We're not letting you out of our sight, remember?"

"I'll wait in the car." She pointed at the MINI Cooper at the curb. They'd brought a getaway car, so to speak, in case they needed to leave quickly. They didn't want to have to find a cab again. "I'll even lock the doors. Completely safe."

It was Patrick's turn to shake his head. "Remember, we're supposed to not listen to you when you're being stubborn. You're coming with us. It'll be okay. I promise to protect you from the rats and the bugs and whatever spooks live in there."

"It's haunted?" She took a step back from the building.

"Well, yeah, I'm sure it is. The building is old. I'm sure there are a few things haunting the inside."

She turned and tried to make a break for the car, but Patrick grabbed her around her waist, throwing her over his shoulder. She struggled for a second before giving up.

"Sorry, love, we were just taking the piss." Patrick walked them toward the building. "The worst thing in this building is the amount of mold growing from the lack of roof and the wet London weather. I'm sure there are mice and rats, but they won't bother you, I promise." He set her down through the window before climbing through himself.

James followed shortly after.

"Alright, let's light these torches and set them on the floor over here, pointing up, to illuminate the room." Patrick pulled the flashlights out of the bag they'd brought.

She took the flashlights and started setting them up around the room while Patrick and James began pulling out photocopies of items they'd found in the duffel bag. That afternoon, they'd decided they'd needed to bring some of the evidence with them in order to convince PC McCleary to help. And for the first time, she had seen what they had. After all the photographs and fake money, she knew, for a fact, they had an excellent chance of bringing down Fitzgerald.

They needed this officer to agree to help them.

She moved back to the men, and Patrick put his arm around her shoulders, pulling her close. After their date the night before, he always seemed to be touching her in some way throughout the day. Whether it was an arm around her shoulders or holding her hand, it was like he wanted to make sure he was keeping her close.

She looked at him and smiled. She was enjoying every second of this new aspect of their relationship. She was going to bask in the glow for as long as she was here.

There was shuffling outside the building, causing all three heads to turn and look toward the windows.

The sound stopped, and the beam of a flashlight illuminated the frame of the window to the left of the door. Patrick removed his arm from around her shoulders and moved her so he positioned her behind him. He was so much taller than her she had to peer around his body to get a view of what was happening.

Patrick and James shifted into defensive stances, each holding a pocket knife, the closest thing they had to weapons in their flat that could do some damage. It wasn't much, and they would never win a fight if the officer brought a gun into it, but it made them feel better to not go into the meeting empty-handed.

The flashlight got tossed through the window, making a large clunking sound as it hit the concrete floor of the building. A man climbing through the window followed closely behind it.

James and Patrick gripped their knives, ready to move into action if the man attacked them. The man bent down and picked up his flashlight before turning around and looking at them.

The lights that were set up around the building helped illuminate his features. He was young, younger than the three of them. He was fit. You could tell he had recently finished all the physical training it took to become an officer. He had blond hair, cropped close to his skull, and he was still dressed in his uniform, like he had just gotten off a shift or he was on his way to start one. And he wasn't very tall. In fact, he was shorter than both James and Patrick.

When he noticed the two large men holding knives, ready to move at him, he held his arms up in surrender. "I come in peace."

"Please state your name," James said, neither one lowering their arms with the knives.

"Police Constable Joseph McCleary. I believe you are expecting me. You have the distinct advantage of knowing who I am, as I have no clue who you are." McCleary was still raising his hands.

James and Patrick slowly lowered their knives, but didn't put them away.

"Sorry," Patrick said. "We can't be too careful, not with the case we're about to share with you."

PC McCleary shook his head. "I understand. I would have done the same. When I arrived at the building, seeing its state, I almost walked past it. I only have my baton on me, and I was worried this was going to be an ambush. But my curiosity got the better of me. I need to know what this case is and how it will make my career."

James and Patrick took a couple of steps forward, making the gap between them and the officer smaller. Patrick reached behind him, grabbing Evelyn's hand, and pulled her along, making sure she stayed close.

"My name is Patrick Miller, and this is my business partner, James Moore. We are local private investigators. We've been working on a case against the Fitzgerald family. Are you familiar with them?"

He nodded. "I'm pretty sure everyone knows of the Fitzgerald family. They're not exactly secretive about their activities. What sort of case are you building? From what I've learned in my time on the force, they're untouchable."

"They're untouchable because every police officer in the borough, except for you, is in the pockets of the family," Patrick stated.

McCleary shook his head. "I don't believe you. Every officer can't possibly be getting bribes from them. I mean, the superintendent is the best person I know."

James walked forward, offering him one of the photocopies from the bag.

McCleary took it and shone his flashlight on it. His jaw dropped open as he looked at the photo of Mickey Fitzgerald paying off the superintendent.

"Impossible. If I wasn't looking right at it, I would still say you were full of shit. I just, I can't believe this."

"Like we said, every officer in the borough is lining their pockets with Fitzgerald money in order to look the other way and let the family have the run of the place."

"How do you know I'm not lining my pockets?"

"We've looked into your background thoroughly," James replied.

"Tell me about the case you're building because my interest is admittedly growing by the second."

"We're working with a local solicitor's office to try Mickey Fitzgerald on the crimes he's committed once he's arrested. We have enough evidence to put him behind bars for the rest of his life. The trouble is, we don't have anyone to make the arrest and press the charges," Patrick said.

"Until now."

"Until now," Patrick confirmed.

McCleary studied the photo for a few seconds before lifting his flashlight and shining it around Patrick and into Evelyn's face. "Who's the girl? What's she got to do with the case?"

"The girl is none of your business. You don't need to know anything about her. Let's just focus on the case."

"If she has something to do with the case, I'm going to have to know. Looking at the fading bruises on her face, she is either tied to the case or you're beating the shit out of her, and I'm going to have to take you in on suspicion of assault. So, which is it?"

Patrick's hand tightened on Evelyn's. "She's involved with the case, and until I know we can trust you, that's all you'll know. The last person we met with wasn't exactly trustworthy, so we'll be keeping things close to our chest until the right moment. I hope you understand."

"Clearly," McCleary stated.

"Good. Now, are you going to help us, or do we part ways now?"

McCleary moved his flashlight back to the picture, investigating it once more. "The rest of the evidence in your possession is this same quality?"

James and Patrick both said, "Yes."

"In the message you sent me, you said this case would make my career."

"If you arrest Mickey Fitzgerald, the media will hail you as a hero and you will get all the credit for breaking up the most notorious crime family in London. You will get the fame, the glory, and the promotions that come along with that title," James explained.

"Or," McCleary went on, "since the three of us will be going into the lion's den to arrest the bugger without backup, we'll gain notoriety as the fools the most infamous crime family murdered because they were stupid enough to think they could bring them down on their own."

"There is a risk we won't walk out of there alive, yes," Patrick agreed. "We'll understand if you walk away now and don't look back."

"What is your plan if I walk out of here right now?"

"We would somehow find a way to get Fitzgerald into another borough, get him to commit a crime, and have that borough's officers arrest Fitzgerald."

"And that officer would get the fame and credit for bringing the man to justice," McCleary added.

"Well, yes."

Evelyn watched as McCleary looked at the photo once more and then at the group.

He handed the picture back to James. "I'm in."

CHAPTER 31

PATRICK

The three friends breathed a sigh of relief as they looked at the man standing in front of them.

"Are you sure? Absolutely positively certain you're willing to do this?" Patrick inquired.

McCleary nodded. "Absolutely. I've been looking for a way to advance my career since I joined the force. There haven't been many cases popping up in Tower Hamlets to really show what I can do since most of the major crimes are committed by the Fitzgeralds, and strangely, we do nothing about those. And whenever I ask about them, I'm always being brushed off by my superiors. This is my chance to make a name for myself and make my borough safer at the same time. I'd be a fool to let this opportunity pass."

James and Patrick turned to each other and shared a look of victory before turning back to McCleary.

"That's good to hear. We have a few details to iron out, like finding where the Fitzgeralds are holed up, but as soon as we know, we'll contact you with a time and place so you can make the arrest."

McCleary nodded. "Do you need my number?" He shook his head and laughed. "Of course, you don't. You already have all of my information."

He took a step toward Patrick, his hand outstretched.

Patrick accepted it, shaking it.

"It was good to meet you, and I look forward to hearing from you soon," McCleary said.

Patrick nodded and released his hand.

McCleary turned and climbed out the window.

Patrick, James, and Evelyn stood quietly and waited for the light to disappear along with the sound of shuffling before they let their guards down and relaxed. Patrick almost couldn't believe what had happened. It was almost too easy. Could things finally be moving in their favor?

"Oh my God." Evelyn moved around to stand next to Patrick. "I just, wow, that went better than our last meeting."

Patrick nodded. "Yeah, I made it through without getting shot. I'd say it went loads better than the last meeting."

James laughed. "Didn't I tell you that with his high ambitions he would take the bait and agree to help us out?"

"Yeah. Good work telling him our original alternate plan of letting another borough take the credit for the arrest and take all the fame and glory. You could definitely see his ego inflating with that one," Patrick replied.

James smiled. "I had a feeling it would push him over the edge, and I was right. I'm pretty sure it was the bit of information that helped make him agree."

"I think you're right," Evelyn agreed. "God, my heart is still beating so fast from when he shone his light on me. I was certain he was going to say something about me and we were going to realize he was a fake, like Harry."

"Me, too, but I didn't appreciate him implying I beat you, though."

Evelyn smiled. "You have to admit, if you didn't know what happened, and the way you were being defensive about who I was, it would give the impression you abuse me."

Patrick sighed. "Next time I take you in public, we need to do your makeup a little better. Make you look less like a domestic abuse ad, yeah?"

"We can try, but I don't think any amount of makeup will fix this."

"You finally looked in a mirror, love?"

"I'm really surprised it still looks as bad as it does. I've never seen so many different colors of blue and green on my face before."

Patrick put his arm around her shoulders, pulling her in close and kissing the side of her head. "The man is a professional. He knows how to hit someone and how to cause certain types of damage. Fitzgerald said to rough you up a little, so he held back. If Fitzgerald didn't give him those directions, I'm sure you would look much worse or be much worse. You should feel lucky."

"I do. I just hope this clears up completely before we have to stage tourism pictures for my parents."

"Evie, I'm a pro at Photoshop, I can fix up anything, so I don't want you worrying about a thing." James moved around the room, picking up the torches they had set out and putting them in the bag.

"I'll keep that in mind. So, what now? What's our next step now that we have found our arresting officer?"

They moved to the window, where Patrick helped her climb through before climbing through himself.

"Now we go back to the flat and start trying to find the evil lair." James stepped through.

"How are we going to do that?" she asked as they got to the car.

Patrick unlocked the car, and they all climbed in. "Well, first we start with you describing, in detail, everything you remember about where you were held, and then we expand upon that with anything else we can find, like from the pictures in the duffel, and hope we hope we find a match."

"But I already told you I was held in a room. An extremely ordinary, plain room."

"Yes, but you'd be surprised at how much you can learn from something like that," James explained. "I'm prepared to amaze you with my internet searching skills.

CHAPTER 32

EVELYN

Evelyn stretched and looked at the clock on James's bedside table. She groaned. It was already early evening. Where had the time gone?

All morning, James and Patrick had sat at their respective computers and shouted street names and locations around town to each other where they suspected Fitzgerald could have his evil lair.

Originally, she had tried to work in the room with them. But after the third time one of their outbursts had made her practically leap from her skin, she'd excused herself to the farthest part of the flat to try to work in peace.

She shut her laptop and stood from the bed. Her bladder and her stomach made her aware of how long she had been sequestered in the room. Time to venture forth and seek sustenance.

She opened the door and immediately ducked into the bathroom. With her immediate need met, she began walking down the hallway. As she did, she noticed it was blessedly quiet. The boys were no longer shouting.

Just as she caught sight of the living room, she stopped in her tracks.

A dozen candles illuminated the room. They seemed to be spread on all the surfaces in the kitchen and living room. Someone had moved the table. She didn't know where, but in its place, they had spread a blanket out.

"Patrick, what's going on?"

He came out from behind the counter wearing an apron. "Fuck. You're early."

"Early?" she asked. "How can I be early when I have no idea what is going on?"

He grinned, gesturing around the room, his right hand encased in an oven mitt. "Date night."

"Date night?"

"Yeah. I wanted to surprise you with another stay-in-the-flat date."

"If you were going to surprise me, how can I possibly be early?" She crossed her arms over her chest, one side of her mouth rising into a half smile as she lifted an eyebrow.

"Okay, okay. This was all a bit last minute, so I may have forgotten the minor detail of telling you not to come out until a certain time," Patrick said sheepishly.

"Where'd you ship James off to?"

"He is on a stakeout. He was frustrated with the lack of progress on finding the secret lair, so he scrolled through the agency's emails until he found something he could knock out easily."

"It's been twenty-four hours since we met with McCleary."

"It has."

"James realizes finding my non-descript warehouse is like finding a needle in a haystack, right? That it's going to take some time?"

"He does," Patrick said, turning back to the kitchen to finish prepping the food. "However, neither of us have any patience, so we need distractions. He has chosen to throw himself into work, whilst I have chosen to woo my lady with my cooking skills."

She walked over and leaned against the counter. "I have to admit, I didn't think you could cook."

He turned to look over his shoulder. "Now, why would you think that?"

"I don't know, perhaps it was the complete lack of food in the flat the day I arrived?"

"Hmm. Yes, I can see why that would lead you to that conclusion. However, I would like to assure you, I am a fantastic cook, and you're going to love what I've made."

"What have you made?"

He turned fully and grinned widely. "Bangers and mash, with Yorkshire pudding. And I've made a tart for dessert."

"I'm going to circle back around and ask you about what the hell some of these foods are, but holy shit. When did you start cooking in order to make all of this?"

"Just about two hours. Nothing I've made is too difficult, and it's all dishes one would find on any British table at any night of the week."

"So, explain. What the fuck is a banger?"

He threw his head back and cackled. Actually cackled.

She frowned. "I didn't think what I said was that funny."

He shook his head, controlling his laughter. "No, it wasn't really. I just find it amusing, is all. A banger is a sausage."

"Why on earth would you call a sausage a banger?"

"Because, love, it makes a bang in the pan."

She shook her head. "I don't know if I'll ever get used to the differences in what you call things here versus in the States."

"Eh," Patrick replied as he spooned the mash into a large bowl before placing two sausages on top. "It's not too different. I think you're figuring everything out just fine. By the time you leave, you'll be a natural." He handed her a bowl and gestured toward the blanket on the floor.

She sat on the floor, careful to not spill her dinner. He untied his apron before grabbing his bowl and a plate with what she guessed were the Yorkshire puddings and walking over to join her.

"What made you think 'picnic in the living room' for our second date?" she asked as she cut her sausage with the edge of her fork.

He shrugged. "Dunno. I guess I was trying to think of something that would make us forget we were stuck in the flat. I can't take you to Vicky Park right now, so I figured I would bring Vicky Park to you."

"Maybe when this is all over, we can go to Vicky Park and have a real picnic?"

He smiled. "Of course. It would be a sin to leave here without taking you to London's first public park."

"Well, that definitely sounds like it would be something I wouldn't pass up if I were here for a planned visit."

She stabbed a piece of the banger, scooped it up with a bit of mash, and took a bite. She closed her eyes. Fuck. He wasn't kidding. He was an excellent cook.

"Good, innit?"

She opened her eyes to find him watching her with a cheeky grin on his face. "It is."

"Now, Evelyn, I've thought we've come so far in our relationship that it wouldn't be so difficult to give me a compliment."

"We have. It's just, I'm pretty sure your ego is big enough. You really don't need me stroking it with compliments."

He bit his lip and looked like he was about to burst out into uncontrolled laughter.

"What on earth..." She trailed off, realizing immediately what was making him react the way he was. "Oh, for fuck's sake. What are you? Twelve?"

"Please, can I just say it, just to get it out of my system?"

"No, because you are a grownup, and you should act like one."

He sighed dramatically. "Fine. Have it your way."

"Now," she said, bringing them back to the date. "I was going to say, before you decided to act like a pre-teen, I can add your cooking to the list of things I'm going to miss when I leave."

He looked at his bowl. "Well, I can teach you how to make all of this before you leave. And maybe we can schedule a night where we cook the same meal and eat it over a video call? Like a long-distance date night?"

She froze, her next bite not quite making it to her mouth. "Long-distance date night?"

"Yeah," he said, his gaze still fixed on his supper. "You know, to vary things a bit."

She set her fork back in her bowl. "You see us continuing past me leaving?"

He finally brought his gaze up to meet hers. "Of course. I would like to give it a try, at least. Do you not?"

"I do, I just wasn't sure where you stood on the whole long-distance relationship thing. I know the other night you said you had feelings for me, but I didn't know if that meant longevity, or just for now."

"Longevity. Definitely."

"Okay, same. Longevity here, too."

He grinned widely. "I'm glad we're on the same page."

"Me, too."

They sat there, staring at each other.

She didn't know who moved first, but bowls were thrust aside, mash spilled on the blanket as they crashed into each other, joining themselves at the lips.

Unlike their previous kisses, this one was more frenzied. She could hardly keep up with whose hands were where.

She broke away to catch her breath as he trailed kisses down her neck.

He moved so he could lay her down on the blanket, shifting on top of her. He recaptured her lips with his, and she gladly returned the kiss with fervor.

He used his knee to spread her legs wide enough for him to settle between them, pressing himself into her.

She could feel his arousal as he moved his hand up to cup her breast through her shirt.

Those two actions caused a panic to rise in her chest.

She was not ready for this.

She pulled away from the kiss, placing her hands on his chest, pushing him off of her.

He immediately moved off of her body, giving her space.

"Are you okay?" he asked, concern lacing his voice.

She nodded. "Yes, it's just I—"

"I know," Patrick said gently, "I know."

She pulled herself into a sitting position and drew her knees to her chest, wrapping her arms around them. "I'm sorry."

He shook his head. "You're sorry? Why are you sorry?"

"For leading you on. For stopping us."

"It's fine. You told me what your boundaries were the other night. I tried to push them. Are you sure you're okay?"

"Yes, I'm fine."

"Then why are you crying?"

She brought her hand to her cheek. It was wet. She wasn't even aware she had started crying. "I guess it's because I feel terrible, and I'm worried I'm fucking up our new relationship with my lack of experience."

He moved closer, wrapping her in his arms and pulling her against him in a hug. She tucked her head under his chin, resting it on his chest. She loved how they fit together, and how this one action immediately put her at ease.

"You're not fucking up our relationship because you don't want to have sex right now," he said, his voice firm.

"In the past..." She started, flashes of angry dates in her undergraduate years calling her a prude flew through her head.

"Fuck the past," he interrupted. "Whatever any other man before said, fuck them. Like I said the other night, there are other ways to be intimate. We can wait until you're ready before we shag. You're worth the wait. And let me tell you, when you're ready? It's going to be fucking amazing."

"What if I'm not ready before I have to leave in three weeks?" she asked, voicing aloud the fear she was holding inside.

"Then we're just going to have to find time to visit one another, right?"

Warmth spread through her body. Never before had anyone understood her insecurities surrounding sex and not being ready. But Patrick did. And that made her fall for him even more.

CHAPTER 33

PATRICK

"Fuck, fuck, fuck." James threw a pencil at his computer screen.

"Still no luck?" Evelyn sat on the couch, working on her thesis.

Her feet were on Patrick's lap, where he was absentmindedly rubbing them as he worked his way through the evidence in the bag, looking at every photograph closely, trying to pick out details in the background that might help them narrow down a location. He knew there had to be a clue in these pictures somewhere, but so far, nothing. Rubbing her feet was a pleasant distraction from the growing frustration he was feeling.

"Do you know how many fucking warehouses have multiple rooms and aren't used commercially in Tower Hamlets?"

"No, I don't."

"Too fucking many." He sighed and dropped his head into his hands.

"Relax. You've only been looking for three days. It took you a week to find McCleary, and you knew where to look. You need to stop putting so much pressure on yourself."

James sighed. "I know, but the sooner we find the evil lair, the sooner we can storm in and take out the super villain."

"Will you please stop calling it an evil lair? We're not living in a comic book." Patrick didn't stop looking at the picture he was inspecting or take his hand off the foot he was rubbing.

"If I keep thinking of this as a comic book, it makes it less scary that we're going to willingly walk into a room full of armed criminals with one police officer with a baton and pocketknives. Remind me again why we think this is a good idea?"

"Because we get to be the superheroes." Patrick kept up with James's comic book analogy.

"Yeah, except when they shoot us, we'll die," James mumbled.

She stiffened next to Patrick.

He looked up from the picture and shot daggers at the back of James's head. He was trying so hard to keep her relaxed and have her forget about the risk they were taking, but James kept bringing it up without thinking.

She shut her computer, removed her feet from his lap, and stood. "I need to go to the bathroom." She scurried off to the back of the flat.

Patrick waited to hear the door shut before turning on James. "You need to fucking stop with the negative shit. I'm trying to keep her calm so she can focus on her schoolwork, and you bringing up the fact we can die isn't helping, at all."

"I'm sorry. I can't help it. It's hard for me to ignore the fact we're essentially walking into a firing squad."

"You don't know that. They could decide to not shoot us as we walk in."

"Do you honestly believe that? Do you really think Fitzgerald isn't going to take one look at us, hear us tell him he's under arrest, and laugh as he signals for his men to shoot us? And then they're going to throw our bodies in the Thames."

"That is a valid scenario. However, I'd like it if you stopped laying out those plausible scenarios in Evelyn's presence."

"I'm sorry. Yeah, I'll do better. I'm just getting frustrated because I'm not finding anything that even remotely looks like it could be the evil lair."

"Stop calling it the evil lair. And I know you're frustrated. I'm frustrated, too. But we need to not think about what can happen when we walk into the hideout and focus on finding the hideout first."

"Have you found any photographs that show any outside details? Because we really need something that shows the outside of the building to narrow my list down."

"Unfortunately, when Megan was spying, she only took photos of the inside of the building."

"Well, bugger. I have a short list. I say we split up and do some old-fashioned investigating. That's my only solution. Normally I'd suggest we go together, but we can cover more ground if we separate and regroup back here."

"That's a brilliant idea, actually. However, we should go out in pairs, not alone. And if one group happens to find the lair, no one acts until after we've regrouped. No impulse invasions. Just make a note of where you found them and move on."

"Agreed. On all points. I'll give McCleary a call and get him here. You take Evie, because you know she's not going to sit back and let us do this on our own. And maybe if you take her, something will jog her memory."

Patrick sighed and watched as she quietly emerged from the bathroom, shutting the door behind her. "You're right. As much as I don't want to take her, there's no way she's going to sit back and let us do this without her."

James picked up his phone. "I'll call McCleary. You go prep Evie."

Patrick followed her to his room. She was lying on the bed, staring at the ceiling.

"Hey." He moved into the room.

She sat up. "Hey."

"So, we've decided sitting here isn't helping our situation, and we're going to do a little field work. Want to join?"

She narrowed her eyes. "Is this a trick? You're not going to drive me over to your dad's and ditch me there, are you?"

He shook his head. "Not a trick. James and I were talking, and we decided we need to go out and see if we can actually find the warehouse where the Fitzgeralds are hiding. But we don't think we should go alone. He's calling McCleary right now, and we decided you should come along with me. Maybe something will jog your memory."

She shook her head. "I've already told you. I was unconscious both times. I was never able to see the outside of the building."

"Are you seriously arguing against coming along? Who are you and what have you done with my girlfriend?" Patrick joked.

Her eyes widened. "What did you say?"

He laughed. "Relax, love, it was a joke. I don't actually believe you've been body snatched."

She shook her head. "Not that, the other part. The part where you called me your girlfriend."

He paused. He hadn't realized he'd said it. It had come out so naturally. He didn't even need to think about it. And now that it was out there, he didn't sense any sort of panic arising like he'd thought there would be. In fact, it felt right.

"Yeah." He smirked. "You're my girlfriend, aren't you?"

She got really quiet, like she was thinking things over, and he panicked. Had something changed in the last forty-eight hours? What if she didn't feel the same anymore? What if she didn't want to adopt these labels? They had talked about being long distance, but they never discussed labels and being exclusive. What if she didn't want to be tied down to just him when there were thousands of miles between them?

"Well, yeah, I guess I am. You've just never said that word before."

"I've always been a little terrified of it, to be honest."

"And now you're not?"

He shook his head. "It's funny, but I said it without thinking about it. It seemed natural."

"And what happens when I leave?"

"Long-distance dates. Remember? Until then, let's just enjoy being together."

She smiled. "Okay. I can do that."

He returned her smile. "Great. Should we get ready to go?"

She shook her head, taking a step toward him, closing the gap before reaching up and pulling him down to bring her lips to his. It didn't take long for their kiss to move from tender and tentative to something more intense.

In the days since they'd admitted there was something there, they had shared some kissing and heavy petting in bed at night, but it never moved past that, and he was okay with taking things slow. This was all unfamiliar territory for him, and he didn't want to fuck things up.

But this kiss was different from all the other ones they'd shared in the past few days. It was intense and full of fire. Hands roamed, and Patrick couldn't help his body reacting to the passion. He moved them until her legs met the edge of the bed, and then he gently maneuvered them onto the mattress, all without breaking the kiss.

They pressed their bodies as close together as they physically could, and as she snaked her hand up the back of his shirt, caressing his skin, he pulled away, panting.

"Love, we need to stop," he said while gasping for breath.

She shook her head. "Please don't stop."

He looked at her, a vision of beauty lying beneath him. "Are you sure?"

"I've never been surer of something in my whole life. Just, be gentle. I've never done anything like this before."

Patrick looked at the woman he held, who he'd grown closer to than anyone else in his life in the short time he'd known her. He didn't want to say he was in love with her, but he had intense feelings for her. She was amazing and kind and beautiful and was choosing him, *him*, to share this crucial moment with.

Not trusting his voice, he nodded and showed her, through his actions, how special she was to him and how he was right. Shagging was going to be fucking amazing.

***

"Which building did James say was the one we're supposed to be looking for?" Evelyn asked as they approached the street James had sent them to.

"Twenty-five seventy-six," Patrick read from the printout.

They continued walking, looking for the building. As they walked, he noticed each building was identical to the other warehouses surrounding it, and looked like the other five they had already seen that day. He kept that observation to himself. It wouldn't do any good to voice his frustration. They were both feeling it after the day they'd had. Every place they had been to so far was very obviously not where the Fitzgeralds operated their crime syndicate. Two were completely abandoned, and the other three housed small businesses.

"I wonder if James and McCleary have had any luck," she said as they made their way down the road.

He shrugged. "I don't know. I guess we'll find out after we check this one out and head back to the flat."

They continued down the road until they stopped in front of the building they were looking for. It looked abandoned. Patrick held in the curse he wanted so badly to exclaim.

"Well, this was a total waste of time," she stated.

"Now, we can't think like that. This probably saved us time, if you think about it. By going to all these places, we were able to effectively eliminate them from the list of likely locations the Fitzgeralds were operating out of. Now we can go back to the flat, report to James and McCleary, and tell them we weren't successful. Who knows? Maybe we'll get back to the flat and James will say they were successful, and were able to find what they needed."

"True. But I'm still a little disappointed we weren't the ones to find the warehouse. I mean, I was held there. I wanted to have an 'a ha' type moment and save the day. I guess after my experience these last couple weeks, I've started to think about our lives as being in a spy movie."

"Because of you and James, I'm starting to feel that way, too. Between you talking like Nancy Drew and expecting James Bond to come around the corner, and James talking secret lairs and thinking Superman is going to come flying in, I'm half expecting there to be some sort of exciting, grand, unexpected showdown between us and Fitzgerald."

"Sorry. The last couple of weeks have been completely surreal. I mean, I can't believe what has been going on. I'm still having a hard time wrapping my head around things."

"You're probably going to need to write everything down that's happened in order to make you believe this wasn't all a dream when you return home."

She scoffed. "I'm definitely not going to have that problem. I'll have the image of Megan's severed head etched into my mind forever. Not to mention, it'll be impossible to forget being kidnapped and abused by a major crime boss."

"You're right. With as surreal as it all seems, some dangerous shit has happened to you. Some scary, dangerous shit." He paused and forced a smile on his face, trying to lighten the mood. "If you ever decide to start writing fiction, however, you'd have plenty of experience to build on."

"I've never thought about fiction writing. Maybe that will be my fallback if academics fail me."

"I can see you as a writer. It's a solitary activity and the best part is you can do it from anywhere."

"I might have to consider it. A career I could do from anywhere might not be that bad."

They were almost to the main road when a man stepped in front of them, blocking their path.

"Excuse me, but do you have the time?" He was dressed in jeans and a tight black shirt worn underneath a sport coat.

"Um," Patrick patted down his body, making a bit of a show, "I'm sorry, but we do not. Now, if you'll excuse us." He took Evelyn's hand and tried to move around the man.

However, he moved back into their path. "I'm sorry, but I really must know the time. Don't you have a mobile or something? Everyone has a mobile nowadays."

Patrick's grip tightened on her hand. "Unfortunately, we both left our phones at our flat so we could have a nice walk without interruptions. But we really must be going. We have somewhere to be." He tugged on her hand and tried to move around the man to be on their way.

The man in front of them blocked their path again. This time, lifting his sports coat to show off the gun he had holstered at his side. "I'm sorry, but unfortunately, I'm not going to be able to let you go."

Patrick whipped Evelyn behind his back and, at the same time, he grabbed the pocket knife he was carrying in the back pocket of his denims. He held the knife in front of him and assumed an offensive stance, crouching down with both arms out, ready to fight.

The man in front of them laughed. "You think a puny knife will be any match against us?"

He stood up straight. "Us?"

Just then, Evelyn gasped. He whipped around as she was pulled into the arms of a second man. She screamed as he held her tight.

Patrick moved to attack the person holding Evelyn, but he stopped short when the guy pulled a gun and held it to her temple.

"Ah, ah, ah. One wrong move, and your Yank girlfriend's brains will decorate the sidewalk."

Patrick stopped short and held up his hands. "Please don't hurt her."

"Drop your weapon." The first man had drawn his gun and directed it at the couple.

Patrick hesitated for a second, but one look at his girlfriend's terrified face as they held her at gunpoint solidified his decision, and he set the knife on the ground before straightening and putting his hands in the air.

Both men laughed.

"That was too easy." The first one took a step toward Patrick. "I think the boss has overestimated you both. He thought you were valid threats, but you're both cowards."

Patrick glared and wanted to open his mouth to retort, but feared they would retaliate by hurting Evelyn, so he kept his mouth closed. He tightened his jaw and swallowed his pride.

The men laughed again.

"I can't wait to put you both in front of the boss and see what he has planned for you," the first one stated again.

Patrick looked on helplessly as the man who held Evelyn brought a white cloth in front of her face, pressing it against her nose and mouth.

"Oi!" Patrick yelled, trying to get to her, but the first man grabbed hold of his arms. He watched on, helpless, as she struggled for a second before her eyes rolled to the back of her head and she passed out.

"Easy there, mate. She's fine, just a bit sleepy. We can't have you seeing our operation. And we are under strict orders to not physically harm the girl. But we are under no such orders for you." The man chuckled before bringing his arm back and striking Patrick in the head with the butt of the gun.

He was out before his body hit the pavement.

CHAPTER 34

EVELYN

Evelyn came to with a familiar feeling of fuzziness in her head and cotton in her mouth. She had been knocked out again by chloroform. Her eyelids were heavy as she opened them.

She blinked as her eyes tried to adjust to the bright lights around her. This wasn't the same room she was held in before. This was a much larger room, and she wasn't alone. She was still tied to a chair, but Patrick was in front of her, his arms held above his head with a rope tied to the rafter. They'd stripped him of his shirt, so he was only wearing his jeans and shoes. His head hung limp, his chin to his chest, blood trickling down the right side of his face from a wound on the side of his head.

"Patrick," Evelyn croaked. Her tongue was heavy in her mouth, her throat dry. It was difficult to get anything out. She swallowed and cleared her throat. "Patrick."

He didn't stir.

She blinked, trying to clear her head. But it was difficult. Waking up from the chloroform was much harder than the last time. She must have been dosed heavier. She pulled at the restraints on her wrists, but only succeeded in giving herself rope burns.

She looked around the room, trying to figure out where she was. It looked like a normal warehouse. An *abandoned* warehouse.

"Fuck," she muttered.

They must be in one of the warehouses they visited today and wrote off as abandoned. They hadn't been careful.

She tried to struggle in her restraints again, but the knots seemed to just get tighter and tighter.

"I'd stop struggling if I were you." Mickey Fitzgerald was behind her. "The more you struggle, the tighter the knots will become, and you'll lose circulation to your hands and feet. And it would be a shame to have your hands and feet amputated."

Fitzgerald sauntered into the main part of the room, carrying a metal poker and a cricket bat. He wasn't wearing the tailored three-piece suit he wore the last time he'd kidnapped her. Instead, he wore a black sleeveless shirt and jeans. His hair was still in its slicked-back style, but the change of attire really made him look different. He looked younger. And with the sleeveless shirt, his arms and chest were on display, showing he never missed a day at the gym. If he wasn't a cold-blooded killer, she would have been attracted to him.

She took his words of advice and stopped struggling. She sat still and stared at the man in front of her as her head began to clear. He set down the weapons on a table off to the side before pulling a chair over and taking a seat in front of her.

He sat straddling the chair, folding his arms on the back and resting his chin on them. "Hello again, Ms. Stevenson. I'm sorry we've had to meet again under such terrible circumstances."

"Why are you doing this? I've told you I don't know anything."

Fitzgerald smiled. "Oh, I know. I know you know nothing. And that's why my associates were under strict instructions to not hurt you. It was just an unfortunate accident you were with the person who knows something. Someone who we specifically warned to drop the case he was working on. Someone who blatantly ignored said warning. Yes, it was unfortunate, indeed. But I don't want you to worry. I'm not going to hurt you, nor will any of my associates. You're not the one we want."

"Then what are you going to do to me?"

"Well, first, you're going to watch so you can see what happens to people who don't follow my instructions. Then you'll stay here. As I said in our previous meeting, I find you very attractive, and I love the fire you have. I want you to be mine."

Her eyes widened. "Yours?"

"My new lover, of course. You're so young and fit. I will enjoy fucking you until you're obedient."

"Don't you fucking think about it," a voice growled.

Fitzgerald stood, and Patrick was now awake, glaring daggers at Fitzgerald.

She breathed a sigh of relief. He was alive.

Fitzgerald chuckled. "Well, well, well, look who decided to join us. Welcome to the land of the living, Detective Miller. I was worried my associates were a little too eager with their strike and that you were lost to us. This is a wonderful occurrence."

Patrick struggled with the ropes tying him to the rafter. "Let her go."

Fitzgerald chuckled before moving behind Evelyn's chair. He put his hands on her shoulders, rubbing them, before moving them down in front of her chest, massaging her breasts while planting kisses on her cheek.

She tried to pull away, but couldn't, his embrace too tight around her. She cringed as his tongue slid up her neck and stopped at her ear.

"Get the fuck off of her!" Patrick yelled from across the room as he struggled with his restraints. "Get off of her!"

A tear ran down her cheek before Fitzgerald pulled away, chuckling.

"This is easier than I expected." He moved away from her.

She breathed a sigh of relief, but it was short-lived. Fitzgerald walked over and picked up the cricket bat from the table before moving to Patrick.

"I'm going to enjoy this about as much as I'll enjoy fucking your girlfriend for the first time." He lifted the bat into a swinger's stance.

She screamed as the bat made contact with Patrick's stomach for the first time. And the second and the third. At the fourth contact, she closed her eyes, listening to her boyfriend's yells as she prayed for a way to get out of the situation they were in.

Suddenly, the screaming stopped, and she opened her eyes. Fitzgerald had walked away from Patrick, casually swinging the cricket bat back and forth at his side, as he moved to the table.

"Patrick." She tried to get his attention, but he didn't look at her.

His eyes were trained on Fitzgerald.

She followed his gaze and failed to hold back a gasp. He had picked up a metal fireplace poker. He walked over to a barrel she hadn't noticed before. One of the henchmen must have brought it in and built a fire inside. He stuck the metal poker in the barrel, all the while whistling "God Save the King." It was revolting how casual he was about torturing a man.

Once he was satisfied with how hot the poker was, he pulled it out. The tip glowed an orange-red as he made his way back to Patrick.

Evelyn tried to be brave, but as Fitzgerald brought his arm back, she squeezed her eyes shut. She couldn't watch the man she cared for get impaled. She just couldn't.

Patrick's scream echoed through the warehouse as Fitzgerald pressed the hot metal poker into his side.

She opened her eyes. Her boyfriend hung limply from the ceiling. He was beaten and bloody, and Fitzgerald showed no signs of stopping the torture any time soon. She was pretty sure he wasn't going to stop until Patrick was dead. And it was looking like it wasn't going to be long until that happened.

She moved her wrists and winced when the ropes tightened even more. She growled in frustration. There had to be a way she could get out of these restraints and stop Fitzgerald from killing Patrick. She moved her hands closer together, and her eyes widened as the ropes loosen a little.

She smiled. Struggling brought the ropes tighter together, as she was pulling her hands outward to try and break through the ropes. However, doing the opposite, bringing her hands inward, seemed to have the opposite effect. She began to quickly move her hands in and out—out a little, in a lot—and the ropes loosened. She almost let out a victorious cheer as her first hand broke free, but held it in to not draw Fitzgerald's attention to her. She quickly freed her other hand and, after a quick glance to make sure Fitzgerald was still focused on Patrick, bent down and undid the ropes at her ankles.

She watched Fitzgerald walk back to the barrel to heat the poker. He shoved the instrument into the fire and waited. She looked over to the table where he had traded the cricket bat for the poker. The bat was still there. Keeping her eyes on his back the whole time, she tiptoed over to the bat. She picked it up as quietly as she could and continued on her journey to where Fitzgerald still had his back to her.

She crept up behind him and, as she got closer, she glanced at Patrick, who had lifted his head and was staring at her.

He shook his head. He mouthed the word, "no," his eyes wide with fear.

She ignored him and turned back to Fitzgerald. It was the only way for them to get out of there. She had to try. She had to do it for their safety. She brought the bat up and swung it with everything she had. It made contact with his back. He stumbled and fell to the ground with a curse.

She turned around and ran to where Patrick was hanging, knowing she had little time. She dragged a chair over to him, climbing on it. She began to undo the ropes holding him to the rafter.

"You need to run. You need to get out of here and save yourself. Leave me."

She shook her head as she struggled with the rope. "I'm not leaving you."

"You need to go," Patrick wheezed. "I'm only going to slow you down. Get out of here and go find James. Get him and McCleary here. This is your chance."

She shook her head again and cursed the fact her hands were shaking too much to get the ropes undone quickly. "I'm not leaving you."

She was near tears as she struggled with the rope and let out a whoop of excitement when she could get it loose. "We're almost there, love. We're almost there, and then we'll both get out of here to get James and McCleary here after we get you to the hospital."

"Evelyn, watch out!" Patrick gasped.

"What?" She turned around as Fitzgerald barreled down on her, tackling her off the chair to the ground.

The air left her lungs as her back made contact with the concrete floor, Fitzgerald's hard, heavy body landing on top of her.

"You bitch." He pinned her down, her arms above her head. "You'll pay for what you've done." He let go of one of her hands, slapping her hard across the face. "I suppose it would be best to let your boyfriend watch the first time. To watch as his bitch gets fucked by his enemy." He reached between them, struggling to undo the fly and button to her jeans with one hand.

Panicking, she brought her knee up and, with all her force, smashed it into his groin.

Fitzgerald keeled over, groaning, bringing both hands to protect his manhood.

She took advantage and wiggled her way out from between his legs, crawling away from him.

"Not so fast, you slag." With lightning quick speed, he reached out and grabbed her by her hair, dragging her back to him.

She screamed and kicked as he dragged her across the floor and deposited her at Patrick's feet. He had been screaming at Fitzgerald to let Evelyn go, but his screams were falling on deaf ears.

She looked at Fitzgerald, and icy fear ran down her spine at the look he gave her. Gone was the smug arrogance, replaced with a look of utter evil. She had a fleeting thought that James wasn't too far off when he declared Fitzgerald an evil villain, but the thought was replaced with sheer terror when Fitzgerald reached for the hot metal poker he'd placed in the fire.

She tried to scramble to her feet, but she wasn't fast enough. Fitzgerald approached her in seconds, stabbing the metal poker into her shoulder.

The pain was worse than anything she had ever experienced. She screamed until her throat was hoarse, tears streaming down her cheeks as she sobbed through the pain.

Fitzgerald removed the poker, stabbing her in her other shoulder.

More pain, more screaming, more sobbing.

"You fucking bitch." Fitzgerald removed the poker from her other shoulder. "If you had just done what you were told, you would have remained unharmed. But I guess I'll have to teach you the valuable lesson of respecting the man in your life. I promise, I won't kill you, but you'll be wishing I would by the time I'm through with you."

He raised the poker and brought it down hard across her face, knocking her flat on the ground. The pain was blinding, and the bones in her face cracked. She lay on the floor, trying to curl up into a ball to protect herself, but it was impossible to move.

She was sluggish. Her head swam, and she had never experienced so much pain in her life. All she wanted to do was go to sleep and forget about everything that was happening.

Yes. Sleeping would be good. She should go to sleep.

She cried out as Fitzgerald's boot made contact with her stomach. He kicked her, again and again, jolting her back to consciousness and causing her to struggle for breath. She didn't know how much more she was going to be able to stand.

She could hear Patrick in the distance. He sounded so far away, even though he was right there. Right next to her.

As quickly as it had started, it stopped. Fitzgerald stopped his attack on her, and through the fog, she thought she could hear him moving away. She tried to open her eyes to confirm, but they were swollen shut.

She was able to pry one eye open. Everything was blurry. She could make out Patrick, who remained tied to the rafter. She thought she could see him looking at her, but she honestly did not know. He was mostly a blur. The mere act of holding her eye open became too exhausting, so she closed it, her head rolling back on the concrete.

She moved in and out of consciousness, the only things she was fully aware of were the pain in her head and torso. Somewhere through her haze, she thought there was a sound of a door crashing open and shouting, but she was sure she was dreaming.

CHAPTER 35

PATRICK

Patrick groaned as he woke up. He opened his eyes and was greeted by florescent lights, which could only mean one thing. He was in the hospital. He groaned, and immediately regretted it. Everything about his torso ached. He brought his hands to his face and rubbed. He was trying to remember how he got here. The last thing he recalled was Evelyn passing out at his feet, hearing a loud noise, and then nothing. He must have finally succumbed to his pain and passed out.

He looked around the room. Colin was asleep in the chair beside his bed.

"Colin." He winced as his throat burned when he tried to talk. Colin didn't move. "Colin," he said a little louder. Still nothing. "Dad," he said as loud as he was able.

Colin stirred, opening his eyes. "Patrick, thank God you're awake. How are you feeling?"

"Like I've been hit by a truck. How long have I been here?"

"A couple of days. They had to put you in a medically induced coma for a day so your injuries would have time to heal, and we've been waiting for you to wake up."

"What's the prognosis?"

"You'll live. You had a collapsed lung and a couple of broken ribs. You needed loads of stitches, but you'll be fine."

"Where's Evelyn?"

"She's here, but she's in the intensive care unit. She was worse off than you were, unfortunately."

"I need to go see her." He struggled to get up.

Colin put a hand on his shoulder, pushing him down. "You're not going anywhere. You need to rest."

"I need to make sure she's okay." He still tried to get up.

"Even if you could get down there, they're not allowing anyone but family to see her."

Patrick shook his head. "She has no family here. I need to go down there so she's not alone."

"They flew her parents in. They arrived the morning after you were admitted."

Patrick froze. "What?"

"Are you ready to hear what happened?"

He nodded, settling back into the bed.

"James and that police officer, PC McCleary, called in the CIA after they discovered you both were taken by the Fitzgeralds. Turns out, they'd been tracking the Fitzgeralds for a while. They had nothing concrete to bring them in on yet. When they got word from James of an international kidnapping, they stormed the warehouse where you were being held, since, by some miracle, Mickey Fitzgerald's lackies didn't leave your mobile lying on the ground where you were taken. They arrested everyone who was there, including Fitzgerald himself. They rushed you both here. Since Ms. Stevenson is an American citizen, the embassy was notified, along with her parents, since they were listed as her emergency contacts. They were flown in, and they have been by her side ever since. James was able to talk to them and discern her condition is pretty serious. Besides her shoulders both being impaled by a hot iron and needing extensive repairs, she sustained a severe head injury. She has yet to wake up, and they don't know when, or if, she ever will."

It was as if someone had punched Patrick in the gut. His girlfriend was in the ICU, with her parents, whom she'd lied to about everything since she landed in London, and they weren't even sure if she was ever going to wake up.

"I need to see her. Please, Dad, talk to her parents, convince them to let me see her. I need to be there with her."

"I can try, but her parents weren't too happy from what James said. They refused to let him in to see her. I don't know if they'll let you in."

"But she's my girlfriend. Doesn't that count for something?"

Colin shook his head. "Not to them. They don't want anyone who isn't family to see her."

Patrick closed his eyes, tears threatening to spill. "Fuck. Fuck them all."

"Why don't you get some more rest? I'll see what I can do."

Patrick kept his eyes closed. "I need to see her for myself. I need to make sure she's okay. She tried to save me, you know."

"What?" Colin paused at the door.

"She tried to save me. She managed to get out of her ropes and, instead of making a run for it like I told her to, she attacked Fitzgerald and tried to get me out of there. That's why she's hurt. Because she tried to save me. It's all my fault." He sobbed quietly.

Colin moved from the door to the bedside. "It is not your fault, son." Colin took Patrick's hand. "Don't you dare blame yourself for what happened. You don't know what he would have done to her even if she hadn't tried to save you. You could both be dead. She bought you both time, and I'm grateful to her." He sighed. "I came too close to losing my son this week, and I'm so very thankful you're still here with me. I'll convey all of this to Mr. and Mrs. Stevenson as soon as I see them."

"I understand what you're saying, but I still can't help but think it's my fault. I shouldn't have brought her with me. She should be safe back at my flat—"

"And you'd be dead. Look, son, you know I don't enjoy talking in circles. I've said my piece. All I can tell you now is, feeling guilty about the situation isn't going to change anything. You can feel guilty until you give yourself an ulcer, but that's not going to change the fact Evelyn is fighting for her life somewhere in this hospital. What you *can* do is focus on getting better so you can try to help *her* get better."

"How can I help her get better if her fucking parents won't let anyone see her?" Patrick growled.

"Restrictions have never seemed to stop you from getting what you want before, now, have they? I think we can find a way around her parents. But we can't do that if you're still bedridden."

"How much longer until they let me out of here?"

Colin frowned. "A fucking madman tortured you. I don't think you're going to get out of here anytime soon, so I'd get comfortable for the next few days."

"You can't pull any strings and get me out of here sooner?"

"I have no sway over medical personnel. Even if I did, this is one thing we won't negotiate on. You'll be here until the doctors say otherwise. And then you'll go home, relax, and allow James, Mrs. Moore, and myself to take care of you until you're completely healed. Do you understand?"

Patrick rolled his eyes, and even that one little motion seemed to cause his entire body to light up with pain. "Yes, sir."

"Good. Now, I'm going to head down to the intensive care unit and see if I can have a chat with Mr. and Mrs. Stevenson about allowing us to wheel you down to sit with Evelyn for a little bit in the next couple days when the doctors allow you to get out of bed."

Colin leaned over and squeezed Patrick's hand. "I am truly, truly relieved you're okay. Pissed off you didn't drop the case like I asked you to weeks ago, but relieved that not only are you okay, but the bastard who murdered your mother will finally be behind bars."

Patrick turned his hand over, squeezing his dad's in return. "Me, too, Dad. Me, too."

Colin gave Patrick's hand one more squeeze before leaving the room.

As soon as the door closed to the hospital room, Patrick leaned back and closed his eyes again, trying to relax, but all he could see behind his closed lids were visions of Evelyn being hit repeatedly and stabbed with the hot metal poker. He brought his fists up and pressed them against his eyes as hard as he could. But try as he might, the image of her with a metal rod through her shoulder wouldn't leave him.

Hot tears welled up behind his eyes, and he didn't fight them as they found their way down his cheeks. It was all his fault. He had one job: to protect Evelyn. That was all he had to do. Instead, he led her right into the Fitzgeralds' clutches and allowed her to get tortured by their hands.

The door to his room opened, and he opened his eyes. James walked into the room.

"Hey," he croaked out.

"Hey." James walked over to the chair Colin vacated a few minutes before.

At least Patrick thought it had only been a few minutes. He really had no concept of time right now.

"How're you feeling?" James settled in.

"Like I've been hit by a fucking truck."

"Yeah, but honestly, if an *actual* truck hit you, you'd probably be in much better shape." He smiled.

Patrick smiled and laughed. And then winced. "You're probably right."

James sobered. "Seriously, how are you feeling?"

"Bloody awful. I can't stop seeing Fitzgerald and Evelyn together. Fitzgerald was fucking sadistic. And I was totally helpless. Fucking helpless. I had to watch as he...he groped her and beat her and stabbed her. It's all I can fucking see when I close my eyes. And Colin says her parents won't even let anyone see her who isn't family, but all I want is to see with my own eyes that she's okay. That she's alive." He fought back tears. "It's all my fault."

James sat silently next to his best friend and partner, not interrupting him to tell him it wasn't his fault, which was exactly what Patrick needed, someone to *listen* as he ranted. He was already feeling better being allowed to get everything off his chest, without being corrected and reassured.

"You're right. This whole situation is your fault."

Patrick reeled. "What the fuck?"

James shrugged. "You were the one who grabbed Evie at the airport in the first place, drawing attention to her. You're the one who then led the Fitzgeralds on a chase through Heathrow. And you trusted Harry, which again, put Evelyn on the Fitzgeralds' radar."

"Well, yeah, all those things happened, but—"

"Now, it was my fault they took her the first time," James continued, as if Patrick hadn't tried to interrupt. "I let her leave the flat on her own. But *you* partnered with her for the secret lair hunt, so, of course, it's your fault they captured you."

Patrick stared at his best friend. This wasn't what he wanted. He just wanted to be listened to. Not agreed with. He opened his mouth to protest once more, but James just kept on fucking talking.

"If you want to go back even further, you can even say your fucking crazy vendetta against the Fitzgeralds put this whole thing in motion, so I guess, yes, we can definitively say the fact Evelyn is in this hospital fighting for her life is very much, one hundred percent your fault, and you should spend the rest of your life feeling sorry for yourself and asking for forgiveness."

"You know, mate, this isn't helping. You're making me feel fucking worse."

"Mate, I hate to be the one to break it to you, but as long as you're blaming yourself for everything, you're going to feel like shit. The guilt is going to eat you alive."

"Then what do you suggest? Like you said, everything *is* my fault."

"We can accept that Evelyn would be in this mess, or worse, with or without you."

"What?"

James readjusted himself in his seat, leaning forward, resting his elbows on the bed. "Think about it. She had the bag of evidence. The Fitzgeralds knew what they were looking for, and they weren't going to stop. They thought she knew things she wasn't supposed to know. If you hadn't intervened, they probably would have picked her up in Heathrow and we would have been reading about her body washing up on the banks of the Thames by the end of the week, feeling sorry for the young American girl who got mixed up with the wrong people before moving on and trying to come up with the next step in our march to nail Mickey Fitzgerald to the wall."

Patrick stared at him. A tightness formed in his chest. "You're right," he squeaked. "You're right. If I wasn't there, she would be dead."

"Of course, I'm right. I'm always right," James joked.

Patrick didn't smile. Even though he shouldn't feel guilty, he couldn't help it.

The smile slipped from James's face. "You can't sit here and feel sorry for yourself. You need to accept this happened and move on. Yes, Evelyn is fighting for her life, but she's *alive* because of you. You need to remember you've played a large role in her survival, and you need to focus on that. Stop blaming yourself for things beyond your control and start thinking of the things you've done for her that have kept her alive this whole time."

When James stopped talking, it was like a dam burst inside of Patrick. All the guilt he had been harboring since Evelyn had first been taken to when he woke up here in the hospital just burst out of him. Part of him wanted to blame whatever pain medication he was on for crying again, but he knew the real reason was because he had been holding so much in for so long.

James moved from his spot in the chair and placed himself on the side of the bed, put his arm around his best friend's shoulders, and let him cry until there weren't any more tears left.

"So," Patrick said. "How in the world did you and McCleary know where to find us?"

James had returned to his chair and leaned back, placing his feet on Patrick's bed, crossing them at the ankle. "When you and Evie didn't return when you were supposed to, we retraced your footsteps, so to speak. We found your pocket knife on the ground, so we knew we had to be close. McCleary called in the CIA, and since you had your mobile in your pocket, they could use their super fancy technology and track you down. Led us right to your location."

Patrick shook his head. "We were lucky."

"Damn lucky," James stated.

The two were quiet for a minute.

"Have you been able to see her? I know Colin said she's pretty heavily guarded by her family, but he also said you've been up there."

James took his feet off the side of the bed, sitting up straight. "Yeah, actually. I sneaked in when they were all out eating together and the nurse wasn't looking."

Patrick swallowed hard at the jealous lump that rose in his throat. "How did she look?"

James sighed, leaning forward to place his elbows on his knees. "About as good as you'd expect."

"That doesn't tell me anything."

James sighed again. "Not good, Patrick, not good. When I visited her, she had all kinds of tubes and machines hooked up to her, and she looked so small and pale. I've never seen anything like it. I broke down and cried. I don't know if you should go in there. I don't know if you can handle it."

Patrick shook his head. "I need to see her. I need to be there. I need her to know I haven't deserted her. I'm still here, waiting for her to wake up."

"Mate, I don't know if you realize this, but you're also in the hospital. It's not like you can just waltz to her room and see her. Plus, her room is guarded more tightly than the Crown Jewels. Her parents don't want anyone who, and I quote, 'got her into this situation,' to see her."

Patrick balled up his fist and slammed it on the bed. "Fuck," he shouted.

"Language, my friend. You don't want to be scandalizing any of these sweet nurses, now do you?" James smiled.

Patrick couldn't help but crack a smile before sobering. "It's not fair, you know? She's going to wake up, and she's going to ask for me, you mark my words, and then they're going to *have* to let her see me."

"You're right. You're absolutely right. And until then, you need to focus on getting better because if you want to sneak about and get into her room, you need to not be in a room of your own, hooked up to all of these gadgets."

Patrick nodded. "Hopefully she'll wake up before I get released and they'll allow me to be wheeled down to see her."

He leaned his head back on his pillow, closed his eyes, and fell asleep.

***

A couple days later, Patrick was sitting up in bed, tying his trainers. They finally cleared him to leave the hospital, with strict orders to go home and continue resting. His ribs were healing nicely, and any vigorous physical activity would set him back.

As the doctor was giving him his discharge instructions, Patrick dutifully nodded along in agreement with everything the doctor said. Go home and lie around in bed and on the couch, sure. Don't drive for at least another week, got it, doc. But the whole time he was listening to the doctor prattle on, he was focused on getting down to the intensive care unit as soon as possible.

He finished tying his trainers and stood. Colin and James were both in the intensive care unit's waiting room, waiting for him. The doctor had given him the option to use a cane, a walker, or to be wheeled in a chair, and Patrick opted for the cane. He was stiff from having lain in bed for a week and a half, and he wasn't sure how far he could walk on his own with his healing ribs and newly inflated lungs. So, he grabbed his cane and winced as he stood fully upright.

Yeah, he'd be going slow. Very. Slow.

He hobbled out of his room and down the hall to the lift. He pushed the button, and when the doors opened, he pushed the button for the third floor and tapped his foot as the lift moved slowly to its destination. After what seemed like an eternity, the doors opened and let him out.

They opened into the waiting room. James and Colin were sitting in the back, whispering to each other. They looked up as he came in, James standing from his chair and moving to help him.

"I wish you would have let us help you make your way here." James took his friend by the arm.

"Well, I needed to see if I could do it on my own. Can't have you two with me all the time. If I have to piss, I'll have to make it to the loo on my own."

"You're not planning on staying here full time, are you, son?" Colin asked as the two young men made it to where he was sitting.

"I was." Patrick hissed as he settled into his chair.

"Are you out of your fucking mind?" James asked. "You'll be going home with me at the end of the day, mate, and I won't hear any arguments from you. You're still healing and there's no way you're going to sleep in these god-awful chairs with broken ribs while you're still healing."

"I'm not leaving. What if she wakes when I'm gone?"

"Then she'll still be awake when I bring you back."

Patrick opened his mouth to protest, but Colin interrupted him. "James is right, son. You'll be going home with either him or myself, and you will rest. One of us will bring you back each morning. But you need to continue to rest and listen to the doctor, even though you're no longer being held hostage, so to speak."

Patrick sighed. "Fine, but you can drop me off and leave. I'm sure you both have work you're needing to catch up on after spending all this time here."

James shook his head. "We have nothing pressing on our plates right now as far as detecting goes. We have a couple cheating spouses, but other than that, the payout we got from Colin's solicitor's office for bringing in Fitzgerald and most of his gang is going to keep us fat and happy for quite a while."

"And I can do any work I have here," Colin replied. "We're not going to let you sit here and wait by yourself. We want to be here for you, Patrick. Let us."

Patrick nodded. "Thank you. Both of you."

"Don't mention it," James said.

Before either of the men could speak up again, a door opened down the hall before closing again. There was a series of footsteps before a middle-aged couple and two young girls came around the corner, heading to the lift and pushing the button. The doors opened, and they stepped in.

As soon as the doors closed, James turned to Patrick. "Now's your chance. That's the Stevensons. They're headed for dinner. You need to hurry if you want the full thirty minutes with Evie."

Patrick took in a deep breath and stood carefully, picking up his cane. "Which room?"

"IC twenty-five. Just down the hall, to the right."

Patrick nodded, taking a deep breath. "Alright. Well, then, here I go."

Slowly, he made his way down the hall and around the corner. He came to the door to Evelyn's room sooner than he thought he would. He paused in front of the tightly closed door before taking a deep breath, looking both ways to make sure no one was watching, and forced his hand to take hold of the handle. He slowly pulled the handle down and pushed the door open. He took two slow steps inside the room before turning to shut the door behind him, just as quietly as he opened it. After taking another deep breath, he turned around.

He wasn't prepared for the sight in front of him, and he nearly collapsed where he was standing when he caught sight of his girlfriend lying on the bed. He could barely see her with everything she had hooked up to her. There were IVs going into her arms, along with blood pressure monitors, heart monitors, catheters, and many other wires coming from her body to machines on either side of the bed. The most glaring thing he noticed was the breathing tube emerging from her throat and the sound of the machine breathing for her.

He walked slowly to the side of her bed and fell into the seat. He looked at her, really looked at her for the first time since he was last with her at the warehouse. She was pale, and her eyes were gently closed, as if she were sleeping. She wasn't broken and bloody like she was the last time he'd seen her, but she looked even smaller and weaker, if possible. Her hair was brushed back, away from her face, and straight down behind her head. Without her fringe on her forehead, she almost didn't look like herself.

Patrick reached out tentatively and brushed her fringe back to where it belonged, making her look a little bit more like herself. However, instead of making him feel better, seeing the woman he was falling in love with, lying in bed, lifeless, was almost too much to handle. He grabbed her hand and, feeling how cold it was, he lost it. He couldn't hold the tears back anymore. Huge sobs erupted out of him.

"I'm so sorry. I'm so, so sorry." He laid his head on the bed next to her and cried.

Soon, Patrick's sobs subsided as he was able to pull himself together. He took a deep breath and sat up. He looked at her and smiled a small smile.

"Hello, love," he breathed, as if he spoke any louder, he'd wake her. "I'm sorry I didn't come and visit you sooner. I was being held hostage in a hospital room of my own. Nothing like this, though. Yours is much louder than mine. You should have a talk with management about that. Get rid of some of this beeping so you can rest easier." He swallowed the lump forming in his throat.

"You're looking much better than the last time we were together, which isn't saying much since you looked bloody awful then. Well, we did it, and I wish you'd wake up so we can go out and celebrate. I owe you a night out on the town to show you London properly. Obviously, we won't need to stage tourist photos for your parents because I'm sure you know they know you've lied to them. But that doesn't mean we still can't go out and have a good time. Show you the sights and eat something a little fancier than fish and chips or curry. Have a proper date." He wiped at a stray tear rolling down his cheek.

"You were really reckless, love. Not that I don't appreciate it. You saved my life, but you really shouldn't have. You're stubborn, like me, and you care too much, and that is your downfall. If Mickey Fitzgerald wasn't behind bars, I'd hunt him down and beat the fucker to death with my cane for what he did to you.

"You need to wake up soon, Evelyn. Your parents won't let us see you. I had to sneak in here like a bloody criminal to be by your side. And I don't have much time left. So, you need to wake up and tell your parents how you want James and me and even Colin to come and visit you so I can be here with you as you get better. But until then, know I'm here. I'm just outside your door, waiting. I haven't left you. Please don't think that. If I could stay, God, if I could have been here since the beginning, I would have. I want to be here with you. There's nowhere else I'd rather be. I love you. Please get better soon."

He leaned over and placed a kiss on her cheek before slowly standing with the help of his cane. He walked to the door and turned to give one last look at her before turning back to the door. Just as he put his hand on the handle, the door flew open, causing him to lose his balance and take a step back, trying to catch himself before he fell. As he caught his balance and stood, he came eye to eye with a middle-aged man with dark hair and olive skin.

He glared at Patrick. "Who the hell are you?"

"I'm, I'm..." Patrick tried.

"What are you doing in my daughter's room?" the man shouted.

Patrick swallowed and took a deep breath. "I had to see her, Mr. Stevenson. I was worried."

"You're him, aren't you? The man they found in the warehouse with my daughter."

"I am. My name is Patrick Miller. It's a pleasure to make your acquaintance." He extended his hand.

Evelyn's father looked at his offered hand, but didn't take it. "I don't understand why you're here. The police made it sound like you're a random person who happened to be there at the same time as my daughter. And some lawyer came and talked to me about how my daughter risked her life to save yours. And now you're sneaking into my daughter's room because you have to see her. So, tell me, Mr. Miller, what is your connection to my little Evie over there?"

Patrick took a deep breath, trying to decide how much he should really tell her father. He decided to be honest, but minimal. Evelyn could fill in the details when she woke up.

"Well, I actually rescued your daughter from Heathrow when the Fitzgeralds were after her. I've been taking care of her since her first day in London. I'm a private investigator who was working on the Fitzgerald case for my father, that lawyer you met with earlier. Evelyn was staying at my flat, and she insisted while she stayed, she helped with the case. I tried to discourage her, but your daughter is very stubborn. She went out on a reconnaissance mission with me, and they caught us. Your daughter could have stayed where she was and watched while Fitzgerald tortured and eventually killed me, but that's not the kind of woman she is. She figured out how to break free of her ropes, and she tried to save me."

Mr. Stevenson narrowed his eyes. "Why would she risk her life to save a detective she barely knows?"

"Because we're in love," Patrick blurted. "I'm in love with your daughter, and she's in love with me. At least, I'm pretty sure she is."

Mr. Stevenson drew his mouth into a frown. By the look on his face, Patrick was pretty sure he was picturing all the ways he wanted to beat the shit out of him.

"That's why she risked her life to save mine," Patrick rushed to say, "and that's why I snuck in here. I couldn't stand not being able to see her for one more day. My best friend and my father have both been by to beg for you to let me visit while I was admitted to the hospital, but you refused. So, I did what I had to do. I needed to see her again, to try and ease the nightmare I see every time I close my eyes of her being tortured at Fitzgerald's hands."

While he had been talking, Mr. Stevenson had folded his arms across his chest. He grew redder and redder as Patrick kept talking. But Patrick wasn't ready to give up just yet.

"I'm sorry you had to find out this way. I'm sorry we had to meet under these circumstances. I had really hoped to meet you on a trip to visit Evelyn in the States, but it seems Fate had other plans for us. So, I'm asking you to let me come back and sit with her again."

"Out," Mr. Stevenson said quietly.

"Excuse me?" Patrick couldn't quite believe what he was hearing.

"I said, get out," he said a little bit louder. "I don't want to see you anywhere near here again."

"What's going on?" A woman entered the room from behind Mr. Stevenson. She was about Evelyn's height, with long strawberry blonde hair. "Who's this?"

"He's the reason Evelyn's in the hospital. It's his fault our daughter may never wake up."

"What?" The news that there was a chance of Evelyn not waking up hit Patrick like a fist to his stomach. "What do you mean, never wake up?"

"What's he doing here?" The woman, probably Mrs. Stevenson, ignored Patrick's question.

"He claims he and Evelyn were together, that they're in love. He's a private detective whose job it was to capture the man who tortured Evelyn. He dragged her into this whole thing and got her hurt in the process, and then he had the nerve to ask to come back and sit with her until she wakes up."

"That's not what happened. You've got it wrong." It was as if the two people in the room couldn't hear Patrick.

"You need to leave. And you need to take those other two men with you," Mrs. Stevenson said. "I don't want to see any of you here again. If we see you here, we'll call security and have you escorted out. If we see you again after that, we'll call the police and have you arrested for harassment. Is that understood?"

Patrick could only nod.

"Good. I think it would be best for all involved if you forget about our daughter and whatever notions you have that you two are in love. Now, get out."

Mr. and Mrs. Stevenson moved out of the doorway, clearing a path for Patrick to exit.

He gripped his cane tightly and straightened his shoulders before reaching into his back pocket to pull out one of his business cards. He set it on the table nearest him. "That's my number. When she wakes up and asks for me, and she *will* ask for me, call me, yeah?"

He didn't even wait for a reply. He moved slowly past the elder Stevensons, past the younger ones waiting out in the hall, and back out to the waiting room. He didn't even stop to greet James or Colin. He moved directly to the lifts, smashing the button to take him to the car park.

"Patrick?" James shouted, but he didn't turn around.

As soon as the doors to the lift opened, he stepped inside, smashing the floor level he needed with his fist. The doors began to close, but were interrupted by an arm coming in between them.

James and Colin entered the lift with him. They were silent as the doors shut.

"What happened?" James asked.

Patrick didn't say anything.

"Are you upset about seeing her? I know it's a bit hard to look at her with all of those machines, but—"

"Her parents came in. I took too long. I wasn't watching the time and her parents caught me in the room as I was trying to leave."

"Oh," James replied, "and I take it they weren't pleasant."

"We're not allowed to be at the hospital anymore. They said if they see us, they will have us arrested."

"What?! Can they even do that? Is that even possible?"

"Unfortunately, it is," Colin responded. "Did they say why? It's not like we're harassing them by sitting in the waiting room. They've not even glanced our way once since we started holding vigil there a week ago."

The elevator doors opened, and the three men walked out, James and Colin leading the way to the car, with Patrick taking up the rear.

"They blame me. Evelyn is in a critical condition, and they say it is my fault. They said it would be best if I go home and forget about her."

"Did you explain that you two are, you know, together?"

"Yes, and it made things worse. I left my card. They have my number. Evelyn will wake up, regardless of what they believe, and she'll ask for me, and as soon as my mobile rings, I'll be on my way back. I can then rub it in their fucking faces she wanted me there, and I'll make it very bloody clear to her how my absence wasn't my choice."

James and Colin stood back and watched as Patrick stood by his car, trying to catch his breath.

"Now, who's crawling into the backseat? I think it's against doctor's orders for me to climb back there."

CHAPTER 36

EVELYN

For a long time, everything seemed fuzzy and felt heavy at the same time. The surrounding sounds seemed muffled. There were voices, but she couldn't pick out the words or identify the voices. She could hear lots of beeping and whirring of machines, but couldn't quite place where she was. She tried to open her eyes, but it was as if her lids were weighed down.

Eventually, she could pinpoint the voices. Her dad. Her mom. Both of her sisters. And then Patrick. For some reason, when he came to visit her, he had been the clearest voice. She made out some words he said. He was trying to explain what had happened. Trying to take all the blame for what happened to her. She wanted to reassure him it wasn't his fault, that she didn't blame him, but she couldn't get the words out. It was as if something trapped her in her own body. No matter what she did, she couldn't communicate with him. So, she laid there and listened to the soothing sound of his voice. He pressed a kiss to her cheek, and then it was over. The chair shifted as he got up to leave.

Then there was an argument with her parents, and he was gone.

She waited and waited for him to return, but he never did. The only voices left in her room were her parents, her sisters, and her doctors. The doctors kept saying she probably would never wake up and her parents would need to accept it.

No, she screamed in her mind. *I'm here. Why can't you hear me?*

Every day, she tried and tried to wake herself up, and then one day, in the middle of the afternoon, surrounded by her entire family, she did.

"Evelyn?" her mom asked as she blinked her eyes open in the bright hospital room.

She tried to speak, but couldn't. There was something down her throat.

She turned her head. Her mom was sitting next to her bed with a relieved expression.

Evelyn turned her head again and her dad and sisters were all around her.

She scanned the room again, confused. Where was Patrick? Why wasn't he here? She lifted an arm, and that one movement took almost more effort than she could handle. But she did it, and she made a gesture with her hand as if she wanted to write. Her middle sister, Elizabeth, seemed to understand right away, and rushed to grab a pen and pad of paper for her. She placed the pen in Evelyn's hand, holding the pad for her to write.

Evelyn struggled. She was trying to do too much for just having woken up. Finally, she finished the one word she wanted to write. Her arm dropped like a lead weight back to the mattress.

Elizabeth turned the pad around and read it aloud. "Patrick?"

Everyone exchanged glances.

"He's not here, dear," her mom replied. "We sent him away."

Evelyn lifted her arm with the pen again, and Elizabeth brought the pad back. She could write what she wanted more quickly now.

Elizabeth read it. "Why?"

"Because only family should be here. Because it's his fault you're in here to begin with. We didn't want to watch you fight for your life with the man responsible for your condition sitting right there," her mom explained.

Evelyn shook her head, her eyes filling with tears. She gestured at the tube in her throat.

"Tony, dear, go get the doctor. Tell them she's awake."

Her dad nodded and left the room.

The four women who remained sat in silence. It didn't take long before Dad re-entered the room, a team of doctors following.

Evelyn tried to keep up as they all talked, but her head still was fuzzy, and all she wanted to do was go back to sleep.

The doctors finally determined she should be okay breathing on her own, and before she knew it, she was coughing up the breathing tube and taking a deep breath.

The doctors and her parents exchanged a few more words, and the doctors exited, leaving the family alone again.

"How long?" Evelyn rasped, finding it both difficult and exhausting to talk.

Michelle brought her a cup of water and held it for her as she sipped from the straw. Her throat immediately relaxed as the cold water slipped down.

"A week," her mom replied. "A very, very long week."

"How did you find out?"

"The embassy called. As soon as the CIA found you and they brought you to the hospital, they contacted the embassy, who contacted us, and they flew us out right away. We've been here ever since," her dad explained.

"What we don't understand is why you *lied* to us about why you were here," her mom stated.

"Sue," her dad started. "She just woke up. Give her some time."

"No, I need to know. I need to know why she told us she missed her flight and was spending some time sightseeing in London before getting re-booked on her way to Greece when she was really here acting as if she were Nancy Drew or in an Agatha Christie novel or something. Putting her life in danger. Or how about why she's been living with two strange men instead of at a hotel, and one of whom had the gall to sneak into the room while we were away and claim the two of them are in a relationship?"

"Mom," Evelyn started.

"Why did you lie to us, Evelyn? What would have happened if you didn't get hurt? Were you going to continue to uphold the lie?"

Evelyn closed her eyes. "That was the plan, yes."

Her mom gasped.

Evelyn spoke up before her mother could get in another word. "Do you want to know why I lied? Because I didn't want you to worry."

She started coughing. Michelle rushed to pour her a cup of water. She brought it over and helped Evelyn take a sip.

"She has a point, Mom," Elizabeth pointed out. "You and dad were already really worried about her going on her trip to begin with."

"'Don't talk to strangers or we'll be seeing you on an episode of *Dateline*,'" Michelle mimicked her mom's voice.

"'Don't look strange men in the eye or you'll be *Taken*, and I'm not Liam Neeson, so I won't be able to rescue you,'" Elizabeth said, lowering her voice to mimic her father.

"Was I supposed to call you and tell you a high-ranking London crime family wanted me?" Evelyn continued, her voice raspy. "But don't worry, two handsome private detectives rescued me and now I'm living in their flat. I'll call you when I'm heading home."

Michelle helped her take another sip of water.

"I'm pretty sure you would have taken the news very well."

"We would have understood. We would have tried to contact the CIA. We would have contacted the embassy. You should have trusted us to help you!"

"I'm an adult, Mom. I can take care of myself. The situation was under control. I had it under control."

"Obviously you didn't or else you wouldn't have been lying in the hospital for a week, fighting for your life!"

Evelyn closed her eyes as tears sprang to them immediately. "I'm sorry," she whispered.

Her mom immediately dropped her bravado and fell into comforting mode. "Oh, sweetie. I'm sorry. A week of watching you struggle for your life, and I just built all of that up. You have nothing to be sorry for. I'm sure if you hadn't gotten hurt, you would have told us, and we would laugh over all of your misadventures."

Evelyn reached up and wiped a stray tear from her cheek. "I have quite a few stories to tell, but those can wait. I need to see Patrick."

"Honey," her mom started.

"No, Mom, listen. I need to see him and make sure he's okay and make sure he knows me being here isn't his fault."

"I'm sorry, but I'm going to have to disagree with you on that. Of course, it's his fault! He dragged you into all of this. He put you in the situation to get hurt," her dad bellowed.

Evelyn shook her head. "No, he didn't. I did."

She didn't continue for a long time. The urge to cry was very strong, and holding it back made her throat ache. But the thought of crying made her even more exhausted than she already was.

"Maybe we should just let this go for now and let her sleep," Elizabeth suggested. "She just woke up, and all you're doing is upsetting her."

"We're just trying to make sense of what happened," their dad defended.

"Right now? This could have waited until Evie was a little better. Able to talk more and defend herself," Michelle pointed out.

"We would have waited, but how could we when she immediately brought up the man who put her here?" their mom whisper yelled, gesturing wildly at the bed Evelyn was currently lying in.

"I'm the one who ran into the woman in the airport and swapped bags." Evelyn spoke as loudly as her throat would allow. "I was the one who didn't listen to him and tried to leave. I'm the one who insisted on being a part of the investigation. I'm the one who tried to distract Fitzgerald in order to save Patrick, causing Fitzgerald to lash out at me. It's my fault I'm in this bed. Not his, and you need to stop blaming him."

"Fine, it's your fault. You're in control of your own actions. But we're not calling him in here. You're not going to see him. You need your rest. You need to focus on healing so we can get you home," her mom said.

"But—"

"No buts. You're resting without a strange British man at your side, and that's final."

Evelyn closed her eyes and leaned back against the pillow, knowing it was fruitless to argue with her mother.

"Are you hungry?" her mother asked.

"A little. I'm mostly thirsty."

"The food here is decent. Why don't I go down and pick something up for you from the cafeteria? And then, if you get hungry, it'll be here for you to snack on."

"That sounds okay."

Her mother smiled. "Good. I'll be right back."

"I'll go with you," her dad stated, and the two of them left.

They left Evelyn alone in her hospital room with her sisters. Her best friends.

"All those emails and not one mention you were living with a hot Brit?" Elizabeth moved to the chair beside her bed.

"You were holding out on us, Evie. You let us go on and on about celebrities and movies, and not once did you tell us you were living in a James Bond movie." Michelle took the other chair.

"I'm sorry," she said weakly. "Next time, I'll make sure to keep you in the loop."

"God, I hope there isn't a next time. This was some scary stuff, Evie."

"I'm sorry, Lizzy."

"You don't need to apologize. Just know the parents are upset mostly because it's an emotion they can express their extreme fear through. Shelley and I are adults, and they haven't let us leave this hospital to go sightseeing. It's here or the hotel. That's it."

"Are you trying to make me feel guilty? Because I'm already feeling that in troves."

"No, what she's trying to do, and failing spectacularly at, is trying to illustrate that Mom and Dad's sudden protective streak is coming from a place of love," Michelle replied.

"I know that. I knew going into this whole mess they'd be angry. But they weren't supposed to find out about it until they were like ninety and on their deathbeds. When they wouldn't be able to react so forcefully."

"So, tell us about that British hunk we found crying over your bed a few days ago." Elizabeth leaned forward, putting her elbows on her knees.

"Yes, dish!" said Michelle.

"Okay. Well, his name is Patrick, and he's a private investigator."

"Yes, yes, we know all of this. Get to the good stuff." Elizabeth made a motion with her hands to try and move the story along.

Evelyn laughed, which caused her to cough.

Michelle immediately handed her a cup of water. She took a sip.

After a pause to make sure she wouldn't start coughing again, Evelyn started listing everything she loved about Patrick. "He knows how to drive me crazy and push all my buttons. I don't think I've ever fought with anyone like I've fought with him."

"Not even us?" Elizabeth asked, grinning.

Evelyn shook her head. "After like the first day, it became a sort of game to rile each other up. He's incredibly stubborn."

"No wonder you two get along," Michelle joked.

"I can picture him at home with his best friend, James, pouting about being sidelined." Evelyn paused and swallowed. Her throat was so raw from the breathing tube. She took another sip of water.

"He stepped in front of a gun for me, and he's done nothing but try to protect me this entire time." She tried to ignore the gasps her sisters made at the mention of the gun, but couldn't. It was pretty fucking scary to look back on. To see the danger they were in.

"He's gentle and caring, and I love him." Her voice cracked, a combination of emotion and from being on the breathing tube. "It's not fair that Mom and Dad won't let me call him because, right now, he's the only person I want to see in the entire world, and I can't," she finished, her voice not much louder than a whisper.

"We can fix that."

"What do you mean?"

"He left his card. We can call him for you. And then we can distract Mom and Dad so you can see him. Once you're better, you'll be able to see him as much as you want. You're an adult. They can't stop you," Elizabeth replied.

"You'd do all of that for me?"

"Of course. You're our big sister, our best friend, and this is something straight out of a love story. And some day, when you're sitting down with your children, you can tell them that Aunties Liz and Shell totally made your future happen."

Evelyn laughed. "Deal. Although, I think we're getting way ahead of ourselves here. We're not quite at the discussing children part of our relationship yet. We've barely defined it, and I haven't told him I love him."

"Oh, I don't think we're getting ahead of ourselves. The look on your face when you talk about him says it all. You're destined for a beautiful future," Michelle stated.

"You watch too many rom-coms."

The door to the room opened, and their parents entered, carrying a tray full of every single one of her favorite foods and beverages.

"We didn't know what you might want, so we got you a bit of everything we thought you might like." Her dad set the tray in front of her.

"Thank you."

"You're welcome, Evie."

As her parents fussed around her, making sure she was comfortable, Evelyn peeked around her mom's body and watched as Michelle grabbed Patrick's card off the side table and snuck out of the room.

CHAPTER 37

PATRICK

Rehabilitation and relaxation were two things Patrick didn't do well. After three days sitting in his flat with nothing but the internet and James to keep him company, he was getting a major case of cabin fever. He was getting restless. He needed to go for a walk or take some reconnaissance photos of cheating spouses, something. But James wouldn't let him out. Either Colin or James were constantly around to make sure he followed the doctor's orders and did nothing too strenuous.

So, there he sat. Either in his bed or on the couch, and he read. He was so bored, he actually read Evelyn's thesis at one point, which he found increasingly fascinating. He couldn't wait to talk to her about it and have her explain a few things she wrote about he didn't quite understand.

At the thought of Evelyn, he glanced at his phone again. The damn thing had only rung once since he'd left Evelyn's room a few days ago. And it was some lady asking for some help because she was certain her husband was fucking the nanny on the side and needed proof. He immediately handed the call off to James, who set up a time and date for him to stalk the cheating husband. The phone had been silent since.

He reached for his cane, leaning against the table beside his bed, and scooted himself so he could stand. He needed to take a lap around the flat. Get some new scenery for a bit and stop staring at his bloody phone. He swung his legs over the side of his bed and stood. He'd taken two steps toward the door of his room when his phone rang. He paused before turning around and moving quicker than he probably should have, as a sharp pain shot through his ribs. He rushed over to his phone to answer it before he missed the call.

He pressed the button. "Hello?".

"Hello? Is this Patrick?" the voice of a woman with an American accent came through the phone.

"This is Patrick."

"This is Michelle Stevenson, Evelyn's sister. She's awake, and she's asking for you."

Patrick couldn't believe his ears. "She's awake?"

"Yes."

"And she asked for me?"

"Yes, but my parents refused to call you. We wanted to make sure you know so you can come down here. Once you get here, we'll distract my parents so you can see Evelyn."

"Okay, yeah, thank you. I'll get someone to drive me there right away."

"You're welcome. It's really quite romantic, don't you think? You were the first person she asked for when she woke up. I really hope you feel half as much for her as she does for you."

"She did?" Patrick couldn't hold back his smile. "You tell her I'll be there as soon as I can, yeah?"

"I will. Shit, my parents are looking for me. See you soon." There was a click, and the line went dead.

Patrick stared at the phone, taking a moment to try to absorb what Evelyn's sister had just said. She was awake.

"Woohoo!" he shouted, throwing his hands above his head, unable to hold in the intense feelings flowing through him at the news.

James threw open his door and stuck his head in. "What's going on?"

"She's awake."

"What?"

"Didn't you hear me, you bloody idiot? She's awake!"

"How do you know? Did her parents call you?"

Patrick shook his head. "Her sister."

James let out a laugh and his own cheer. "This is great news! What are we waiting for? I'd think you'd already be in the car waiting for me."

"Well, I would be, but you're blocking the doorway."

Patrick had the biggest grin on his face since before his kidnapping.

"Now, if you're going to stand there, make yourself fucking useful and help me down to the car. We need to stop somewhere and get Evelyn the biggest fucking teddy bear in all of London. Think it will fit in the Coop?"

James laughed and shook his head. "We may have to get the second largest teddy bear in all of London in order for it to fit in the car, but I think we can make do."

Patrick grabbed the cane leaning against the night table and grimaced as he straightened, his ribs still making it hard to move around. But he wasn't going to let that get him down. She was awake.

And she asked for him.

CHAPTER 38

EVELYN

Evelyn was lying on her bed in a thankfully empty room. Her sisters had begged their parents to take them somewhere to sightsee for a couple of hours. Michelle had whispered to Evelyn that she had managed to make a call to Patrick. The plan was in motion.

So, now the family was off to go look at the guards in front of Buckingham Palace and see Big Ben. Evelyn had recommended an enjoyable walk along the Southbank Promenade, as well. She sounded so local when she said it. And once everyone had left, she realized how nice it was to be in a mostly quiet room, with just the sounds of machines rather than the constant chatter which had been buzzing around her since she'd awoken. Between her parents fussing over her every time she flinched or said she was thirsty to the nurses coming in every thirty minutes to check on her, she was glad to be alone.

Although, she hoped Patrick came by soon.

She tried to roll over, but every time she moved, the damn machine sounded alarms and the nurses came rushing in to make sure she was okay. So, she laid still. On her back. Enjoying the silence. She was just closing her eyes as footsteps came from outside her door.

"If you're a nurse, please keep walking," she whispered to herself.

The door opened slowly, and one set of footsteps came in the room before quietly shutting the door behind them. And then nothing. She opened her eyes and slowly turned her head.

"Oh my God," she whispered, tears immediately springing to her eyes.

"I didn't wake you, did I? I was trying to be quiet," Patrick whispered back.

"I wasn't asleep, I was just resting my eyes."

She watched him slowly walk to the side of her bed, noting the cane he used before settling in the chair closest to her bed.

"Your sister, Michelle, called and told me you woke up. So, I had James drive me down here right away."

"James is here? Where is he?"

"In the waiting room. He wanted to give me a chance to see you alone first." He placed a hand on her cheek.

She brought her hand up and covered his.

"How are you feeling, love? The last time I was allowed in, your parents implied you may never wake up. I've been so scared for you."

"I hurt everywhere. I'm exhausted, which makes no sense since I was basically sleeping for a week. And even though I've only been awake for a few hours, I'm already tired of this hospital. All I want to do is go back to your flat and curl up in your bed and sleep for a month."

"Well, you need to hurry up and get better, and we can make that happen. I'm on strict relaxation orders from the doctors. We can curl up in bed together and make James wait on us hand and foot until we're allowed to do things on our own. Or until he catches on that he doesn't have to be our personal slave anymore."

She laughed, and then grimaced. "Ouch. Don't make me laugh."

He smiled. "I'll try not to, but it's so tempting. It drives home the point you're going to be okay when I see you laughing."

"Are you okay? How long were you in the hospital?"

"A few days. I'm fine. I woke up after two days, and the rest was the doctors making sure my lung re-inflated properly and my ribs were healing. My injuries were nothing compared to yours."

"But you're using a cane." She gestured at the offending object.

"Oh, that's only because trying to walk with broken ribs fucking hurts. I can't stand up straight, so I use the cane to support myself so I can walk and breathe at the same time. It's bloody awful. I've been spending a lot of time in bed and on the couch."

"Oh, man, again? How are you managing? Does James want to kill you yet?" she teased.

"Ha, ha. I'll have you know I'm going bloody insane. I'm running out of things to keep me occupied, so you better get released from this place soon so you can keep me company. I was so bored, I read your thesis the other day."

"You didn't!"

"I did! I didn't understand seventy-five percent of what you wrote, but I found it immensely interesting. You'll have to explain what most of it means."

"It's not finished."

"Doesn't matter. I enjoyed it all the same."

"Well, when I get out of here, I'll have to explain it to you, and you'll have to read the rest of it when I get it finished. Which will hopefully happen before my parents whisk me back home."

He looked at his lap.

"What's wrong? You had to know that, with my parents involved, I wasn't going to get to stay here as long as we originally talked about."

He shook his head. "It's not that. It's that I hope your parents are aware of the legal implications of your involvement with the case."

"Legal implications?"

"You're a witness in the case. Not just a witness, but what Colin keeps referring to as a 'star witness.' He and the rest of the solicitors at his firm are adamant you not leave the country. You'll need to stay here until the end of the trial. They don't want to take the chance you won't come back and testify. Especially since they're bringing Fitzgerald up on international charges."

"Oh."

"What? You're sounding a little bit disappointed."

"I'm not disappointed. Believe me, I'm happy to have whatever time I can here with you and James and the chance to explore, but my parents may not agree."

"Ah, no one's talked to them about the case."

"Well, now, I don't know that per se, but I do know they haven't mentioned anything about the case to me since I woke up. It may be because they don't want to stress me out. I mean, I just woke up from a coma a few hours ago."

"Oh, yeah, the coma thing. That may explain why you're not up to date on current events."

She laughed, grimacing again at the pain. "I told you to stop making me laugh."

"Can't help it, love. Reminds me you're alive."

The two of them sobered.

"I'm so sorry, Evelyn."

"You don't need to be sorry."

"Yes, I do. I was supposed to protect you, and I did a piss-poor job at it. A really piss-poor job. I mean, I couldn't have failed more spectacularly at my one job than I did."

She gave him a weak smile. "You didn't fail. I would have been dead long ago if it weren't for you. You could have left me in the airport on that first day to fend for myself. But you didn't. Ever since then, you've done amazing at trying to help me and keep me alive. I've been the one making things super difficult for you. I haven't stayed in one place. I've ventured out on my own, which got me kidnapped the first time. You essentially took a bullet for me. I don't think you failed, Patrick. I think you did the best you could under the circumstances. And the circumstances weren't the best. The odds were stacked mightily high against us."

He shook his head. "I can't believe you're stuck in a hospital bed hooked up to dozens of machines and you're still fucking optimistic."

She shrugged. "Can't help it. It's in my nature."

He leaned over, placing a soft kiss on her lips. "I'm glad you're okay," he whispered.

"I'm glad you're okay, too," she whispered back. "I was so worried about you. Watching Fitzgerald do what he was doing, I just I had to stop him, you know? I was so worried that if I didn't, he'd kill you, right there, in front of me."

"I appreciate it, love, I do. I just wish you'd stayed put. James and McCleary and the CIA came in not much longer after you came to my rescue. If you had just waited it out—"

"You could still be dead. We didn't know James and McCleary were coming. We didn't even know they knew where we were. I couldn't gamble with your life. Yes, hindsight is twenty-twenty and all that, but you have to remember, in that moment, when it was us versus Fitzgerald, we didn't know we were going to have backup. We didn't know rescue was imminent, and so I did what I had to do to make sure some psycho didn't murder the man I love right in front of me."

"By placing your own life in danger!" Patrick almost shouted. "Do you know how many times I've replayed that scene from the warehouse since that day? Every time I close my eyes, I see Fitzgerald stabbing you with that fucking metal poker. Over and over and over again. You can't even imagine how I've felt since I snuck in to see you and your parents told me you may never wake up. To have the last image of your girlfriend alive be of a man fucking stabbing her, that's brutal."

"I'm sorry!" she said as forcefully as she dared. "I'm sorry. I really am. I'm sorry for putting myself in a situation that worried both you and my family. At that moment, I wasn't thinking about myself. I didn't think about what Fitzgerald would do to me. I could see you hanging from a rope, bloody and beaten, and I did what my instincts told me to do. I'm so sorry," she sobbed. Each sob sent a sharp pain through her chest.

"Hey." He took her hand. "Hey, don't cry, love. Please don't cry. I get why you did what you did. I do. I really do. It's just hard, you know? Remembering the last week. But that's past us, yeah? You're awake, I'm getting better, and you'll be getting better. We'll be back at my flat before we know it, recuperating together, and we'll be able to look back on this whole thing with whatever the opposite of fondness is."

She nodded, bringing her free hand up to wipe the tears from her face. "You're right. You're absolutely right. We need to focus on getting better, making sure Colin and his partners have an airtight case against Fitzgerald and everyone else they arrested, so they can stay behind bars for a very long time."

"That's the spirit, love!" He smiled. "Let's lock those fuckers up for a very, very long time. From what Colin was saying the other day, they have a pretty airtight case already, as long as you're sticking around and willing to testify."

"Oh, I'm willing. I'm very willing."

"Good. Because they're building their entire case around you. The CIA is bringing him up on some major charges. Kidnapping, assault, attempted murder of an American national, and Megan's murder. McCleary is bringing him in on some of the lesser local charges. Either way, the fucker is going away."

"What happened with the police who were being paid to look the other way?"

"They're suspended without pay, pending an investigation. Scotland Yard is pissed. They're scrambling to fill the borough's office. James and I even got calls to convince us to rejoin the force."

"Yeah? And you said?"

"Piss off. What do you think we said? I'm bloody injured, and James is my nursemaid, and he's trying to keep our business afloat while I'm laid up. Poor bloke has had to go on two whole stakeouts on his own in the last week."

"Oh man, two whole stakeouts in one week. He sounds pretty overworked. You better give him a vacation."

"Love, when this whole thing is over, I think we should all go on holiday somewhere warm and sunny, and with alcohol. Lots of alcohol."

"Sounds marvelous."

"So, it's a date, then? When the trial is over, and we're all healed, the three of us on holiday, funded by the fee from a bunch of rich solicitors?"

"It's a date."

Epilogue

EVELYN

One Year Later

The airport was busy. People were rushing to check into their flights, store their luggage, get through security, and get on their flights. Besides all the people milling about, there were the people standing in the lobby, trying to say goodbye to their loved ones before boarding their flights.

"I don't know what I'm going to do without you." Patrick wrapped his arms tighter around Evelyn, who had her arms wrapped around his neck, her head pressed into his chest.

The trial had ended a few days earlier. It was the trial of the century. Every television network aired it as it happened. Evelyn, Patrick, and James spent several days each on the stand being questioned and cross-examined repeatedly. When it was all done, the jury didn't even take a full day to deliberate before coming back with a guilty verdict for every single member of the Fitzgerald family on trial. Fitzgerald, of course, had the most charges brought up against him. They sentenced him to whole-life order, which was a term Evelyn grew familiar with as the trial progressed. He yelled he would get revenge against the trio as they dragged him out of the court. They tried to shrug it off, but inevitably decided it would probably be a good idea to be vigilant for a while, always looking over their shoulders.

"I'm only going home for a week. Then, I'll be meeting you and James in Tahiti. I think you'll be fine."

"It's going to be weird not having you here all the time. I don't know why you need to go back home, anyway."

"You know why. I need to pack and start shipping things over. And besides, this will give you and James an opportunity to pack all of your things. The new flat is available as soon as we get back from vacation."

"I still don't know why we need to move. I thought our flat was very adequate."

"It's too small for the three of us, and you know it."

"True. Your bear takes up half the living room. I don't know why we bought you that fucking bear."

"Because you love me. That thing kept me company for the long days I was alone in that hospital room after my family went back home, and you and James had to work."

"Yeah, that's a good bear."

She laughed. "You're so fickle. I better see that bear right where I left him when we get back."

"Don't worry. I won't hurt your bear. Are you excited about seeing your parents? I mean, it's not like you haven't seen them. You guy's Skype every other night, but *really* see them?"

"Yeah, I am. I can't wait to get back to Iowa and eat at my favorite restaurants and see some of my friends. Defend my thesis, get my degree, you know, the little things."

"I wish I were going with you. To support you, you know. Help you out."

"I do, too, but you know this is the right plan. My parents and sisters have already started sorting through my things, so it'll be easier for me to pick what's important enough to ship over and what to pack or what to give away. Shit. You're right, I wish you were coming. I think I've overestimated what I can accomplish in a week."

"Hey." He leaned down, placing a kiss on her forehead. "You'll be fine. You've got this. You have plenty of help there. And then we'll be in Tahiti, with sands and beaches and alcohol. Lots of alcohol."

"Hmmm," she murmured. "That sounds absolutely marvelous. Okay, I think I can get through this week now, knowing what's waiting for me at the end of it."

The clock in the airport rang twice.

Patrick sighed. "You better get going if you're going to make it through security and to your flight on time."

She held him, tears springing to her eyes. "Why is this so hard? I don't want to say goodbye to you."

He held her tight. "I don't want to say goodbye, either. But it's not forever, yeah? We'll see each other in a week for our holiday, and then you're back here and we can start planning for the rest of our lives together."

She smiled through her tears, lifting her left hand from his shoulder, holding it up where she could see it. The ring on her third finger caught the light and gleamed.

"You're right. This isn't goodbye. We'll be back together before we know it, and we have our whole lives ahead of us."

She pulled back before pressing her lips to his. "I love you," she whispered.

"I love you, too."

One more kiss, and they parted.

Evelyn headed toward the security gate, turning back to take one more look at her fiancé and her future.

LONDON DETECTIVE AGENCY BOOK TWO
BE MY LITTLE BABY
STEPHANIE R. CAFFREY

For Matthew, the hero of my love story.

Acknowledgements

Mistaken Identity was supposed to be a standalone novel, however, a year or so after turning it into my agent, I couldn't let James go. I loved him too much. And so, the story of *Be My Little Baby* came to me.

Thank you to the late Dawn Dowdle for encouraging me to write this sequel and agreeing that the story wasn't finished.

Thank you to Kelly and Shelly at Rowan Prose Publishing. It has been so wonderful working with you on this series, and I know that my books are in great hands.

As always, thank you to Louise for being an amazing Brit Picker. My characters would be so much less British without you, and London would be so inaccurate without your keen eyes.

To Sydney, Laura, and Ally – Thank you for being amazing readers and pointing out all my huge plot holes and pieces of the story that simply didn't work. This book wouldn't be half as good as it is now without your help.

To Arthur, who wrote alongside me during November as I worked on this book. Thanks for being an amazing son and writing partner. I love our writing sessions together.

Beatrice for being such a tolerant toddler during the time this was written and doing her best to entertain herself while I was trying to write with friends in various restaurants.

Sharon, Jamie, and Sarah for being my ride or dies. Can't wait for our next writing retreat and everything that comes with it. I couldn't do any of this without you all by my side.

My parents and sisters for always encouraging me in continuing with my writing.

And finally, to my husband, Matthew. You have always been so supportive of this dream of mine, and none of this could be achieved without you. Thank you, and I love you.

CHAPTER 1

JAMES

"I am hearing what you're saying, Mrs. Williams, but I am going to tell you one more time, we don't really do this sort of work." James Moore ran his hand through his red hair and rolled his eyes. This was the third time this week Mrs. Williams had called their office, so this was the third time he would have to turn down her business.

"But Muffy has been missing for a week. I want to find my Muffy."

"Mrs. Williams?" James' partner, Patrick, mouthed at him from the desk opposite his in the small office.

James nodded.

Patrick rolled his eyes and motioned for James to hand the phone over to him. Which he gladly did.

"Mrs. Williams, is poor Muffy still missing? Did you check at the RSPCA?"

While Patrick took care of Mrs. Williams and the Case of the Missing Tabby Cat, James turned to the computer with their shared document to go over what other cases they had still open at the moment.

A year and a half ago, he, along with Patrick and his fiancée Evelyn, helped take down a notorious crime family in London. Since that time, their meager little private investigator agency that barely scraped by had exploded because of the publicity of the case. Not only were they earning enough to live off of comfortably, they could move their business out of their flat and into its own space, which made the work life balance a little easier.

Well, easier for Patrick. James had nothing else really taking up his time. While Patrick and Evelyn had moved into a new flat together, stating they needed a fresh start in their own space, James had moved in with Joseph McCleary, a police officer, to help pay the rent and to make the flat feel not so empty. The two had gotten along ever since Joe had helped with the case the year before. Living together was pretty easy as they kept the same schedule: neither was ever really home.

James kept busy with work. He loved the thrill of the chase and the satisfaction of solving a case brought him. Nothing could beat how he felt while he worked. He pulled double the cases Patrick did, mostly because Patrick actually separated work from the rest of his life.

Patrick hung up the phone and sighed. "Well, I think I just promised Mrs. Williams one of us would go over and help her find Muffy."

"Patrick!"

"I'm sorry! I apparently have a really hard time saying no to little old ladies. And easy money. I have a honeymoon to pay for soon."

"So, does that mean you're going over to take Mrs. Williams to the RSPCA?"

"Fuck. I guess it does." He stood from his desk and grabbed his coat as he moved toward the door. "I'm going to head over there now and get this over with. And then I'm going to head home from there. Watch the time. Don't stay here too late. It's a Friday night. Go home, grab Joe, and hit a pub."

"You have big plans for your Friday night?"

"Oh yes, Evelyn and I have the exciting plans of putting together a seating plan and making sure we have all our vendors in order."

James pulled a face. "Oh yes. Very exciting."

"Have you written your speech yet?"

"Not yet. But it will get written."

"The wedding is in two weeks, mate. I'm just going to tell Evelyn you have everything done. Let her cross something off her bloody list."

"Works for me. Now, you enjoy the RSPCA, and I promise I will leave the office before it gets too late, and I will not work the entire weekend."

"And you will go to the pub and pick up a bird."

"And I will go home and watch a movie."

Patrick shook his head. "As long as it's not here, I honestly don't care what you do. You're working too hard, James. We're allowed to let some of these cases go. We don't have to work every single one that falls into our lap."

"Logically I know this. However, we don't know how much longer this Fitzgerald Bump is going to last. I want to milk it for all it's worth, and build up my savings for when it all falls flat again."

"It's been nearly a year and a half. I think it's safe to say, any bump from the Fitzgeralds has run its course. This is more than likely our new normal based on our reputation and word of mouth. We'll be fine."

"Yes, well, I'm going to keep on keeping on, so to speak. You're the only one uncomfortable with my workload."

"Not the only one, Evelyn worries about you, too."

"Well, Evie is a gentle soul who worries about everyone. Tell her to stop worrying about me and focus on your wedding. She can worry about me after you return from your honeymoon."

"I will pass that along. And now that my job of telling you to work less is done, I have a date with an old lady and an animal shelter."

"Good luck, mate."

"Ta." Patrick gave him a mock salute before exiting the office.

James shook his head and turned back to the computer. They started using a shared spreadsheet in order to keep track of cases and their status. Besides their open cases, they had an overflowing email inbox with potential cases. Patrick was probably right. Any bump from the publicity of taking down Mickey Fitzgerald and the subsequent trial had probably already worn off. Their overflowing email and the need to juggle half a dozen cases at a time was because they were fucking good at their job and word was finally getting around London. They were *the* team to go to if you needed to employ the services of a private investigator.

After finishing up some notes about a cheating spouse case they were working on, he shut down his computer and began packing up for the day. He looked at the clock. Nearly six. A very reasonable time to sign off and go home. As he put his laptop in his backpack, he wondered if maybe Patrick was right. Maybe he should go out to the pub. It had been a while since he tried to pull a bird. If anything, it would be nice to at least chat up someone new.

He pulled out his phone and texted Joe. He wasn't sure what his work schedule was this week. Sometimes he worked days, and sometimes he was on nights. He couldn't remember which he was on currently. As soon as he finished composing the text, but before he could hit send, there was a knock on the door.

He frowned. No one really ever came to their office. While it was exciting, they had an office separate from their flat, the office was quite small. Barely enough room for their two desks and an extra chair for when Evie would come and visit when she had time. They did most of their business via telephone or would meet off site. Knocking on their door was not normal.

He finished packing his bag and moved around his desk to go answer the door. He opened it to find a young woman, probably around his age, late twenties, early thirties, standing there, hand poised to knock again. She had her black curly hair pulled back into a ponytail, but it still ran down to the middle of her back. Thick rimmed cat-eyeglasses framed her brown eyes, the purple a bold contrast to her copper skin. When she saw he opened the door, her face broke out into a smile, however it didn't reach her eyes.

"Can I help you?"

"Yes, is this Miller and Moore Investigations?"

"It is. I'm James Moore." He offered his hand, and she took it. Her smaller hand easily engulfed within his.

"Tessa Lopez," she replied.

"What can I do for you, Ms. Lopez? I have to admit, we don't get very many clients knocking on our door."

"Well, I had emailed you two days ago about my case, but I have yet to hear anything from you, so I thought I would try my hand at coming down in person. My case is rather urgent."

"Our email is pretty backlogged at the moment, so I apologize. We would have gotten to your email in the next day or so. If your case is urgent, wouldn't you be better served to go to the police about it?"

"Well, that's the problem now, isn't it? I went to the police, but they told me they can't do anything until a crime is committed. When I asked them if my case would fall under harassment, they asked me if I knew who the harasser was. When I told them I didn't, they told me they couldn't do anything. Since then, things have escalated a bit, and I've gotten worried about my safety. My friend told me about you and your partner, and so here I am."

James frowned. "I was about to leave for the night, but now you have me both intrigued about your case and worried about your safety. Please come in."

He stepped out of the way, letting her into the office. As she passed, he caught a whiff of coconut and vanilla. She moved to sit in Evie's chair as James shut the door and went back to his desk. Rather than pull out his laptop again, he found a legal pad and a pen pulling both in front of him. He opened the pen and poised it, ready to write everything she said. He nodded to her to show he was ready.

"Well, a couple of weeks ago, I started getting letters to my place of business. Like actual letters. I almost never get letters to my shop. People mostly communicate to me through email, my website or review sites, so I was already thinking it a little odd."

"What's your business?"

"I own a bake shop, here over on Redchurch Street. It's called Cake Me Home Tonight."

"You own Cake Me Home Tonight? You make the best Victoria Sponge."

She blushed as her eyes strayed down at her hands. "Thank you."

"You're welcome. Anyway, you were telling me about the letters?"

"Yes, they started off innocently enough, praising me for something I had baked. Asking me if I would make something specific to have in the shop the next day. Things like that. Then they got more personal. Asking me if I had a boyfriend. Asking me what my favorite position to fuck is. Things like that. It was when they turned in this direction I went to the police. But because whoever is sending these letters is doing it anonymously, and they have never come in contact with me, the police say they can't really do anything. They called it a prank."

"And you don't recognize the handwriting on the letters? Could it be someone you already know?"

Ms. Lopez shook her head. "They're all typed. And I think they're all hand delivered through my letterbox, none of the envelopes have been addressed. Just blank on the front."

"Hand delivered? That makes things a little easier. I'll put in a request to get the CCTV footage from in front of your shop. If the letters were hand delivered, we'll be able to see who did it."

"Really? That simple?"

"Hypothetically. I mean, any number of things could occur. We'll get a really clear picture of the bloke's face, case closed. Or it will be a grainy image and we won't be able to tell who it is, but it will be a lead. Now, you mentioned something earlier about how the harassment has escalated, which is what brought you here in the first place?"

"Yes. Hold on, let me show you." Ms. Lopez pulled her handbag, which had been slung across her chest hanging at her hip, into her lap. She opened the flap and pulled out an envelope. It was a little larger than a standard envelope, but not A4 sized. She set the envelope on the desk and pushed it across to him.

He picked it up and opened the flap. There was a folded sheet of A4 paper next to a glossy photograph. He unfolded the paper and frowned when he read it. "That color looks good on you." Then he looked at the photograph and his hands formed into fists, almost crushing the picture between them.

"Do you live above your shop?"

She nodded. "I do."

The picture was a spy shot, taken from the street up through what appeared to be Ms. Lopez's bedroom window. Framed perfectly in the window, between the crack of her curtains, was Ms. Lopez, shirtless, and poised with her hands behind her back, taking off her emerald green bra. Completely oblivious to the cameraman below.

CHAPTER 2

TESSA

Tessa could feel her face warm as she watched Detective Moore look at the picture she gave him. To be honest, she had left out the more risqué ones. She couldn't bear watching a stranger look at her bare chest. It was already incredibly embarrassing to have to come in here. She should be able to handle a few letters. She got worse in reviews around the internet. People felt bold enough to say many horrific things while hidden behind the anonymity of a screen. However, there seemed to be something a bit more sinister about these letters. Whether it was the content, the frequency they arrived or the manner in which they were delivered, she couldn't decide. She knew something was off way before she got the surveillance pictures two days ago. She simply couldn't put her finger on what.

She pulled her bottom lip between her teeth and shifted her gaze down to the photographs in the detective's hands. She drew her eyebrows. He was gripping the photograph tightly. The pictures were quite upsetting to her, but she didn't think they would upset other people.

"So, you have a stalker."

"I have a stalker."

"Stalking is a crime in the UK, but I don't think I need to tell you that."

"Like I said, I have gone to the police, and they've shrugged it off. Told me it's probably a prank. That I should be flattered."

"Here's the thing. It is after six on a Friday night. I can't do much until after the weekend. Have any of the letters been threatening?"

She shook her head. "No. No actual threats."

"Good. On Monday morning, I will put in the request to get the CCTV footage from outside your shop. Once we get the footage, I can go through and see if I can find anything that feels suspicious. On Monday I would like you to bring in everything he's sent you. I'm assuming you kept everything."

"I did. I am at the shop from 3:30 am until a little after midday baking. I will bring you everything in the afternoon on Monday if that is okay with you?"

He wrote notes on his legal pad. "Are you in the shop at 3:30 every morning?"

"Every morning except Sunday when the shop is closed."

"Are the letters already delivered in your letterbox when you arrive? Or do they appear later on in the morning?"

"They are already there when I arrive."

"And the shop closes around midday?"

"No, I leave around midday. The shop closes at five each night. I have a manager and a girl who helps run the shop. They're usually there alone between midday and five. Tonight, I stayed and closed because my manager is on holiday."

"So, sometime between the shop closing at five and you arriving at three-thirty, our mysterious author is delivering letters in your post."

"Yes, that seems right."

Detective Moore set his pen down and looked at her. His green eyes locked with hers. "Since the letters are being delivered to your place of business and not your home and they are not of a threatening nature, while it's concerning, I'm not overly worried. Go about your weekend as normal. If anything changes before Monday, please give me a ring, and I will come sort it out. Your stalker seems to be acting the role of a secret admirer at the moment. If you start getting letters that are more threatening, call me." He slid his card across the desk to her. She picked it up and slid it into the pocket of her jeans.

"Thank you. I know you're busy, so I appreciate you taking the time, on a Friday night, no less, to meet with me. And I appreciate you moving quickly on this."

"Most of our cases right now deal with cheating spouses or money laundering, which are cases that, while important, don't quite have the urgency attached to them as 'man who sends letters to woman and takes her picture unknowingly.'"

"You keep referring to my stalker as male. Do women tend to not do this whole stalking business?"

"Oh, I'm sorry. How heteronormative of me. I just assumed. Well, yes. Women do, do the stalking thing. When I get the CCTV, I can expand my search to men and women exhibiting suspicious behavior."

She tried to hide her smile as his face grew red, accentuating the freckles that peppered his nose. Not for the first time since she entered his office, she noticed how attractive the red-headed detective was. His shaggy rusty hair covered his ears and swooped across his forehead, while his beard was light enough it was almost impossible to see. He was taller than her, which she noticed from when he answered the door, and she had to look up to meet his gaze. Even though he came off a little nerdy, he was definitely out of her league. And now he thought she wasn't into men because of the way she worded her question. She had meant it to be playful. Instead, she seemed to be offended.

"I'm into men," she all but blurted out. She closed her eyes and let out a silent groan.

"What?"

"I'm simply putting it out there. I'm into men, so would it likely be a male?"

"Likely. But like you pointed out, it could be a woman. Someone who has fallen in love with you through the bakery and knows your preferences and maybe feels jilted. And for the record, it doesn't matter to me, men, women, both, whoever you prefer, we're not discriminatory around here."

She opened her eyes and met his gaze. He was smirking at her, like he knew her gaff completely embarrassed her. "I'm glad to know I'm doing business with such a forward-thinking group." She moved to get up. This seemed as good a time as any to excuse herself before she embarrassed herself any further. But then something he said hit her. "Do you think my stalker has come to my shop regularly? As like a customer?"

"It's likely. I honestly wouldn't be surprised if they came in at least once a week. They might even be one of your regulars."

Tessa closed her eyes and mentally sorted through everyone who came in regularly. There were so many loyal customers. People came to her when they were hosting parties, when they needed treats for the office, or craving a sweet treat. For the past five years Cake Me Home Tonight had grown in reputation for having affordable cakes and pastries that didn't skimp on the taste or the looks. She had poured her heart and soul into that bakery, and was thrilled the first day they ever sold out of goods because of having so many customers. Word of mouth built her a loyal customer base, and some blogger posted about her shop on a travel website and now tourists come out of their way to visit her. To get a slice of her famous Victoria Sponge.

She tried to pick out one person who stood out to her. Someone who would look a little creepy. Someone who screamed, 'I'm a creepy stalker,' but no one stood out.

"Would it help if I made a list of my regulars? At least those whose names I know?"

"It very well could. If you got me a list, I could try to cross reference them with the CCTV footage, see if any of them are poking about in the night."

"Brilliant. I'll work on my list on Sunday. Is there anything else you need? It's nearing the middle of the night for me and I'm completely knackered. I'm going to head home and get some rest before my alarm reminds me it's time to head back to the kitchen for baking.

"Oh yes, please feel free to leave. I'm going to work on typing up my notes and uploading them into a shared folder for my partner to look at. First thing Monday morning, I will put in my request for that footage. It will take a couple of days to come in, but I would love for you to bring in the list of names and all the letters. And if you think of anything over the weekend that you think might help, no matter how small it may seem, jot it down on a notepad and bring those in as well. My partner will be in the office Monday afternoon and two heads are better than one, and we'll go over the case."

"Thank you." She stood from her chair and made her way to the door. "Thank you so much. I can't even thank you for everything you've already done. Knowing you're taking me seriously and going to work on figuring out who this is, I think I may actually sleep tonight."

"I'm glad I could do that, at least. Please keep my number close. If things escalate over the weekend, call me. If the stalker makes contact physically, call the police. My flat mate is a police officer here in Tower Hamlets, his name is Joseph McCleary. If you need to call, ask for him."

"McCleary. Got it."

"Have a good weekend, and I will see you on Monday."

"See you on Monday."

Tessa left the office and made her way down the stairs of the building to the street. She wasn't lying when she told him talking to him had eased her mind. The idea of her having a stalker still freaked her out but having Detective Moore tell her just receiving a few photographs and letters that did nothing to outright threaten her was nothing too worrisome helped take a weight off her shoulders. She could breathe slightly easier.

She walked down the sidewalk toward her home. She was glad the notorious detectives who took down an entire crime family lived in her borough. She hated the Tube. She enjoyed walking through the neighborhood.

She pulled her coat around her tighter as she walked. The wind had picked up and, combined with the mid-October temperature drop, she was regretting her choice of the lighter coat. As she neared the street with her shop, she could feel her pulse quicken. The nights were already longer, so the sun was disappearing over the horizon, streetlamps were lit, and the world was full of shadows. She never enjoyed being out after dark, but with the whole stalker business, she especially disliked being out.

She picked up her pace and breathed a sigh of relief when she could see the shop. Almost there.

As she walked down her familiar street, she looked across the street where whoever was taking pictures of her through her window had to be staked out. Right now, the street was filled with cars. It was Friday night and there were shops and restaurants that stayed open much later than hers. People bustled about, ducking in and out of storefronts and up and down the sidewalk. It was impossible for her to pick out anyone familiar. Anyone who could be watching her. Waiting for her to go upstairs and change. A shiver ran down her spine that had nothing to do with the cold.

Finally, she was at her shop. She pulled out her keys, letting herself in. As she shut the door, she glanced at the post basket and breathed a sigh of relief to see it was empty. Whoever delivered her daily letters obviously hadn't been there yet. Maybe they were busy. It was a Friday. They could be out on the town. On a date. With someone else forgetting all about her. She could only hope.

She locked the door and moved through the shop to the back stairs. Ascending them, she was exhausted. She didn't realize how much this whole situation was taking out of her. Unlocking the door to her flat. She smiled at the silence of the flat. It was a pleasant contrast to the chaotic bustle of her shop.

She walked into the kitchen, flicking on the kettle to make some tea. After devouring a small bag of crisps, also known as dinner, she prepared herself for bed. As she walked into her bedroom, she checked and double checked her curtains. A routine she started two nights ago after receiving those photos. Not one crack. No one would see into her sanctuary tonight. No one.

CHAPTER 3

JAMES

The cursor blinked on the screen of the computer as if mocking him. Blink. Blink. Blink. Nothing. Nothing. Nothing. James had been sitting at his computer for the better part of the hour, and he had checked his email, checked his social media, read the news headlines, but had yet to write one word of his best man speech. He didn't understand why he was having such a hard time putting words on paper. Patrick was his best friend, and after living with her for a year, Evie was as well. But why couldn't he find it in him to put anything down? Evie told him last night at dinner to just say something short and sweet. To stop putting so much pressure on himself. Told him to make it funny. Throw in some pop culture references.

But that was the problem. He didn't want to make jokes about their friendship. They meant everything to him. He wasn't close to anyone like he was to them. And how did you convey everything he felt about them into a brief speech? He sighed and ran his hands down his face. To this day, he still could see their battered bodies in their hospital beds after they were rescued from the Fitzgerald lair. The images seared on his brain. The relief when he learned they would be okay was probably the strongest feeling he had ever felt.

Being able to convey that all in one brief speech? Impossible. Maybe he would simply have to write a speech for the masses and a separate letter for Patrick and Evie to read later. He perked up. That was exactly what he would do. First, he would write the speech for the crowd and get it over with. Get Evie off his back.

Then, once the wedding was over and they were on holiday, he would work on the longer letter and deliver it to them when they got home.

Brilliant idea, James. Well done, chap, he thought to himself as he prepared himself to type. As soon as he pressed down the first keys, mercifully filling the blank page he had been staring at for what felt like forever, his phone buzzed, showing an incoming text. He sighed. It was probably Evie asking him about his progress. Not even twenty-four hours since he left her flat after dinner and a movie night, a Saturday night tradition, they continued even after they moved out of their shared flat, and she had to check in on his progress.

He picked up his phone and did a double take when he noticed it was not from Evie but from an unknown number. He frowned and opened the message.

UNKNOWN: Hi this is Tessa. The woman with a stalker. Wanted to remind you before you went in tomorrow morning I live above my shop. CCTV footage from one location only.

James smiled. Tessa. Ms. Lopez. His new client. Even though his weekend had been filled with helping Patrick finish his list for the wedding and movie night, Ms. Lopez had never been far from his mind. He worried things would escalate over the weekend. If the person was truly stalking her, would they have seen her go into his office and decide now was the time to act? Her being on his mind had absolutely nothing to do with how beautiful she looked even after working a long day in the bakery, or how when she smiled, her entire face seemed to light up...

He shook his head, banishing those thoughts from his mind, and answered Ms. Lopez.

JAMES: Thank you for reminding me. My memory isn't as bad as you're making it out. I had remembered. I'm not that old.

He sent the message and then immediately wrote another.

JAMES: Quiet weekend?

He set his phone aside and turned back to his document, working on his speech. His phone buzzed before he could write more than three words.

TESSA: Complete opposite. My manager is still on holiday, so I worked a full day at the shop yesterday. And today we opened the shop for a special event. I'm completely knackered.

He smiled.

JAMES: I didn't realise your shop did special events. When do you sleep?

TESSA: Right now. It seems sleep comes when I can no longer hold my eyes open while I watch the telly after work. Special events are a recent development. May need to rethink. We hosted a six-year old's fairy party today. Never. Again.

JAMES: Oh, come on, it can't have been that bad.

TESSA: Detective Moore, I have sprinkles in places there should not be sprinkles.

James blushed at the image of sprinkles in inappropriate places.

JAMES: James. Call me James.

TESSA: Tessa

James smiled down at his phone. Tessa. He didn't know why it thrilled him to be on a first name basis with her. She was a client. And one he had only met once. He shouldn't be this involved with her already.

JAMES: Any escalation this weekend with our mutual friend?

TESSA: No. In fact, I have received nothing from them this weekend at all. Is that a good thing? Has he given up?

JAMES: There's no way of knowing. Even if we're entering a lull, it will still be good to figure out who this person is.

TESSA: I agree. My manager will be back from their holiday tomorrow. I will bring everything I have tomorrow around one. Will that work for you?

JAMES: It will.

TESSA: Well, I better sign off. My eyes are struggling to remain open. See you tomorrow?

JAMES: Sleep well, Tessa. See you tomorrow.

James set his phone aside and laughed a little. He wondered if all of their conversations would go that smoothly?

"You've got quite the goofy grin on your face? Meet a bird this weekend, Jimmy?"

James nearly leapt out of his skin before whipping around to see his roommate, Joe, leaning against the kitchen counter, arms folded across his chest. A big grin spread across his face.

"Fucking hell, Joe. When the hell did you get in?"

"About a minute ago. You were completely absorbed in whatever you were doing on your phone to notice. Did you meet someone? Because if you did, good for you."

"No. I was only messaging with a client."

"Bullshit. You don't look all moony eyed at your phone when you're simply chatting with a client. This is something more."

"I promise you, it's only a client. She came in as we were closing on Friday. Stalker. We were arranging our meeting tomorrow afternoon."

Joe shook his head as he stood up from the counter and began unbuttoning his uniform shirt. "Sure, keep telling yourself that. I give it a week before you're no longer just client and detective and you've got her bent over your desk. Mark my words."

"Fuck off. You know we don't date our clients. We keep things completely professional."

Now Joe truly laughed. "Sure, you do. I think I'm in a wedding in a couple of weeks that completely contradicts that statement."

"That's different."

"How? Evie was a client, wasn't she? And then Patrick went and fell in love with her. And now they're getting married. Please explain to me how it's different. I'm waiting."

James opened his mouth to tell him *exactly* how it was different, but faltered. It really wasn't different, was it? Evie may have fallen into their lives by accident, but before she and Patrick fell in love, she was a client. A nonpaying client, but still technically a client.

"Fine. It's not different. But I am not Patrick. Tessa is a client, and nothing more. Now, where were you all weekend?"

"Oh, no. We're not changing the subject. I want to talk more about how you're apparently on a first name basis with this client."

"Were you working all weekend, or did you meet someone? I don't think I've seen you around the flat all weekend."

"Both. I worked over night on Friday, but went to Clint's flat when I got off. I was there the rest of the weekend."

"Clint, eh? That's two weekends in a row with him. Things getting a little serious for you two?"

"Nah. Well, at least on my end. He may be getting a little more attached than I am. I will probably have to end things between us soon. Which is a shame, since he lives so much closer to the station than I do."

"Is that why you're dating him? You don't have to go as far to get home?"

"My primary goal in life is to not have to ride in some weirdo's Uber at four in the morning. You know this. And how did we get on the subject of my complete disaster of a love life? We were talking about you following in Patrick's footsteps and falling in love with someone who has come to you to protect them."

James shook his head. "You're reaching and you know it. Hey, I have a question for you. If someone came into the precinct with letters that had been delivered to them that were stalkery but not threatening, what would you do?"

Joe walked over to the couch and flopped down on it. "Well, if the letters were not threatening, we wouldn't be able to do much of anything, unfortunately. Stalking is a crime, so I would probably take the person's information and ask to read a letter or two, maybe make a report to create a paper trail. But beyond that, I wouldn't be able to do anything."

"At what point would the police be able to do something?"

"When the issue became so serious that the letter receiver was in danger. If the letters started having obvious threats. Or if the author of the letters made physical contact with her. Is this your stalking case?"

James nodded. "Yes. She told me she had already talked to the police prior to seeking our help. And it went just as you said. They couldn't help her. In fact, they laughed her off, told her it was probably a prank. But what's bothering me is that when it escalated, she didn't go back to the police. She came to us, thinking you wouldn't be able to do anything."

"In what way did it escalate?"

"Her stalker has graduated from leaving fairly harmless letters in her post to taking pictures of her through her windows from the street."

Joe sat up on the couch and leaned forward, resting his elbows on his knees. "Any threats attached to these photographs?"

"None. Only the photos and the same non-threatening letters."

"Well, we probably wouldn't have done anything if she had brought those in. Other than maybe to send someone out to patrol the area the following night to see if we could spot anyone suspicious. Where does she live?"

"She lives above her bake shop, Cake Me Home Tonight."

"Wait. Your new client owns Cake Me Home Tonight?"

"She does."

"She makes the best Bakewell tarts in the whole fucking city. That's it. I'm done taking the piss. You need to marry that girl like yesterday."

"Joe."

"If you get married, would I be able to get a discount on baked goods, you think?"

"How often are you going to her shop?"

"I'm there at least once a week."

"You're a walking stereotype, mate."

"Fuck off."

"Can we get back to the case?"

"Fine. Knowing the area her shop is, depending on the time of day, it would be damn near impossible to tell who was there staring at her shop and who was there simply going about their business. That's a busy part of town."

"I know. I'm going to put a request in tomorrow to get the CCTV footage of the street to see if I can get anything from that. But like you said, with how busy it is, I'm worried I'll get nothing."

"And a lot of it really depends on the location of the camera on the street to her storefront."

"Exactly. I'm afraid I may have gotten her hopes up too early that I could figure out who is delivering her letters."

"I'm sure she knows it's a long shot. If she's a born and bred Londoner, she knows how shitty some of the CCTV footage could be."

"Yeah, I'm sure you're right."

"Of course I'm right. I'm always bloody right. And now I'm going to go take a shower and pass the fuck out, because I am on the morning shift tomorrow."

"A year and a half and they still can't even things out over there?"

"It's fucking insane, mate. We're still short staffed after getting rid of all the corrupt bastards. And they still can't get us on a consistent schedule. Bloody exhausting. Cheers mate."

Joe got off the couch and walked to the back to the back of the flat to where his room and the bathroom were.

After he left, James turned back to his computer and tried to work on his speech. But he couldn't get a cute girl with purple glasses out of his mind, causing him to be distracted the rest of the night.

CHAPTER 4

TESSA

"Guess who's back! Which means it's time for you to get the hell out of this kitchen and out of this shop."

Tessa smiled as she finished drying the bowls she was holding. Freddie, her best friend, business partner, and manager of her shop, was home. "I'm finishing up in here, and then I plan on leaving. I've got to meet that detective I was telling you about."

Freddie let himself into the kitchen wearing a frown. He looked as meticulously put together as he had every day since they met in Year 2. Always wearing grey pants, even when he wasn't in school uniform, a button-down shirt with a jumper pulled over and his dark brown hair styled just right, he was the yin to her yang. Logical where she was emotional. Organized to her disarray. When she talked about opening Cake Me Home Tonight, he took care of lining up the business side of things, explaining to her how everything worked, showing her how he had organized everything, while she worried about the baking side of things. Their twenty years of friendship were the most precious thing to her. He was the sibling she always craved.

"I'm so glad you went to the detective."

"I'm glad you found their information for me. I never would have thought to go to them without your nudge. So, thank you."

"You're welcome. It makes me uneasy you are receiving these letters in the first place. But when you called me and told me he was taking pictures of you without knowing? That was the last straw. You mentioned something about CCTV footage in your texts?"

"Yes, he was putting in a request this morning to get the footage from our street. He's hoping it will be a lead."

"Are you going to view the footage now?"

"No, I'm going over there to bring him all the letters and photographs I've received."

"Good. Maybe he can make sense of them. I can't believe the fucking police refused to do anything."

"Yes, you and me both."

She set the bowl on the shelf and used the rag to wipe down the counters.

"How did the birthday party go yesterday?" Freddie asked with a little apprehension. It was his idea to open up to special events. And prior to this weekend, it was mostly old ladies who wanted to come in with their friends and decorate cakes and gossip over tea. This was the first child's birthday party, and when he realized it had been booked for his weekend away, he offered to cancel his holiday. She had turned him down.

"How do you imagine it went?"

"Little girls high on sugar, swinging from the rafters while screaming, 'More cake, Mummy! More cake!'"

Tessa laughed, taking off her apron and hanging it on the hook near her baking station. "You're not too far off. It was chaos. So many tears. I had the wrong color icing, even though it was exactly what they had requested, and the birthday girl was inconsolable and the mum kept acting like I was deliberately ruining her princess's special day. By the end of the party, I felt I needed a strong drink, and you know I don't drink."

Freddie winced. "I'm so sorry. I promise, no more little girl birthdays. Only old ladies and tea from now on."

"It's fine. We can do another one, but maybe those are a two-person operation party, yeah?"

"Done. I will double and triple check my calendar before we book another to make sure I am in town."

"How was your holiday?"

"Exactly what I needed. I could relax and read a book, and I took in the new art installation at The Louvre."

"And you could get she who will not be named off of your mind?"

"We can name her. It doesn't hurt as much anymore. Maybe it's a good thing Alice broke our engagement two weeks before the wedding. I rather enjoyed going on our honeymoon alone. Lots of time for self-reflection."

"I'm glad. I'm still sorry it worked out the way it did. I'm almost glad I never finished writing my best man speech. I was always stuck on something nice to say about Alice."

"You two never got on. I should have seen the writing on the wall. If someone can't get along with my sister, they're not worth marrying. That is the lesson I've learned from this whole endeavor."

"I'm just glad she called it off before I made the massive cake she wanted."

"Honestly, missing out on the cake is my one regret from this total fiasco. I was really looking forward to it. The vanilla sponge with the mango? Probably my favorite thing you've ever made."

"What would you say if I make one up for our Sunday brunch this weekend? But a miniature version of it?"

"I would say I love you and I don't know what I would do without you. I'll make veggie omelets to balance out the cake. Make us feel less guilty."

"Deal. Now, I must run. I told him I would be there at one. I'll be cutting it close." She grabbed her coat off the hook next to her apron, pulling it on. Then she grabbed her messenger bag, slinging it across her chest until it rested against her hip.

"Yes, good luck. I hope he's able to catch this bastard. Are you sure you don't want to come stay at mine for a while, just until he's caught?"

"I'm sure. I will not let this prick chase me from my home."

"I love that about you. Not letting some creepy nutter get you down. Now go. I have cake to sell."

Tessa gave Freddie a quick hug and dashed through the back door. If she left through the front, she was sure to stop and talk to whatever customers were currently in the shop, and she didn't have time to stop and talk to Mrs. Haberdash about her grandchildren.

She moved down the street and shivered. The sun was out, but the temperature did not reflect the vision of the beautiful day. The breeze cut through her light coat. She really needed to pull out the thicker one and give up the hope of warmer weather sticking around just a tad longer. She should fully give herself over to the inevitability of winter. At least the sun was out. It could have been rainy.

Luckily, the walk to the detective agency didn't take long. She opened the door to the building and sighed as her glasses fogged up. Easily the most annoying thing as the weather grew colder. Once she could see again, she walked to the office and knocked on the door. She glanced down at her watch. Right on time. Her shoulders relaxed. It was a point of pride for her to be on time everywhere she went.

"Come in."

She turned the knob and pushed the door open. As she stepped into the small office, she was a little taken aback. She had assumed she was going to be meeting with James. She'd forgotten he had told her his partner was going to be there. She didn't know why her stomach dropped in disappointment at the thought she wouldn't be alone with James, but it did.

"Hello."

"Tessa, this is my partner, Patrick Miller. He's going to be working on the case as well."

"Nice to meet you, Ms. Lopez. I'm sorry to hear about your situation, but we're going to work this out."

"Actually, we've already met. I'm making your cake for your wedding. Please call me Tessa."

"That's right! I'm so sorry. I can't believe I didn't remember you. You make the best cakes. Evelyn gets this dreamy look on her face whenever she is on a video chat with her mum and they talk about the cake."

Tessa laughed, "It's alright. You were only at the initial cake testing, and honestly, the cake is the genuine star of the shop. It's understandable you wouldn't remember me."

"We've put in the CCTV request this morning, and they have told me we will get it by the end of the week," James explained, gesturing to the empty seat in front of the desks, bringing them back to the reason they were there.

She moved to the chair and sat down. She pulled her messenger bag around to rest it in her lap. She felt awkward with everyone's eyes on her. "That is good, right? Do you know how far from my shop the camera is situated?"

"We don't. But we know your street has at least two cameras. We requested all the camera footage for the last month. Unless the letters started arriving earlier than that?" James asked.

"No, they started arriving about three weeks ago? Two and a half. I have them all here." She reached into her messenger bag and pulled out the manila envelope she put together the night before with all the letters and photographs and handed it over to James.

James took the envelope and opened it, pulling all the contents out. "Holy shit, did they deliver a letter every day for the last two weeks?"

"Yes, nearly."

He let out a low whistle and handed part of the stack to Patrick. The room was silent except for the rustling of papers, which made Tessa feel even more awkward. Should she go? Was she expected to stay?

"The author of these letters isn't very chatty, is he?" Patrick commented, not looking up from his letters.

"No, he is not."

"These letters only have one or two lines. No punctuation, but otherwise perfect grammar. Which, on the one hand this doesn't give us a lot to work with as far as identifying factors. On the other hand, the style could be something we could easily identify."

James handed Patrick one picture. "Patrick, does it look like they took directly these photos across the street from the flat?"

Patrick took a second and studied the picture. "Could very well be. The angle is pretty direct. We'll scrutinize the pictures and see if we can pinpoint where exactly they took them."

"You'll be able to tell only from the picture?"

"Maybe. We'll also need to go to the shop and confirm. Stand where he probably stood. Things like that," James explained.

"Brilliant."

"If we can work out the angle, then when we look at the CCTV footage, it may be possible for us to identify the photographer. Which could be another way to identify him if we can't get a clear picture off of the front of your building," Patrick explained further.

"What are the odds of us getting a clear picture of the letter writer?"

"I'm going to be very conservative about our odds and say it's about 50/50. We could get really lucky and find the footage and show it to you and you'll be able to tell us exactly who it is, and case closed. Or we could get the footage and it will be clear footage and you'll not recognize them, and that will add a little extra work, because we'll have a clear picture we can ask around with. Bad news would be we don't get a clear picture at all, and we'll be back here where we started," James explained.

Tessa nodded. "Right. I have also included a list of all my regulars who I could identify by name. I don't know how much it will help, but I wanted to give it to you, too."

"This will help, thank you," James turned his gaze to her, and smiled.

Their eyes locked, and Tessa's heart quickened. What was wrong with her? Why was this happening? She was paying him to find her stalker. She wasn't here to find a boyfriend. *Maybe after they solved the case...*she shook her head to clear that thought away.

She wasn't here to find a boyfriend. Full-stop. She was here to get rid of the creep, leaving her brief letters in her post and taking spy shots of her from her bedroom window. Which when she laid it out like that, it seemed rather silly she was hiring them at all. She could save her money and let this whole thing fizzle out. Why did she let Freddie talk her into this?

"Do you have everything you need?" She spoke up, startled at how loud it came out. She was nervous. She needed to go home and get some sleep and wait for James and Patrick to do their jobs.

James looked down at the pile in front of him and then back at her. "I think so. Thank you again for bringing everything in. We'll be in touch later this week, once we have all the CCTV footage."

Tessa stood up and hurried to the door. "Thank you again. I look forward to your call."

James stood from the desk and quickly moved around it, opening the door for her. "Have a good night, Tessa."

As she left the building, all Tessa could think about was how James' hand lingered on her arm as she walked out the door.

CHAPTER 5

JAMES

"She's cute," Patrick commented after the door to the office closed.

"Is she? I hadn't noticed."

James walked back to his desk and picked up the papers and pointedly looked at them.

"Bullshit. You have absolutely noticed. You went all heart eyes the second she walked into this room."

James scoffed. "I did not."

"You did. I didn't think you could have had a goofy look on your face, but as soon as she walked in, you looked all dopey."

"Fuck off."

"I'm sorry, I don't mean to take the mick, but seriously, it's okay if you think she's cute. You're allowed to have a crush. In fact, I encourage it. Have a crush. Have several crushes. For the last several years, you've become quite the workaholic. When we close this case, ask her out for a drink or something. Pretty sure if I tell Evelyn, you have a crush on the cake lady, she'll be completely behind this match. Especially if it means baked goods will start arriving on Saturday nights."

"You're impossible."

"I'm optimistic."

James shook his head and focused on the letters in front of him. "It doesn't matter. We don't date clients."

"The future Mrs. Evelyn Miller would like to disagree with that statement."

"She wasn't really a client. We both know that. We don't date paying clients."

"By the end of the week, we'll have solved her case and then she won't be a paying client. Then you should ask her to be your date for the wedding."

"I thought you and Evelyn finalized the details over the weekend?"

"Well, she's already coming to the reception. We offered her a plate since she has to bring the cake in and set it up. But we could have her sit at your table. You know what?" he pulled out his phone and started texting. "I'm going to have Evelyn put her at your table. We can move someone around."

"Don't bother Evelyn with something like this. She's probably very busy."

"It's afternoon. She doesn't teach in the afternoon. She has office hours. I'm sure she's sitting in her office working on research or wedding plans or something. This is not a bother."

Patrick's phone chirped, signaling an incoming message. "And she has agreed it's a good idea. And she wanted me to tell you to wait until after the wedding to sleep with her, otherwise if things go pear-shaped, she doesn't want the cake lady to fuck up the cake as revenge."

"Nice. Very nice, Patrick. Can we please move on and discuss the case? You know the whole reason she's come into our lives in the first place?"

"Fine, spoil sport. Looking at the letters, I can't really tell if this is someone who knows her really well, or someone who is only casually acquainted with her."

"I agree. When she mentioned she was getting letters daily, I thought this would be someone with a lot of time on their hands, but if all they're doing is writing one sentence on a page and delivering it through a letterbox, they honestly don't need that much time. This person could spend one afternoon making a batch of letters and portion them out to be delivered throughout the week."

"It's the photography that takes some time."

"But not much more. If they know her schedule, they could easily time it to be at her window when she would change and then leave. Print the photos at home and then deliver."

"But if they didn't know her schedule, he or she would have to spend a lot of time on the pavement waiting for her to appear."

James sighed. "It all comes down to whether we think this is someone who knows her really well, or someone who barely knows her."

"Pretty much."

"Statistically, a person who stalks a woman like this is someone who knows her."

"True. Write this down: exes, jilted lovers, unrequited love. We need to ask Tessa if there is anyone who falls into these categories. We need their names so we can scour their social media and get images to compare to the CCTV footage."

"We should also add angry customers, loyal customers who seem a bit too loyal, and business competition."

The door to the office opened and Evelyn walked through. She gave the boys a smile as she shut the door and made her way into the small space. She leaned over and greeted James with a quick peck on the cheek, and then greeted Patrick with a proper kiss before settling into her chair.

"What are you doing here? Aren't you supposed to be keeping those Uni students in line?" Patrick asked.

"No one signed up for my office hours today, and once I got your text about James and our baker, I needed to come down here and get some more information."

James narrowed his eyes. "Why would you need more information?"

"Because it appears you're crushing on my baker, and I need to make sure you won't scare her away. I need her cake, James. It is very important."

"I won't scare your baker away. You'll get your precious cake."

"Good. Because her cake is life."

"You're being ridiculous."

"I am the bride. I'm allowed to be ridiculous. Now, tell me about her case. Is it pretty easy? Someone stealing from the shop?"

Patrick held up one of the tamer pictures. "Someone is stalking the creator of your new favorite food."

Evelyn reached over and grabbed the picture out of his hand. "No! Poor Tessa! Any leads?"

"None yet. We're waiting for footage and we're making lists of suspects," James explained.

"Have you looked into her business partner?" Evie asked.

"She has a business partner?" Patrick leaned forward, resting his elbows on his desk. "Did she tell you she had a business partner?"

James shook his head. "First, I'm hearing of one."

"Oh, so, apparently, she and her best friend from childhood went into business together. He handles the business side of things, and she handles the baking. He was engaged to get married and then poof! Two weeks ago, the fiancée dumps his ass like a week before the wedding."

Patrick looked at her, confusion written all over his face. "How on earth do you even know all of this?"

"I'm an American and I have no boundaries. Anyway, apparently the fiancée never really liked Tessa. She would say all kinds of rude things under her breath. Tessa told me she was pretty sure she was jealous of how close she and the partner are."

"All of this came up during your cake tasting session?" James asked, bewildered.

"No. So, don't judge me, but Cake Me Home Tonight isn't very far from both our flat and the University. It's way too close to the University for my waistline to still fit into my dress in a couple weeks. I've been stopping in on my lunch hour at least once a week since our tasting two months ago, and Tessa and I have been eating together. Or sometimes just having a cuppa and a biscuit and calling it lunch."

"You're friends with our baker?" Patrick was incredulous.

"Yes. I like her." She swiveled and pointed an accusing finger at James. "And if you, fuck things up with her and I can no longer have tea with one of the few girlfriends I have managed to make here I will not be held responsible for my actions."

James held his hands up in surrender. "Oi. Let's not get ahead of ourselves, yeah? I will admit, I find her attractive. The few times we interacted have been pleasant, but I have no intention of trying to start a romantic relationship with her. Not as long as she's a client."

"Ah hah! You admit you have a crush on her and have an interest in asking her out!" Patrick shouted, pointing his finger at him.

"Oh, my God. Are we back in secondary school? Are you going to sing rhyming songs about me and Tessa in a fucking tree?"

"K-I-S-S-I-N-G!" Evie and Patrick sang loudly through laughter.

The three of them dissolved into hysterics after that, and James' chest was warm, and his heart grew full. He loved his friends, and he knew they had to move on to the next stage of their life as they were getting married in a few weeks, which meant they wanted their own space, and a space to grow at that. Even though he knew all of this, and it made sense on a logical level, he missed the days of the three of them crammed in the small flat, shouting and laughing over stupid shit. Saturday nights were nice, and he held them close to his chest, never making other plans on a Saturday night but nothing could compare to a random Wednesday when all of them would be home from work, arguing over dishes and who the better Darrin on *Bewitched* was.

"Are you two done taking the piss? Can we please move on?"

"Yes, yes, sorry." Patrick took a deep breath, and wiped under his eyes. "She has a business partner with a jealous ex. This all seems very promising."

"But are we looking at the partner or the ex? Who looks good for it?"

"That's the thing, isn't it? If we could get this person to make some threats, this would be a lot easier to figure out. Or be a little more aggressive in their interest in her. These are all very bland for stalking notes. So, I think it could be either or neither at this point."

"How long has she been getting letters?" Evie asked, pulling her feet up under her.

"Two weeks daily, except this weekend."

"Her partner was on his honeymoon this weekend, alone. If he was out of town, he couldn't deliver letters."

Patrick clicked his pen and wrote something down on his legal pad. "Business partner is looking fantastic right now."

"Motive?" James asked, leaning back in his chair.

"Unrequited love. His fiancée guessed correctly, he loves her, she only sees him as a friend. He tries to get in her good graces by passing on these flattering letters, testing the waters. They don't go as well as he would like, and so he escalates to taking photos, but not for malicious reasons. He feels they could be a compliment. He does like that color on her. He goes away for the weekend, and obviously can't deliver letters while he's gone," Patrick explained.

"Sounds plausible. But I'm also liking the ex-fiancée for this. She has a motive. And maybe she wants to scare Tessa into wanting to quit or move or something," James pointed out.

"Not as strong a motive, and really doesn't fit in with the timeline. Why would she stop writing letters for a weekend after consistently delivering them every day?"

"I don't know. Maybe you're right. Maybe it is the business partner," James turned to Evie. "What's his name? Maybe we can get a search going on him and see if he has anything suspicious."

"Freddie, but I don't know his last name."

"That should be enough to go on. We can also pull business licenses and get a last name from that." Patrick pulled out a pen so he could take notes. "This is a good lead. Thank you for being a nosey American and becoming friends with our cake lady."

"You're welcome."

James' phone chimed, and he pulled it out. It was a text from Tessa. He frowned. He wasn't expecting to hear from her. Maybe she thought of something and wanted to let him know. He opened up the message, and it was a picture. His heart skipped a beat.

"So, I'm thinking maybe we can scratch Mr. Honeymoon on his own, off our list of suspects."

"Why?"

James turned his phone to show the other occupants of the room. Patrick immediately leaned forward and grabbed the phone out of his hand to get a better look.

"Oh, my God," Evie gasped, bringing her hands to her mouth.

James didn't need the phone in front of him to know what she was reacting to. The image seared itself into his brain. It was a picture of Tessa leaving their office on Friday night, coat wrapped tightly around her body, looking somewhere to the left of the camera. But that wasn't the shocking part. No, the shocking part was someone had taken a red pen and put a large X across her face and scrawled, "YOU'VE MADE A MISTAKE," across the photo.

CHAPTER 6

TESSA

JAMES: Are you safe?

Tessa stared at the message from James for several minutes, debating how to answer. Was she safe? Technically, she was. She was not in any immediate danger. Did she *feel* safe, though? That's where things got fuzzy. She knew logically she should be fine. She was in her flat, Freddie was downstairs, this person had not made themselves physically known. They were still contacting her through letters in her post. However, this felt different. This wasn't someone perched outside her house where they knew she would be. This was someone following her around the city.

Taking pictures of her.

And now they're threatening her. Because she sought help? But was it a threat? 'You've Made a Mistake' wasn't a direct threat against her. It was more of a warning? A warning of what she didn't know, but she was less anxious if she thought of it as a warning and not a threat, so she was going to choose to think of it as a warning. For now.

TESSA: I'm fine.

JAMES: That doesn't answer my question.

TESSA: I'm safe. As far as I know.

JAMES: Evie told us about Freddie and his fiancée. Any chance it's either of them?

Tessa was completely taken by surprise. Freddie and Alice were suspects? She shook her head. Impossible. Freddie was her best friend, and he would never do something like this. Besides, he was out of town on Friday. There was no way he could have followed her to the detective agency. He was in Paris enjoying his honeymoon with himself.

Alice hated her, but why would she go through all of this trouble? Tessa was pretty sure she didn't blame her for the dissolution of her relationship with Freddie. Unless Freddie really downplayed her role in the breakup.

Tessa thought back on every interaction she had with Alice and tried to determine if it was an interaction where they would have been at odds. But nothing seemed out of the ordinary. Most brunches, Alice kept to herself. She rarely came into the shop, citing she was trying to keep her figure, and the two of them spent no time alone together if they could help it. On the rare occasion Alice and she were alone together, Alice would often comment about how she better remember her place. Whatever that meant. It was easier for her to avoid being alone with her.

TESSA: I don't think it could be. Freddie was in Paris for the last week, and honestly, I don't think Alice could be arsed to care this much about me.

JAMES: We should still look at them. Make sure they have strong alibis. It always helps to mark off the people closest and then expand the search from there.

She bit her lip. Of course. She watched enough crime shows to know they always look at those closest to the victim first. But the thought of having to investigate Freddie felt wrong to her. Really wrong.

TESSA: I'm sure it's protocol, but I promise you, Freddie can't be the person doing this. He would never do something like this.

JAMES: Then it will be a quick investigation.

Tessa let out a growl of frustration. Apparently, there was no talking them out of looking into Freddie.

TESSA: You're just going to be wasting your time.

JAMES: I'm just going to call it being thorough and move on.

TESSA: You're very frustrating

JAMES: I'm going to take that as a compliment. Trust me. You'll appreciate us being thorough.

TESSA: The CCTV footage will clear him and prove he was out of town all weekend.

JAMES: Which is when the letters stopped. Fits the timeline.

TESSA: Now you're contradicting yourself. Whoever took the latest picture of me was in town on Friday. He left Thursday night. It can't be him.

JAMES: What are Freddie and Alice's full names?

TESSA: Freddie Kaur and Alice Lewis.

JAMES: Great. Leave the investigating to the professionals.

Tessa glared down at her phone, frowning. And instead of responding to the last message in a way she wanted to, she instead acted like the grown up she was and put her phone in her pocket. She needed to take a break from James. Obviously, they would not agree on the matter, and arguing with him was just going to make things worse. She was paying him to solve the case of who is stalking her. Why would she hinder the investigation? Because deep down somewhere inside of her, she worried about what they might dig up. What if it was Freddie?

She shook her head. "Stop it, Tessa. You're letting this mess with your head," she muttered to herself.

She glanced at the clock. It was only three. The shop was still open, Freddie was down there with Mariel, and she really needed to keep her mind off everything. She slipped on her shoes and walked down the back stairs into the kitchen. Clean, exactly how she left it two hours before. She pushed her way into the shop, and it was bustling. Mondays were not a typically busy day, but now that they were firmly in autumn, her pumpkin flavored items were becoming hard to keep on the shelf. It was a risk, making pumpkin flavored items when they weren't super popular here in the UK. However, she wanted to take a page from the Americans and try something new for the season. Apparently, the risk was paying off.

She did a quick glance into the display case and noticed even with two hours until close; they were running low on most of the items. She would have to make sure she baked more supply tomorrow.

"What are you doing here?" Freddie asked from behind her. "You're supposed to have your feet up and reading a book before finally calling it a night as the sun sets."

"I know, but I was feeling antsy, and I didn't really want to be alone."

"Fuck. Another one? When the hell did it get delivered? I was here ever since you left."

"I found it in the post when I got back. I checked this morning when I opened, and it wasn't there."

"So, you're telling me this fucker delivered the letter in broad daylight, with me and Mariel working five feet away?"

Tessa nodded.

"He's getting bolder, Tess. I don't like this. What was in the letter this time?"

"A photo. Of me leaving the Miller and Moore agency on Friday. With vaguely threatening words scrawled across it."

Freddie brought his hands up to his hair, grabbing it by the fistful before dropping his arms back to his sides. "Did you tell the detectives?"

"I did."

"Great. After I close up shop, I'm going to go grab a few things and I'm going to stay on your couch for a couple of days."

"You are not!"

"I am. I would feel better if I did. They're escalating, Tess. It's getting worse. Now they're following you around town? What the fuck is up with that?"

"I'm an adult, Freddie. I can take care of myself. I don't need you going all toxic masculinity on me. I'll be fine."

Freddie sighed. "Fine. But maybe you should sign up for one of those self-defense classes you've always talked about wanting to take. It might help you feel safer, and it would definitely ease my mind knowing you could drop a man twice your size."

Tessa smiled. This is what she was trying to tell James. There is no way Freddie is the culprit. Why would he be offering to sleep on her couch or suggest she get better at defending herself if he were the one causing the mischief?

To throw you off his scent, the small voice in the back of her head piped up, sounding an awful lot like James. She shook her head to clear it. There would be none of that.

"I'll think about it. The problem is they're all after normal people get off of work and I'm well on my way into the middle of my night."

"I'm sure they have some sessions for people who work the night shift or just stay at home during the day. We'll investigate it. Listen, this conversation isn't over, but it looks like Mariel needs some backup. What the hell did you make that has everyone swarming in here like they're going to miss out if they don't get it?"

"Nothing out of the ordinary. I really leaned into the pumpkin spice craze this year and made pumpkin bars. Those are new."

"Pumpkin bars. I bet that's it." He leaned over and placed a kiss on her forehead. "It's going to be okay, Tess. I promise you. You've hired the best detectives in London. They will find whoever is doing this. I know it."

And they think it's you, she thought as she watched him move back to the counter to help Mariel. She smiled a bit forlornly. How well could you really know a person? She didn't know Freddie and Alice's problems were so bad that she was going to call off the wedding until after the wedding had been called off. The problem was, she was too trusting. She should learn to be more suspicious.

But he was not wrong. Miller and Moore were the best in London. Ever since they took down the Fitzgerald family and cleaned out all the corrupt cops in their borough, they had been all anyone could talk about. Their faces were a mainstay in the tabloids and news during the trial. Back then, she thought they were very attractive men, but thought nothing beyond that. And then she landed the coveted role of making the wedding cake for Patrick Miller and his American fiancée, Evelyn Stevenson, a key witness to the case. It was going to be the biggest wedding of the year. And she was going to make their cake. And then she and Evie became friends. Never in her life did she think she would hire them to solve a case. These things didn't happen to people like her. They happened to more interesting people.

"Good afternoon, Ms. Lopez. You're not usually in the shop at this time of day."

Tessa turned around and smiled when she noticed one of her favorite customers. "Fraser! You're here later than usual. And unless I'm mistaken, it's not Wednesday."

"Yeah, me mum heard about pumpkin bars in the shop from one of her friends, and she sent me out to pick some up before you sold out. Grabbed the last two. These are new, aren't they?"

"Yes, I made them on a whim this morning. Didn't know they would be so popular."

"Ah, well, word is getting around if me mum heard about them."

"Well, I guess I'll have to keep them on for a bit, then. How is your mum?"

"She has her good days and her bad days. She's had a good week so far. She's hoping to make it into the shop on Wednesday for tea. She had me block off a full hour in my schedule that morning. Will you be making pumpkin scones again? I remember those were a favorite of hers last autumn."

"I will be. Tell her I'll save one just for her, so she doesn't have to worry about rushing in here."

Fraser smiled widely, his eyes lighting up. "Oh, that will be wonderful. If she can't make it on Wednesday morning, I'll swing by and pick it up for her after I finish work. Though she is determined to make it. She misses her chats with you."

"I miss her, too. Please send my love to her."

"I will, Ms. Lopez. I best be going. She's going to feel like she's won the lottery when I get home and tell her we scored the last two pumpkin bars. I'll be seeing you."

"Be seeing you Fraser."

Tessa watched as he pushed his way through the crowd and out the front door. Fraser and his mum were some of her first customers, always coming in on Wednesday mornings to have tea and eat scones. She looked forward to seeing them every week. And then his mum grew ill and their visits grew infrequent. Fraser still stopped in once a week to get a treat for his mum, but she didn't get to see him very often because he usually stopped in after work.

She closed her eyes and sighed. Both of their names were on the list she gave to James this afternoon, which meant Patrick and James were looking into them. It made her so angry. Thinking about everyone she loved on the list, she really hoped Patrick and James hit brick walls with everyone on them, and once they got the CCTV footage, she would see a perfect stranger leaving her notes. The idea of someone she cared for stalking her devastated her more than if it were a stranger doing the stalking. She could trust no one again if that were to be the case.

CHAPTER 7

JAMES

"They're here," Patrick spoke up as soon as James walked into the office on Thursday morning.

"A day early, they're getting quicker."

Patrick shot him a look. "I'll forward you the files. We can both go through them and make notes to go over together later."

It had been a long week. After texting her on Monday, concerned about her safety, James hadn't heard from Tessa the rest of the week. Looking back over the texts, he was pretty sure she was annoyed at him. Which was fair. He was a bit of a tosser there at the end. At first, he was okay not hearing from her. She was only a client, after all. But as the week progressed, he tried to think of an excuse to message her, but really couldn't think of any.

With her case paused until they could get the CCTV footage, he had kept busy with the dozens of other cases they were juggling at the moment. They closed three in the last few days.

He pulled out his phone and opened up the text thread with Tessa. He hesitated for a brief minute before typing.

JAMES: CCTV footage arrived

TESSA: (...)

James frowned. He could see her typing as if she were going to respond. But then, nothing. He set his phone aside, opening up his computer. He clicked open the shared files and sighed. It was a lot of footage. A lot. He knew it was going to be a lot, based on the number of days they requested, but seeing it all lined up was daunting.

He clicked open the first file, put in his ear buds, opening up Spotify. He clicked open his 'Back in the CCTV' playlist and settled in for the long haul.

***

James took out his ear buds and rubbed his eyes. He checked the time. They had been at this for three hours and he'd barely made a dent in the footage. His stomach growled. Lunch time. Well, close enough.

He tapped on the desk, getting Patrick's attention. He took out his own ear buds and looked at him quizzically.

"I'm going to get some food. Want something?"

"Where you going?"

"Just the chippy. And I may swing in and get something sweet."

Patrick narrowed his eyes. "Something sweet?"

"She's still not answering my texts, mate. I need to make sure she's okay."

Patrick just nodded. "I would like lunch. And a pumpkin bar. Evelyn had tea with Tessa yesterday and said they were the best she's ever eaten."

James grinned. "Fish, chips and a pumpkin bar. Coming right up."

He stood from his desk and stretched. His back always protested to long periods where he would just sit still. He was getting old. If you could call early thirties old. He grabbed his jacket, and as he was putting it on, he eyed his umbrella. He looked out the small window and frowned. It was autumn, and the sky was grey. Plus, it *was* London. He grabbed the small umbrella, stashing it in his pocket. He opened the door and walked out of the office and out into the world.

It was nippy and windy. He was glad he had upgraded to his heavy coat the day before. There was also a mist in the air. It was the right decision to grab the umbrella.

As he walked down the pavement, his mind turned to the case, as it always did when he was alone. It really bothered him that Tessa wasn't texting back. Evie was the only reason he knew she had received nothing else from the stalker since the photograph on Monday. Which worried him to no end. It was never a good sign when the perpetrator went off script. For weeks, they had been delivering letters daily. And now, nothing? It could mean one of two things: they gave up, they had achieved what they wanted to achieve, or they were building up to something that was much more sinister. He really hoped it was the first one. The first one made their job easy. However, his gut was telling him it was the second. The stalker was gearing up for something big. They were probably watching and reveling in the anxiety that was more than likely building up in Tessa's anticipation for the next move.

He hit up Cake Me Home Tonight first. Nobody wanted cold fish and chips. As he approached the shop, a knot formed in his stomach. He reached up, scratching his beard. He was making a mistake. A big mistake. She obviously didn't want to talk to him, and here he was, forcing himself into her life like some kind of caveman? This was exactly why she stopped talking to him. Unfortunately, it was too late to turn back now. He was at the shop, and he had promised Patrick a pumpkin bar. If he came back without it, he was pretty sure Patrick would kill him. He was surrounded by a group of people who were completely and utterly obsessed with sweets. Every time he and Joe were in the same room, Joe asked him if he was sleeping with Tessa yet and could he get him a discount at the shop. Obsessed.

As he reached out to open the door, the hairs on the back of his neck stood up, and he froze. He dropped his hand and glanced around. The street was bustling. It was the lunch hour, and this was a busy part of the borough. People were ducking in and out of shops up and down the street. He turned around and looked directly across the street with narrowed eyes. He took in everyone, but no one really stood out to him. Everyone seemed to be going about their business as usual.

It was as he turned back toward the shop; he caught a glimpse of him out of the corner of his eye. Dressed in black, with a black beanie pulled down low, sunglasses perched on his face. He was standing in the shadows of the alley between two of the shops across the way. Barely noticeable, but watching. James whipped back around, dashing across the road, dodging traffic. He cursed as a lorry nearly took him out, but he didn't slow his stride. He kept running directly to where the man had been standing. As he approached the alley, he knew he was too late. He hadn't been remotely stealthy. The alley was empty. The man was gone. Instead, laying on the ground where he once stood was a discarded receipt from Cake Me Home Tonight with 'Nice Try' hastily scrawled on the back.

"Fuck!" James shouted into the sky. Many people stopped to look at him, particularly mums and their young children. James smiled sheepishly at them as he quickly snapped a picture of the offending piece of paper before picking it up and shoving it in his pocket.

He made his way safely back to the shop, and this time didn't even hesitate before opening the door and marching inside. The shop was busy, and the girl behind the register seemed overwhelmed. There was also a man about his age manning the baking case, pulling orders for people. That was probably Freddie. And unless he was the fucking Flash, he was not the man standing and watching the shop in the shadows.

He approached the counter.

"What can I get you today?" possibly Freddie asked.

"Two pumpkin bars, please."

"Anything else?" he asked as he boxed up the goods.

"Is Tessa around?"

The man narrowed his eyes. "Who's asking."

James reached into his pocket and pulled out his card, handing it over to him. "James Moore."

The man looked at the card and reached his hand over the case. "Freddie. I'm Tessa's business partner. Follow me. I'll take you back to her."

"I still need to pay for these pumpkin bars."

"They're on the house. Tessa wouldn't want to charge you for them. Come on back."

James shrugged and followed him around the counter. They walked through a doorway with hanging beads and back into the kitchen. His breath caught in his throat as he caught sight of the vision in the kitchen. Tessa was in her element. She was wearing denims, a purple form fitting t-shirt, with an apron over her clothes and had her long curls pulled up into a haphazard bun on the top of her head, with a wide purple headband to keep her hair off her forehead. With flour smeared across her cheek, you could tell she'd adjusted her glasses more than once. She was fucking adorable. And he realized all the teasing Patrick and Evie had put him through was for nothing. He had feelings for her. He was fucked.

"Tessa, Detective Moore is here to see you," Freddie announced.

Tessa startled and turned around. "James."

"Tessa."

"*Ooookay*. I'm going to go back out front. Leave you two to be all awkward together." Freddie didn't wait for a response. He turned and left.

Tessa and James stood there, their shuffling feet the only sound to break the silence.

"You weren't answering my texts."

"I didn't think it was a requirement for you to solve my case."

"It's not. But I was, am, worried about you. Evie told me you haven't received any more letters?"

She shook her head. "No, which is probably worse than if they were still sending me daily letters. The anticipation of waiting for the letter to arrive. Will it be a letter? Another photograph? Something worse? It's the not knowing that's killing me."

"That's part of what gives stalkers the thrill. Keeping their victim on edge. What's troubling me is how they've switched their M.O. suddenly."

"Really?"

"Yeah. When a criminal switches their M.O. it usually leads to an escalation. In order to ensure your safety, you should always be on the lookout and taking note of your surroundings, alright?"

"You really think they're going to escalate things? Further than they have already done?"

James only had to think for a second before deciding he should tell her what he saw when he arrived. "I caught someone lurking in the alley across from your shop. However, when I ran across to catch them, they were already gone, but they left this." He produced the receipt and handed it to Tessa. "Do you recognize the handwriting?"

She shook her head. "Maybe? I don't know. I just—"

He lifted his arm, placing his hand on hers, causing her to move her gaze from the receipt to his. "It's going to be okay."

"Did you get a good look at whoever it was?"

James shook his head. "Not really. He had his face covered. The only thing I can say with certainty is he was male. The good news is, unless your friend, Freddie, has super speed, he can't be our guy, so we can cross him off our list of suspects."

Tessa gave him a tight smile before turning her attention back to the receipt. "This is from today. The person who is stalking me came to my shop *today* to buy sweets, and then stood outside and watched the shop. What was he doing? Waiting for me to leave? Staking the place out?"

"Maybe a little of both? I don't know. If I hadn't been looking for someone suspicious, I would have never seen him. However, now I know what to look for, it'll make scouring all the bloody CCTV footage easier. We can look at the alley and see how often he is skulking there."

Tessa brought her gaze up from the receipt to his face. "Do you think he's been out there often?"

"Can't say, but I'm guessing if we scour all two weeks of footage, we'll find him at least daily. I'm nearly certain he took the spy shots of you in that exact location."

"Oh, my God." She brought her hand up to her neck. "It was scary before, but why is it scarier knowing for certain he's watching me?"

"When we have evidence to back it up, these types of situations become more real."

She shook her head, and brought her hand up to wipe away tears on her cheeks, which only smeared the flour around even more.

James moved closer. He brought his arms up as if to embrace her, but stopped himself short. He didn't know if his comfort would be welcome. "Hey, do you want me to go out and get Freddie? You look like you need someone."

Tessa moved until she stood right next to him, and she didn't stop. She stepped into his space and wrapped her arms around his waist. She laid her head against his chest and started crying.

James' heart raced in surprise, and he only needed a fraction of a second for his brain to catch up to his body. He quickly brought his arms up, wrapping them around her trembling body, holding her tight against him. He ran his hands up and down her back, trying to soothe her.

"It's going to be okay," he whispered. "You're going to be okay."

CHAPTER 8

TESSA

Her shop was being watched.

When James left to return to his office to go through more footage an hour ago, she busied herself cleaning up her kitchen. The only thing going through her mind was James seeing the person who has been stalking her. Saw him. With his own eyes.

The only good news from his visit was that Freddie was now off the hook. He couldn't be her stalker. He was in the shop when James had seen the person hiding in the shadows. That was an enormous relief for her. She now knew she could continue to trust him. She needed a friend right now, and one she could trust.

She finished drying her bowl, set it up on the shelf, and threw the towel she was using into the dirty laundry before taking off her apron and hanging it on the hook. She stood there, frozen. Her face was heating, tears were welling behind her eyes. She brought her hands up to either side of her face, willing herself not to cry. This was not who she was. She was a strong, independent Latina. When her mother left her and her father when she was ten, she held it together for her father. Three years ago, when her beloved father was diagnosed with stage four cancer, she became her father's strength. If she could make it through those tragedies, she can make it through this. Some arsehole who wanted to be some kind of fucking movie villain would not be the thing that broke her. She wasn't willing to let that happen.

She looked around the kitchen. She built this. This was her accomplishment. Her dedication to her father, the man who taught her how to bake and love being in the kitchen. If someone was trying to scare her off of this dream, it would not work. At least, she thought that was the stalker's goal, wasn't it? To scare her into closing the shop? She couldn't think of any other reason someone would take the trouble to harass her. She had seen some comments and reviews around the internet. There were people who didn't like a Latin woman, the daughter of an immigrant, becoming a successful business owner. As much as people liked to think the world was a less racist place, it really wasn't. And she lived it every day. This stalker was just another one, hiding behind his anonymity in order to be a horrible person. Even though none of the letters had been overtly racist, they were still misogynistic.

She rubbed her temples, feeling her chest tighten. The whole fucked up situation was going to give her an ulcer. She needed to get away. Go somewhere else to clear her head. What she really wanted was to go back to her childhood home and curl up with her dad and cry. Unfortunately, she couldn't do that, but she could do the next best thing.

TESSA: Heading out to see Dad.

FREDDIE: Want me to come?

TESSA: No, stay and help Mariel. I'll be fine.

FREDDIE: If you're sure.

TESSA: I'm sure.

FREDDIE: Text if you need anything.

Tessa grabbed her coat off the hook along with the large black umbrella she had leaned against the wall. She dashed out the back door of the shop and into the alley. She hated the alley; it gave her the creeps. But if the front of her shop was being watched, she would brave the rear to make sure her stalker wouldn't follow her.

As she walked to the Tube station, she constantly looked around her, scrutinizing every person she met on the street. James told her to be aware of her surroundings, and she was hyper aware. Even once she made it to the Underground station and hopped on, she stood holding the bar, constantly looking around for a man dressed all in black following her. If anything, she was more upset about the stalker stealing her sense of safety rather than the act of stalking itself. The anxiety she had whenever she left the flat, the feeling of always being watched, it was worse than anything the stalker had actually done. And she hated it.

She breathed a sigh of relief when she got off at her stop and started walking. Her body and mind became further relaxed as the crowds thinned out, and the buildings began to line only one side of the street.

She let herself in through the wrought-iron fence of the cemetery, quickly making her way along the path she had long ago memorized, letting the overgrown trees and bushes that filled the cemetery become her protection, only stopping when she was in front of the headstone.

Javier Lopez

Her dad.

She knelt on the ground and cleaned the headstone a little before settling in. Today's visit was going to be longer than normal.

"Hi, Dad. I know it's been longer than normal between visits, but I've been really busy with the shop. I never would have guessed autumn to be my busiest season. I always thought summer would be my busiest time with wedding season, but I was wrong. Apparently, my pumpkin bars are so delicious people are traveling from all over the city to get one, and fight over them. I had to special order cans of pumpkin from the States to keep up on production. Yesterday, I watched as Freddie had to break up a fight between two grannies about who would get the last pumpkin bars. I've started making triple what I started and still can't keep up with demand. When I switch from autumn to Christmas, I don't know what will happen. I'm worried the nans will start a riot in the street.

"But that's not the reason I came here today. Well, not the entire reason. I did come here to boast a bit. I mean, come on, grannies are fighting over my pumpkin bars. How wicked is that? No, I came here because there's something wrong, and I don't know what to do. Well, I do know what to do. I hired someone to take care of it, but I don't know what to do. Am I making any sense? I don't think I am."

Tessa took a deep breath and let it out slowly.

She needed to get this off her chest. To tell someone who wasn't Freddie what was happening.

"Someone has been harassing me for the last few weeks. It started off innocently enough. Only a few letters, but..." She took a breath, trying to calm herself.

"He's following me, Dad." Her voice cracked as she tried to hold back her sobs.

"Following me. James, one of the detectives, actually saw him posted outside of my shop just *watching*. I don't know what to do. It makes me never want to leave my flat again. But that's what he wants, isn't it? For me to be too afraid to do anything. But how do I carry on? I don't want him to win. I want to carry on with living, but what if the next time I go out he doesn't simply snap a picture of me? What if he grabs me? Or hurts me? Kills me?

"I wish I knew what to do, how to feel. Freddie has offered me to stay at his, or he would stay at mine, but I don't want to inconvenience him. And having to rely on him defeats the purpose of being independent and solving my own problems.

"If only you were here, to tell me what I should do. I wish I could lay my head on your lap, and you could run your hand along my head, smoothing my hair, like we did when I was younger. You always gave me the best advice. Please, send me a sign about what I need to do next. I need a little nudge."

Her phone dinged, showing she had received a text message. She pulled her phone from her coat pocket and smiled at who it was from. James. She swiped it open, and her grin grew wider.

JAMES: Just checking in to make sure you're okay.

And below it was a GIF of a little ghost giving an air hug with the phrase, 'Ghost hug, you can't feel it, but it's there.'

Smiling, she typed back:

TESSA: I'm doing okay. Any luck on the CCTV footage?

JAMES: None yet. So. Boring. May need more sugar. (Snoring Emoji)

Tessa laughed. This was exactly what she needed. She looked back at her dad's headstone. "Thanks, Da. I best be going, so I can get home before it gets dark. It gets dark so early these days. I love you, and I'll make sure I don't leave so much time between visits."

She stood and before she started heading back to the shop, she sent one more text to James:

TESSA: Do you need me to make a delivery? I don't know what's left at the shop. I just know there are no more pumpkin bars.

JAMES: (Crying emoji) No more pumpkin bars? Why must you be so cruel? Patrick is telling me to say no to a delivery. My stomach is saying yes. Please don't inconvenience yourself. We will soldier on.

TESSA: Don't you think you're being dramatic?

JAMES: I'm always dramatic. It's in my nature. Just ask my mum.

TESSA: That will be the first thing I ask if I ever meet her.

JAMES: I can't wait.

Tessa blushed at that last message. How had they gone from being goofy and flirty to something so serious as meeting the parents so quickly? She tucked her phone back in her pocket and began her walk back to the train. She didn't need to be distracted while she walked. Even though she was certain no one had followed her, it was prudent for her to be aware of her surroundings at all times.

She took the train back to her station. Once she emerged from the station, she was thankful she remembered to grab her umbrella. It had started raining. She put up her umbrella, walking briskly toward her flat. She quickly glanced at her watch and realized it wasn't as late as she thought. The shop would still be open for another half an hour. As she neared the shop, she debated which way she would enter: the front door or the alley?

She thought about her conversation with her dad. Whoever this was, they wanted her scared. They wanted her to hide. Going in and out through the alley would let them win. Under no circumstances would she allow that to happen. She had agency and power in this situation. She would not let some anonymous person dictate how she lived her life. She was fierce. She was woman, hear her roar.

She rolled her shoulders back and strode down the street with her head held high. As the hour was nearing dinnertime, the sidewalks were bustling with people. She looked around, trying to figure out if she could see the man James had seen earlier, but as she looked in the alley across the way from her building, she couldn't see a thing. The crowds were thick this time of night, and it was starting to get dark. If he were wearing all black, like James had said, it would be nearly impossible for her to pick him out of the crowd. He would blend in nicely.

As she went to open the door, she paused. She turned around and stared across the street into the darkening evening. She looked in the general direction she thought her stalker would be. She held her back straight and glared toward the alley, trying to telegraph how not afraid of him she was. Like some sort of leading lady from a thriller film. The one who survived to the end, not the one who died halfway through. After she had given enough of an 'I am not afraid of you' vibe into the abyss, she turned around and let herself into the shop, feeling lighter than she had felt in days.

CHAPTER 9

JAMES

"Bugger. Fuck. Piss," James yelled, throwing his pencil at the computer screen. He and Patrick had been scrolling through the footage for two days now, and he couldn't find his man in black anywhere. They couldn't see anyone approaching the shop. They couldn't find anyone standing across from it. It was like this person didn't exist. Then, just when luck seemed to smile on him, and there was someone all in black approaching the post slot in the shop, it was as if he knew where the cameras were and he kept his back to them. No pictures of his face. And that was the case with every other occurrence of the man on film. The man was an expert at keeping his identity a secret, and it frustrated James to no end.

"Calm down," Patrick chastised from his spot at his desk.

It was Saturday, and they had come into the office to plow through the remaining footage and see if there were any pictures of his face. It was kind of Patrick to do so, especially since his wedding was a week away. Well, it was kind of Evie to let Patrick come with the wedding a week away. With her family due to arrive from the States this morning, and a full day of plans with her sisters and parents, she was happy for Patrick to come to work and help her friend.

Of course, movie night was not on the table for tonight, but James was okay with it. He was going to go have dinner with his mum, who he hadn't seen in a few weeks.

"Don't tell me to calm down."

"I understand being frustrated, but yelling at the computer and tossing things at it won't solve the problem."

"How the fuck does he keep his face hidden in every bleeding shot? Every shot, Patrick."

"He must be familiar with the location of the cameras. Which means he's from around here. Only a local who has lived here would know the exact locations of the cameras to avoid them so easily."

"Which only narrows the suspect pool slightly."

"I think we're going about this all wrong. We need to go back to square one and look at the letters and the pictures again. Maybe have Tessa get her regulars to write a phrase on a paper so we can compare handwriting to the picture and the receipt?"

James perked at that suggestion. "That's brilliant. I wonder if we can have her do a raffle for a sheet of pumpkin bars. We know that would draw in people. Then we can sort through the slips and compare the writing. I knew I kept you around for a reason."

"What it's not for my devilish good looks?"

James shook his head, crumpling a paper and tossing it at Patrick, who easily batted it away. "You ready to get married next weekend?"

"More than. It feels like it's just all for the pomp and circumstance, you know? I already feel like Evelyn and I are married. However, my dad keeps telling me the big do is for the bride, and I will do anything to make Evelyn happy. So big wedding it is."

"You ready for a week with your future in-laws hanging about?"

After everything with the Fitzgeralds, Evie's parents were not too fond of Patrick, and they were not shy about expressing all the reasons. James had been witness to many loud video calls while they lived together. However, Patrick had mentioned the last couple visits had gone really well, but they were short, sweet visits. A full week may prove things may not have completely changed.

Patrick cringed. "Yeah, I'm glad we have this 'urgent case' to keep me busy at the beginning of the week. I think her dad believes I'm going to have a sudden change of heart and leave his daughter in a foreign country. She has a job here. We've been together for almost two years, but it's all still a whim to him. I'm hoping he'll ease up once we've walked down the aisle."

"Fingers crossed."

Patrick leaned back in his chair and locked his gaze on James and grinned. "So, any progress with you and Tessa? Are you two going to be next down the aisle?"

James scoffed. "She's still a client, and I'm sticking with my morals and not dating a client. However, we have been talking a lot, and it's been nice. We've been texting a bit in the evenings before she heads to bed for the night. She's hilarious and can hold her own in a pop culture reference battle."

"You're smitten."

"I will admit. I am."

Patrick did a fist pump. "Finally. You're going to make Evelyn so happy with this news. Especially if things work out well with you and Tessa."

"Because she makes delicious cake, and she would bring it to our get-togethers?"

"No, because she's been worried about you."

"Worried? Why would she be worried?"

"Because you're alone. She cares a lot about you and she wants you to be happy. She wants you to have what we have. We love you, mate, but you've been a workaholic for quite some time and have really neglected your social life. Knowing you're going out of your comfort zone and at least flirting with Tessa was good enough for us. To learn you're actually getting feelings for her? We're thrilled for you. We want you happy."

James reflected on the last few years. Not just the last year and a half with the business booming, but before that, he could definitely see where Patrick was coming from. Yes, he flirted. He was great at flirting. But it never really went beyond that. The last time he was in any sort of relationship was back when he was on the force, before he and Patrick left to start their business. Even then, it was kid stuff. They were so young, and it wasn't very serious. He hadn't been thinking about marriage or the future. That was stuff for adults. Then the business started, and he put all his efforts into it. Starting it, maintaining it, helping Patrick as he navigated grief, the Fitzgerald fiasco. Life merely got too busy for him to slow down and try to give himself what he wanted. Except, he didn't know he wanted it, until recently. Until Tessa.

"I think I am happy. I mean, I was never *unhappy*. I love what I do, what we do, and I love spending my time with you and Evie. The times we lived together in the flat were some of the best times I've ever had. I guess I never stopped to think about how I could get that outside of you two. I know you guys are going to want to spend more time just you two, and eventually you'll have kids, but I guess I took for granted you would always be here. I never thought about what it would be like to be left here, alone."

"You know we would never abandon you, and you know we aren't trying to get you married off so we could go off into our little world. Evelyn wants another girl at movie nights to even the score a bit. She loves it being the three of us, but she would also love it being the four of us. You know what I'm saying? She has all these elaborate fantasies of us double dating, going on couples' holidays, our kids growing up together and going to primary school at the same time. Nothing we talk about involves us all going our separate ways. In fact, it involves us getting even closer."

James hadn't even considered it a possibility that they would get closer. He always assumed he was going to be left behind as his friends moved on. He liked the vision of the future Patrick laid out for them. The funny thing was, he could picture it. Double dates, couples holidays, all of it. Funnily enough, he could picture it all with Tessa by his side. He shook his head. He was really getting ahead of himself now. He knew he liked her, and he could assume she felt the same way. At the very least, she flirted right back at him, but did she picture her future with him in it?

"That all sounds really nice. Makes me want to try hard to solve this case so I can ask Tessa out on a date."

"Just ask her out. It's such an arbitrary rule, not dating your clients."

James shook his head. "I made this rule and I'm going to keep it. And this way it doesn't interrupt your wedding. You will have an unproblematic cake. And then we will solve the case and I will ask her out for a proper date."

Patrick smiled. "I like it. Now that you've calmed down and have something to look forward to, can we get back to finishing this footage so we can move to the next step?"

James nodded and turned back to his computer. He was feeling better about the future, and more motivated to catch this bastard than ever before.

CHAPTER 10

TESSA

Tessa smiled as she set her phone down. Taking the time to visit her father the previous Thursday provided a welcome distraction and was beneficial for her mental health. Her week started off a little lighter because of it. Also, the random texts from James helped. Although, his hinting at meeting his mom sat with her all weekend. She could barely concentrate on making Patrick and Evelyn's cakes throughout Sunday. And now he wanted to know what she was wearing to the wedding?

She was a little out of practice on the dating scene, but knew he was flirting with her. She was a hundred percent open to it, but was now really the time to be thinking about being in a relationship? Was it OK to date the guy you hired to handle your stalker situation? Maybe it would be a bad idea to get into a relationship with James right now. It would feel too much like she was paying someone to be her boyfriend. She should wait until he caught her stalker.

TESSA: What color are you wearing?

She tucked her phone into the back pocket of her denims and turned back to the several batches of pumpkin bars she was frosting. She'd started making several large batches in the mornings before the shop opened and another round about halfway through the morning in order to have enough to last until close.

The kitchen was hushed, but she could still make out the faint buzz of conversation from the customers at the front of the shop. Freddie was no longer just the numbers guy. He was full time behind the counter boxing up customer orders while Mariel rang everyone up. It was a good thing Brits knew how to queue. Less chaos in her shop. Didn't have to go out and buy ropes to contain the crowds. Not only were the pumpkin bars selling out, nearly everything was. She was used to making some of her items in batches that lasted a day or two, and now she was having to make things daily. The whole thing was mad.

On the one hand, it was good her business was succeeding in ways that she never could have imagined. On the other, if this continued, she was going to need help in the kitchen. She could barely keep up with demand as it was. If the demand continued to rise, she would either need to hire another baker, or cut hours at the shop. Less time the shop was open, the fewer items being sold, the less she would need to make.

Hopefully, once autumn ended, and she retired the pumpkin bars for the year, things would slow down. At least she hoped it would work that way.

Her phone buzzed in the back pocket of her denims, and she willed herself to not check it. She needed to finish the baking and go upstairs and take a nap, not banter with James.

The phone buzzed again. And again.

She frowned.

Grabbing a towel, she wiped her hands from any of the cream cheese icing that found itself on them and reached behind, pulling her phone out of her pocket. She laughed. In a series of texts, James had sent her several pictures of what he was going to be wearing to the wedding on Saturday. Screen shots from the website. Pictures of the tux laid out on his bed. And finally, some selfies of him wearing the tux in the mirror, making silly faces.

She shook her head and typed a reply, telling him she would go through her own wardrobe to find something suitable that would match his tux, and for good measure, she turned on the camera and took her own selfie. Her hair was up in a messy bun, with tendrils frizzing out around her head in almost a halo, and there was flour smeared down her face she didn't know was there, most likely from her adjusting her glasses as they slipped down her nose. She stuck her tongue out the side of her mouth and snapped the picture, sending it before she changed her mind.

James' reply came almost immediately, and it was only one word: stunning.

Blushing, she returned her phone to her back pocket and focused on her baking. She glanced at the clock and sighed. There was no way she was going to leave at her normal time today. Not if she was going to finish everything she had planned for the day and get slightly ahead for tomorrow.

She looked toward the door to the bakery, knowing Freddie was out there working the till. When the store closed, she was going to need to talk to him about their finances and see if they could afford to hire some more help. Logically, they should be able to with this uptick in business, and it didn't need to be permanent. It could just be through the Christmas rush, and then, when things settled down, they could go back to the way it was before. Just the two of them.

The part of her that liked control didn't like the idea of having someone else in her kitchen, but the part of her who liked sleep really needed to have some help so she could have a functioning brain.

Her phone buzzed again in her pocket, and she was determined to ignore it. She knew it was probably James, sending her more teasing texts. Or telling her about whatever they were doing today. He had warned her over the weekend the case would be a little slow going this week. Patrick had taken the week off to spend time with Evelyn's family and to prepare for the wedding, and James was also going to be spending time with his best friend's fiancée's family. He had explained they were practically his family, too, and he rarely got to see them, so he was going to do some touristy things. She had assured him it was fine. Her case was at a dead end anyway.

The phone in her pocket was vibrating again and despite this, she reminded herself that she had to ignore it. She needed to finish her baking so she could go upstairs and collapse until she could talk to Freddie about the shop.

As if her very thoughts summoned him, Freddie walked into the kitchen. His usually slicked into submission hair was out of control and the natural curl was very prominent. He looked exhausted.

"Mariel and I flipped the sign so we could go for lunch. I hope you don't mind."

Tessa shook her head. "Good for you. You deserve a break. Was it mad out there?"

"Mad would be an understatement." He walked over to the stool sitting in the corner and collapsed on it. He leaned back against the wall and closed his eyes. "When I close my eyes, all I see are pumpkin bars. Sometimes they have little wings so they can fly themselves off the shelves."

Tessa laughed. "Pumpkin season is ending soon and so will your nightmares of pumpkin bars."

"Don't get me wrong, Tess. I'm positively chuffed with how these bars are selling. The cafe is well into the black. But bloody hell am I exhausted."

"I've been thinking we should hire some more help." Tessa suggested as she frosted another set of pumpkin bars. "Another person for the front and maybe someone to help me back here. If things don't slow down after pumpkin season, I'm never going to keep up."

Freddie opened his eyes and set up a little straighter. "Absolutely. That's a brilliant idea. We can sit down with the book on Sunday and see what we have in the budget, but if things continue to go as well as they are, I don't see why we couldn't at the very least hire someone to help back here."

"If we only have the budget for one person, we should honestly hire someone for the front-"

"No," Freddie interrupted. "I can always help in the front. We should focus on finding someone for back here. You work hard enough as it is, you deserve the help. You don't need to martyr yourself over sticky toffee pudding."

Tessa smiled. "Thank you, Freddie. For not only believing in me enough to risk everything to open this shop with me, but for also caring for me when I would just let myself go."

"You're welcome, but you really don't need to be thanking me. I love you, Tess. You're my best friend, practically my sister. You know I have your back, no matter what."

Comfortable silence fell between them as Tessa cut the bars and placed them on the sheets to go into the display case and Freddie sat resting.

"Has your detective found anything more?" Freddie asked, breaking the silence.

"No. He messaged earlier to tell me they have hit a dead end. They couldn't get anything from the video. Whoever it is must know where the cameras are because they kept their face turned away."

"Fuck, I'm sorry, Tess. Has there been any other contact between you and the stalker?"

She shook her head. "No, I haven't heard from them in a couple days. Not since James caught them across the street hidden in the alley watching the shop."

Freddie sighed. "Are you sure you're fine staying here? I have an extra room in my flat. You're more than welcome to it until they catch him. I am worried about you staying here alone."

"Thank you for the offer, but I think I'll stay where I am for now. Nothing has been outright threatening, and they have stayed outside the shop for now."

"Except the time they bought something here and then used the receipt to write a threatening letter to your PI."

"Touche."

"Can I at least install some cameras inside your flat? They are inexpensive and it will make me feel better if you had something vaguely resembling security."

"How would cameras inside my flat help you feel better?"

"I would have access to the cameras and get an alert when they go off. Then I can—"

"Ew, Freddie, listen to what you just said. All of it together."

Freddie contemplated in silence for a moment, but then it seemingly all made sense to him and he involuntarily shuddered. "Yeah, I heard it, so, we won't be doing that. Maybe on the outside of your flat? The front door? That's less creepy and stalkery, yeah? And you would also have access so you can arm them at will. Think about it, please."

Tessa nodded. "I will. I'll think about it. Thank you for being so concerned about me."

Her phone dinged in her back pocket, signifying another text message. She ignored it and kept lifting the pumpkin bars from the pan to the trays. It dinged again.

"Aren't you going to see who that is?"

She shook her head. "I'm sure it's only James. He was texting me earlier about what he is wearing to the wedding on Saturday so we can coordinate since we're sitting together. I'm sure it's just him."

The mobile dinged again.

Freddie stood up from the stool and walked over to her, picking the phone out of her pocket. He looked at it and frowned. "Does James have an unlisted number?"

It was Tessa's turn to frown. "No, he should show up as himself."

Freddie turned the phone to face her. Three unread text messages from an unknown number.

"That's odd." She reached out to take her phone, but looked down at her cream cheese covered fingers and frowned.

"Your passcode still the same?"

"Yes."

Freddie input her code and the way his eyebrows drew in almost made her heart stop.

"What is it?" she asks.

"You'll want to call James."

"What is it?" she repeated, grabbing a towel to wipe her hands off.

Freddie turned the phone toward her, and she could feel her legs collapsing from under her as she read what was on the screen.

UNKNOWN: I can see you.

UNKNOWN: Why are you talking to him?

UNKNOWN: STOP IGNORING ME!!!!

CHAPTER 11

JAMES

"Is your mobile number on your website or tied to anything with the shop?" James asked.

Even though he technically had the week off to prepare for Patrick and Evie's wedding, he dropped everything at Tessa's frantic call, letting him know her stalker had escalated yet again.

"It's not. I set up a phone line only for the shop so I wouldn't get calls to my personal line. It's not on my business cards, it's not on the website, it's not on my Google search results. Nothing."

James held out his hand, and Tessa immediately handed her phone over. They were sitting in Tessa's flat to give them some privacy. He was sitting in an armchair upholstered in a burgundy and gold floral pattern and bloody comfortable. It was sitting directly across from a matching love seat on which Tessa sat perched with Freddie, who draped his arm over her shoulders.

James had to remind himself he had no business being jealous of the casual way Tessa and Freddie interacted. Tessa had told him she and Freddie were just friends. Besides, he didn't date clients.

He looked at the messages. He pulled out his phone and copied the number to his phone. Then he forwarded the messages to himself.

"When I get back to my flat, I'll run the number through my software. However, I'm not very optimistic I'll be getting any hits."

"You think the bloke used a burner phone?" asked Freddie.

"Yeah. I'm almost certain of it. He's been covering his tracks so far. If he used his own number to send this, it would be a huge mistake on his part."

"And he doesn't seem the type to make mistakes," Tessa filled in.

"He does not," James agreed.

Tessa ran her hands through her hair. James took the time to actually notice her for the first time since coming in. Her normally put together appearance was anything but. Her curls, usually pulled back into some sort of bun, were riotous and seemed to have a life of their own. She was still wearing her apron from the kitchen, and there was flour on her face, right below her left eye on her cheek. She had dark circles under her eyes, which were red from crying.

"I don't understand. Why me?" Her voice was tight, as if she were trying not to cry again.

"Stalkers are narcissistic people who want something and go for it," James explained. "Someone noticed something in you they liked and latched onto it. It became an obsession."

"But what could I have done to encourage him to do something like this?" she gestured to her phone.

"It could have been something as simple as being nice to someone. Giving them a smile, saying hi. People like this are attention starved. They live an unhappy life, or they're treated unfairly by people around them. Any sort of kindness sent their way will feel like a lifeboat," James explained.

"And they latch onto that string of hope and become obsessed, yeah?" Freddie asked.

"Yeah."

Tessa took off her glasses and handed them to Freddie before bringing her hands to her face and groaning. "I'm trying to think of people who I would have been nice to in the last couple months who I see regularly enough that seem suspicious, but I can't think of anyone." Her hands muffled her words, but James could easily hear the emotions getting the best of her in her voice.

"It may not even be someone you see regularly. Your stalker could have come in once, bought a cake. You would have smiled and thanked them, told them to have a good day, and thought no more of it. And that one interaction could have meant the world to them." James wasn't sure if his words were making things better or worse at this point. Would it be better if the stalker were a regular customer or a one off? He didn't know, honestly.

Freddie moved his arm so he could rub Tessa's back. "You have an amazing smile. Lights up the whole bloody room, always has. Ever since we were kids. I can see someone becoming obsessed if you were to smile at them and they had no one else in their lives who smiled at them."

Tessa removed her hands from her face. "Oh, God," she muttered.

"What?" James inquired.

"What if it isn't a customer at all? What if it's someone from my past who was a little sketchy?"

Freddie stopped rubbing her back and sat up straighter. "Who are you thinking..." His eyes widened. "Oh fuck, I think I know who you're thinking of."

James leaned forward, opening the notes app on his phone. "What's his name?"

"Bruno Nelson," Freddie declared, without hesitating. "He was our friend, well, former friend, and he had this weird obsession with Tess."

"I wouldn't call it an obsession—"

"You caught him fucking spying on you in the loo, Tess," Freddie practically yelled. "He was a tosser. Her dad thought about pressing charges after the loo incident, but his parents begged him not to."

"He was my friend," Tessa explained. "He, Freddie, and I were all best friends in primary. In the summer before year nine, he went on an extended holiday on the continent and when he got back, he was different. Freddie and I had sort of grown apart from him. We were still friendly. We just weren't hanging round him much anymore."

"He became a bit of a loner. Very stereotypical, early 2000s goth and emo sort of thing." Freddie continued. "Except he would always make sure he was sitting next to Tess in every class they had together."

"He was my friend. We hadn't been hanging out outside of school very much, but we were still friends."

"Except he would get really fucking weirdly jealous at parties."

"Explain," James pulled out his phone and began frantically taking notes. This was the most promising lead they had. He didn't want to miss anything.

Freddie handed Tessa her glasses, leaned forward, and began talking with his hands. "So, whenever we were at a party or a club and some bloke would come and talk to Tess to try to pick her up, Bruno would walk up, looking like Richmond from the *IT Crowd*."

"And he would just stand there." Tessa took over. "He would just stand there and hover. He wouldn't say anything and inevitably, whoever I was chatting with would simply walk away."

"Tell me about the loo incident." James opened his voice recording app. Since it seemed the 'loo incident' was a significant event which seemed to have a stalker tendency to it, it seemed important to make sure he didn't lose one word.

"I was in band, and so was Bruno. We would have practices after school. And being kids, we would mess around. One day, I was doing a dance with a friend before practice, and bumped into someone drinking a red drink. Spilled it all over my shirt. Naturally, I went into the loo to try and salvage my white shirt. I had just taken my shirt off when I heard a sound from inside one of the stalls. I knocked on the door to ask if the person was ok and they hadn't shut it. It was slightly ajar. It opened even wider after I touched it."

"And when it opened, there was fucking Bruno, his trousers around his bloody ankles, having a wank," Freddie finished.

"What happened after you caught him?"

Tessa and Freddie were both quiet for a second as they turned to look at one another, neither seeming to want to talk about the next part.

"I need to know what happened next. It could be important. This is the first lead we've had in this case. Whatever you tell me, I will only share with Patrick in the context of solving the case. I won't tell Evie or anyone else."

Tessa closed her eyes and turned her head back toward James. "He didn't say anything. He looked so embarrassed. He sort of tucked himself away and made a run for it. I sort of stood there, baffled."

"Our teacher caught him coming out of the girl's loo, and when the teacher walked in to make sure everything was okay, she noticed Tessa there and raised fucking hell."

James stopped the recording. "Well, I would say we have a suspect."

"Really? It was so long ago," Tessa remarked. She was skeptical, he didn't blame her. "And it was all most likely a misunderstanding. I kept telling people there was no way he could have known I would be in there changing. But, no one would believe me. They thought I was covering for a friend."

"Do you still have any contact with him?"

"No, that was the last time either of us talked to him. His parents took him out of college before he could get expelled, and Tess's dad didn't press charges, but he didn't want him to come near her. And then we left school and went to university and that was that," Freddie answered.

Tessa drew her bottom lip between her teeth and looked down.

"Tessa?" James inquired.

Freddie turned, so he was looking at Tessa. "Tess? That was the last we saw of him, yeah?"

"Well," she started.

"Tess!" Freddie exclaimed.

"He reached out after my dad died. And we're sort of friends on social media now."

Freddie closed his eyes and allowed himself to fall back onto the couch. "Oh, my God, I can't believe you're in contact with fucking Bruno. Bruno!"

"I know! But he seems okay now. At least from what I've seen on his socials. He's not dressed like a vampire anymore."

"Appearances can be deceiving," James pointed out. "Forward me links to his socials. I'll check them out. And I'll do a thorough background check on him as well. We'll either rule him out as a suspect or he may very well be our guy."

Freddie immediately perked back up, pulling himself into a sitting position. "You really think he could be our guy? Like we catch him, and Tessa will be safe?"

"Possibly," James explained. "Or he could simply be a bloke you knew from school."

"Even just having this lead makes me feel a little better," Tessa affirmed.

James checked the time on his phone before tucking it back into his pocket. "At the very least, I now have something tangible to follow up on, rather than just spinning circles with faceless people in black on surveillance tape."

James stood from the chair. He needed to get back to Patrick and Evie and the wedding preparations. He and Evie's sisters had a lot of items on their lists as best man and co-maids of honor. "Are you alright staying here?" he asked. "Because the Stevensons are paying for us to stay in a hotel for the next few nights leading up to the wedding, so we're all together. My flat is empty if you would rather stay somewhere else."

"I'll be fine," Tessa insisted. "I will not let some arsehole scare me out of staying in my home."

"Are you sure?" Freddie asked. "If you're only being polite because you don't want to impose on James, my spare room is empty. Alice moved all her stuff out this past weekend."

"I'm not only being polite. I'm really, really sure. As long as he's not breeched my door, I feel safe here. I want everything to stay as normal as possible."

James gave her a smile. "If, you're sure."

"I've said, I'm sure! Now go. I talked to Evie this morning to finalize a few things, and it sounds as if you are in for a busy week. So, go. Run nothing through your programs until after the wedding. This can wait."

James locked his gaze with hers. The fear and defeat he saw mere moments ago seemed to have vanished. It was as if the promise of a lead, the idea this could all be over sooner rather than later, invigorated her.

"I can't promise to wait until after the wedding, but I'll at least wait until my duties for the night are finished."

"After the wedding. I'm going to be busy with wedding baking. I won't have time to worry about whether you found anything. Promise you'll wait until the wedding is done?"

Her eyes never left his as her mouth quirked up into a smile. He shook his head, returning her smile with one of his own. It was impossible to tell her no. "Fine. I promise to not look into anything until after the wedding."

"Thank you."

"You're welcome."

James was the first to break away as he moved toward the door. "Keep an eye out round here, yeah?" he asked, directing it at Freddie.

"Always," the man James now respected answered.

James gave them a nod and opened the door and left.

As he made his way out of the shop and began his walk down the sidewalk toward the underground entrance, he couldn't shake the feeling he was being watched. But as he turned around to check behind him, there was nothing.

CHAPTER 12

TESSA

The door had barely closed behind James before Freddie turned toward Tessa. "Are you sure you'll be okay here?"

"Yes, I'm sure. Please stop worrying."

Freddie shook his head. "As long as this person is out there threatening you, I'm going to worry. You're my best friend, my sister. It's my job to worry about you."

Tessa smiled. "Well, try not to worry too much tonight. So far all he's done is leave notes and text. He's never tried to approach. I don't think he'll choose tonight."

"If he does, please call the police, and then either me or James," Freddie urged. "I'll come as quickly as possible."

"Okay. I will."

Freddie looked at his watch. "I better go. I promised my mum I would be home so she could pick up Alice's something borrowed."

Tessa frowned. "How are you doing? I feel like we swept your crisis aside for mine."

Freddie shrugged. "Dunno. I'm alright, I guess. Alice came by while I was working at the shop to clear out the rest of her things so she wouldn't have to see or talk to me. It feels surreal. We were supposed to be married, yeah? And now we don't even talk."

"I can't help but feel a little responsible for your breakup. It was me she didn't like."

Freddie shook his head. "Don't. Everything is on her. Giving me a fucking ultimatum. She had to know what I would choose. She was looking for an out and used you as a scapegoat. Ten quid says she was fucking around with some other bloke."

"You really think she would cheat on you?"

He shrugged. "She accused me of cheating on her with you. Usually, accusations reflect the actions of the accuser."

"Well, either way, I'm sorry. Were you able to get any of your money back?"

"Most of it. Turns out vendors feel sorry for a bloke left at the altar. Played up the wounded soul a little."

"At least something good came out of the mess."

"Yes, the glass is half full or whatever. Now I really must be going. You know my mum. If I keep her waiting, I will never hear the end. And I'll already have to have an earful of her telling me all the ways this wouldn't have happened if I had simply let her set me up with a nice Indian girl."

Tessa gave him a sympathetic smile before walking to her fridge and pulling out a container. "Would some gulab jamun take a little heat off?" She gave the container a little shake.

"I'm not going to ask why you have a secret stash in your fridge, but yes, it would. It absolutely would. You know my mum takes pride in teaching you how to make all the traditional Indian sweets and loves that you carry them in your shop. Of course, the flip side is instead of lecturing me about not accepting an arranged marriage, she's going to spend our time waxing poetically about how she wishes you were her daughter-in-law and why I haven't I married you already."

"Well, I don't have to give this to you." She turned to make it look like she was going to put the dessert back in the fridge.

"No, wait, I'll take it. Listening to the monologue about you is preferable to the arranged marriage one."

Freddie walked over and took the container from her hands. He leaned forward and gave her a quick peck on her cheek. "Thanks, Tess. I owe you one. And I was serious. Call. Any time." He gave her a little wave and walked to the door. "Lock up behind me." And then he was gone.

And she was alone.

She walked over to the door and flipped the lock into place. The click sounding louder than it should.

Had her flat always been so quiet?

She glanced around.

Seriously. Had it always been this quiet?

Her phone buzzed in her hand, and she jumped.

She tentatively looked down at her hand. Was it him? Was he messaging her again?

When James's name was on the screen, she sighed, letting out the breath she was holding, her heart still beating a kilometer an hour. She opened the text.

JAMES: Just making sure you're doing okay. Don't forget to send me the socials for Bruno when you get a chance. See you at the wedding... X

Tessa closed out the message. Her hands were shaking. Was this going to happen every time someone texted her from now on?

First, she feared the post. Then she couldn't have her curtains open, lest she have her picture taken. Now she couldn't even get messages on her phone? What would be next? What else would this arsehole steal from her?

She threw her phone at the armchair and let out a primal scream as she fell to her knees onto the carpet. Hot tears spilled down her cheeks, causing her vision to blur behind her glasses. She had never felt so helpless and trapped before. Never in her life did she think she would become a prisoner in her own home. A prisoner in her life. Fearing shadows, always wondering if the customer she was serving was the one making her life a living hell.

All she wanted was to live her life. For everything to go back to normal.

***

The next morning, Tessa was in the kitchen at her normal time. She'd barely slept the night before. Every time she drifted off, she would relive that moment in the loo during school. Telling James about it must have drudged up her suppressed emotions about the entire ordeal. She hadn't slept more than a handful of hours.

She put her hands under her glasses and rubbed her eyes, immediately regretting it.

She had forgotten she had moved the pumpkin bars onto the display tray. Now she had cream cheese icing all over her face.

She walked over to the sink and washed her hands and her face before grabbing the tray and carrying it out into the store. She placed it in the position of honor, front and center. Over half the display was with pumpkin bars, and she had even more in the back. Plus, another batch in the oven. She really hoped she had enough.

She walked to the front door and turned the lock and flipped the sign, officially open for the morning.

As soon as she made it back to the counter, the bell sounded, announcing a customer.

She turned around to see Fraser walking in.

"Good morning!" he announced, sounding way more chipper than anyone should at six thirty in the morning.

"Good morning, Fraser. You're not usually in so early."

"Yes, well, mum had a rough night, so she asked if I would run over and pick her up a couple pumpkin bars. She was worried if I waited until the afternoon, they would be all gone."

Tessa smiled. "Well, I think I made enough pumpkin bars to last through the afternoon, but with the way things have been going, it's probably a brilliant decision to come so early."

She moved behind the counter and pulled out a box. "How many?"

"Four. Mum was very specific. It needs to be four, and I can't eat any," he moved toward the register, pulling out his wallet.

Tessa smiled. "Well, I'll throw in a fifth one, on the house, so you can have one. I'll even put it in a separate bag. It'll be our little secret." She gave him a wink as she carried the bars over to the register.

"Are you sure? I can pay for it. It's not a big deal."

"It's fine. You and your mum are some of my best customers. So, on the house."

Fraser smiled his crooked smile, his right side going higher than his left. His blue eyes twinkling. "Thanks, Ms. Lopez. I really appreciate it. You know me mum loves you, and loves coming here for tea."

"Well, I look forward to seeing her every week."

She rang him up, and he handed over his credit card.

"Are you doing, okay?" Fraser asked as she handed his card back.

"I'm fine. Why do you ask?"

He shrugged. "You don't seem like yourself. You look tired."

"I had a rough go at sleeping last night. Pumpkin bars are showing up in my nightmares. At one point I dreamt there was a riot in my shop because they had sold out." She fibbed, not wanting the others to know the real reason. All they would do was worry, and she didn't want that.

Fraser let out a low whistle. "Sounds rough. Well, I will cross my fingers no one riots over pumpkin bars in your shop today."

Tessa laughed. "Thanks."

He reached into his wallet and pulled out a card. "If you need any help, or just want to talk about anything, this is my number."

Tessa picked up the card. Fraser Hudson, Software Developer.

"I work from home, so I'm almost always available," he continued.

She tucked the card into the pocket of her apron. "Thank you. I will definitely keep this in mind. I appreciate it."

He gave her one more smile. "Well, I better be off. Take care, Ms. Lopez."

"Thank you. Have a good day."

He gave a little wave and walked out the door.

Tessa turned back around and walked back through the kitchen. Mariel would be there soon, and until then, the bell would alert her to any customers. She needed to get started on Patrick and Evie's wedding cake preparation, since the wedding was this weekend.

She was pulling down her large mixing bowl, when she had an epiphany.

She pulled out her phone and the business card. She snapped a picture of it and sent it to James.

TESSA: Could be nothing, but he's a regular. Do you think it's worth checking out?

She was about to tuck her phone away since it was still early. She wasn't expecting a reply when it dinged.

JAMES: It's worth checking out every lead. I'll look at him when I look into Bruno.

TESSA: Thanks. What are you doing up so early?

JAMES: Wedding stuff.

JAMES: How many pumpkin bars did you make this morning?

TESSA: Too many. Counting the days until December.

JAMES: It'll be here soon enough.

JAMES: Counting the days until I see you again.

Tessa smiled down at her phone. All the stress she was carrying in her shoulders melted away, and she was relieved. She was falling hard for this man. And she was hoping he was falling for her, too.

TESSA: Me, too.

CHAPTER 13

JAMES

The sun wasn't even up yet, but James couldn't sleep. He spent the last couple of days worried about Tessa and her stalker. He knew he was supposed to be on "holiday" so to speak, but it didn't stop him from worrying.

He sat on the couch in the living room of the hotel suite he was staying in. It was early, so no one else was up yet. He opened the laptop he had retrieved from his flat and booted it up.

"You're not supposed to be working," a voice from behind James spoke up, causing him to jump.

"Fuck," he muttered under his breath after he turned to see Evelyn standing behind him.

She was wearing Patrick's old robe and holding a cup of coffee wrapped in her hands. She hadn't brushed her hair, and she was smirking.

"I'm honestly surprised. I know you've been throwing yourself into work lately, but this feels like a very Patrick move," she pointed out as she moved closer to the couch.

"You know I wouldn't normally be sneaking in work on holiday like this, but there was a development in the case."

Evelyn stiffened. "You're kidding. You have a lead?"

"I have a lead."

Evelyn quickly moved around the couch, sitting herself down next to him. "Patrick mentioned the CCTV footage was a bust."

"It was. This lead came from talking with Tessa the other night. After she received the text message threat."

"What did you find?"

James quickly filled Evie in on what Tessa and Freddie had told him about Bruno and the loo incident.

"I honestly don't know what I want to do more right now, hug Tessa or punch this Bruno bastard in the face," she seethed once James finished.

"Yeah, well, Tessa gave me this Bruno bloke's socials to look into. Apparently, they reconnected after her father died."

"We can circle back to the fact Tessa friended him on social media after everything he did. First, tell me what you're hoping to find? Do you think he's posted declarations of love to Tessa? Posted pictures of his black hoodies?"

James shook his head. "No, nothing like that. Mostly, I'm hoping to grab a picture or two to plug into our facial recognition software."

"And run it against the CCTV footage." Evelyn filled in. "Smart."

"Yeah, hoping he's been hanging around the shop without his full regalia. If I can catch him at the shop as Bruno, then maybe I can compare him to the person in black."

Evelyn leaned her head on his shoulder and watched while James began inputting the URLs Tessa sent him into his search engine.

"What are you doing up so early?" James asked. "What's on your mind?"

Evelyn let out a soft laugh. "You know me so well."

James shrugged. "We lived together for a year."

"It's more than that, and you know it." She grew quiet as she watched him scroll through Bruno's Facebook page. "I guess I'm a little nervous about tomorrow."

James stopped scrolling, turning his head to look at her. She was looking down at her coffee, so all he could really see was the top of her head.

"What do you mean?"

She shrugged. "I don't know. Something about standing up in front of everyone I love and committing to someone I've only known for a year and a half for the rest of my life."

James frowned. "You're not having second thoughts, are you?"

She shook her head. "No?"

"You don't sound very sure."

"No, I'm sure. I just...I don't know. I love him, and I moved halfway around the world for him, but...you don't think we're moving incredibly fast, do you?"

James set his laptop down onto the table and moved so he could wrap his arm around Evie, pulling her into a side hug.

"No. I don't. If it were anyone else, I would be hesitant to say you were moving anything but fast. However, I was there. I was there when you two first met. I've watched you fall in love, and I will say, with absolute certainty, you're not moving too fast."

Evelyn looked up at him, her eyes shining with unshed tears. "Yeah?"

"Yeah." He bent his head down to place a kiss on the crown of her head. "Has anyone been telling you otherwise?"

She shrugged. "My parents have spent the last four months asking why we were moving so fast. Repeatedly asking, 'What's the hurry?'"

"Citizenship? Visas?" James enumerated.

"I told them as much, and they worried I was marrying him *only* to stay in London."

"Your parents have completely lost the plot."

"They're just concerned—"

"Mate, they've been fucking 'concerned' about all of your choices you've made in the last year and a half."

"That's not fair," she argued, lifting her head from his shoulder.

"It is. You're forgetting, I lived with you, and I was around for your video calls."

Evelyn closed her mouth and frowned.

"During the trial, they were 'concerned' about how long it was taking. When you transferred to finish your masters here in London, they were 'concerned' about whether you were making the right choice. When you called to announce your engagement, they were 'concerned' you were being too hasty."

"Alright!" Evelyn whisper shouted. "I get it. They are very concerned."

"I'm wondering if that concern is creeping into your head, making you have doubts. You're not planning to stand Patrick up at the altar tomorrow, are you?"

"Absolutely not," she rushed to say.

James smiled. "See. Nothing to worry about. If you weren't sure about your choice, or thought you were moving too fast, you wouldn't have answered that question so quickly or so surely."

Evelyn smiled at him. "Thank you."

"For what?"

"For listening to my neurotic thoughts before the sun is even fully up."

"You're welcome."

James bent over and picked his computer back up.

"Anything interesting on Bruno over there?"

He shook his head. "It's all innocuous. He doesn't seem to be extremely active. I'm going to nab this picture of him and upload it to the facial recognition software and let it do its thing."

"How long until you get any results?"

"Probably not until after the wedding."

"That's so long."

"It's a lot of footage. A lot."

Evelyn pulled a face. "At least this time you won't have to comb through it all yourself."

"Silver lining."

He finished inputting the settings into his software and minimized the screen. He opened the text from Tessa he got the other day and looked at the picture of the business card she sent him.

"Who's Fraser?" Evelyn asked.

"A regular of Tessa's at the shop. He comes in every week with his mum."

"Oh! I think I know who you're talking about."

James turned, so he was facing her. "You do?"

"Yeah, they come in on Wednesdays for tea. His mom is the sweetest. She helped me decide which floral design I wanted on my cake."

"What about this Fraser bloke?"

"Friendly. He's a little older than us, maybe late thirties, possibly early forties. Dotes on his mother. Makes great conversation. Seems like a genuinely nice guy."

James nodded. "Good, good."

"Why did Tessa send you his card?"

"Since we've hit such a brick wall with this case, we discussed potential suspects. What to look out for. I told her and her business partner to look for people who may be from the past, or people who are regulars at the shop, but not necessarily someone who would be overtly suspicious."

Evelyn nodded. "And Fraser Hudson is a regular, who spends a lot of time in the shop, but he doesn't act as if he's stalking Tessa."

"Exactly."

"What are you going to do with this information?"

"Same as with Bruno. Head to his socials, get a picture, put it in the facial recognition."

"Won't he show up if he's a regular?"

"Yes, but we'll also be looking for him if he shows up and does something weird."

James typed Fraser's name into all the social media apps and came up empty.

"Is that a worrying sign?"

"Nah, Patrick and I don't have social media. Many people don't. It's not a red flag. It's just disappointing because I can't get a picture of him to run through the software."

"You should dance with Tessa at the wedding," Evelyn blurted out.

James' head turned so quickly in her direction he was pretty sure he gave himself whiplash. "What?"

"You should dance with Tessa at the wedding," she repeated.

"I heard you the first time, but I don't understand why?"

"Because you like her."

James opened his mouth to reply.

"Don't deny it." Evelyn interrupted. "It's written all over your face when you talk about her. And you've all but admitted it in the past. Dance with her."

"I don't date clients. It's unethical."

Evelyn held up her left hand and wiggled her left finger where her modest engagement ring sat. "Is it though?"

James shook his head. "You were different."

"Was I? You both helped solve the case of the notorious crime family who wanted to murder me."

"You weren't paying us. We did it because we're kind and generous..."

"And you could tack me onto the case someone else was paying for you to solve," Evelyn finished.

"Exactly. Not a client. An adjacent client."

Evelyn shook her head. "James. For the last year, you have been working yourself to your bones. You never go out. You're not allowing yourself to live your life outside of the agency."

"We've been really busy."

"Not too busy to take a break. I know. I'm marrying your partner."

James sighed, running his hand through his hair. "I don't know. I guess I have been feeling down lately."

"About what?"

"You and Patrick."

Evelyn gasped. "What?"

"Not like that. It's just, I guess I'm feeling left out. I knew it was inevitable. The three of us couldn't live together forever, but ever since you moved out, it's been a little lonely? We picked that flat out together. And then you two just...left."

Evelyn gave him a sad smile. "I'm sorry. We didn't know us moving out would be that big of a deal. Honestly, we moved out because we didn't think you enjoyed being the third wheel. Maybe we should have talked to you about it before moving forward with our plans."

"I've never thought of myself as the third wheel, for the record."

"I know. But don't you want to have something of your own?"

"I do, but—"

"Then why won't you let yourself be happy with Tessa?"

James shrugged. "I don't know. Because you're right. I do really like her."

"Then why won't you do anything about it? And don't feed me some bull about not dating clients."

"Because what if she doesn't feel the same and rejects me?"

"Then she rejects you, and you move on. But you'll never know for sure until you do something. Ask her to dance with you tomorrow."

James looked into Evelyn's face, which was so sincere in her desire to see him happy that he could feel himself caving.

"Fine," he sighed. "I'll ask her to dance."

Evelyn's face broke into a wide smile, and she was practically bouncing in her seat. "Yay! I'm so excited."

James shook his head and stopped fighting the smile spreading on his face.

Evelyn moved to stand up. "I need to head into the shower before someone else claims it. Everyone else will wake up soon and we have a busy day."

"That we do. Rehearsal and the hen and stag parties."

Evelyn wrinkled her nose. "Yes, don't remind me. I tried to finagle my way out of having a hen party, seeing as I don't have very many girl friends here, but my sisters insisted, and I'm not entirely sure what we're doing tonight."

James laughed. "It will all work out. I promise. You'll have fun."

Evelyn's eyes widened. "You know what they have planned."

"I do. But before you ask, they've sworn me to secrecy."

"Traitor," Evelyn whispered, narrowing her eyes.

James laughed. "Go. Take your shower. You're not getting anything from me."

Evelyn started walking toward her room, and James turned back to his computer.

"James?"

He turned around.

"Thank you." Evelyn gave him a sincere smile.

"Thank you," he replied.

Before he could get back into doing what he was going to do, his phone went off. He picked it up and there was a text from Tessa. He opened it and laughed.

TESSA: May I present to you, wedding cake! Think they'll like it?

Attached was a picture of Tessa, sitting on the counter in her kitchen, two tiers of cake on either side of her. She was gesturing to the cake, her arms wide open, presenting it to the camera, and her face had a streak of blue icing down one cheek, and there were multiple colors of icing staining the front of her white apron. She was wearing a traditional chef's hat, which she must have put on for the picture because, unlike the rest of her, it was pristine. The cake tiers looked amazing, with their cascading blue and purple flowers on white icing, but he only had eyes on the baker.

James continued to stare at the picture on his phone.

This was a side of Tessa he hadn't been able to see through most of the case. She looked happy and playful. Everyone was right. He had it bad for her.

He touched the box to type in his reply and didn't even stop to think before he hit send.

JAMES: Beautiful

He tucked his phone into his pocket and stood from the couch. He ran a hand through his hair and for a split second worried about what he sent.

Almost immediately, a reply sounded, and he rushed to take the phone out of his pocket.

TESSA: (Heart Eyed Emoji)

James smiled.

Satisfied, he tucked the phone back into his pocket and whistled lightly as he sauntered to the bathroom to claim the first shower.

He had forgotten what it was like to start something new with a girl. He could get used to this feeling.

CHAPTER 14

TESSA

Tessa carefully set the cake topper Evelyn and Patrick had picked out on the top layer of the cake and stood back. She let out a sigh of relief. The cake was straight, and it looked sturdy. She smiled to herself. She had lined the flowers up perfectly on the first try.

The cake was white, with a line of dark purple and cerulean flowers cascading down the right side of the top layer and moving across the other three layers in a way that made them look like they were swirling down the cake. Placed on top of the elegant cake she and Evelyn had designed sat two cartoon characters Patrick had paid someone to make to look like him and Evelyn.

She bent down and picked up the boxes she had carted the cake in and walked to the back of the reception hall where the kitchen sat. She stowed the boxes and quickly untied her apron and tucked it away with the boxes.

She ran her hands down her navy dress to make sure everything was sitting right. The men were wearing the cerulean color, so Tessa thought the navy would pair well with what James was wearing without making it look like she was part of the wedding party.

There was movement at the front of the hall and Tessa peeked out the door of the kitchen to see guests already arriving.

She took a deep breath and let it out slowly.

Why was she so nervous?

She waited as everyone filed in and began mingling as waiters walked around hors d'oeuvres for people to snack on.

Finally, the DJ came on and announced the wedding party. She watched as the first couple walked in. She assumed it was Evelyn's youngest sister and James' roommate, Joseph, the police officer. Next, James walked in with Evelyn's other sister. He had the biggest grin on his face. His red hair slicked to the side, showing off his blue eyes. He looked fit. Really Fit.

Finally, Patrick and Evelyn came in, and everyone cheered. He was wearing a tux that matched the others, black, with a cerulean waistcoat and tie. She was in a simple white dress. It was floor length, with a small train, a lace sheath overlay on the white silk underneath. Her hair was curled and a small veil perched on her head. Both wearing the largest smiles possible.

The wedding party made their way to their separate tables, and when James got to his, he stopped and looked around.

Tessa took another deep breath and stepped out of the shadows of the kitchen. As soon as she moved into James' eye line, he noticed her and froze. His grin widened as he moved his gaze along her figure. When his gaze returned to hers, he drew his bottom lip between his teeth and shook his head.

As she walked to the table, she could feel her cheeks warm under his scrutiny. If she didn't know better, she would swear every eye in the room was on her. Everyone was talking amongst themselves, waiting for their dinner to be served.

She finally made it to her seat at the table the rest of the wedding party was sitting and looked up at James.

"You clean up nicely," she complimented.

"Oh, this old thing?" He joked as he pulled on the lapels of his suit jacket. "You look amazing. Hardly recognize you without the apron."

Tessa grabbed hold of her skirt and held it out. "Turns out I exist outside of the bakery and have fancy dresses."

"Who knew?"

"Who. Knew."

James moved and pulled out a chair for her. "Milady."

She laughed, shaking her head. "Thank you, my kind sir."

He pushed in her seat and then took the seat next to hers. "Let me do some introductions. Everyone, this is Tessa. She's the owner of Cake Me Home Tonight, and she made the cake we'll get to partake in later. Tessa, this is Joe, my flat mate and our friend. Next to him is Michelle, Evie's youngest sister, and next to her is Elizabeth, Evie's middle sister."

Everyone greeted her with smiles, and she held up a hand in a small wave back.

"How was the ceremony?" she asked.

"Beautiful," Elizabeth answered. "Evelyn cried during the vows, which made Patrick cry."

"Which made me cry," James pointed out. "Not a dry eye in the house."

"Are you ready for your speech?" she asked. He had texted her the night before, worried about it. Couldn't decide if he should go funny or serious. She had convinced him to mix it up and do both.

He patted his breast pocket. "As ready as I'll ever be. I bloody hate public speaking."

Joseph let out a guffaw from next to James. "You? Hate public speaking? The most extrovert of extroverts I know?"

"Hey, just because I'm extroverted doesn't mean I'm okay with hundreds of eyes on me."

Elizabeth made a show of looking around the room. "Hundreds of eyes?"

Tessa glanced around and noticed that the "big crowd" of guests she had seen come in earlier was really only fifty people.

"Each of these people has two eyes, don't they?" James emphasized.

The table laughed and then settled into comfortable conversation. Tessa had turned to Elizabeth and was talking to her about Uni. She was getting ready to graduate. As she chatted, she could feel the warmth radiating off of James' arm, which he had slung on the back of her chair. Her heart thrilled at the proximity. It was the second time they had been so close, and it still thrilled her as much as it did the first time. She found it hard to concentrate on her conversation with Elizabeth.

She had to stop herself from pouting when the food arrived and he moved his arm from its position.

"Does this meat look dodgy to you?" he asked, poking around his plate with his fork.

"It looks fine." She picked up her knife and cut through the piece of chicken in front of her.

"Are you sure? I don't want to get food poisoning and miss out on giving my speech."

"For fuck's sake, James, eat the fucking chicken," Joseph stated, not bothering to look up from his own food.

"Alright, alright."

She shook her head. "Are you always this difficult?"

"Not always. Must be the nerves."

They ate and chatted, and before she knew it, someone was clinking their glass, announcing it was time for speeches.

James leaned into her, whispering in her ear, "Wish me luck," but before she could answer, he was already up and moving toward the front of the room.

Tessa grabbed her wineglass and turned so she was looking at James.

James took the microphone from someone and turned so he was facing Patrick and Evelyn.

"I thought really hard about what I was going to say today, and I couldn't decide if I was going to be funny or sincere. But when I looked back on our friendships, I thought, of course I need to be sincere. You two are my best friends. And I'm so happy for the two of you finally making it to this moment right here.

"Patrick, you're my brother, mate, no question. Evie, you're the little sister I've always wanted. Together, we're the Three Musketeers. All for one and one for all."

Patrick and Evelyn said that last line with James, and the room erupted into laughter.

"As you move on to this new chapter of your lives, remember where you came from. And all the trials you faced at the beginning of your relationship. You've already tried out the 'sickness and in health' portion of your vows and made it through. Anything else you face will be a breeze comparatively."

Patrick raised a hand to his forehead while Evelyn brought her hands to touch her ribs. Tessa noticed a large scar on Patrick's forehead she hadn't noticed before. They must be remembering the injuries they got while fighting the Fitzgeralds last year.

"You two are the perfect example of what love should be," James was wrapping up his speech. He turned his head until his gaze met hers, holding it as he said the next part. "I could only dream of having what you have." He turned back to Patrick and Evelyn, raising his glass. "To Patrick and Evie."

"To Patrick and Evie," everyone repeated.

As Tessa raised her glass to her lips, she could feel butterflies in her stomach.

As she lowered her glass, she glanced up as James passed Elizabeth the microphone. As he caught her gaze on him, he gave her a wink and a smirk, and her face warmed.

Shit. She had it bad.

***

The music blared over the speakers, and everyone was dancing to the latest pop hit.

The cake had been cut and enjoyed. The important dancing had happened, and now the party had truly begun.

Tessa was sitting on a chair and swaying back and forth to the music. Laughing as James and Patrick were doing some weird half break dance, half secret handshake, she wasn't sure, but it was very physical, and the men had shed their suit jackets two songs ago.

The song stopped and everyone who had gathered to watch the men do their dance applauded and they took dramatic bows.

The next song queued up was a much slower song than the previous one.

When the initial notes of Ed Sheeran's "Thinking Out Loud" began, Patrick and Evelyn found each other on the dance floor, as if they were two magnets that couldn't help but be attracted to each other.

As everyone on the dance floor paired off, she watched as James made his way over to her.

His shirt sleeves rolled up to his elbows, his tie hanging loose around his neck, his once perfectly styled hair, hanging damp across his forehead, he kept his predatory gaze on her as he made use of his long stride to move quickly to her side.

He held his hand out, and didn't have to say anything. She knew what he wanted, and she wanted the same thing.

She reached her hand out and grabbed his.

He pulled her out onto the dance floor, pulling her into his arms. She wrapped her arms around his neck while he placed his hand on her waist, pulling her in close.

As Ed Sheeran sang about people falling in love and kissing under the stars, they moved together. She brought her hand to play with the hair at the back of his neck as his hands moved from her waist up her back, pulling her in even closer.

He laid his cheek onto the top of her head, and her heart skipped a beat. Just as Ed sang about finding love where he was, she couldn't hold it in anymore.

"James?"

"Hmm?"

"I like you. I really like you, and it's okay if you don't feel the same. It was something I thought you should know…"

James pulled back from her, moving one of his hands from her waist until it was under her chin, lifting her face until she was looking at him.

As he looked down at her, she could see everything he was thinking written on his face, and she didn't need his next words to know he felt the same way she did.

"I like you, too," he murmured.

Her breath caught in her throat, and she barely noticed they were no longer dancing, but standing still in the middle of the dance floor.

But it didn't matter. Nothing did. Not when he was bringing his face down to meet hers.

She held her breath in anticipation as his lips stopped a fraction from hers, waiting for her to make the last move, waiting for her to grant consent.

And grant it, she did.

She closed the gap, bringing her lips to his, sharing their first kiss.

CHAPTER 15

JAMES

They were kissing.

Tessa's lips were on his.

That's all his brain could think of as they stood in the middle of the dance floor, connected at the lips.

When his brain began working again, he moved the hand that had been cupping Tessa's chin until it was behind her head, pulling her in closer.

She wrapped her arms around him tighter, pushing her body flush against his.

He ran his tongue along the seam of her lips, and she opened to him, deepening the kiss.

It had been so long since he had kissed a woman, let alone made out with one. It had been even longer than that since the last time he'd had sex, and his body was reacting in ways he was unprepared for.

He could feel himself swell against her and adjusted his lower body. He didn't want her to think he expected more.

They were kissing on the dance floor, which was surprising all on its own.

The song changed, a loud bass began beating out of the speakers, causing the two of them to jump apart, breaking the kiss.

With everyone around them jumping around and dancing to whatever song was playing now, James and Tessa stood there.

James watched her chest rise and fall as she tried to catch her breath. When he moved his gaze back to her face, he could see her eyes widen behind her glasses, uncertainty creeping in.

"C'mon." He reached for her hand.

She didn't hesitate. She took his hand, linking her fingers with his.

He turned and pulled her from the dance floor, dragging her along with him. He pulled her toward the back door into the kitchen, weaving them through the counters where the caterers were busy cleaning up.

"Slow down," she panted from behind him. "I'm going to twist my ankle, moving so fast in heels."

"Sorry," he apologized, slowing down.

He pushed through the door, and they emerged outside, the cold air a shock against their hot, sweaty bodies.

"Wait." She stopped them. "I've left all of my things."

"We'll be back." He tugged on her hand and led them further into the alley.

Once they were far enough away from the door and ensconced in the shadows, he pushed her gently against the wall, immediately trapping her lips with his.

She returned the kiss with as much fervor as he gave.

He moved his hands up her body, and she rewarded his touch with the most tantalizing moans he had ever heard. He grew achingly hard. When he tried to move away from her, she moved her hands to his hips and held him there against her.

It was his turn to moan.

He reached down and tugged her by her thighs, lifting her so her legs wrapped around his waist. He moved in closer, pressing her firmly against the wall.

He pulled away from her mouth and moved his lips down her neck. One of her hands gripped his shoulder while the other threaded its fingers through his hair, holding tightly as they moved against one another.

He pulled back, looking at Tessa, her head thrown back against the wall, her eyes closed, panting.

"We need to stop," he breathed out.

"What? Why?" She opened her eyes, meeting his gaze. She looked distraught at the thought of stopping what they were doing.

"I don't want the first time we fuck to be in the alley."

She nodded her head vigorously. "Good point. My place or yours?"

"Yours," he answered, without hesitation. "You're closer."

He gently placed her feet on the ground and reluctantly stood back from her. They took a second to straighten out their clothes and fix their hair before James took her by the hand and led her back toward the reception hall.

"We should say goodbye to Patrick and Evelyn before we disappear." James looked back at her, his mouth curling up into a sly smile.

"And I need to get my things. I have cake boxes and my apron."

James nodded. "We won't forget those."

They made it back to the door that led into the reception hall, and James stopped them before they entered. He turned, so he was in front of her. "Before we go any farther, I wanted to check and make sure you're okay with all of this. You're a client, and you're paying me to catch a stalker. I don't want to cross any boundaries." Tessa smiled up at him. "I told you I liked you first, remember? Of course I'm fine. Are you okay with this?" James nodded before leaning down, capturing her lips in a searing kiss.

She instantly responded.

James didn't think he would ever grow tired of kissing her.

Reluctantly, he broke the kiss and led them into the reception hall.

Inside, he parted from Tessa and went in search of Patrick and Evelyn. He found them talking with her parents.

Evelyn noticed him first, her face brightening. "James! Where have you been? I need you to settle an argument for me."

James returned her smile. "What?"

"My dad thinks the best Doctor was Smith, but we all know the best is clearly Tennant. Right?"

James laughed. "What did Patrick say?"

"Whitaker, obviously," Patrick scoffed. "She and her fam made the show amazing."

James rolled her eyes. "Well, I'm sorry to say you're all wrong, because the best Doctor is Eccleston. Hands down. That is, if we're strictly speaking of New Who. If we open up the discussion to all time, the answer is completely different."

Evelyn playfully shoved James' shoulder. "Ugh, you're so annoying. You couldn't once agree with me?"

"Evie, my dear, sweet Evie, if the three of us were ever to agree on the best of anything, I'm certain the world as we know it would end. You don't want us bringing upon the apocalypse now, would you?"

Instead of answering, Evelyn launched herself at him, wrapping her arms around him, placing a kiss on his cheek. "I love you, you know."

James, taken aback, hugged her back just as tightly. "Of course I know that."

"Thank you for the beautiful speech, and for being here today, and just for everything in the past year. You're my best friend."

"You're most welcome."

She gave him one last squeeze, but before she moved away, she put her mouth up to his ear and whispered, "Now say goodbye and get back to snogging Tessa."

As she pulled away, he stared incredulously at her, his mouth moving, but no words coming out.

"Oh, don't look so surprised," she whispered. "I saw you two kiss on the dance floor and then run out of here like horny teenagers. I'm honestly surprised you're still here."

James shook his head and leaned down, placing a kiss on her cheek. "Can't get anything by you. You're not annoyed?"

"Annoyed? Why would I be annoyed?"

"It's your wedding."

She let out a stream of air and waved her hand. "I don't care. If you and her finally are acting on your feelings and it happened at *my* wedding, I get to take full credit and have bragging rights. And I'll never let you two forget I was the one who brought you two together."

"But—"

She held up her hand, stopping him. "I get full credit."

He shook his head, his grin widening. "You get full credit. Which I guess isn't too far off from the truth. I don't think I would have acted on my feelings right now without the aid of your wedding reception." He paused and thought for a second. "And if we're giving credit where credit is due, we should also credit Ed Sheeran. Because it was his song—"

"Oh, be quiet." Evelyn laughed. "Now, go. Don't keep Tessa waiting."

"Where's he going?" Patrick asked, moving to put his arm around his bride's shoulder.

James opened his mouth to answer, but Evelyn beat him to the chase.

"He and Tessa are leaving, so they can go shag like bunnies."

He caught the glint in Evelyn's eye and heard the words come out of her mouth, and wondered how long she had waited to pay him back for the teasing he'd thrown on her and Patrick way back at when their relationship was just beginning.

Patrick smiled. "Alright, James. But what happened to," Patrick held his hands up and made air quotes, "I never sleep with a client?"

James shrugged. "Something Evelyn said yesterday, combined with seeing her here tonight, made me rethink everything."

"Good. I'm glad. Now go. We'll see you when we get back from our honeymoon," Patrick drew him into a hug, "and if you need anything—"

"I'll ask Joe, because you're on your honeymoon and your mobile will be off while you spend the next two weeks relaxing and shagging your wife," James finished, giving Patrick a pointed look.

Patrick shook his head, and Evelyn laughed.

"Have a safe trip, and I'll see you in two weeks," James waved to them before turning around.

He made his way back to the kitchen and walked through the door to see Tessa standing there, wearing a large coat and holding a bag. Boxes were sitting at her feet.

"Ready?" she asked.

James bent down and picked up the boxes. "Ready."

"Brilliant, I parked Freddie's car out back. We can take it back to mine." She smiled.

James returned her smile. "Lead the way."

***

Later, James lay in the dark of Tessa's flat looking at her. She lay on her side, facing him, asleep. They hadn't pulled the blankets all the way up, baring her shoulder and most of her back to him. He smiled as he ran a hand down her bare skin.

They had come back to the flat and had barely made it across the threshold before they were shedding clothes and moving toward her bedroom.

The sex was everything he could have hoped for and more.

The pillow talk, even better.

She was in the middle of a sentence when she drifted off, and just the sight of her made his heart flutter.

They'd only known each other for a week, but he was falling in love.

His bladder took the opportunity to make itself known, so, reluctantly, he stood up from the bed, careful not to disturb her. Bending over, he picked up his boxers from the floor and pulled them on.

Quietly, he opened the door to her bedroom and made his way into the main living room. It was pitch black, and he struggled to see anything.

He moved to the curtains and opened one, letting the streetlight flood into the flat, allowing him to see the furniture. The room was still unfamiliar. He didn't want to pull a Dick van Dyke over an ottoman. He scampered around the chair and headed to the loo.

After doing his business, he moved back into the living room and walked to the window.

He took the curtain in his hand so he could draw it, but stopped short when something outside caught his eye.

It was late, and the pavement was clear, except for one lone figure standing directly across the street.

James squinted, moving closer to the window, trying to make out who it was.

The figure was all in black, with a hood pulled up over their head. They either had something over their face, or the shadows covered it, because James couldn't make out any features.

They were standing still, looking in his direction.

James cursed under his breath. His phone was in his trousers, somewhere in the flat. He glanced behind him. They were right outside the door to the bedroom. Two feet away.

He wondered if he went and got his phone, if the figure would still be there.

He turned back to look out the window.

The figure was still there, but now had something in their hand.

James frowned. He couldn't make out what it was. It seemed rectangular and thick.

He turned back and ran to his trousers, fumbling with the pockets, trying to get his phone out.

"What's going on?" Tessa asked, her voice scratchy with sleep. She moved into the doorway, her sheet wrapped around her body. She was not wearing her glasses and her hair was in an absolutely beautiful state of disarray.

"There's someone outside. Watching your flat," he told her.

She stood up straighter. "What?"

"They're dressed all in black, just standing there."

"What are you going to do?"

"I'm going to take some pictures," he stood, moving back toward the window, "and then I'll call down to the CCTV office and have them send me the footage right away." He was standing at the window, his back to it. "Maybe we can—"

A loud crash sounded through the flat, cutting him off.

"James!!" Tessa screamed.

He turned toward the window, but it was too late.

Something had flown through the window. He was alert enough to think "brick" right before it impacted his head.

The pain seared through him and knocked him off balance. As he fell, it was like he was moving in slow motion. His body hit the floor, and everything went black.

CHAPTER 16

TESSA

Tessa's heart stopped as she heard the sound of shattering glass and watched as James fell to the floor. It all happened in a flash. In a single moment, James went from walking towards the window to being thrown to the ground as glass exploded in her living room.

She moved toward him to make sure he was okay, but stopped before she even started. There was glass everywhere, and she wasn't wearing any shoes.

She also wasn't wearing any clothes.

She turned as quickly as she could and ran into her bedroom, throwing off her sheet. Before she did anything, she grabbed her glasses from her bedside table. Now she could see. Next, she ran to the wardrobe and grabbed the first thing she found and pulled it over her head. She reached in and grabbed some slip-on trainers and ran back out to the living room.

She went to the window and looked outside. She knew James would want to know if the person was still there.

They weren't. The street was empty.

She turned back and knelt down next to James.

He had been hit in the head with whatever had flown through the window. Blood was pooling next to his head, and he was unconscious.

She reached down and felt for his neck pulse. It was there, and it was strong.

She let out the breath she was holding.

His face was pale and his red hair stood out against it more starkly than normal. Blood pooled from his head onto her floor at what seemed like an alarming rate.

She ran into the kitchen and grabbed a towel.

She knelt back down next to him and pressed the towel firmly against the wound on his head.

"You're going to be okay," her voice was tight in her throat, "you're going to be okay."

Satisfied with her first aid attempt, she reached down and picked his phone up out of his hand. She scrolled through the contacts and stopped at Joe's name. She moved her finger over his name and then hesitated.

She looked at the clock. It was after two in the morning. She drew her lip into her mouth. He should be back from the wedding, but how much had he had to drink?

She called him anyway.

She pressed call and brought the phone up to her ear.

"'Lo?" a groggy voice came through the speaker.

"Joe? It's Tessa. Someone threw something through my window and hit James in the head. He's on the floor of my apartment unconscious. There is a lot of blood, and I don't..."

"Call 999 and touch nothing," Joe sounded more alert than when he first answered the phone. "I'm going to get dressed and I'll be right there. Don't panic."

The call disconnected before she could say anything else.

She immediately called 999 and told them what had happened. They told her they were sending an ambulance around at that moment.

She set down the phone and stood up. Looking down at James, with the bloody towel against his head, she decided he would be okay for a minute. She went into her room and picked up her phone and hit the first name in her contacts.

"What's wrong?" Freddie answered on the first ring.

"James." Her voice broke at the sound of her best friend's voice, and she was unable to say anything more.

"What did he do?"

"He didn't do anything. Someone threw something through my window, it hit him..."

"I'm on my way."

"The police and ambulance are on their way—"

"I'm on my way," Freddie repeated.

"Okay."

"Tessa?"

"Yeah?"

"Everything is going to be okay."

The call ended and Tessa set her phone down. She needed to go down and open the shop door so the emergency services could get in. Looking at James, she threw open her door and ran down the back stairs entering into the shop. She rushed through the shop to the front door and flipped the lock before hurrying back upstairs into her flat, immediately back into the living room to kneel next to James.

Joe told her not to touch anything, but stopping James' bleeding didn't count. She pressed her hands against the towel again, hoping pressure would stop the blood.

Tears rolled down her cheek. She tried to wipe them away with her shoulder, but it didn't really help.

Lights flashed through her windows and the sirens grew louder. The ambulance. That was quick.

She listened as the door to the shop opened and there was a rhythmic pounding coming up the stairwell. Followed by a knock on her front door.

She stood and rushed to the door, throwing it open.

She stepped aside and everyone rushed in. There were two EMTs. Following them were two police officers, followed by Joe, who was still wearing his tux pants and dress shirt.

"Tessa," he stopped in front of her, "this is PC Randolph and PC Davies. They're going to move around your flat and collect evidence. I'm going to take your statement."

"You're still in your wedding clothes."

Joe looked down at what he was wearing. "I am. And you're in an oversized t-shirt with a Tardis on it."

Tessa looked down at what she was wearing and noticed she had grabbed a shirt dress with the Tardis and the Tenth Doctor on it.

She shrugged. "I don't see a problem with what I'm wearing."

"And I don't see a problem with what I'm wearing."

The two stood there looking at one another, neither one wanting to voice what the other suspected the other of having done.

Joe gestured to the hall. "Let's stand out here and talk."

Tessa looked around him at where the paramedics were lifting James onto a stretcher to move him from the flat.

"He'll be fine," Joe reassured her.

Tessa nodded absentmindedly and moved out into the hall, not taking her eyes off of James.

"Tell me what happened."

"I was asleep, and I heard something moving in the living room. I noticed James wasn't in bed with me anymore, so I got up to look for him. When I moved into the doorway of my bedroom, I saw James digging in his trousers to get his phone. That's when he told me he could see someone on the pavement watching the flat. He wanted to take some pictures and then call the CCTV people to send him the footage. He had just turned around to walk back to the window when the glass sort of imploded into the room. And something, whatever caused the glass to break, hit James in the head and he fell to the ground."

Joe looked up from the notepad. "Did you see what broke the window?"

Tessa shook her head. "I didn't. Just heard the glass breaking and then I watched James go down. After that, I was too concerned about James to bother looking. Especially after you told me not to touch anything."

Joe nodded. "You did the right thing."

"Tess!"

Tessa turned around to see Freddie jogging up the stairs and down the small hallway to her flat. He was wearing pajama bottoms and a shirt that matched hers.

"Freddie." She met him halfway and embraced him.

"Scuz us."

They moved apart to let the paramedics by as they carried James away.

Tessa tried to follow them, but Joe stopped her with his hand. "They'll let us know which hospital he's taken to, and I'll bring you with me when I go over there."

Tessa nodded, turning back to Joe. "Is there anything else you need to know?"

"Did you see anyone on the street?"

She shook her head. "No, um, I went to look as soon as I put shoes on, since I know James would have wanted to know, but the street was empty."

"Why didn't James say he was going to call the police on the person watching your flat?"

"Oh, c'mon, you know why," Freddie stated. "You all are bloody useless when it comes to stalking. Tessa and I called about the letters multiple times."

"I was told the police couldn't do anything until the stalker escalated and actually threatened me," Tess wrapped her arms around her body.

Freddie stepped forward and wrapped his arm around her shoulder, pulling her close. "And they told us sending letters was technically not against the law."

"And I'm pretty sure standing on a public street in the middle of the night isn't breaking any laws either." Tessa's fear started transforming into anger. "The whole reason I had to hire James and Patrick in the first place was because the police were no help. So, I'm guessing that is why calling you was the last thing on James' mind before someone destroyed my flat."

"So, has the situation escalated enough for you lot to finally get off your arses and do something about this tosser?" Freddie asked, malice in his voice.

Joe held his hands up. "Look, I'm on your side. I even talked to James about your case the day he took it on. My hands were tied. But, you're right. This has escalated enough to warrant me to sign on and work the case from an official capacity."

Tessa perked up at what he said.

"However," Joe continued. "Unfortunately, this is going to be categorized as a vandalism case, since they threw something through your window. James and Patrick, when he gets back from his honeymoon, are going to still need to work on the case from a stalker angle. But since we're obviously looking for the same person, we'll be working on the same case."

"That's fucking bullshit," Freddie bit out. "Her fucking life is in danger, and unless the stalker is in here holding a gun to her head, you can't do anything. Throw something through her window, and we've got vandalism when it's obviously tied to the stalker. The law is shit."

"Yeah, well, take it up with your MP and get them to change the law," Joe stated with infinite patience. He was probably used to people going off on him.

Freddie and Joe stood in the hall, staring at one another. Their eyes locked. Tessa could sense the palpable tension radiating between the two men.

Freddie opened his mouth, like he wanted to say something else, but PC Davies stepped into the hallway holding a plastic bag in his hand. Inside the bag was a brick.

"What's that?" Tessa asked.

"Looks like it was what smashed in your window and smacked into your boyfriend's head."

"A brick? Where would he even find a brick?"

"We're in London. I don't think he would have had to go very far to find one," Joe stated.

Tessa and Freddie shrugged.

"What's interesting about this brick is it's no ordinary brick. It's an angry brick," Officer Davies explained.

Tessa tilted her head. "I'm sorry. Did you say it's an *angry* brick?"

"What on earth makes a brick angry?" Freddie asked.

PC Davies turned the bag around in his hands until the opposite side was facing them. "When someone scrawls cruel words on them."

Tessa brought her hands to her mouth as it dropped open.

Scrawled in black ink in big block letters spelled the word 'WHORE.'

CHAPTER 17

JAMES

James opened his eyes to be met with a bright light that was so intense it made him instinctively shut his eyes. He was obviously not in Tessa's flat anymore.

Shutting his eyes, he used his remaining senses to assess the situation. The air smelled of sterility and antiseptic, and his head fucking hurt.

Slowly, everything started coming back to him. The wedding. Tessa. The stranger on the street. The window smashing.

His eyes flew open. "Tessa," he whispered, struggling to sit himself up.

"Whoa there, mate. Let's lay back down. Tessa is fine."

James turned to see Patrick next to his bed.

"What are you doing here?" James asked.

"I'm your emergency contact."

"Shit," James muttered, settling back on the bed. "You're supposed to be on your honeymoon."

Patrick laughed. "It's four o'clock in the bloody morning, the day after my wedding. I'm supposed to be in bed with my wife. We don't leave on our trip until tomorrow morning, remember?"

"I'm sorry."

Patrick scoffed. "Sorry? What do you have to be sorry for? You didn't put yourself in the hospital. It's the arsehole who threw a brick through Tessa's window who should be sorry."

"A brick?"

"A brick."

James lifted his hand to his head, feeling the bandage on the left side of his forehead.

"You know," Patrick dragged the chair closer to James' bed before sitting down, "getting a head injury is completely unnecessary in pursuing a mate."

James looked over at Patrick. His scar from when he got shot last year was still red, not quite to the point of fading. Before the accident, Patrick had kept his hair short, but ever since, he had grown it out, wearing his hair over his forehead, covering the scar. The publicity surrounding the trial made them minor local celebrities, and everyone wanted to see the scar left by a top police officer in their borough.

"It's not like I tried. Didn't expect a brick to fly through the window at me, did I?"

"No one expects a brick to be thrown through a window." Patrick laughed. "Why would you?"

"How bad is my injury?"

"Four stitches and a minor concussion. You'll be fine."

"Tessa?"

"Uninjured, but extremely worried for you. She was here for a little while, but Freddie took her back to his to take a nap. She'll be back in a couple of hours."

James closed his eyes. "I didn't get a picture of the bastard."

"Joe is getting the CCTV footage as we speak. We'll be able to see the person standing there and throwing the brick. If we're lucky, other cameras caught him through the city."

"He had his face covered, and he was wearing a hoodie. We won't get anything."

"His face was covered at *Tessa's*," Patrick explained. "There's a possibility he could have uncovered his face at any time to and from the shop."

James opened his eyes. "When did you become the optimistic one?"

Patrick shrugged. "I think Evelyn is rubbing off on me."

"Was she angry you had to leave?"

He shook his head. "Nah, mate. She was worried about you. She wanted to come, but we didn't know if they would allow her to come back. We didn't know how serious your injuries were. She and her sisters are going to clean out the suite and take our stuff back to the flat. Your stuff will be at ours. You can let yourself in with your key and get it whenever you need. After, she's helping her family get off to Heathrow, and then she'll stop by here."

"My laptop was running the facial recognition software."

"It was done by the time we got back to the suite. I saved the files before I shut your computer down. I packed it into your bag."

"Is there any way you can convince Evelyn to bring the computer with her when she comes to visit?"

Patrick frowned. "Mate. Do you really think you should work right now? You're in hospital. Someone hit you in the head with a bloody brick. You should be resting."

James shook his head. "I just need to check the facial recognition. It's going to bother me if I don't. I want to make sure Tessa is safe."

Patrick didn't say anything. He just pulled his mobile out and typed something into it. "I'm only doing this because if it were Evelyn in danger, I would make the same choice." After he tucked his phone back into his pocket, he looked at James and smirked. "So, you and Tessa..."

James smiled while shaking his head. "Me and Tessa."

"That's great news!"

"Thanks. But don't be getting ahead of yourself and planning double dates. It was one night, and it ended with her window shattered and me in hospital. She's probably already told Freddie what a mistake it was to bring me home."

Patrick shook his head. "Quite the opposite, actually. Bringing you home caused the stalker to escalate to committing a crime the police can actually investigate. She was telling Freddie she should have made a move on you sooner."

"The police are investigating? Who's in charge?"

"Joe."

"Thank God."

"My thoughts exactly."

"How long until they let me out of this place?"

Patrick shrugged. "They didn't say. Considering you've been unconscious, my best guess is you'll be stuck in here for a while longer. They'll probably set you free later today."

James leaned his head back on the bed and closed his eyes. He was exhausted. "Sounds great. I think I'm just going to rest my eyes for a bit, if that's okay with you?"

He didn't hear Patrick's reply. He was already asleep.

***

When he woke again, someone else was sitting in the chair next to his bed. He smiled once his eyes adjusted, and he could see who it was.

"You're here."

Tessa looked up from the book she was reading and smiled. "I'm here."

"Where's Patrick?"

She set her book down on her bag next to the chair. "Evelyn called, saying she was on her way and bringing food. He went to meet her so they could eat before coming up. How're you feeling?"

"Like a brick hit me." He looked up at her and grinned.

Tessa shook her head, not cracking a smile. "Not. Funny."

"C'mon, it's a bit funny."

She shook her head again, still not smiling. "Someone threw a brick through my window with the word 'whore' scrawled on it. The same someone they're thinking who has been stalking me, although Joe can't comment on it in any sort of capacity. My flat no longer has a front window. You're in hospital because said brick smacked you in the head. And you're sitting here, cracking jokes."

James sobered. "I'm sorry. I'll stop if it makes you feel better."

"Thank you."

"Wait, did you say they'd written on the brick?"

She nodded. "They did."

"So, it's my fault."

"What do you mean?"

"He must've seen me go home with you. In a fit of jealousy, he hurled the brick through your window."

"Or, he was angry I'm not appreciating his advances and lashed out." Tessa reasoned.

James sighed. "You're right. That's the more logical explanation."

Tessa tilted her ear toward him. "I'm sorry. I don't think I heard you clearly. You said that I'm what?"

"You're right." He chuckled.

"That's what I thought. Now seriously, how is your head?"

"It aches. Patrick told me I have a concussion. I don't know how much longer I'll need to stay in here."

"I'm staying at Freddie's for a bit. I don't want to stay in my flat right now."

"I don't blame you. What about the shop?"

"It's Sunday, so we're closed today, but I'll open as normal tomorrow as long as the police say it's okay."

James nodded. "I can work from the shop tomorrow, if you'd like."

"If you're not here, you should be at home resting."

"I just want to make sure you're safe."

"I'm an adult, James. I don't need anyone watching out for me. Besides, I won't be there alone. I'll have Freddie and Mariel. And about five hundred people in search of pumpkin bars. Whoever this is won't try anything whilst I am working at the shop."

"I know, but—"

"No," Tessa interrupted firmly. "No. If we're going to move forward in some kind of relationship, then we need to have an understanding. I'm not some fucking damsel in distress and you're not a white knight riding to my rescue."

James sat up taller in his bed. "Look, I'm not trying to be a white knight, I'm just concerned—"

"Then be concerned. That's fine. Don't hover. I am thirty years old. I don't need a babysitter. If you're going to be concerned, do it from afar."

James frowned. "So, you don't want me around at all? How will that foster any sort of relationship?"

"You can be around. I would love for you to come 'round and hang out. But I can't have you just sitting in my bloody shop hovering."

"When Patrick was protecting Evie—"

"I don't need protecting, though, do I?"

"You have a fucking stalker! You are in danger!" James worked hard to keep his voice down, being mindful they were in a hospital room.

"He's *never* threatened me outright," she defended, using her pointer finger to emphasize her point.

James' face tensed, and he had a powerful urge to shout. He closed his eyes and inhaled deeply, feeling the tension in his face dissipate. "The brick through your window would beg to differ."

"Calling me a whore is not a threat," she argued.

"It's not the word, it's the action that is the threat."

Tessa drew her lips in tight, forming them into thin lines, her nostrils flaring. "If we can't agree on this, I don't think we are going to work as a couple. And I may need to request Patrick take over the case full time, and you step back."

James opened his mouth to argue, but she cut him off.

"No. This is non-negotiable. And before you invoke Patrick and Evie, their situation was completely different. Completely. There was no other choice other than her living with you, and there were active violent threats against her. My stalker seems to just want to be with me, not want to kill me, as that would be counterproductive to their agenda."

James was silent. He wanted to argue, but she was making some good points. Their situation differed from Patrick and Evie's.

He really wanted to protect Tessa. His gut was aching to keep her safe. However, he also wanted to see where whatever this thing between them was would go. He didn't want to lose the case.

The only solution would be to put away his chauvinistic instincts to protect, and to just stand back and give her the space she needs.

"Okay," he stated.

"Okay?" Tessa asked, her body relaxing as the anger seemed to drain from her body with that one word. "That's it? Okay? No more arguing?"

James shook his head. "No more arguing. If we're going to explore whatever this is, then we need to listen to each other and trust one another. So, okay. I won't set up a spot at your shop to work. I will text you periodically throughout the day to make sure you're doing okay."

"But not excessively texting." Tessa tacked on, holding her finger up, giving him a pointed look.

"Not excessively. Maybe when I know you're winding down for the day at the shop? And when I finish up at the office? And before I know you go to sleep?"

Tessa smiled. "Sometimes before I go to sleep and when you leave from the office is the same."

"True. So that would mean only two messages a day. Reasonable?"

Tessa pretended she was thinking it over. "It's good for now. We'll give it a trial run and reevaluate in a few days."

James relaxed as he laughed at Tessa's negotiation skills. "I can still come in for sweets, yeah? Before pumpkin season is officially over, I would like to get one or five more pumpkin bars before you bring in the different treats for Christmas."

Tessa leaned forward until her arms were resting on his bed, folding them perpendicular to her body, tilting her head, her gaze locked on to his. "Or," she started, her voice low, "I could come to yours and bake you an entire batch of pumpkin bars of your very own, and..." she trailed off, raising her eyebrows, looking pointedly into his eyes.

He caught her meaning.

"Yeah," he cleared his throat. "I like that plan. Come to my house and we can," this time he paused, tilting his head forward, almost conspiratorially, really leaning into emphasizing the next word, "bake."

When Tessa's face colored at his declaration, his chest swelled with pride. Along with other parts of his body. He leaned back into his bed, relaxing into his pillow and willed those other parts to calm down. They were in no position to do anything. They were in hospital, for fuck's sake.

Tessa practically jumped in her seat when they heard the knock on the hospital room door, like whoever it was had caught her in the act.

The door swung open, revealing Patrick and Evie, the latter with James' laptop bag slung over her shoulder.

"You look a lot better than I imagined when we got the call in the middle of the night," Evie walked over to give him a quick peck on his cheek.

"'Tis but a scratch," James teased.

"Well, I didn't know that when Patrick got called to go to A&E. All I could picture was you lying in a pool of blood, bleeding out from a gunshot wound."

"To be fair, he was lying in a pool of blood," Tessa spoke up. "There was *so* much blood."

Evie moved into the room until she was standing next to Tessa. She gave the other woman a quick, tight hug before pulling back into her own space. "It was the same when Patrick got injured. Head wounds bleed so much."

"I think I remember reading about him being injured during the trial," Tessa said.

Evie nodded. "During the Fitzgerald hoopla, his mentor shot him in the head."

"The bullet grazed me," Patrick clarified, lifting his hair to show off his scar. "Same spot as this bloke, only deeper. Now we match."

Tessa shook her head. "Thank goodness it was a brick and not a bullet."

"The way the glass of the window exploded, for a split second I was worried it was a bullet," James said.

"Me, too," Tessa agreed.

The four friends grew somber thinking about the close calls both men had.

"Hand it over," James gestured to the computer hanging from Evie's shoulder.

Evie slid the strap of the bag down her arm before handing the bag over to James. "Let the record show, I completely disagree with you working from your hospital bed."

"Noted," James extracted the computer from the bag.

Tessa removed the bag from the bed, setting it on the floor while James balanced the computer on his lap, booting it up.

Patrick moved to the head of the bed so he could see the computer screen. "So, are we hoping the software found something or not?"

James shrugged. "Honestly, I don't know."

He pulled up the files Patrick saved and opened them.

Patrick let out a low whistle.

"What is it?" Tessa asked, leaning forward in her chair again.

James turned the computer so both she and Evie could see the screen.

"Apparently, your old friend Bruno is a regular at your shop."

CHAPTER 18

TESSA

Tessa stared at the computer screen.

There was her old friend, Bruno. He looked almost exactly like he did when she had last seen him back in school. Except older. His blond hair, which he wore long and messy in school, was cut shorter and styled nicely. He was wearing slacks and a button-down shirt. The video was a profile, but she would recognize his Roman nose anywhere. It was a feature he was very insecure over when they were teens.

She struggled to find her voice, or any words to convey what she was feeling by what she saw.

James' facial recognition program found two dozen instances of Bruno visiting her shop.

Two. Dozen.

"Have you ever seen him come into the shop?" Evelyn asked, quietly.

Tessa shook her head. "I haven't seen him in person since we left school."

"How? If he's been coming to your shop so many times?"

James turned the computer back to face him. She watched as he clicked around before turning it back to face them.

He clicked on a video. "So, I went back to the video feeds where the program pulled these photos. And look at this."

The video played, and they all watched as Bruno would approach the shop, stand staring in the front window for a few minutes before turning and walking away.

"He didn't go in." Tessa couldn't believe what she was seeing. "Why didn't he go in?"

James read the date and time. "Do you remember if you were working the counter?"

Tessa shook her head. "I don't know. It's been so mad in the shop the last few weeks. I can't pinpoint whether I was in the front or back at that exact moment."

James peered over the top of the computer and clicked another video.

It was the same as the first. Bruno walked to the shop. Stopped. Spent several minutes looking through the shop window before walking away without going in.

James clicked through all twenty-four videos. They were all the same.

"He's never been in the shop," Tessa commented. "Not once."

"In some videos, he seems to spend longer looking in the window than others," Patrick pointed out.

"Do you think those times he spends longer are when Tessa is working the counter?" Evelyn posed.

"It seems logical," James answered.

"I don't understand why he would stop by so often, only to *never* step foot inside to talk to me. What reason would he have?" Tessa asked.

James looked at her over his computer, and the way he was looking at her, she didn't even need him to say anything else.

"Is this proof he's my stalker?" she asked, pointing at the computer.

"I mean, it's not definitive proof, but it's pretty compelling," James stated.

Tessa let out a breath. Bruno. Really?

"What do we do with this?"

"James can stake out his flat. Follow him around a little. See if he's the one coming and snooping around your flat at night. We can pass this lead along to Joe and he can question him," Patrick explained.

"So, you will stalk him, like he's been stalking me?" she asked.

"I wouldn't phrase it like that, but basically, yes."

Tessa bit her lip. "How long until the police will have CCTV footage of last night?"

James shook his head. "Dunno. I can call Joe and get an update on the case. Or I'm sure he or another officer will be here to question me about last night."

Tessa slumped back in her chair, throwing her head back against the headrest. She closed her eyes.

Most of the time, she could tuck this whole stalker thing to the back of her mind and carry on. But now? Now it was taking over her life.

She was supposed to wake up this morning curled up in James' arms before getting out of bed and making Chelsea buns.

Instead, she was sitting next to his hospital bed.

"When will this all be over?" she asked without opening her eyes.

She felt Evelyn place a comforting hand on her shoulder. "These things take time."

"I know," she took a breath, calming herself. "I know. But I just want everything to go back to normal."

"And they will," Evelyn gave her shoulder a squeeze. "Or, if not normal, maybe something close."

Tessa opened her eyes and looked up at her new friend. If anyone knew even remotely what she was going through, it would be Evie.

And as she looked at Evie, she could see someone who was happy.

Tessa sat up and looked at James, and smiled.

Maybe this entire experience would have one positive outcome after all.

***

Tessa knocked on Freddie's door.

She was exhausted, and all she wanted to do was go to sleep.

She had stayed at the hospital until it was clear James was going to be released.

The police had come and questioned him and after he told them the same things she had; they had also informed them they had just received the CCTV footage, but it would be several hours until they heard anything about it.

Once the hospital released James, Patrick and Evelyn had taken him home and she headed to Freddie's.

Freddie's door swung open, revealing her friend. He was wearing a t-shirt and sweats, his feet bare. Sundays were lazy days when you worked at a bakery.

"You could have used your key." He stood aside so she could enter.

"I didn't want to just barge inside in case you had a girl, or a guy, here." She entered his flat, undoing her coat as she walked.

Freddie scoffed as he closed the door, and dead bolted it. "I am far from ready to be entertaining any paramours. Especially when my best friend is in crisis."

Tessa dropped her bag next to the couch before falling onto it. She waited for Freddie to sit before she dropped the bombshell on him.

"Bruno has been stopping by the shop, staring through the window and walking away."

"What?" Freddie exclaimed. "How often?"

"Two dozen times in the time frame of the CCTV footage James and Patrick have."

"The fuck?"

"You never saw him? All those times you were manning the counter?"

He shook his head. "No. Although to be fair, I started helping at the front of the shop once it became a madhouse, once word of your pumpkin bars spread. Mariel might have seen something. If he was coming to the shop during the summer, before the autumn rush, she might've noticed something."

Tessa perked up. "Freddie, you're brilliant."

She pulled out her phone and opened to Bruno's social media and took a screenshot of his picture. She then opened up her messages and sent the picture to Mariel, asking if she had ever seen this man around.

"How's James?" Freddie asked once she had tucked her phone away.

"He's fine. They let him go home with orders to rest."

"That's good. I'm glad he's okay," he paused. "How are you?"

"Frustrated," she answered immediately. "Angry. Scared."

Freddie looked at her, nodding. "These are all understandable and very valid emotions that you are feeling. I am also frustrated and angry. I really wish there were more I could do for you."

"You're doing plenty, letting me stay here."

"Well, it's the least I can do. Unfortunately, staying here is going to be a huge inconvenience to you tomorrow."

Tessa groaned. "Oh, fuck. I'd forgotten. You live so far from the shop. I'm going to need to get up so fucking early," she moaned.

"Hopefully, it will only be for a few days. I've left a few messages with some window people and with insurance. Since your flat is part of the shop, we should be able to cover fixing it through the insurance."

"Thanks for taking care of everything. You didn't need to."

"I'm the money guy. It's my job. Besides, I needed to keep myself busy, otherwise I would be worried about you and James, or pacing around angrily wanting to punch whoever it was who threw the brick."

"Don't go beat up, Bruno. We don't even know if he's the one stalking me." Tessa cautioned Freddie, shooting him a look that left no room for argument.

"I'll promise I won't seek him out, but I can't guarantee I'll leave him alone if he walks into the shop."

"You can't just accuse him of stalking me."

"I won't. But I will tell him to get the fuck out of our shop. He's not welcome there after what he did in our last year of school. I'm glad I haven't run into him since we left. I would have probably already walloped him. Fucker deserves a beating for what he did."

"You already beat the shit out of him while we were in school, immediately after the incident," Tessa pointed out.

"Yeah, well, I didn't get it all out of my system. Teachers pulled me off of him way too quickly."

Tessa shook her head. "You're mad."

"What I can't understand is what happened to him. We were all such great friends, and then he drifts away, and comes back into our lives inappropriately obsessed with you. How many times had he watched you in the loo before you noticed?"

She made a face. "I try not to think about it."

Her phone buzzed, and she picked it up, checking the texts. It was from Mariel. When she read her reply, her stomach dropped.

Mariel: Oh, yeah! He used to stop by the shop all the time! Hasn't been in a for a while though.

CHAPTER 19

JAMES

James answered the phone on the first ring.

"You just spent all day with me in the hospital. Are you missing me already?"

"Bruno used to come into the shop all the time, but stopped once it became too crowded," Tessa's voice came through his phone. She was speaking hurriedly, a panicked edge to her voice.

"He what?"

"I sent his picture to Mariel, and she told me he used to come in and have a chat. When the shop started becoming busy, he stopped," Tessa repeated, slower this time.

"Did she say what he would come in and chat about?"

"She said it was small talk, mostly. He would come in and buy something and chat about the weather or which football team was playing. Then, a week before he stopped, he started asking questions about me."

"What sorts of questions?"

"Dunno. Mariel couldn't remember specifically. All she said was she didn't answer any of them because he was acting dodgy."

"Have you ever told Mariel about your stalker?" James asked.

"No. I don't know her well enough to tell her something like this. And with Freddie working the counter once the stalking escalated, I never saw the need to fill her in."

"Which would explain why she never thought to tell you about the man who was coming 'round the shop asking questions," James surmised.

"Exactly."

"This new information is pretty damning. He's been around the shop a lot. He very well could be the one dropping off pictures and letters."

"Is there any way to know for certain?"

"I'm on my own for the next couple of weeks while Patrick is on his honeymoon. There are two things I can do, and I'll do them in whichever order you would like. First, I can compare the images and video we have of Bruno to the ones we have of the stalker. See if they have any similar physical features."

"That sounds like a lot of tedious work." James could hear the pity in her voice.

"Yes, and it may be fruitless."

"What's the second?"

"The second is I can tail him. See where he goes. We know the stalker spends time outside the shop, watching it. I can follow him around for a couple of days and see where he goes and see if he favors dark alleys near your shop."

Tessa grew quiet on the other end of the line. He could tell she was weighing the two options, trying to figure out which one would help her life go back to normal the soonest.

"Do the second one," she answered after a minute.

"The stakeout?"

"Yes. I think that would give me the most definitive answer of the two, and you won't be stuck in front of a computer screen for hours."

"Thanks for looking out for my eyesight."

"You can't read a recipe if you can't see."

James grinned. "You're really going to teach me how to bake?"

"Of course. I can't be the only baker in this relationship."

Warmth spread in James' chest at the discussion of their relationship in terms that sounded long term.

"How about we hold my first lesson this week?"

"How does Tuesday sound?"

James tried to be stoic, but the thrill in his voice was unmistakable. "Tuesday sounds great."

"And I want you to know, I'm not just using you because your flat is closer to the bakery than Freddie's. I truly want to teach you how to bake the pumpkin bars." Tessa teased.

James had to bite his bottom lip to stop the groan from coming out. "I would never accuse you of using me."

"Glad we're on the same page. I better go. I need to get to sleep since I'm no longer living above my place of work, and Freddie's place is so far away it's like he lives on another planet."

James laughed. "Sleep well. I'll keep you posted on what I find out about Bruno."

"I appreciate it. Stay safe."

"You, too."

They hung up, and James couldn't help but perform a happy dance. As he spun around, stomping his feet, his gaze caught on the kitchen. He and Joe had been so occupied with their jobs and the wedding preparations, the dust and grime had started to accumulate in their flat. The kitchen would not pass a health code inspection in its current state.

"Oh, fuck."

He stopped dancing and walked into the kitchen, grabbing the cleaning supplies along the way.

***

James pulled the MINI-Cooper up next to the curb across the street from Bruno's residence.

According to LinkedIn, he worked from home. It took minimal sleuthing to find his house. Yes. House. Not flat. Whatever Bruno did, it must pay well.

James had woken early to make sure he arrived at the house before a normal work hour would have begun, just in case Bruno didn't work from home.

He settled in, making sure his camera with the long-range lens was ready to go and within reach in case he needed to grab it in a hurry. Reaching into the center console, he grabbed a breakfast bar, tearing it from its wrapping.

As he ate, he fought to keep his eyes open. He had stayed up pretty late, making sure the kitchen and the rest of his flat were immaculate before finally falling into bed to grab a couple of hours of sleep.

His phone buzzed.

TESSA: Good morning.

He smiled and looked at the clock. The shop had been open for a few of hours already, so that must mean Tessa had some downtime.

JAMES: Good morning. How's the shop?

TESSA: Just finished the morning rush. Mariel arrived minutes ago, so I'm back in the kitchen to get ahead on the baking.

TESSA: Are you at Bruno's?

JAMES: I am.
TESSA: Be safe.
JAMES: I will be.
TESSA: X

James smiled down at his phone. The kiss was a pleasant surprise. Without thinking about it, he sent one back.

He set his phone down and picked up his canister of coffee, taking a large sip. As he was setting it back down, the door to Bruno's house opened and the man in question stepped out, wearing track pants and an old T-Shirt.

James picked up his camera and snapped a few pictures as Bruno made his way to a red Corsa parked directly in front of his house. James smiled. A red car. Easy to tail.

He set the camera down on the passenger seat and turned the car back on. When Bruno pulled away, James pulled out into traffic and stayed a reasonable following distance behind him. Traffic was still a little thin, thankfully, so it should be easy to follow him.

The hunt was on.

***

The hunt was fucking boring.

James leaned his head back on the headrest of the Cooper and closed his eyes.

After Bruno left the gym, he had come straight back home and never left.

The curtains were all drawn, and all James could do was sit and wait. He planned to stick it out into the night, as Tessa's stalker seemed to watch her flat when it was dark.

But so far, Bruno seemed to live an extraordinarily boring, normal existence, and James was worried he was going to have to sit out here again another day to see if there was a break in the pattern.

But not tomorrow.

Tomorrow was for baking with Tessa.

The passenger door swung open, and Joe slipped into the seat.

"Oh, thank fuck you're here," James exalted.

"Being a bit melodramatic, are you?" Joe laughed.

"Mate, nothing has happened in the last four hours," James explained. "Nothing. He walked back into the house and hasn't left or opened any blinds. I'm starting to go mad."

"Only because you're hungry." Joe handed over a bag from The Deli Downstairs.

James immediately tore it open and pulled out his sausage roll, taking a big bite.

"Thank you so much. I was starving," he said, talking around the food in his mouth.

"Yes, I gathered that when I got your text, which read," Joe pulled out his phone and read, "Mate, bring me food. I'm feeling rumbly in my tumbly." Joe shot James a look that screamed annoyance.

James gestured out his window at Bruno's house. "Nothing has happened, remember? Bored. So, fucking bored."

Joe reached into the pocket of his jacket and dropped an old music player onto the dash. "Also, grabbed that out of your room and added the next couple of books in your Wheel of Time series onto it. Next time, be a better scout next time and come prepared."

"Thank you," James tried to sound sincere this time. "I honestly thought this would be a bit more exciting."

"The bloke works from home. What on earth did you think would happen?"

James shrugged. "Dunno. Maybe working from home was what he wrote on his profile and he lived some sort of torrid double life as an MI6 agent?"

Joe rolled his eyes. "Next time go into it assuming what you see is what you get and bring your fucking book player."

"Yes, mum," James took another large bite of his sausage roll.

"Before I head back to work, I should let you know we have been going through the CCTV footage, and while we have the perpetrator on film loitering in front of Tessa's and throwing the brick through the bloody window, we have yet to find any footage of them without the hoodie or the face covering."

"Bugger it all," James growled. "Did he bring the brick with him, or did he go off and find the brick after loitering?"

"See," Joe started, adjusting himself so he could fully face James. "That's the interesting part. He had been loitering near the flat for a full hour before you and Tessa arrived at the shop from the wedding. And when we watched him walking down the street, he was already carrying the brick."

James sat up straighter, setting the sausage roll down on the dash, before turning to face Joe. "What?"

"He had already been there. With the brick."

"That doesn't add up. Logically, the order of events should have been as followed: he's already there, we arrive together, he leaves to find a brick and scrawl whore on it, returns and throws the brick through the window when he sees me looking out at him."

"I agree. It doesn't make any sense. However, it is what happened."

James furrowed his brow, picking up his sausage roll. As he ate, he ran a variety of scenarios through his mind. As he was stuffing the last bite into his mouth, it came to him.

"Get more CCTV footage," he said quickly after swallowing his food.

"How much more? And what are we looking for?"

"I would go two nights back," James explained. "Look to see if the stalker has been standing outside the flat. Then track to see when he first brings the brick with him."

Joe pulled out his notepad and took notes. "What's your theory?"

"Three nights before the wedding Tessa called because the stalker had escalated to sending text messages. I went over to her flat and spent a while with Freddie and her going over scenarios in which the stalker could text her. I left alone. He might have seen me go in and out and started drawing conclusions."

"Why would he suddenly decide she was sleeping with you now rather than all the other times you had been over?"

"I had never been up to her flat until then," James explained. "She's always come to my office."

Joe nodded. "Fair point, but Freddie was also there."

"But I don't think he knew that," James explained. "Freddie typically arrives and leaves through the back entrance in the alley. There's no way he could have known whether or not Freddie was there."

Joe nodded again, making notes. "I'll have them pull CCTV footage from the street. What day does the footage you have end?"

James gave him the date.

Joe wrote it down. "I'll have them pull from that point forward. We'll see if we notice any patterns. Did you notice any in the footage you have?"

James shook his head. "It's all erratic. Nothing consistent other than he obviously knows where the cameras are and has been good at hiding his face."

"Do you only have the cameras around the shop?"

"Yeah."

"We'll pull from the shop to the tube station. He comes and goes in that direction. I'll have some rookies comb over all the extra footage and see if we can find anything."

"Do you have all the footage now for the night of the brick incident?"

"We do."

"And he has hidden his face in all of them?"

Joe nodded. "He knows where all the cameras are. He comes out from a building, we're not sure which one, and as he walks, he puts on the face covering, keeping his face away from cameras."

"I wonder when the face covering began." James mused.

"My guess is when Tessa hired you to find the bastard."

"Any other leads?"

Joe set down his pen and grinned. "That's what else I wanted to tell you. They got a print from the brick."

CHAPTER 20

TESSA

Tessa sighed as the strap on the canvas bag she had slung over her shoulder slipped down her arm again. She had had a successful journey to James' flat from Freddie's via the tube, yet the walk from the station to the flat was proving to be a challenge.

She had two tote bags with ingredients to cook dinner and bake pumpkin bars in addition to an overnight bag. Taking the overnight bag seemed a little awkward and presumptive, but all their texting and calls since the wedding implied that she would stay the night, and she didn't want to risk not being ready.

She made it to the door of James' flat and knocked.

The door swung open and Joe was standing there, his police shirt unbuttoned, exposing his white vest. He had a bottle of beer hanging from the fingers of his left hand.

"'Ello, Tessa," he greeted with a smile.

Tessa's stomach dropped. Had she completely misread the situation? Why was Joe here? And why was he the one answering the door?

"Hello."

"Come in. James is still getting ready."

Tessa pushed her way past Joe, walking fully into the flat. As she stepped into the living room, she was pleasantly surprised.

The flat was much cleaner than expected, considering two young bachelors lived there. It was also larger than she expected.

"I know you're probably wondering why I'm still here, but don't worry," Joe moved to perch himself on one of the stools set at the kitchen island to finish his beer. "I'll be out of your hair soon. Came home to clean up before heading out to the clubs."

Tessa frowned. "It's Tuesday."

"Yeah, but it's my Friday," Joe explained, taking a sip of his beer. "It kind of sucks being off in the middle of the week. The clubs are mostly empty, but I'm usually able to pull, so it all works out in the end."

"So, you're not in a serious relationship, I take it?" Tessa asked, moving into the kitchen to set down her canvas bags of food.

Joe shook his head. "Nah. I don't know if I'm the 'serious relationship' type, to be honest. Too many men out there to just commit to one."

Tessa smiled. "If you say so."

Joe took another drink of his beer before setting the empty bottle down on the counter and pointing at her. "Hey, your friend Freddie. Is he single? If so, think I could pull him? He feels a bit out of my league, but a man could dream, yeah?"

Tessa laughed. "He is single. He just got out of a long-term relationship. His fiancée broke off their engagement a couple weeks before the wedding, in fact. We were talking last night, and I'm not sure he's ready for a serious relationship."

Joe nodded. "Rebound sex is the hottest sex." He spoke those words as if they were a sacred mantra.

Tessa wrinkled her nose. "Boundary number one. Freddie is like my brother. If you pull him, I don't want to hear about it."

Joe laughed. "No problem." He mimed zipping his lips. "We'll keep our torrid affair under wraps."

Tessa shook her head, pulling out her phone. "What club are you starting at? I'll send a text to Freddie to meet you there. He could use a fun night out, and a good flirt from someone good looking."

Joe told her the name of the club and she sent it to Freddie.

"Done."

"Thanks. You're making out to be a good wing woman."

"Don't thank me yet. He hasn't agreed."

Her phone dinged.

FREDDIE: Tell him I'll be there. I need a good night out.

"Well, he says he'll be there."

Joe did a fist pump and stood from the stool. Gotta get ready and put some extra thought into my look. Wish me luck."

Tess laughed. "Good luck."

She watched as Joe walked out of the kitchen and down the hall toward the bedrooms with a bit of a spring in his step, laughing and shaking her head.

Tessa had just started unloading groceries on the kitchen counter when she heard a door open from the back of the flat. She could feel her stomach flutter with anticipation.

Spontaneously sleeping with James after the wedding was last minute and unexpected. Coming over to his house to cook dinner and dessert together, knowing what the expectations were for the evening was different. This was a date.

Their first.

She could hear James' soft footfalls on the hardwood floors as he made his way toward her.

"Hello," she greeted, not turning away from her task.

James wrapped his arms around her waist from behind. His body stepped into hers and she could feel his heat on her back. He bent his head forward, placing a kiss on her neck before resting his chin on her shoulder, their cheeks touching.

"Hello," he breathed.

His cheek was scratchy against hers with his beard, and she couldn't resist rubbing her own against his.

"It surprised me when you didn't answer the door."

"Sorry about it. But to be fair, you are a bit earlier than I expected."

"I was nervous, so I left early."

"Nervous? We don't have to do more than cook together."

Tessa pushed on James' arms until he loosened his grip on her waist. Once they were loose, she rotated herself until she was facing him. She brought her hands up to rest on either side of his face, making sure she was looking directly into his eyes.

"I wasn't nervous about our night leading to sex," she asserted. "I was nervous because this is our first date."

She couldn't hold back the laugh that formed as James' eyes widened almost comically.

"Shit, it's our first date! And you're cooking in my flat, when I should have wined and dined you somewhere in the city!"

Tessa leaned forward and placed a quick kiss on his lips. "I don't want to be wined and dined in the city. I think this is the perfect first date."

James smiled and leaned forward to place a quick kiss on her lips. "You're right. This *is* the perfect first date."

He leaned forward and caught her lips with his again, but this time, it wasn't quick. He deepened the kiss as he pushed her back against the counter. Tessa opened her mouth, and he entered. She moved her hands from his face until she threaded her fingers through his hair.

She could feel the edge of the counter digging into her lower back, but she didn't care.

James pressed himself closer to her, using his knee to push her legs apart so he could slip his leg between hers.

She could feel his hardness against her hip as James' hands wandered until they rested on the curve of her arse. He clenched his fingers around her, and she broke away from the kiss with a moan.

"Don't mind me."

James and Tessa leapt apart as if they were on fire.

She looked around James to see Joe standing near the front door, putting his coat on with an impish grin.

"Fuck off, Joe," James growled, running his hands through his hair. He was breathing heavily and staring at the ground.

"If you didn't want to be interrupted, you shouldn't have been trying to fuck your girlfriend in the kitchen."

James grabbed something off the counter and threw it toward Joe.

Tessa cringed as she watched her bag of carrots slam against the wall inches from Joe's head.

All Joe did was laugh.

"I'm off. Stop throwing veg at my head," he laughed hysterically. "And don't wait up. I won't be sleeping here tonight. With any luck, I'll be at Freddie's." Joe waggled his eyebrows as Tessa groaned, covering her face with her hands.

She heard the door open and close quickly, and knowing Joe was already gone, she removed her hands in time to see James holding the double cream in his hand, ready to throw it.

"If you keep throwing our ingredients at your roommate, we won't have anything left to eat."

James at least had the decency to look embarrassed. "Sorry." He set the double cream down on the counter and moved to get the carrots from the floor near the door.

Tessa turned so she was facing the counter. She began putting away the foods she didn't need right away, before looking around to find the pans she would need to make their dinner.

"So, I'm guessing Joe officially killed the mood?" James asked, moving to place the carrots on the counter.

"Yeah, you could say that. You throwing our food around didn't help matters either. Besides, I'm famished. Stay here and be my sous chef, and I'll teach you how to make the best roast dinner you've ever had."

James smiled as he opened a drawer and pulled out two aprons, handing one to her. "Challenge accepted."

***

Later, as she lay in bed next to a dozing James, she smiled as she replayed their evening together. It really had turned out to be a really nice first date. They laughed, they cooked, they snogged while the dinner was cooking. Baking the pumpkin bars turned out to be more foreplay than anything. But at least they pulled the bars out of the oven before succumbing to their lust.

She looked over at the clock on James' bedside table. It was only seven, but she could feel sleep pulling at her.

"You can go to sleep," James wrapped his arm around her, spooning in behind her. "You won't offend me. I know what time you have to wake up to go into the shop, especially now that you're not staying above it."

Tessa snuggled back into James' body, closing her eyes. "Mmm," she hummed. "If I fall asleep, the day will be over."

"Yes," James whispered into her ear, "but the next day will begin, and we'll have a new adventure to explore."

"I like the sound of that." She paused, already feeling the pull of sleep dragging her down. "If I sleep, what will you do?"

"Good thing we're in my flat, yeah? I'll probably go catch the end of the Arsenal game on telly, and turn in myself. I have a long day of tailing Bruno tomorrow."

"Unless the fingerprints come back clearing him."

"Yes, that. Part of me is hoping it's not him, so I don't have to spend another day sitting outside his house."

"You're getting a lot of reading done."

James chuckled. "Yeah, that I am. Gonna make my way through the whole *Wheel of Time* series if I sit outside his house any longer."

It was Tessa's turn to laugh. "Well then, it will be worth it. Those books are amazing, especially the part—"

James gave her a playful squeeze to cut her off. "Eh, no spoilers."

She laughed. "Fine, my lips are sealed."

James planted a kiss on her bare shoulder. "Seriously. Go to sleep. I'm closer to the shop than Freddie's place, but not above the shop close."

"Come into the shop for tea tomorrow if you can get away from Bruno's.".

James placed another kiss on her shoulder. "I'll be there. Now go to sleep."

She lifted his hand and placed a kiss on his palm. Lying there in his arms, it took no time at all before she was asleep.

CHAPTER 21

JAMES

James rolled over in his bed and touched the space where Tessa had slept next to him. He sighed. He wished he could have woken up with Tessa in his arms this morning, but unless it was a Sunday or if he wanted to wake up in the middle of the night, that wouldn't happen.

He had brief memories of her leaving and saying goodbye, but he wasn't fully awake for it, so it was all fuzzy.

He ran his hands down his face, rubbing his eyes to wake up a little more.

Perk of running your own business was not having to get up before the sun. However, he needed to get to Bruno's early enough to catch him coming home in case he was sitting in an alley across from Cake Me Home Tonight.

That's why he was up at five in the morning.

He got out of the bed, threw on a pair of boxers and walked out of his room. He walked down the hall toward the kitchen, his stomach growling, knowing he had an entire sheet of pumpkin bars waiting for him in the kitchen.

He rounded the corner to the kitchen and stopped dead in his tracks.

"No," he breathed out.

Freddie turned from where he was pouring himself a cup of coffee at the counter. His brown eyes were wide, his mouth dropped open as he struggled to find words.

"What are you doing here?" James asked, even though he knew the answer.

Freddie's dark cheeks flushed with red, and he hung his head to hide his eyes behind his untidy hair. "Fuckin' 'ell," he muttered under his breath. And then quickly whipped his head up, locking his gaze with James'. "Oh, fuck, is Tess here?"

James shook his head. "Left around three to get to the shop."

Freddie visibly relaxed.

James laughed. "Ashamed of fucking my mate?"

"Ashamed? No. Embarrassed? Yes."

"Embarrassed? Why? Joe is a catch."

"Because I ended a long-term relationship with my fiancée a month ago, and now I'm in bed with the first bloke to flirt with me post-breakup? How sad is that?"

James shrugged. "Mate, it's been a month. You're allowed to move on. Have some fun. No one is saying you and Joe need to get serious or anything, and no one is expecting you to remain chaste until you're ready for a new relationship. We're young, we're allowed to live a little. Have some fun."

Freddie leaned against the counter, holding his coffee in his right hand. "Is that what you're doing with Tess? Having a little fun?"

It was James' turn to sputter. "What? No!"

"I mean, it's fine if you are. Having fun, that is. Just as long as you're both on the same page," Freddie paused and took a sip of his coffee, never removing his gaze from James. "If she thinks what you're doing is something serious and you think it's casual, she's going to get her heart broken, and I just can't allow that."

"It's not casual," James rushed to defend. "I'm not sure how serious it is, but I know for sure it isn't casual. At least not to me."

Freddie broke into a wide grin, "Oh thank fuck. I didn't want to have to give you a threatening speech."

"Threatening speech?"

"You know, 'if you ever hurt Tess, I'll find you and beat the shit out of you,'" Freddie intoned, deepening his voice and wagging a finger. "All a bit rubbish," he changed back to his normal voice, "innit? But as her non-brother brother, it's my duty to threaten the love interest."

"I'm pretty sure Tessa can take care of herself."

"Oh, absolutely, but I enjoy doing the speech. Tessa gets a kick out of giving hers to whoever I'm currently seeing."

This time, it was James' turn to smile. "So, is she going to need to give it to Joe?"

Freddie narrowed his eyes. "No." He paused with a frown. "Maybe?" He sighed. "I don't know. Last night is all blurry."

"You were drunk."

"Yes, I was drunk. We were at a bar. And Joe looked even hotter than he did in his uniform on Saturday night. One minute we were talking and drinking, and the next..." he trailed off and gave James a pointed look.

"I get the picture," he replied with a laugh. "If you're looking for something non-committal, then Joe's your guy. He has a phobia of commitment."

"Oi," Joe's voice came from behind him. "Don't be spouting shite." He walked into the kitchen, in just his boxers, and made a beeline for the kettle. He squeezed in close to Freddie to pour himself a cup, and as he turned back around, he placed a kiss on Freddie's cheek. "I don't have a phobia of commitment. I'm willing to commit to the right person."

He said all of that with his gaze locked on Freddie.

Freddie's cheeks colored.

He cleared his throat. "Well, I'd best be off. I hate leaving Tess to deal with the morning rush on her own."

"You have my number?" Joe asked.

Freddie nodded. "And you mine?"

Joe nodded.

"So, I guess I'll see you around?"

Freddie set down his mug and moved to leave the kitchen, but Joe stopped him. He placed his hands on either side of Freddie's face, pulling him in for a kiss. It didn't take long for Freddie to give in and reciprocate. The kiss grew heated, and James turned his head and looked away, giving the two men some privacy to say their goodbyes.

James heard them break apart and whisper something to one another before Freddie pushed past him on his way to the door.

"See you around," Freddie said.

"See you."

When Freddie had left the flat, James whipped around. "What the fuck was that?" He pointed his finger at the door.

Joe shrugged and brought his coffee up for a sip. "I don't know what you're talking about."

"Fuck off," James chastised him. "You and Freddie?"

"Don't know what you're talking about. Tessa asked Freddie to meet me at the club."

James shook his head. "And?"

Joe shrugged. "And it didn't go exactly how I had planned."

James laughed. "You caught feelings for the bloke after one night?"

Joe shrugged again. "Maybe. I don't know. When I met him Saturday, I was like, 'hmm, he's handsome, pretty sure he's queer, I would like to hit that.' And then last night, he got to the club, looking better than anyone ever deserves to look, and we hit it off. Confirmed he's queer, and after hours of talking, I brought him here for a shag."

"See, this is the part where I know you've caught feelings, because you never bring a bloke home. You always go to theirs."

"I know!" Joe asserted. "I know. This is completely out of character. And Freddie has just gotten out of a relationship with a bird he was going to marry. And I just ended things with what's his name,"

"Clint," James supplied

"Clint, yes. It must be some sort of punishment for my promiscuity for me to find a man I would like to have a relationship with, only to have that man be completely unavailable."

"I mean, I wouldn't consider him completely unavailable. He came home with you, yeah? And from what I know of Freddie, he doesn't seem like that one-night stand kind of bloke."

"What're you saying?"

"I'm saying keep an open mind. Don't write anything off yet. Text him later."

Joe cringed. "Same day? Seems desperate, doesn't it?"

James shook his head. "Not desperate. Interested."

"I'll keep that under consideration."

James moved into the kitchen to help himself to some of the coffee Freddie had brewed and cut himself and Joe each a pumpkin bar.

"What are you doing up so early on your Saturday?"

"Got a message from the lab about the fingerprint on the brick," Joe answered after taking a bite of the pumpkin bar.

"They got a match?"

Joe shook his head. "Inconclusive."

"Fuck."

"Yeah, sorry, mate. I really thought this would clinch it."

"Inconclusive because the print was rubbish or because the person isn't in the system?"

"The second one."

"So, if we can somehow get some fingerprints..."

"We can run them against the brick," Joe finished. "But and this is a *huge* but, we have to consider the person who threw the brick, that might not be his print. For all we know, he found that brick lying about and it's some random person's fingerprint."

James groaned, throwing his head back. "I know, I know."

"We still have all the CCTV footage still to look through. It's not completely hopeless."

"I'm not frustrated by the lack of progress. I'm frustrated because I need to go sit in front of Bruno's house again today."

Joe cringed. "Yeah, I can see why you're upset. You need me to swing by with lunch again today?"

James shook his head. "I'm meeting Tessa at the shop for tea. I'll just pack some snacks to tide me over."

"Think he'll do something more interesting today than Monday?"

James scoffed. "I highly doubt it. I'm prepared to sit in the car, listening to my book, one hand on the camera, waiting to take a picture of absolutely nothing."

"How long do you plan on sitting outside Bruno's?"

James shoved the rest of his pumpkin bar in his mouth and picked up his coffee so he could go get ready in his room. "For as long as it's going to take."

CHAPTER 22

TESSA

Tessa wiped the counters down in the shop and let herself relax for the first time all morning. It was their mid-morning slow down, and she'd let Mariel and Freddie take their breaks while she manned the counter.

She was literally counting down the days until November ended and she could switch to Christmas treats and retire the damn pumpkin bars.

She had hung a sign the day before declaring pumpkin bars were to end on the first of December, and people had apparently heard about it. She didn't know how it was possible, but business had increased. Originally, she thought this new uptick was because of the damn pumpkin bars, but now she was selling out of everything. People were coming in specifically for items other than the pumpkin bars, and she was wondering if this level of business was going to carry on through past the pumpkin bar phase.

She glanced over at Freddie, who was sitting at a table, smiling into his phone.

The day she had left James', he had walked into work and confessed that he had slept with Joe and there was *something* brewing between them. She had given her his blessing, which he felt she needed, and for the last two days he's spent every spare moment texting back and forth with Joe.

Which she loved for him, but she had to wonder if Joe ever worked.

Freddie must have sensed her gaze on him because he looked up from his phone, a sheepish look on his face. "Sorry."

She waved him off. "Don't be. I don't think I've ever seen you this happy."

Freddie frowned. "Really? Not even at the beginning of my relationship with Alice?"

Tessa shook her head, frowning. "Not that I can recall, although I spent most of the beginning of your relationship with Alice being interrogated by Alice."

"Why don't I remember any of this?"

"Probably because she did it when you weren't around."

"Weren't you dating what's his face when I started seeing Alice?"

"Ben? Yes. Did it matter to Alice? Absolutely not."

"The more you tell me about how Alice treated you, the more I wonder why you didn't back me into a corner two years ago and tell me to break it off."

Tessa shrugged. "You were young, and in love, and I didn't want to stand in the way of your relationship. No matter how many times she accused me of fucking you behind her back."

"Ugh, she was the worst, and I'm only noticing it now, because hindsight is twenty-twenty and all that shit, but fuck, I'm feeling much less sad she basically left me at the altar." He looked down at his phone again, grinning. He typed in a quick reply before glancing back up at her. "Okay, tell me. Are you seeing any red flags with Joe? Before I get in too deep?"

Tessa remembered back to the day before when the four of them had sat together in the I and enjoyed tea together. "None."

"Really?"

"Really."

"You're not just saying that because I'm happy and you don't want to crush me? Because I want you to be brutally honest with me."

"I am being brutally honest. I really like Joe. He's funny, he's nice, and he's not jealous of me. Honestly, I can't think of anyone better as a partner for you."

"You don't think I'm moving on too quickly?"

"Absolutely not. It's been a month. And if you think about it, probably even longer since you were remotely happy with Alice. You're allowed to move on."

Freddie smiled. "I'm really glad you're in my corner, because things are moving really fucking fast, and I don't know who I would have talked to about it if you were against it."

"Well, who better to talk to about going from zero to one hundred in a relationship than me?"

Freddie's eyes widened. "Oh yeah! You and James! Joe and I are you guys two weeks ago, except instead of just giving into your attraction, you denied it for weeks."

"Weeks? You make it sound like we danced around each other for months. It was two weeks, and, yeah, we were idiots. What do you want?"

"At least you can admit it now."

"Yes, well, to be fair, I've had a lot on my plate, can't be thinking about starting a new relationship when I've got a nutter stalking me."

Freddie frowned. "Joe said they're still going through the CCTV footage and he will get a full report when they're finished. He's thinking any day now."

"Are they really going through everything Patrick and James had already gone through?"

Freddie shook his head. "Not the same footage. They pulled from surrounding streets and from down by the tube, since they think he lives around there. They're hoping to catch the bastard's face on camera." He held up his crossed fingers. "Here's hoping they find something and this whole thing can end."

"Yes, please. I think the most unnerving aspect is the stalker hasn't reached out and made any contact since the night of the wedding."

Freddie sat up straighter, setting his phone face down on the table. "Really?"

"Nothing. No letters, no text messages."

"You're not staying here. Maybe he knows and doesn't know where to find you?"

"He has my number, remember? And the shop has been open every day like normal."

"Wait."

Tessa leaned on the counter in anticipation. "What?"

"James has been at Bruno's every day since the brick incident, yes?"

"Not round the clock, but off and on, yes."

Freddie leaned on his arms on his table, pushing himself closer to Tessa. "What if your stalker has stopped contacting you because he can't without James finding out?"

Tessa frowned. "Are you thinking Bruno is really my stalker? And because James is outside his house, he's stopped so he won't incriminate himself?"

"Why not? It feels like it could be logical."

"But Bruno doesn't live near our tube station. He lives elsewhere in the city."

"Maybe your stalker simply makes it look like he lives around here? Circles back around to hop on a train after taking his disguise off?"

"All that seems pretty logical. However, James assured me Bruno wouldn't notice him. He's a professional."

Freddie laughed. "The mini isn't exactly the most inconspicuous car, and James has had it parked outside Bruno's house for days. If Bruno *is* your stalker, I'm pretty sure he would recognize James, and know he's being followed."

Tessa moved around the counter and sat in the chair opposite Freddie, resting her elbow on the table and her chin in her hand. "Fuck, I was really hoping it wasn't Bruno."

"After everything he put you through in school?"

Tessa slouched back in her chair and crossed her arms across her chest. "Yeah. Mostly because of everything we'd gone through when we were younger. We were best friends, Freddie. Best friends. We were inseparable for years. Even though we grew apart, there was some part of me hoping maybe we could reconcile, despite that one incident at school."

"That you know of."

"What?"

"One incident that you know of," Freddie clarified. "We don't know what else he was doing in school. And what if, all these years later, he is still not over whatever obsession he had for you in school, and it's escalated to full-blown stalking?"

"But if it is him, why now? Why start now? Why wait so long?"

"Fucked if I know."

Tessa was about to open her mouth to answer when the door to the shop flew open.

In walked the subject of their conversation.

"Bruno?" Tessa exclaimed, leaping up from her chair, almost causing it to topple over.

Out of the corner of her eye, she could see Freddie typing something on his phone frantically. She knew he was messaging Joe, who would message James, to get the fuck over here.

They had decided James could take the day off from tailing Bruno and work on another case. And now he's here in her shop.

"Why are you having me followed?" Bruno shouted as he approached where Freddie and Tessa were standing.

"What?" Tessa asked, truly at a loss for what to say.

"The bloke parked in front of my house in the mini. He's the ginger detective who brought down the Fitzgeralds last year. He's fucking famous. I recognized him the minute I saw him. What I want to know is why are you having him watch me?"

Tessa found her voice. She stood up taller and crossed her arms in front of her chest. "What makes you think I hired him to watch you? We haven't even spoken in ages."

Bruno reached into his back pocket and threw down a copy of The Mirror on the table. The tabloid was open to one of the center pages. There was a picture of Patrick and Evelyn at their wedding. Behind them stood James and Tessa sitting at their table, James leaning over and whispering something in Tessa's ear.

"Because you were with him at this wedding. Plus, I can't think of anyone else in my life who would hire a fucking private detective to follow me around. But, like you said, we haven't spoken in ages, so I can't seem to figure out why you would do it."

"You know why," Freddie spoke up.

Bruno wrinkled his brow, his dark eyes narrowing. "Because of the incident in the loo? I've apologized for that. And it was over a decade ago."

"Not the loo incident," Freddie dismissed.

"I honestly don't know what you're referring to. I've done nothing."

"You haven't? Then why are you so worried about whether James is following you? If you have nothing to hide, then it shouldn't matter," Tessa spoke up.

"Of course, it bloody matters!" Bruno shouted, running a hand across his shortly cropped black hair. "Like I said, he's not exactly unknown, and my neighbors are talking."

"Why do you come to the shop and never walk in?" Tessa blurted.

Bruno stopped short, looking at her like she lost her bloody mind. "What?"

"You come to the shop, and just stand here, staring in, but you never come in. Well, at least not anymore. The girl who runs my register says you used to come in all the time."

Bruno looked truly confused. "Are you accusing me of something? Because last I checked, looking in the window of a public place is not a crime."

"Just answer the fucking question, Bruno," Freddie practically growled out.

Bruno raised his arm and pointed a finger at Freddie. "Because of this. Right here."

"What? Can't take a bit of disagreement?" Freddie challenged.

"You beat the shit out of me before we left school. I've had no desire to be around you since."

Tessa shook her head. "Enough," she scolded the two men before turning her attention back to Bruno. "You didn't come in because you were worried Freddie would beat you up?"

"Not exactly. But I knew there would be some sort of confrontation. I stop by the shop to talk to you, Tessa. Ever since we reconnected through social media, I've wanted to reconnect with you in person. I learned about the shop, but every time I came in, you weren't here. And then the shop grew busy, and every time I stopped by after, Freddie was working the counter."

"You could have called," Tessa threw out.

"I don't have your number, and it's not listed anywhere. How could I call you?"

Before Tessa could answer, the door to the shop flew open and James strode in, followed closely by Joe, who despite it being his day off, was wearing his full uniform.

James didn't stop until he was standing right next to Tessa.

She was really proud of him when he didn't put his arm around her like he was trying to claim her for his own. Their talk over the weekend really did a number, and she really appreciated it.

"Is this man bothering you, Tessa?" Joe asked.

"Um, not really?" she answered truthfully.

Joe turned to face Bruno. "Sir, do you mind if I ask you a few questions?"

"What the fuck?" Bruno was stunned. "You called the police on me? For coming into your shop? Are you mad?"

"I didn't call the police," Tessa reassured him. "This is Officer McCleary. He works closely with James."

"He's the lead officer investigating who threw a brick through Tess's window Saturday night," Freddie filled in.

Bruno sputtered. "And you think I had something to do with that?"

"Where were you Saturday night?" Joe asked. "Between the hours of midnight and two a.m.?"

Bruno shook his head. "I'm not answering that."

"Why not? Guilty?" Freddie taunted.

"Freddie, don't," Tessa chastised him.

"Am I under arrest?" Bruno asked.

"You are not," Joe answered.

"Then I don't need to answer any of your questions. I'm out of here. I don't need any of this." Bruno turned to walk out the door, but stopped and turned back. He marched back, stopping inches away from James.

"You stay the fuck away from my house. Stop. Following. Me."

James didn't say a thing. Tessa was pretty sure he didn't even blink.

Bruno turned on his heel and marched out the door.

No one stopped him.

CHAPTER 23

JAMES

James watched Bruno storm out of the shop, his eyes narrowed.

He couldn't say with a hundred percent certainty Bruno was innocent, but he couldn't say he was guilty either. The only thing he *could* say was he seemed really fucking shady.

"Can Bruno have you arrested for loitering?" Tessa asked, her gaze still locked on the door where Bruno had just exited.

"No," James and Joe answered at the same time.

"Loitering isn't a crime in the UK," Joe explained.

"So, he can call, but all it will do is allow me to have a nice social break in the middle of my observations."

"Are you still going to watch him?" Tessa asked.

"I wasn't going to, but after this exchange, I kind of want to just to spite the bastard."

"He was really pissed," Freddie piped up. "Like really pissed."

"Did he say why he's been loitering at the shop window?" James asked, turning toward Tessa.

"Told me he wanted to reconnect with me," she answered, finally turning away from the door.

James frowned. "If he wanted to reconnect, why stay outside?"

"He said he was worried I would knock his head off," Freddie answered, crossing his arms in front of him.

"Would you have?" Joe asked.

Freddie shrugged. "Dunno. Before the stalker stuff? Probably not. I would've just given him the stink eye. After the stalker stuff? Maybe."

"What do we do now?" Tessa asked. She was antsy. Crossing and uncrossing her arms. Tucking stray hairs behind her ears.

James stepped closer to her, wrapping an arm around her shoulder, pulling her in closer. "Now, we wait for the CCTV footage to come in. And from there we'll decide the next steps. Has he contacted you at all since Saturday night?"

Tessa shook her head. "Nothing."

"Maybe the police presence has spooked him," Joe offered.

"Never thought of that," Freddie said. "Police investigation feels more serious than a PI poking his nose about. No offense, James."

"None taken, because it's true. We can do a lot of legwork, but we still need to turn suspects in to the police. We don't have arresting power."

Tessa rested her head on James' shoulder. "Part of me hopes the police have scared him away. The other part doesn't."

"Why is that?" James asked.

"Because if the police have scared him away, I'll never know who it was. I'll always wonder who had the nerve to stalk me. If he's not caught, could he come back? Could he simply start again once the scrutiny is off?"

"Always looking over your shoulder," Freddie added.

"Scared of the bogeyman in the shadows," Tessa finished.

James dropped a kiss on the top of her head. "We won't give up. If he stops, the urgency is gone, but I promise I'll keep trying to figure out who this is."

"Don't make promises you can't keep," Tessa's voice was quiet, almost forlorn.

"Oh, I bloody well intend to keep this," James almost growled. "The bastard threw a fucking brick at my head. It's personal."

The bell above the shop's door rang, announcing someone entering the shop. Tessa pulled away from him, smoothing her hair, and plastering on a smile for her customer.

"Good afternoon," she greeted brightly. "Welcome to Cake Me Home Tonight."

"Afternoon, Tessa!" the man who entered greeted.

He was about their age, maybe a little older, brown hair combed smartly to the side, a half-smile on his face. He was escorting an older woman on his arm.

"Fraser! Mrs. Hudson! We missed you yesterday!" Tessa moved to the counter and pulled out a plate.

Fraser. This was the man whose card Tessa had sent him. The one who Evie didn't think was worth looking into.

James watched him as he led his mother to a table and helped her sit down.

"Mum was feeling poorly on Wednesday. I couldn't even get away to pick up our treats. I was worried about her breathing."

"He worries too much," Mrs. Hudson answered as she set herself down in a chair, trying to prop her cane against the table next to hers.

"Let me take that, please, Mrs. Hudson," Freddie moved to take the cane and set on the floor next to their table.

Tessa brought over a large plate with a few of their most popular items, placing them on the table.

"I'll be right back with the tea. Fraser, you should have rung ahead. We would have had everything ready for you."

Fraser flashed her a smile. "Although it would have been a kind thing to do, I wasn't certain we would make it. I was worried mum wouldn't be able to handle the walk, and if I had called ahead and we'd had to turn around, I would have felt guilty having you go through all the work for nothing."

Tessa waved him off. "Call next time. We could always enjoy the tea for ourselves if you end up not making it. No harm done."

Tessa gave one more smile before walking into the kitchen to prepare the tea.

"I don't think we've met," Fraser addressed James.

"James Moore," he offered his hand.

Fraser shook his hand and gave him a wide smile. "Fraser Hudson."

"Your name sounds familiar," Mrs. Hudson queried, "have we met?"

"I don't think we have," James turned to face Mrs. Hudson, "I was in the news for a bit. My partner and I were instrumental in the takedown of the Fitzgeralds. The trial was on the telly a lot."

Fraser clicked his fingers and pointed at him. "I *thought* your face looked familiar, but I couldn't put my finger on where I could have possibly seen you. We have the BBC on most of the day. Mum likes the background noise, so I'm sure I saw you on the news."

James smiled. "Yeah, I'm sure that's it."

"Wow," bright smile spreading across Mrs. Hudson's face, "a celebrity in our local shop."

James chuckled. "A celebrity I am not. And it's my local shop, too. I live here in the neighborhood."

Fraser looked around at Joe. "You look familiar, too."

Joe stepped around James. "I'm Sergeant Joseph McCleary. You have probably also seen me on the telly, as I also had a hand in taking in the Fitzgeralds."

"Two celebrities!" Mrs. Hudson declared gleefully. "Fraser, you should have let me do my face before coming down here."

"Mum," Fraser chuckled. "You look fine. And as they mentioned, they're not exactly Prince Harry and Prince William. I'm sure they don't mind you looking the way you do."

"You look beautiful, Mrs. Hudson," Joe complimented.

Mrs. Hudson blushed.

"What brings you down to our little cake shop?" Mrs. Hudson asked. "Are the rumors true? The police fond of their cakes?"

Joe and James laughed.

"While it is true, we love our cakes, and this is the best place in the borough to buy sweets, we're just here to see our sweethearts," Joe answered.

James watched Fraser closely for his reaction. If he were the stalker, he would react to this statement.

Fraser narrowed his eyes and tilted his head to the side. "Sweethearts?"

"Yeah, James here is dating Tessa, and I'm seeing Freddie," Joe explained, slipping an arm around Freddie's shoulders.

James could see Joe out of the corner of his eye, and just by his stance, he could see what he was doing. He knew Fraser was a suspect. He was goading him to see if he could get a reaction. James kept his eyes on Fraser so he wouldn't miss the reaction.

The door to the kitchen opened, and Tessa came out with the tea tray.

"Tessa," Fraser said as she made her way to the table, setting the tea tray down. "You should have told me you were seeing someone."

"Oh," Tessa was a bit taken aback. "It's all new."

"Well, now I feel like a right twat, giving you my card, telling you if you needed to talk, to call me." He turned to face James. "Sorry about that, mate. I didn't mean to ask out your girlfriend. I'm not that sort of person."

James was surprised. "It's not a problem. Don't worry about it."

"James and I weren't even really seeing each other when you did that," Tessa explained. "We knew each other, but were just friends. Honestly, I didn't even know you were trying to ask me out."

Fraser let out a breath with a small laugh, placing his hand on his chest. "I'm thankful that you were single when I tried to hit on you, but I'm embarrassed that you didn't realize what I was doing. I don't get out much," he explained. "Working from home and taking care of me mum gives me little time to go out, so I'm rubbish at flirting. I feel like a numpty."

Tessa rested a hand on his shoulder, giving him a soft smile. "You're not a numpty. You're just out of practice."

"Yeah, mate, you just need to get out and interact with people your own age," Joe piped in. His eyes widened. "You should come out with Freddie and me."

Fraser shook his head. "I don't know."

"You should! We'll go to the straight clubs, find you some girls to pull, and we can be your wingmen!"

Freddie looked at Joe side-eyed. "You're way too excited. Tone it down a notch."

"I think your enthusiasm is scaring him," Tessa whispered.

James stifled his smile when he caught the deer in headlights look on Fraser's face.

"I don't know," his words were stilted, as he stammered a little. "With my mum—"

"Oi," his mom piped up, "don't use me as an excuse. I'm in bed by seven every night. Go out and have fun with your mates."

"There you have it!" Joe exclaimed. He pulled out his billfold and took out a card. He handed it to Fraser. "This is my number. We are going to go out on Tuesday. Let's make plans to meet up."

Fraser reluctantly reached into his pocket, pulling out his own card, handing it to Joe.

Joe looked at the card with a smile on his face. "Brilliant." He looked back up, locking his gaze onto Fraser's. "We're going to get you laid," he declared with full sincerity oozing out of his voice.

James watched as the color drained from Fraser's face, his expression clearly telegraphing he was certain he'd made a grievous error.

"C'mon, I'll walk you out. We're done scaring our best customer for the day," Freddie took hold of Joe's arm and began leading him outside, "G'day, Fraser. Mrs. Hudson."

They watched as Freddie led Joe outside and toward the tube.

"Blimey," Fraser muttered. "Is he always like that?"

James let out the chuckle he had been holding in during the interaction. "Yes. And believe it or not, this was pretty fucking tame for him."

Fraser ran his hands through his hair. "What have I gotten myself into? I can barely talk to a girl. And now he wants me to..." he swallowed. "I will have to tell him I'm not coming when he sends the information."

Tessa laughed. "You will be fine. Maybe it will be good for you."

Fraser turned. "Will you two be out with them? That's a thing, right? Double dates? I am so out of my depth."

James eyed Fraser.

He had been watching him this entire time, and nothing he was doing seemed to be suspicious. He didn't seem jealous. In fact, he seemed like a genuinely nice person. However, he had one more test.

"Sure," James answered. "We can go out with the lot of you on Tuesday. We wouldn't be able to stay too long. Tessa has to get enough sleep in order to wake up early to get into the shop to bake. She's staying with Freddie until her window can get fixed, and he lives eons away from the shop."

"What happened to her window?" Mrs. Hudson asked.

James kept his gaze on Fraser when he said the next part. "Someone threw a brick through it last weekend."

Fraser looked genuinely shocked. "Someone threw a brick through her window? Who on earth would want to a throw a brick through a baker's window? Was it one of those old ladies who couldn't get a pumpkin bar last week?"

James' shoulders relaxed. "We don't know. Joe and I are trying to figure it out."

"It's a good thing she and Freddie are dating men of the law," Mrs. Hudson expressed. "Hopefully you'll be able to catch whoever it is who would do something so cruel."

"That's our hope," James agreed.

"We won't keep you any longer. Enjoy your tea and let me know if you need anything else."

"We will, dear."

"Yes, thank you, Ms. Lopez. I'm sorry about your window," Fraser apologized.

"Please call me Tessa, Fraser."

"Oh, okay. Thank you, Tessa."

Tessa gave him a smile, and she and James moved through the shop and into the kitchen, since Mariel was back from her break.

"So," Tessa began speaking as soon as the door closed behind her. "What do you think?"

"Honestly?" James leaned against the counter. "I feel pretty good about him not being our stalker."

Tessa perked up. "Really?"

"Really. He seemed genuinely surprised about the brick. And he didn't seem jealous when he found out you were dating me."

"You can tell these things?"

"I'm fantastic at reading people. It comes with the job. I don't think he's the stalker."

Tessa let out a breath. "I'm so relieved to hear that, because I really like him and his mum."

"They seem like good people. When I talked to Evelyn about this before the wedding, she told me she didn't think it could be him, either."

"So, that leaves us with—"

"Bruno."

CHAPTER 24

TESSA

Tessa stood in Freddie's bathroom trying to finish her makeup.

She had pulled out all her "going out" outfits from her wardrobe and threw them in a bag Saturday night before leaving the shop for the night. She dropped them off at Freddie's before spending her Sunday with James.

He had really scaled down his tailing of Bruno. The man never left his house, and James thought it was mostly because he was sitting there. He talked to Joe, and this week they were going to stand down, and mid-week, grab the CCTV footage from his block and see if they could see any delineation from the pattern.

Her case was on the back burner for a while, and James was going to focus on a backlog of cases in their email, at least until Patrick got back from his honeymoon next week.

"You almost finished? I need to fix my hair," Freddie spoke through the door.

"Yes, I'm finished," Tessa called back, putting the lid on her mascara.

She rarely wore makeup, since it would all just melt off her face in the heat of her kitchen. But if she was going to go out, she was going to doll herself up. She briefly thought about trying out contacts again, but opted for her simple black-rimmed glasses.

She opened the door to let Freddie in.

He let out a low whistle. "Damn, you clean up nicely."

Tessa waved him off as she pushed past him.

"Seriously. You should go out more often."

"You know, going out is not my thing. I would much rather stay in, wearing sweats and going to bed by eight."

Freddie pulled her into a one-armed hug. "Yes, I know you revel in living like an old lady, but this will be good for you. And for you and James. Besides, I can't reign in Joe all by myself. I haven't learned how to control him yet. I need James."

Tess sighed. "Fine. For just one night I'll pretend to be a thirty-something rather than an eighty-something. But come ten, I'm out. I turn into a pumpkin if I stay out too late."

"More like the Wicked Witch of the West," Freddie muttered, not quite under his breath.

Tessa gave him a playful shove. "Be nice, or I'll cancel."

"You wouldn't," Freddie teased. "You like Fraser too much to sacrifice him to the whims of Joe."

"I hate it when you're right."

"Now, out, I need to make myself look beautiful."

Tessa laughed as she made her way back to the office, aka her room. She immediately went to the full-length mirror propped up against the wall.

She decided simple was better than going overboard. Especially after a full day of work. She was probably going to convince James to sit somewhere. Her feet were tired from spending the whole day standing on them.

She opted for dark wash skinny jeans, and a black asymmetrical tunic length blouse. She wore her hair loose, her tight curls fully on display as they cascaded down her back. Light makeup, no jewelry, and her black and white Chuck Taylor trainers.

She smiled.

She cleaned up nicely.

She opened her purse and pulled out her ID and a card, slipping them into her front pocket, and slid her phone into her back pocket.

One last look in the mirror before she turned off her light and walked to the front of the flat.

Just as she entered the living room, there was a knock on the door.

She opened it to see James and Joe standing there.

As soon as James caught sight of her, she could visibly see his jaw drop.

"Fuck."

She laughed. "I'll take that as a compliment."

"Definitely a compliment. Always a compliment."

"You're acting like you've never seen me in fancy dress before. When it's only been a week and a bit since the wedding, where I was in much fancier dress."

"Tessa, love, I'm going to let you into a little secret." Joe moved in closer, leaning their heads together. "He's speechless because while you looked brilliant in your dress at the wedding, it did not fit your body like a glove like your current outfit. Poor James here is short circuiting because that outfit makes your tits and arse look phenomenal, and that is coming from me, the gayest man in this group."

Tessa's cheeks warmed and her mouth dropped open.

"For fuck's sake, Joe," James growled. "You haven't even started drinking yet."

"Not true," Joe disagreed. "I had a beer from our fridge right before we left."

"You're incorrigible," James grumbled.

"Gonna go find my man." Joe pushed past Tessa into the flat.

"Hi," James drawled when they were finally alone.

"Hi," Tessa replied.

James moved closer and placed a hand to cup the back of her head, pulling her into him, capturing her lips in a kiss.

They broke away before things could get heated.

The beginning of a relationship was always her favorite. Getting to know one another, both in and out of bed, and the newness made it so they couldn't keep their hands off of each other.

"Are you sure you want to go out with these lunatics?" James asked, gesturing toward the back of the flat with his head. "We could stay in, watch a new episode of the latest MCU show on Disney, go to bed..." he lowered his voice as he trailed off, waggling his eyebrows.

Tessa laughed. "While your idea sounds like my ideal evening, we made a promise. And do you *really* want to leave poor Fraser alone with those two?"

She turned her head into the flat where Freddie and Joe were practicing some sort of coordinated dance to something Joe was playing on his phone.

"You're right. We're Fraser's only hope," James shook his head.

"Oi," Joe called over to them when he noticed they were looking at them. "What are you lot looking at?"

"We need to go if we're going to be at the club when Fraser arrives," James answered.

Joe picked his phone up from Freddie's counter and shoved it in his pocket.

"What are we waiting for?" He waltzed past them into the hallway, Freddie trailing closely behind. "Let's go."

Tessa and James exchanged a look before following the two men, Tessa closing and locking the door behind her.

The club's music was too loud for Tessa's comfort, but it wasn't so loud that it drowned out her friends' conversation.

As she settled herself at the table they found, she glanced over at Fraser.

He was wearing dark wash jeans and a dark grey button-up shirt, buttoned most of the way to the top, and French tucked into his trousers.

"You look nice," Tessa leaned in toward Fraser so he could hear her over the music.

She could see Fraser's cheeks color. "Thanks," he shouted over the music. "I wasn't sure what to wear, and even more unsure if I could even wear jeans. I'm glad you're also wearing them, so we can both be in this faux pas together if we were supposed to wear something nicer."

Tessa laughed. "It's not a faux pas. You're fine. You should relax."

Fraser took a deep breath, held it, and let it out. "I'm so nervous. This is my first time at a club."

Tessa tried to hide her surprise, but knew she was failing. "Really? Not even at school?"

Fraser shook his head. "My mum has been ill for most of my life. After my dad left, I was the only one who could take care of her. I've been a bit of a hermit, honestly. Finished my A-Levels and did most of my university courses online, worked from home. I don't want something to happen to my mum and not be there for her."

Tessa reached over and placed a hand on his arm. "You are a good man, Fraser, and an excellent son. But you deserve to have a little time for yourself."

Fraser dropped his gaze to where she had placed her hand on his arm before bringing it back up and meeting hers.

Tessa's gut clenched when their eyes met.

There was something in the way he looked at her that made her feel a little uneasy, but she couldn't quite place it.

She removed her hand and placed it in her lap.

Fraser kept his gaze on her, causing her to squirm a little in her seat.

He was socially awkward; she told herself. He's been isolated in his home. He didn't know how to act around others. That's all this is.

Tessa forced herself to smile, which caused Fraser's smile to widen, and whatever it was she saw in his gaze disappeared.

"We have booze!" Joe announced as he, Freddie, and James made their way to the table.

James had a pint in each hand, as did Freddie, and Joe, well, Joe was carrying a tray of shots.

"You don't have to take one," James muttered, as he took his seat next to her, placing her pint in front of her. "Don't let him pressure you."

"James, I don't like that you are always warning people away from me, as if I'm some sort of bad influence. I'm a well-respected London police officer."

"Who is very charismatic, and who likes to goad people into doing his bidding when out," James observed, "remember the night after the Fitzgerald verdict?"

Joe set the tray on the table and folded his arms, staring off into the distance before shaking his head. "No, I can't say that I do."

"Neither do I, and neither do Patrick and Evie. All I know is it started off with coming to a place like this, and you bringing over a tray exactly like this one, and then it's a blur."

"We were all equal participants in that night of revelry," Joe defended. "I will not take the blame for what you do and do not remember."

Tessa laughed, taking a sip of her pint. "I'm going to pass on the shots. I have to be up at three so I can get to the bakery in time to, you know, bake. I can't be hungover."

James sat back and placed his arm around her shoulders. "I'm out, too. Solidarity."

"Spoilsports," Joe teased. "More for the rest of us. Drink up chaps, we're in for a wild night!"

Freddie and Joe immediately reached for a shot. Tessa couldn't help but smile. This was the happiest and most carefree she'd seen Freddie in a while. Even if his relationship with Joe was short-lived, it was a wonderful experience for him.

Fraser moved a little slower, but he also grabbed a shot.

The three men counted down from three and threw back their respective shots before setting the glasses back on the table.

"Alright, lads, let's away!" Joe shouted, leading the charge, holding tightly to Freddie's hand as they made their way to the dance floor.

Fraser shot her and James a pitiful look before he, too, followed Joe into the abyss.

James tightened his arm around Tessa's shoulder and brought his head down. He used his nose to push aside her hair before planting a kiss on her neck.

"First date outside the home?" Tessa asked, her voice already taking on a breathy quality.

"Mmm," James hummed against her neck as he traced his way up to her ear, giving it a little nibble. "First double date, too." He captured her lips with his.

Tessa felt like a schoolgirl again, sitting in a club making out with a hot guy.

Freddie was right. Getting out was a good thing.

When James' hand traveled to her breast, she pulled away.

"Want to dance?" she gasped out.

"What I want is to leave this place and go home and get into bed with you, but I'll settle for dancing."

James stood and held his hand out for her. She placed her hand in his and he led her to the dance floor.

***

Dancing was not the activity she needed for her overactive libido.

The booming music cast a steady beat for the last half hour as she and James moved together on the dance floor.

Right now, he was behind her, and she could feel his erection digging into her ass as they moved together to the heavy bass line, and she finally had enough.

She knew it was earlier than she had promised, but she didn't care. She wanted to go home and fuck her boyfriend before going to sleep.

She turned around and draped her arms around James' neck, pulling him down to talk to her. "Want to get out of here?"

"Fuck, yes," James growled into her ear.

"I need to use the loo first. I'm bursting."

"I'll go tell the others we're taking off, and I'll meet you by the loos, so we're not wandering 'round trying to find one another and stuck here for eternity."

Tessa laughed. "Good idea."

James gave her one more quick, searing kiss before they parted. She watched briefly as James weaved his way through the gyrating bodies of the fellow club goers before turning herself in the loo's direction.

She pushed open the door and as it shut behind her; she breathed in a sigh of relief. The music was much quieter in here. Her ears still rang as she took care of her business and washed her hands.

She took a second to check out her appearance in the mirror. She had time. It would take a few minutes for James to find Joe, say their goodbyes, and make his way back to her.

As she scrutinized her appearance in the mirror, she couldn't keep the smile off her face. Things were going really well with her and James. They had only been a couple for a week, but boy, what a week it had been.

She tried to tame her hair, but decided it was fruitless, especially given what they planned to do back at his flat.

She bit her lip to hold back the smile.

She tucked her hair behind her ears and practically skipped to the door.

When she stepped back into the hall with the bathrooms, the music playing at its normal volume was too much for her.

She stopped outside the door and looked down the hall.

To her right, there was just a dark hall which led to an emergency exit, the left led back to the dance floor. Both ways were empty, so James must've still been talking to Joe.

She walked the few feet from the door of the women's room to where the hall met the main floor. From here, she would be more visible to James, and they could leave right away.

She stood on her tiptoes and looked around and she could see James' familiar red hair weaving its way through the crowd.

He broke through the crowd, looking around for the hall.

She raised her arm to get his attention, when something wrapped around her waist and neck.

Whatever had wrapped itself around her body jerked her backwards hard enough for her glasses to be knocked off her face.

Arms.

These things, wrapped around her, were arms.

And they were swiftly dragging her toward the emergency exit.

CHAPTER 25

JAMES

James turned when he caught movement out of the corner of his eye.

He smiled as he caught Tessa signaling to him. He couldn't wait to get back to his place and have her to himself for the night.

He started toward her, but stopped short when he watched her suddenly jerk backward into the dark hall.

It only took a second for him to realize she was being pulled. His heart skipped a beat before he took off at a run.

He shoved his way around the drunk people in his way and ran full speed.

His feet skidded on the polished concrete floor as he made the sharp turn into the hallway. Something crunched beneath his feet as he entered the hall. Looking down, he could see Tessa's glasses lying on the floor. The pit in his stomach grew. How hard did the bastard grab her for her glasses to fall from her face?

He looked up from the floor to look for Tessa.

The hall was so poorly lit, and he could barely make out the two figures of Tessa and her assailant.

Whoever was dragging her was trying to be quick, however, dragging a struggling Tessa was slowing him down. Which was good for James.

As James ran toward them, he cursed to himself. He should have thought ahead and put his knife in his pocket. Given him some sort of defense if the kidnapper had a weapon.

James shook that thought from his head. His priority should be to get to them before they made it to the emergency exit and caused the alarm to sound, creating chaos in the club.

Running through the hall, it was as if he were in a dream. Everything seemed to move in slow motion, and the hallway never seemed to get shorter. He was convinced he wasn't gaining any ground. Like he was running in place on a treadmill.

As he got closer, his heart skipped a beat as he could see Tessa being dragged more clearly. Her legs were kicking out from under her, trying to find purchase on the polished concrete floor of the club. It was too dark to make out her expression, but he didn't need to see it to know she was terrified, because he was terrified.

He was just about to close in on them when they stopped, and the kidnapper let go of Tessa and thrust her at him.

James watched as Tessa, not prepared to stand fully on her own, fell, face first, toward the ground.

He sprinted across the gap between them and dove, wrapping his arms around her, holding her tightly as they both went down. As they got closer to the floor, James turned so he would make impact with his side, and rolled onto his back, holding his head up and not letting it smash onto the concrete.

Quickly glancing at Tessa to make sure she was okay, James rolled to his side to see if he could get a look at the kidnapper.

He caught the back of the man just as he reached the emergency exit.

The man turned around briefly, looking toward James and Tessa.

James couldn't make out any features, it was too dark.

And just as quickly as the man had stopped, he pushed through the emergency exit, which didn't set off any alarms, and ran out into the dark of the night.

As soon as he couldn't see the man anymore, he turned his attention to Tessa.

He could feel her shaking in his arms.

He sat them up and moved them so she was sitting on his lap, facing him.

James brought his hands up to her face and pushed her hair back so he could get a good look at her.

She was crying, her mascara running down her face.

"Are you hurt?" he asked. He almost asked if she was okay, which was a stupid question. Of course, she wasn't okay.

She shook her head. "Not really."

"What hurts?" James asked, looking her over, moving his hands down her body as he assessed for injuries.

"My neck and my stomach from where he grabbed me."

James brought his hand up to her neck, moving her hair out of the way. It was hard to tell in the dimly lit hallway, but he thought he could make out some bruising.

"We need to talk to Joe and make a report."

"Joe's drunk."

James shook his head. "Not a report to him. We need him to make the call to someone on duty to come and take the report. Can you stand?"

Tessa nodded. "Yeah, I think so."

James shifted them so he could help Tessa get to her feet, before standing himself.

She was a little wobbly, but that was probably more because she was still shaking than her actually being injured.

"My glasses."

"I'm sorry. I stepped on them when I chased after you. They're broken."

"It's okay."

"How poor is your vision?"

"I can see fine. I won't be able to read anything too far away, but you're not a blur or anything."

James wrapped an arm around her and helped lead her through the crowd.

He scowled at everyone who bumped into them as they weaved across the dance floor.

He'd been having so much fun tonight, and had been looking forward to what was going to happen next, and now, his mood was soured, and all he wanted to do was find the arsehole who tried to kidnap his girlfriend and beat the shit out of him.

Joe and Freddie were where he had left them, with the addition of Fraser. When he had said goodbye, Fraser had been off flirting with some bird, and Joe and Freddie wouldn't stop gushing like proud parents.

Freddie saw them first.

"What happened?" he asked as he rushed toward them, taking Tessa's hand in his.

James waited until Joe had joined them before answering.

"The stalker escalated."

James knew Joe wasn't as drunk as he had made himself out to be when the second he heard this information, he snapped into police mode. "Where?"

"Back by the loos," James answered.

"What'd he do?"

"He grabbed me, and tried to drag me out of the club," Tessa spoke up beside him.

"Fuck!" Freddie exclaimed, letting go of Tessa to run his hands through his hair.

He looked over at Tessa, who stood next to James as new tears ran down her face.

Freddie grabbed onto her and tugged her away from James, and wrapped her in a tight hug.

"Did you get a good look at the guy?" Joe asked.

James shook his head. "It was too fucking dark. Couldn't see a damn thing."

Joe pulled out his phone and dialed a number. "I'm going to call this in. You two will need to give a statement."

"Yeah, I thought as much."

Joe stepped away and walked toward the exit of the club so he could talk on the phone without the bass interfering.

"What's going on?" Fraser asked, reminding everyone of his presence.

James moved around Freddie and Tessa, pulling Fraser aside. "Tessa has had a bit of an incident. We're going to need to go out and meet with the police."

"The police? This sounds serious. Is she okay?"

"Physically, she's okay, but she's really shaken up."

"Does this have to do with what happened to her window?" Fraser asked, folding his arms and bringing one hand up to rest under his chin.

James frowned. He was getting a strong feeling, but he couldn't figure out what it was trying to tell him. "Yes," he drawled. "We're pretty sure it does."

"Oh my," Fraser intoned, "poor Tessa."

"Yes," James narrowed his eyes slightly, almost imperceptibly, "poor Tessa."

James waited for Fraser to say something else, to do something else, mainly to excuse himself from the situation. However, the man just stood there. Staring at him, standing up straight, his chin still resting in his hand.

That feeling in his gut came back.

Suspicion.

"Where were you about ten minutes ago?" James asked.

Fraser didn't even flinch. "I was over at the bar, trying to pull a girl. It didn't work out." He tilted his head. "You don't think I had something to do with this, do you?"

"I wasn't implying you did," James answered. "Trying to get an idea of where everyone was when it happened. Where were you a week ago Saturday? About two in the morning?"

"At home asleep. Like I've said, I don't go out much. This is my first time at a club."

"Can anyone corroborate your presence?"

"Me mum."

James watched Fraser's face and neck as he answered his questions. He wasn't exhibiting any of the tells of a liar. He was telling the truth. Then why was his gut telling him he wasn't?

Fraser uncrossed his arms and relaxed his posture, and just as suddenly James' suspicions rose, they dissipated. He shook his head, as if clearing the cobwebs.

"Right," he drew out, "since you weren't around, you won't need to stay and give a statement, and unfortunately, I think the night's done for the rest of us."

"Yeah, yeah," Fraser nodded, "I guess I'll just take off then."

"Don't let us ruin the night for you. Stay. Have some fun. Find a bird to go home with."

"Nah, I think I've had enough rejection for the night. Tell Tessa I'll see her at the shop tomorrow morning."

James must have looked confused.

"Me mum and I come in on Wednesday mornings for tea?" Fraser reminded him.

"That's right. I've got my days mixed up. Rarely go dancing in the middle of the week," James forced a smile and a short laugh.

Fraser returned his smile. "Same. I'll see you around, James."

James watched Fraser walk out of the club and couldn't shake the uneasy feeling he had.

When he could no longer see him, James turned toward Freddie and Tessa.

"We should head outside. Joe is calling in the attempt. They'll want to question us."

Tessa pulled back from Freddie and nodded. She stepped away from his arms and walked over and took James' hand.

He led them out of the club and into the frigid November night air.

Joe was standing on the sidewalk talking to the bouncer. He had completely sobered, which meant ninety percent of how he acted in the club was more for show, and he really hadn't drunk as much as he led people to believe.

Joe stopped talking when he noticed the group moving toward him. "Good news," he started once the four of them were together. "This bloke here says they have cameras in the alley, and they keep the footage here on the property. He's just called the manager and they're going to prep the footage for us now. PC Davies is on his way and will meet us in the manager's office."

"That was fast," James failed to keep the surprise out of his voice.

"Because it happened in the last hour, it's easy for the manager to pull up the footage. Let's head in."

Joe led the way, with Freddie following close behind. James took Tessa's hand and helped move her through the crowds.

Her grip on his hand was tight, as if she was worried someone could snatch her away from him at any moment.

He gripped her just as firmly, the same fear etched in his brain.

Watching her getting dragged through the hallway was the most helpless he had felt in a long time. He would be damned if he let anything else happen to her ever again.

They reached the manager's office and walked in. The room was small, barely big enough for everyone to fit, but they squeezed in and shut the door behind them.

"PC McCleary?" the manager, a thirty-something woman with a no-nonsense haircut and business suit, asked.

Joe lifted his hand. "That would be me."

She nodded. "I have the footage pulled up for the time in which the incident took place. But I'm afraid it won't be much help."

She turned her monitor around so the room could see. She pressed play, and they watched as the door to the club opened and a man ran out.

The footage was black and white and a little grainy. Because of the lack of color, you could only see that the man was wearing some sort of dark shirt and dark trousers, which was the dress of most of the men in the club. And he was wearing a dark knit hat, covering any identifying features, which weren't many, since he was looking at the ground as he ran.

"What the fuck is it with this guy and cameras?" James exclaimed, pointing at the video. "There's no fucking way he knew there was a camera in that alley."

"Maybe he scoped it out before tonight?" Freddie posited.

Joe shook his head. "We didn't even decide to come here until this morning. There's no way he could have known to come here and scout the alley."

"Then how did he know I was here in the first place?" Tessa asked.

"He probably followed you," Joe explained, "Followed us."

"So, he knows where Freddie lives?" she asked.

"It seems to look that way," Joe apologized.

"I can't go back there," she shook her head.

"You can come stay at mine," James offered, "if you want," he quickly added, remembering their conversation about him being overprotective.

"Yeah, I think I want that," she gave him a small smile, reassuring him he hadn't overstepped.

"I can bring round your stuff tomorrow," Freddie suggested, "after the shop closes."

"Thanks."

There was a knock on the door of the office before it cracked open. PC Davies poked his head in.

"Full house," he commented.

"I'll get out of the way. Stay as long as you like," the manager squeezed her way through to the door.

Everyone shifted and let PC Davies in.

"So," he pulled out his phone and turned on his recording app, "tell me what happened."

They took turns recounting what had happened, but hearing the story told back, James knew it was hopeless. No one had seen his face, or any identifying features.

They still didn't have a suspect.

James stood up straighter. If they were living in a cartoon, he was pretty sure a light bulb would flash above his head.

"Bruno Nelson."

"Who's that?" PC Davies asked.

"He's someone who went to school with Freddie and Tessa. He had an obsession with Tessa in school. I've been looking at him as a probable stalking suspect. I had been sitting outside his house, but obviously I wasn't there tonight."

"Do you think he could have done this?" Freddie asked.

"It's quite plausible. He has motive. He knew I was sitting outside and watching him, so he would have noticed I wasn't there today. Since he and Freddie used to be friends, he could have knowledge of where Freddie lives. It's quite possible he could have left his house, followed you from Freddie's and, when you went to the loo, escalated things."

"Why would he want to escalate things now? Over a week since he would have thrown the brick?" PC Davies asked. "Allegedly," he added quickly.

"He came into my shop and confronted me about having James following him," Tessa added.

"It's not hard evidence, but it's a lead. We'll go round and I'll question him myself."

"Thank you," Tessa said.

"My professional advice is to go home, get some sleep, and don't be too worried. Let us do our job," he made a show of turning off his recording. "My non-professional advice would be to be careful, be aware of your surroundings, and don't go anywhere alone."

Tessa nodded.

"I'll drive you to the shop," James offered.

Tessa shook her head. "I couldn't have you do that. It's so early."

James shrugged. "I can always come back home and go to sleep once you're in the shop."

"And I'll make sure you get to James' after you're done at the shop," Freddie spoke up.

"Looks like you're in excellent hands," PC Davies commented. "I'll be in touch. I'll let you know if anything comes from looking into this Bruno fellow."

He tucked his phone into his pocket and put his hand on the handle to open the door. "Oh," he said, turning around. "Before I forget, earlier tonight, the results of the CCTV search came in. They could find some shots of the bloke with his face uncovered. However, they're terrible shots. Blurry. I sent the files to you both," he pointed to Joe and James, "but I'm afraid they were inconclusive. We're back at square one."

CHAPTER 26

TESSA

Tessa took her glasses off and rubbed her eyes for probably the one hundredth time since she arrived at the shop this morning.

"Tired?" Freddie asked, walking into the kitchen.

"Yes," she placed her glasses back on her face before flapping her hands and jumping from foot to foot to wake herself up.

Freddie moved next to her and set a very large takeaway cup of coffee on the counter. "I figured. I went out and got one of these for each of us."

Tessa stopped her jumping and reached for the coffee on the counter. "You're a blessing."

"Did you sleep at all?"

She shook her head as she took a long drag from the coffee cup. "No. Every time I even drifted off for even a second, I found myself right there, back in the hallway with his arms around me, dragging me to who knows where, and then I would startle myself awake."

Freddie gave her a sympathetic smile. "And James?"

"He didn't sleep at all, I don't think. Every time I woke up, he was awake, watching me."

"He was probably worried about you."

"Yeah, I know. I hope he's getting some sleep now."

Freddie stared at her face, squinting his eyes, before breaking out in a long peel of laughter.

"What's wrong?"

"Have you been rubbing your face a lot?"

"Yes."

He pulled out his phone and opened the camera, flipping it into selfie mode and turning it toward her.

When she caught sight of herself, she about died. Flour and various other ingredients she had been working with all morning covered her face. Even the arms of her favorite purple glasses had flour fingerprints caked all over them.

"Fuck," she rushed over to the sink to wash her face and glasses. "I wonder how long I've looked a mess. I helped customers this morning before Mariel came in."

The admission made Freddie laugh harder.

"It's not funny."

"Oh, it absolutely is," Freddie wiped at the tears forming in his eyes from laughing so hard.

"I'm going to lose customers," she scrubbed her face.

"You're not. They're going to love you all the more because you look like you spent all morning baking delicious things for them to buy. They've probably gone and told all their little grannie friends, and we'll see an influx of visitors at lunch."

"You're trying to make me feel better."

"It's my job as the best friend. Is it working?"

"A little."

"Oh, before I forget, before I came in, I dropped your essentials in your flat so you can grab those when we leave. This way you won't have to wait for me to come back after the shop closes to clean your teeth."

Tessa smiled her first smile since the incident the night before. "Thank you."

"You're welcome. Now down the coffee and let's get to work. The pensioners will swarm this shop soon."

***

Tessa shut James' door behind her and leaned against it.

Freddie was right. Whoever had seen her looking like a mess this morning had spread the word, and they had double the customers they normally had.

She was exhausted.

Freddie was kind enough to walk her to James' flat before heading back to the shop to close it with Mariel.

All she wanted to do was go to sleep.

She took her shoes off by the door and walked through the flat. Joe's bedroom door was wide open, and he wasn't inside. She hoped he was out doing something for himself and he didn't go in on his day off. Not for something for her.

She looked in James' room. Also, empty.

He had probably gone into the office.

She dropped her bag on the floor next to the doorway and shuffled to the bed before falling on it face first.

She was asleep immediately.

***

When she opened her eyes, it was dark outside, and there were sounds coming from the kitchen. She rolled over and looked at the bedside clock. It was after six.

She stretched and sat up.

Her sleep pattern was going to be severely disturbed.

She stood from the bed and made her way out of the room. As she walked down the hallway, she noticed Joe's door was still open and the lights were out. She wondered where he was.

She made it into the kitchen to see James stirring something in a saucepan on the hob.

"What are you making?"

James jumped and turned around, his hand clutching at his chest.

"Bloody hell, Tessa, you're going to give me a fucking heart attack. Walk a little heavier next time."

She laughed. "Sorry, I didn't mean to startle you."

"Admit it. You enjoyed giving me a fright."

"I did."

James turned back to the stove, stirring the pot again. "I'm making ramen. Nothing fancy. I figured we needed a simple comfort meal after last night."

"Ramen actually sounds delicious." She walked over to the bar stools, pulled one out, and hoisted herself onto one, resting her arms on the counter. "What have you been up to today?"

"Spent some time outside of Bruno's. Nada, as usual. Then I went down to see if Officer Davies had found anything."

"Did he?"

"Went and talked to Bruno, and he said he never left the house last night. Which was then confirmed by the CCTV footage from his street. He never left his house. However, Davies pointed out there were no cameras in the back of the house, so they can only say with certainty he never left through the front."

Tessa put her head down on her arms. "We're never going to figure out who's stalking me."

"We will. We just have to be smarter than whoever it is."

"I feel like we're always one step behind them."

"We'll do some brainstorming. See if we can anticipate the next move."

Tessa picked her head up from her arms. "I love your optimism."

"I love you," James proclaimed.

Tessa froze.

James froze.

"What?" Tessa asked.

"Nothing. I said nothing. I love ramen?"

"That's not what you said."

"Just forget I said anything."

"So, you didn't mean what you said?"

James stood at the stove, his back to her. "Do you want me to have meant what I said?"

"We've only just started seeing each other," her voice was hesitant and unsure.

"I know. Just forget what I said."

Tessa watched James stirring the ramen with his back stiff. She thought back to the short time they'd known each other. She knew pretty quickly she felt something more than just friendly toward him. And even with only a couple weeks of dating between them, there was something here that was just... more.

"I don't want to forget what you said."

"What?"

"I said I don't want to forget what you said. Because I'm pretty sure I feel the same."

James set down the spoon he was using to stir and turned off the burner. It was a full five seconds before he turned around, sporting a wide, silly grin.

"You're not having me on, are you?" James asked.

Tessa shook her head.

"Well. Okay then. Let's table this revelation for after we eat our delicious dinner, and then we'll continue it say, in our bed, with less clothing?"

Tessa laughed. "I like the sound of that."

James turned back to the stove and whistled a jaunty tune she wasn't even sure was an actual song or something he had made up.

He dished up the ramen and walked the bowls over to the counter, placing one in front of her and the other in the spot next to his. He went to the fridge and pulled out a pitcher of squash, setting it down on the counter. He then went to the cupboard and pulled out two glasses and gave one to each of them before sitting down next to her on the other bar stool.

It all felt so fucking domestic. Combined with the words they both sort of said to each other, Tessa could feel a warmth spread through her body. This is what her future held for her. She could get used to this.

"How was the shop today?"

Tessa groaned. "It was a madhouse. I was so tired this morning, I kept rubbing my face. And apparently, I rubbed all sorts of flour and pumpkin and whatever all over it, I looked a right mess. Well, I served some grannies first thing. They thought I looked charming and spread the word, and I'm pretty sure every pensioner in London was in my shop this afternoon."

"That's wonderful!"

Tessa shot him a look.

"I mean, it's wonderful for your business."

"It is, it truly is, and I'll always be so grateful for all the people who come into my shop, but we really need to hire more people going into Christmas if this is going to be the normal flow of customers. I'll never be able to keep up with the baking on my own."

"Well, I hope you find someone worthy of working in your kitchen." James raised his glass to her in a toast.

She laughed and raised her glass, and they clinked them together before each taking a sip and turning toward their dinner.

"Did Fraser and his mum come in today?" James asked after they had eaten for a few minutes.

Tessa shook her head. "No. They didn't show. His mum probably wasn't having a good day today."

"I'm going to say something, and I don't want you to get offended. I know you like Fraser and everything, but last night—"

"He was acting strangely," Tessa interrupted.

"Yes, well, not exactly, but there was something strange about him. I don't know. My instincts were telling me to keep an eye on him, but he wasn't really giving me anything *to* suspect. He was telling the truth every time I asked him a direct question."

"It wasn't just you. We made eye contact last night, and there was something in his eyes that made me feel uneasy."

"Be careful around him, Tessa. I know he's one of your best customers, and his mum is really nice, but I don't know. Just be careful."

Tessa nodded. "I will be."

The door to the flat opened and Joe came walking in, carrying a large bouquet of flowers in his arm.

"Where've you been all day?" James asked.

"I went into the office and helped go over Bruno's CCTV footage, and then went around and looked at the alley in the daylight. Then I got peckish, so I swung by Cake Me Home Tonight. Freddie and Mariel were overwhelmed, so I jumped in to help them out until we closed. Freddie and I picked up a quick bite, and went our separate ways because we're bloody knackered after the last couple of days."

"And he gave you beautiful flowers to thank you for working hard in the shop all afternoon?" Tessa grinned.

"Actually, no. These were outside the door. They have your name on them, Tessa."

He walked over and put the flowers down on the counter next to Tessa and walked to the fridge, pulling out a beer.

Tessa frowned at the flowers. "You got me flowers?" she asked, turning toward James.

He shook his head. "I did not. And those weren't outside the door when I got home an hour ago."

Joe didn't even open his beer. He set the bottle down on the counter. "Touch nothing."

"What? Why?"

"Evidence," James explained.

"I'm going to get my kit so we can process everything." Joe left and walked toward his room.

"You think..."

"The stalker sent you these flowers? Yes."

Tessa stared at the beautiful arrangement. It had a variety of autumn-colored flowers and grasses. It looked expensive. And there, nestled amongst the flowers, was a large envelope with her name scrawled on it in red marker.

James must have followed her gaze, because he held onto her hand. "Remember, we can't touch anything, not until Joe processes everything."

Joe came back out into the room, holding a small bag and a camera. "I'll take pictures of everything, and dust for prints. Once I collect the prints, we can open the envelope and take pictures and prints on whatever is inside."

"I didn't think you could work my stalker case," Tessa pointed out.

"I don't fucking care at this point. The bastard tried to kidnap you. You're my friend, and I'm going to process this as evidence. And if I get shit for it, I'll point my superiors to you almost being abducted and your window."

Tessa watched as Joe moved through the motions of cataloging and fingerprinting everything. She had never seen him so serious before. She'd only ever seen fun, happy partying Joe. Watching him work, and seeing this other side of him, she instantly understood why Freddie was attracted to him and why they fit so well together.

"Alright," Joe finished his thorough investigation of the package, "let's open this and see what this bastard has to say now."

Joe plucked the envelope from the flowers, took a couple pictures, lifted a couple of prints and, with his gloved hands, opened the flap.

He pulled out one sheet from the envelope.

He unfolded it and set it down on the counter.

A chill rushed over Tessa as she looked at what came with the flowers.

It was a picture of her and James dancing last night in the club. Over her face, drawn in red marker, was a heart with an arrow drawn through it, bisecting her head. Over James' face, an 'x' had drawn angrily until it had ripped holes in the picture.

What really chilled her were the words scrawled across the bottom of the photo.

"Discard your redheaded twat, or you'll be sorry. If I can't have you, nobody can."

CHAPTER 27

JAMES

For the second night in a row, James couldn't sleep. Every time he closed his eyes, visions of something terrible happening to Tessa flooded his mind. All he could do was lay awake and stare at his girlfriend, and hope she wouldn't just vanish when he looked away.

He could tell she was having trouble sleeping again because she was restless, tossing and turning in her sleep.

He looked at his watch, noticing it wouldn't be long until they needed to be up to go to the shop, so falling asleep now would be fruitless. He debated getting up, but he would feel trapped without something to do.

He felt helpless. At least they had a purpose when they tried to save Evie. They knew who they were protecting her from. With Tessa, there was no suspect. He didn't even know where to start. Every lead they had seemed to come up empty. They had no viable suspects.

Except for Bruno. Who was a suspect, and a pretty good one. Nevertheless, there was no evidence that he was the one responsible for any of this.

"I can hear your thoughts. You're thinking so loud," Tessa whispered from the bed next to him.

James looked down at her and gave her a small smile. "I'm sorry. Didn't mean for my thoughts to wake you."

"I wasn't asleep, really, so there was nothing to wake me from."

James brought up a hand and ran it down her arm. "I'm sorry, love. I hate to be the bearer of bad news, but we need to be up soon to go into the shop."

Tessa groaned. "Another day of looking like a mess in front of customers."

James chuckled. "The upside? More. Customers."

"So many customers."

"Did you ever imagine being *the* bakery in East London when you opened Cake Me Home Tonight?"

"No. We both thought that we would barely make enough to cover our expenses. Which is what we were doing for the longest time. After a year, we were doing really well, and were actually making money for once. If I'd known all it would take were pumpkin bars to skyrocket our business to fame, I would have made them the first autumn we were open."

"They *are* fucking good pumpkin bars."

"They really are," Tessa laughed.

"What are you going to make for Christmas?"

"Well, mince pies."

"Obviously."

"I also usually make mini–Yule Logs, and mini trifles. Traditionally, I set up an order form on my website for Christmas Puddings. I'm hoping we'll have help by then because I'm worried too many people will order and I won't be able to make them all, which wasn't a problem I've had in the past, but with my newfound popularity, I think it very well might be."

"I have stopped at your shop so many times, but I have never gone in around Christmas."

"Do you do your own Christmas baking?"

James laughed. "No. No, I'm not the best baker. My mum usually does the baking and gives me enough to feed an army. Last Christmas, Evie was feeling homesick, so she made so many bakes. It was overwhelming."

"Evie can bake?"

"She can. And she's fantastic at it."

In the dark, he could see Tessa's eyes widen. "Do you think she would want to help at the shop? I know she is teaching at the university, but not during Christmas hols."

"She might. You should ask her when she gets back from honeymoon."

"I will! Thank you."

"For what?"

"Everything. Meeting you has been such a blessing. My life is different now because of you."

James smiled. "I could say the same to you."

"I guess it's a good thing I came into your office asking for help."

"And that I, the ever consummate over worker, had not left the office when Patrick ordered me to."

Tessa moved closer to him, wrapping her arms around his neck, pulling him in toward her.

He helped close the gap, capturing her lips with his.

The kiss was gentle, and he could feel everything she was feeling for him poured into this one kiss. He hoped she could feel everything he was feeling through his kiss.

He really meant what he had said the night before. He loved her. And it scared him how quickly and easily he could fall for her.

He finally understood Patrick and Evelyn and the beginning of their relationship. He never could figure out how they could fall so quickly for one another. And now he did. Sometimes, love needed little time to grow. It could come on suddenly, out of nowhere.

And it was fucking scary.

James broke the kiss and gazed deeply into Tessa's dark eyes.

"I love you."

"I love you, too," she answered with no hesitation.

"Sorry I can't make it any safer for you, but we'll figure it out. I can lean on Bruno, ask him—"

"James?" Tessa interrupted. "No offense, but I *really* don't want to talk about Bruno right now."

She didn't wait for him to answer before pulling him down to kiss him again. This time the kiss was a little more heated, Tessa making it very clear what she wanted to do. And James was completely on board.

He shifted them until she was under him, and he could feel her curves against him.

They moved together in a practiced manner as if they had been doing this for years, peeling clothes off one another, pulling a condom out of the bedside table, and putting it on.

They had slept together almost every night since the first time the night of the wedding, but there was something different about this time. As if neither one was holding back. They didn't need to suppress their feelings, which James, at least, had thought had come on too early, too quickly.

James looked into Tessa's eyes as they came together and knew he would do anything for her. To make her happy. To keep her safe. Even if it meant sacrificing his own happiness. His own safety.

James rolled off of her, pulling her along with him, letting her settle on his chest as they caught their breath.

He ran his hand up and down her back as they caught their breath.

"Wow," Tessa's voice was airy as she tried to catch her breath.

"Yeah."

"I feel like I could sleep now. We should have done this earlier in the night."

James looked over at the clock on his bedside table. "We still have half an hour until we need to be up and at the shop. You should close your eyes and try to get some rest."

Tessa shook her head. "That's not enough time."

"It is. Close your eyes. I'll wake you when we need to leave."

He didn't have to tell her again, as he could hear her breathing grow heavier.

He tightened his grip on her as he, too, closed his eyes, letting her breathing lull him into his own slumber.

***

James looked around the small interior of Cake Me Home Tonight and couldn't believe it could hold so many people at once.

He chose to spend the day working at the shop. To his surprise, he didn't even have to list off his many reasons he should. Tessa agreed immediately. She was likely still rattled from the night prior.

However, after being at the shop for an hour, he realized he wouldn't get much work done. Not when he was watching Tessa try to juggle the influx of customers while finishing her baking in the back.

He set aside what he was failing to work on and sent her back into the kitchen. He handled the till, trying to ease some of the stress, until Mariel and Freddie came in.

And then at lunch, it was an all hands on-deck situation.

So many people.

James watched as the inventory dwindled.

Eventually, Tessa went back into the kitchen to prepare some baked goods to last until the store closed, and the number of customers decreased, and the area became still. James sat in his chair where he had placed his laptop and bag and sighed.

"You okay, mate?" Freddie asked, sitting down in the chair across from him.

"Is it like this, every day?"

"Ever since we put up the countdown to no more pumpkin bars? Yes."

"Fuck."

"I know. Tessa keeps thinking it will slow down once she no longer serves the thing that brought everyone in, but I don't have the heart to tell her this is more than likely our new normal."

"Hence hiring more people."

Freddie pointed a finger at him. "Exactly."

"I think she's going to ask Evie if—"

A scream from the kitchen cut through the shop.

James and Freddie leapt from their chairs and ran in the kitchen's direction. As they pushed through the door, Tessa was standing in the center of the kitchen, staring at the wall directly across from her, her hands up at her mouth, covering it.

James followed her line of sight and anger flowed into him.

Pinned on the wall using one of her knives was another picture, this time taken of them walking into the shop this morning, hand in hand, the knife going through Tessa's face.

"He's following us," Tessa whispered.

"He's escalating again." Freddie pointed out. "This is three days in a row. He's never done things three days in a row. And he's never outright threatened you."

"It's me. It's because of me." James stated.

"Mate," Freddie started.

"No. Look, the brick through the window happened the night we transitioned to a romantic relationship. The kidnapping, our first out of the flat date. The flowers and this now that you're staying at my flat. He upped his game when we started dating each other."

"We all know correlation is not causation," Freddie rationalized. "It could be a coincidence."

"He's jealous. He's jealous that I'm dating you and not him."

"I'm going to call Joe and tell him about this. Touch nothing. I know they're going to want to pull prints." Freddie pulled out his cell and walked to the front of the shop, dialing as he walked.

"When did he have time to do this?" Tessa mused. "He had to have come in the back."

"The shop was so busy all morning. He had ample opportunities to sneak back here. We never would have noticed," James pointed out.

His mind couldn't stay still. He caused the escalation. He just knew it. There was no other explanation.

"Do you even think CCTV would be helpful at this point?" Tessa asked. "We could look through the footage, and see if we can spot anything—"

"I think we need to break up."

The words were out of his mouth before he even realized what he was saying.

Tessa froze.

She stared at him, her eyes darting around his face to see if he really meant what he was saying.

"Wha-what do you mean? Break up? Why?"

"He's spiraling. It's obvious he's escalated because of our relationship. It will be best if we put everything on pause for now."

"Best? How is this the best solution? I love you." Tessa's voice broke. Which broke his heart.

He wanted to take everything back. But he knew this was the only way. The best way to keep her safe.

"I love you, too, but—"

"Then why are you ending things?"

"It's only temporary." James reassured her. "Only until we can catch the stalker. I think it will deescalate the situation. Make the overt threats stop. Once we catch him—"

"What if we never catch him?" Tessa shouted. "Huh? What then? Are we to never be together because some fucking arsehole threatened me? Am I never allowed to be happy as long as he's out there?"

Tears stung the back of James' eyes. He blinked them away. "We'll catch him."

"Is that all you have to say?"

James swallowed the lump in his throat as he nodded, not trusting his voice.

Tessa shook her head, swiping at the tears running down her cheeks, leaving a trail of flour behind.

"I think you should go," her voice was hoarse.

"Tessa…"

"No. I can't have you around. Not when," she swallowed, "not when you've broken my heart. I'll have Freddie come round and get my things."

"I'm sorry," James murmured. "I truly think this is the best thing for us right now."

"Yes. So, you've said. It doesn't matter what I want or what I think. You've decided."

"Don't be like that!" James shouted before wincing. He didn't mean to be that loud.

"Be like what? Upset that the man I love, who I told to not be an overprotective wanker, is doing exactly that? Pulling his man card like some fucking hero? Fuck you, James Moore!" by now she was shouting at him, practically sobbing her words. "When Patrick gets back from his honeymoon, I want him on the case. I never want to see you again."

This time, James didn't stop the tears. He let them fall down his cheek. "If that's what you want."

"It is. So, please respect that."

He nodded. "I will."

The two of them stood there, silence enveloping the room.

James didn't know how things had gotten to this point. He wanted a temporary break, but it had spiraled into Tessa never wanting to see him again.

He needed to fix this.

"I won't bother you, but I'll keep working, and I'll send Joe round if I find anything. I love you, Tessa."

He didn't wait for her to respond. Instead, he turned on his heel and marched out of the kitchen.

He ignored Freddie and Mariel's stares as he gathered his things, and walked out of the door into the street.

He briefly glanced at the alley across the shop. He could have sworn he had seen a figure duck further in the shadows, but when he tried to get a better look, there was nothing there.

CHAPTER 28

TESSA

The only sound in the kitchen after James left was Tessa's sobs. The tears streamed down her face as her heart slowly broke apart.

The door to the kitchen swung open and she could already tell who it was by the sound of the footsteps.

She turned around and crashed into Freddie's chest as his arms wrapped around her, pulling her tightly to him.

"What happened? Mariel and I could hear you two shouting, and then James just stormed out of here."

Tessa tried to catch her breath. "He...he...he broke up with me."

"Are you fucking serious? Are you sure? Because I was talking to him right before we came in here, and he gave no sign he would break up with you. Quite the opposite, in fact."

Tessa swallowed, feeling her tears subside a bit. "He thinks being with me is what caused the stalker to escalate. So, he broke up with me to keep me safe."

"That is complete rubbish," Freddie growled. "Don't you get a say in the matter?"

"Yes. I told him as much. He brushed me off, saying it was only temporary. Once they catch the stalker, we can get back together."

"What if they don't catch the stalker? What then?"

"I told him I never want to see him again."

"Oh," Freddie whispered.

"Will you get my things from his flat?"

"I'll text Joe. I'll have him pack them up and bring them to mine." Freddie let go of Tessa and gave a quick text to Joe. "You're staying at mine again, yeah?"

Tessa shook her head. "I kind of just want to go home."

Freddie nodded. "Yeah, yeah. Right. So, I'm completely on board with whatever you want to do, but let me go buy and install a camera, okay? And clean the place up a little. The window still is just a board, but it's livable, after I hoover one more time to make sure we've gotten all the glass. Can you agree to these terms?"

"A security camera outside my door and my flat cleaned for free? Yes, I think I can be amenable."

"Brilliant. It's way past the time you clock off you should go back to my flat and take a nap, pack up whatever you want that you left behind, Joe will swing by with the rest, and I'll text you once I've finished."

Tessa tilted her head. "You're not going to walk me back and forth?"

"You've just had a man tell you what's going to happen in your life. Do you really want me to do the same? It's daylight, and you're in the middle of London. You'll be fine."

Tessa gave him a wavering smile. "Thank you."

"You're welcome. Now go. I have Ben and Jerry's in the freezer. It's yours."

Tessa moved forward and gave him a tight hug. "I love you."

"Love you, too," he paused. "I'm sorry you've had your heart broken."

"Thank you. I just wish I understood why he thought this was the only solution. He told me he loved me last night."

Freddie took a step back and held her at arm's length. "Here's the thing about blokes like James. He's the heroic sort. People like him are always wanting to do the saving, even if it means sacrificing their own happiness. Unfortunately, it means your happiness gets to be collateral damage."

"I told him not to do heroic shit."

Freddie gave her a wry smile. "And did you actually think that would work?"

She shook her head. "No, but I thought it would manifest in him moving into my flat, or taking up a part-time job at the shop. I didn't realize it would mean him breaking up with me for my safety. How fucked up is that? He actually used those words. For your own safety. Like we're in a film."

"Yes, he's a right twat, and I want to eat ice cream with you and dish about all of this. But later, after we've taken care of everything, yeah?"

She nods.

"Great. Go to my flat. Wallow, take a nap, take a bubble bath with the ice cream, and I'll let you know when it is safe for you to come back to your flat."

She took off her apron and threw it on the counter. She patted her pockets to make sure she had her mobile and keys, and walked out of the kitchen.

"Hey, Tessa?"

Tessa turned to see Mariel standing at the counter, holding her arm with her hand.

"Are you okay?"

Tessa gave her a small smile. "No, I'm not."

"If you want to talk, you have my number."

"Thank you, Mar."

Tessa pushed her way out of the door and made her way to the Tube and to Freddie's.

She was really proud of herself. She didn't cry on the train. However, she barely made it inside Freddie's before completely falling apart. She found her way to the guest room before collapsing completely on the bed and crying herself to sleep.

***

Tessa woke as the sun was setting. She sat up in the bed and stretched. She moved to the edge and listened.

It sounded like no one was here. She picked up her mobile and checked the time. It was a little after five, and she had a couple of missed texts from Freddie.

FREDDIE: All finished here. You can come home whenever.

FREDDIE: Joe dropped your things off here. Talk to you soon.

Tessa breathed a sigh of relief. She could go home.

Freddie was really nice to let her stay, but she just wanted to go home.

She stood from the bed, pocketing her mobile and walking out of the guest room.

She made her way into the bathroom and, after relieving herself, she looked into the mirror above the sink while washing her hands.

Fuck, she looked a fright.

Her hair was a frizzy mess from sleeping in a half bun, and her eyes were all red and puffy.

She took out her hair band and tried to smooth her hair and tame it back into a ponytail. Once she thought she could get on the underground and not be mistaken for a zombie, she dried her hands and exited the bathroom.

She went back to the guest room and threw her clothes into a bag. There were a lot. She didn't know she had brought so much of her wardrobe with her.

After everything was in her tote, she slung it across her chest and walked toward the door.

She hesitated for a second, contemplating whether she should text someone and let them know she was on her way to her flat, and stopped.

The person she wanted to text was James. He was no longer an option. Not anymore.

Tears immediately sprung to her eyes, and she blinked them away. She could fall apart at home.

Her hand reached for the door handle and hesitated. She turned back into the flat and walked up to the freezer and ripped the door open. She reached inside and grabbed a Ben and Jerry's and threw it in her tote. Freddie told her she could have it, and she knew she didn't have any at home.

Determined to make it home before becoming a mess again, she marched out the door and out into the evening.

After an uneventful train ride, she made her way toward the shop. As she turned the corner of her street, a chill ran down her spine. She shivered, coming to an abrupt stop across from her building.

As she gazed up at the window that was covered with boards, a feeling of unease began to settle in the pit of her stomach.

"C'mon, Tessa. Freddie said everything was fine," she muttered to herself.

She straightened her shoulders and quickly crossed the road. She pulled her key and inserted it into the front lock and froze.

She twisted her head and looked behind her into the alley. The one James said her stalker liked to hide in.

It was dark, but she thought it looked empty.

She spun back to the shop, unlocked the door, and pushed her way inside. She immediately locked the door behind her.

The shop had only been closed for an hour, Mariel and Freddie had only been gone maybe half that, but with the sun going down so early these days, the shop gave off an eerie, almost abandoned feel. Or was that just her fears projecting themselves into the atmosphere?

Keeping her keys in hand, she made her way through the shop, through the kitchen, and up the back stairs to her flat.

She made her way through the hall and stopped in front of her door.

She looked up to see if she could spot the camera Freddie had installed and give him a little wave, since she knew he must have activated it before leaving.

She frowned.

There was no camera.

She looked behind her.

Nothing.

The unease that had settled in her stomach earlier rose again.

Something wasn't right.

She pulled out her phone and checked it again.

The messages were there. She hadn't imagined it.

She moved to put the phone back in her pocket when it vibrated.

She looked at it again. A message from Freddie.

FREDDIE: Shop got busy after you left. Helped Mar close it. Just getting round to the shop with the cameras. Sit tight. I'll be back soon. Start eating ice cream without me.

Tessa took a step back from the door.

If Freddie hadn't texted her, who had?

She looked around and breathed a sigh of relief. She seemed to be alone in the hallway.

She looked down at her phone again.

The two texts from Freddie had come in different threads. Why didn't she notice it before?

She clicked on the one she received from Freddie earlier and forwarded it to Joe, telling him she didn't think this came from Freddie and if he could tell who it was from.

After sending the message, she put her hand on the handle to her flat and turned.

Locked.

Tessa let out the breath she had been holding. If the door was locked, she was fine. She was already here, she might as well go in.

She put her key in the lock and opened her door. She took about two steps in before stopping dead in her tracks.

Candles covered every surface in her flat. Hundreds of them, and they had all been lit. It must have taken whoever it was who put them there ages to light them all.

Tessa turned her head, her breathing speeding up as she took in the scene.

Playing over a wireless speaker, loud, but not so loud you could hear it from the hall, was Eddie Money's 'Take Me Home Tonight.' Her dad's favorite song. The song she had taken her shop name from.

The upbeat mood of the song contrasted with every feeling coursing through her right now.

She swallowed a lump in her throat as panic rose.

She fucked up.

She spun around, trying to see who was in her flat. But she couldn't see anyone.

She pulled out her phone and dialed the first number she could think of. One she dialed out of habit. The one person she hoped would come help her during this time.

James.

The phone rang as she brought it up to her ear.

Once.

Twice.

A third time.

The phone clicked as if he had answered it.

Behind her, the door to her flat slammed shut.

"Hello?"

Someone from behind her grabbed her phone out of her hand and threw it across the room. She heard it smash against a wall and cringed.

Whoever was behind her pressed himself against her back until she could feel the warmth of his body radiating against hers.

He wrapped an arm around her waist, pulling her in tight against him. His breath was warm against her ear as he leaned in, and in a voice she clearly recognized, sang along with the song, "Be my little baby."

CHAPTER 29

JAMES

James hadn't wanted to go home after Tessa had kicked him out of the shop. After he had broken her heart.

It was still early afternoon, so he went into the office.

At first, he tried to distract himself with cases from his email. However, his brain couldn't stand it. If he was going to get the case solved quickly so he could get on his knees and beg Tessa to take him back, he had to focus on her case.

He opened his email and pulled up the one from PC Davies.

The blurry photos of the stalker.

He also pulled up the CCTV footage from Tuesday, the alley behind the club.

The clues to identify the person who was stalking Tessa had to be somewhere among these items.

His phone rang.

Joe.

"Hello."

"So, I'm here at Cake Me Home Tonight, because Freddie called and said the stalker had struck again, with another threat, and what to my surprise neither you nor Tessa are here. The two people the threat was aimed at. And when I asked why you two were missing, Freddie comes to tell me you broke up with her! What the fuck, James?"

"I—"

"Freddie told me. And look, I'm going to say this with all the love I can, because I'm your friend. This was probably the stupidest thing you've ever done."

"I know."

"She's perfect for you."

"I know."

"Now that we're on the same page, I wanted to let you know Davies came in and processed the scene, and took the prints back to the lab. I'm sticking around the shop to help Freddie and Mariel since they sent Tessa home. When the shop closes, I'm going to stick around and shop for cameras with Freddie and help him install it. Are you at the flat?"

"No. I'm at the office."

"Think you'll go home at all tonight?"

"Dunno. Why?"

"Tessa needs her things, so I was going to have you pack them up for me."

James sighed, rubbing his eyes with his free hand. "I can make time to go home."

Silence fell over the line.

"Hey." Joe broke the silence. "For the record, if Freddie were the one in danger, I would have done the same thing. It's the cop in us."

James bit his lip, his eyes stinging a little. "Yeah?"

"Yeah. We'll catch this bastard, and we'll help you do the biggest fucking grand gesture there is to win her back."

"D'ya think she'll take me back?"

"If we solve this within the week? Yes. Month? Probably. Years? Nah."

"Fuck, I hope it doesn't take years for us to solve this case."

"I give it a week. He's getting sloppy. We could pull a lot of prints off the knife today."

"Doesn't help if we have nothing to compare them to."

"Davies is going over to print Bruno."

James sat up straighter in his chair. "What?"

"Freddie told him about Bruno's confrontation in the shop the other day. Said that's reasonable grounds and went and got a fucking warrant. I'm feeling a bit like a proud dad at the moment. The new recruits I've been training up are fucking brilliant."

"So, we're going to have Bruno's prints to compare to all the other ones we have?"

"And we'll have an answer by tonight."

James threw his head back onto his chair, slumping down. "Fucking finally."

"We should thank the bastard for escalating to vandalism and attempted kidnapping," Joe pointed out, "without the escalation, no warrant."

"No warrant, no fingerprints."

"No fingerprints. You would still be sitting outside Bruno's house waiting for him to fucking leave and do something interesting."

"Do you think he's good for it?"

Joe sighed. "Look, he's the most likely suspect. He had that obsession with Tessa. He got caught wanking in the girls' loo while watching her change. He's been seen loitering outside the shop. The man shouted at her a week ago. The judge thinks it's enough evidence to get a warrant. I'm feeling good about the odds. It's Bruno."

"I hope you're right."

"I'm always right." James could hear Joe talking to someone on his side of the phone. "Hey, James, I need to go. The shop is getting its last rush, and I'm going to go and manage the till while Freddie brings things in from the kitchen. Send me a text once you've packed Tessa's things, and I'll come round and pick them up."

"Will do. And if you see Tessa...."

"I'll try to talk you up."

"Thanks mate."

"Bye."

"Bye."

James hung up the phone and turned back to the computer. He pulled up the footage from the alley and got to work.

***

As the sun was setting through the office window, James was pretty sure his eyes were going to fall out of his head in protest.

He had watched all the footage he had which showed the stalker so many times; he had each beat memorized.

No matter how many times he watched, no matter what resolution he had the footage at, he could not get a clear picture of his face.

The best he could determine was he was a white man, which in London, didn't narrow his suspect pool very much.

He leaned back in his chair, crossing his arms across his chest. There had to be something he wasn't thinking of. A different angle to look at things. If he couldn't see the bastard's face, how else could he identify him?

He sat up straighter.

James pulled up the footage he had of Bruno loitering outside the shop. He measured his height. He pulled up the footage of the stalker. Measured his height.

It wasn't a match.

"Fuck!" James yelled, his voice echoing in the empty office.

It wasn't an exact science, but it was pretty definitive.

There was a knock on his office door.

He frowned. No one came to their office, except...

"Come in!" he yelled, sitting up straighter, smoothing his hair.

The door swung open, revealing Bruno.

"You fucking bastard!" Bruno shouted, pointing an ink-stained finger at James. "I told you to fucking leave me alone, but today, in the middle of a very important meeting, I had police officers serve me a fucking warrant to get my fingerprints."

"Look, man, I'm sorry—"

"No! You don't get to apologize. They never even told me why. I've done nothing wrong. And now I've been humiliated in front of my employees."

"Someone has been stalking Tessa," James interrupted Bruno's rant.

Bruno froze, his arm sagging. "What?"

"Someone has been stalking Tessa for a few months, and it has escalated. That's why she hired me. To find out who it was. We'd run into a dead end, and I told Tessa to think of anyone in her life who she thought it could be. She and Freddie told me about what you'd done in school, and you were our only lead. You're *still* our only lead."

Bruno shook his head. "I can't believe someone is stalking Tess. I'll kill the bastard."

"Well, join the queue."

"I swear it's not me. I've only just reconnected with her. And I haven't even seen her in person. Well, except last week when I came to yell at her. But only then."

"I know it's not you. I analyzed the footage. You're too tall."

"There's footage?"

James gestured at the computer. "I've got the bastard on tape so many times, but he knows where all the cameras are and has successfully hidden his face. Every time."

Bruno walked over and dragged a chair next to James, sitting down.

"So, it's someone familiar with the area."

"That's what we're thinking."

"For the record? I was trying to go to see Tessa so I could apologize," Bruno kept his eyes on the screen, "when we reconnected after her dad died, I thought it was time to mend fences. I would go round the shop, but I could never really get the courage to go in and talk to her. I had finally resolved to write her an email when I noticed you hanging round outside my house."

"For the record?" James pulled up footage of the stalker. "I think she would be receptive to an apology. She never thought it could be you."

"That's Tessa. Always thinking about others. I'll make sure I take the time to apologize once this is all over."

"Join the queue," James muttered.

He pulled up the blurry images of the stalker.

"This is the best we've got."

Bruno leaned forward and squinted at the screen. "Can you zoom in?"

James zoomed in as far as he could.

His phone buzzed with a text from Joe.

JOE: Prints Not Bruno.

James typed back that he had already figured out it would be the case and set the phone down on his desk.

He looked over at Bruno, who was leaning forward, his hand over his mouth as he inspected the screen.

"I think I know him."

James sat up straighter. "How on earth can you tell from this picture?"

"The hoodie." Bruno pointed at what appeared to James a plain black hoodie. "It's very familiar. Do you have any clearer pictures? Of the hoodie?"

James opened up the stills he took from the CCTV footage of the stalker dropping the letters. He zoomed in.

Bruno leaned in closer.

James' leg bounced, and he brought his own hands up to his mouth.

Bruno leaned back and looked at James.

"I own a software company which is contracted out to several businesses throughout the city. I employ a small crew who I assign to different size companies throughout the city to help develop the software specifically for each company, so it's customized to them."

James nodded. "Are you saying this is one of your employees?"

Bruno shrugged. "I can't say with any amount of certainty, but I have someone who works for me who lives in the same area as Cake Me Home Tonight, and he has mentioned once or twice of frequenting the shop. And whenever I hold a virtual meeting, he's wearing this black sweatshirt."

"How can you tell? It looks like a black sweatshirt."

Bruno pointed at the screen. "See this, right here? There's a weird bleach pattern in the shape of France. I stare at it during all of our meetings. It's distracting."

James could feel the wheels turning in his head. The dots were connecting.

"You're in software development?"

Bruno nodded.

"And you have an employee who is a regular at the shop?"

"Yeah, goes there every week with his mum."

There it was.

James picked up his phone and scrolled until he found the picture of the card Tessa had sent him a couple of weeks ago. He turned his phone until it faced Bruno.

"Is this him?"

Bruno didn't hesitate. "Yeah, that's him."

"The *fucking* bastard!" James shouted into the empty office. "I *knew* there was something wrong with him!"

He dialed Joe, who picked up on the first ring.

"It's Fraser," he spat out the second Joe answered the phone.

"Who?"

"The stalker."

"How do you know?"

"His employer is sitting in my office and recognized his fucking hoodie on the video."

"Fuck!"

"You need to get to Freddie's and tell Tessa to stay there."

"Yeah, we'll head there next. We're at the camera shop now. I'll have Freddie send her a text telling her to stay put."

"Don't tell her about Fraser. We don't want to scare her."

"Good idea. I'll call Davies and have him try to get a warrant for Fraser."

They hung up without saying goodbye.

"Mate, you don't know how much we owe you for this."

Bruno shook his head. "It's nothing. But it's weird, yeah? That someone who works for me is stalking my old friend?"

James frowned. "Yeah, that is weird."

"Do you think there is a connection?"

"I don't know."

"He's odd," Bruno stated. "He has no social skills."

"Yeah, I'm familiar with him. We've spent time with him."

Bruno frowned. "He went out with you?"

"Yeah, to a club the other night."

"That's so strange. He's a bit of a recluse. Only goes out to take his mom to the shop to get sweets. Otherwise, he's got that weird fear of going outside his house. Tells me that when he thinks about leaving, he has panic attacks," Bruno explained.

"He didn't tell us any of that. And if he is the stalker, the bloke has no problem leaving his house. He's in the fucking alley across from the shop all the time."

James' phone rang again, this time Tessa's number came up. He hesitated.

"Aren't you going to answer?"

James swiped, answering the phone.

"Hello?"

Tessa didn't say anything. All he could hear was Eddie Money. He frowned. "Hello? Tessa?"

The next thing he heard was an enormous crash, and the phone went dead.

CHAPTER 30

TESSA

Tessa's head was pounding.

She opened her eyes and blinked.

She didn't remember going to sleep.

She looked around. She was lying on an unfamiliar couch in an unfamiliar room.

She closed her eyes, trying to remember where she was.

The last thing she remembered was walking into her flat after realizing someone had tricked her into coming home by spoofing her number. When she walked in, there were candles and music and...

"Oh, you're awake," a woman's voice said from somewhere above her head.

She turned herself until she could see who was talking.

Mrs. Hudson gave her a wide smile.

"Mrs. Hudson?" Tessa brought her hand up to her head. Her brain felt as if it were in a fog.

"Oh my." Mrs. Hudson set aside the knitting she was working on. "Do you have a bit of a headache?"

"Yeah. I don't know why, but my head is killing me and I'm finding it hard to focus."

Mrs. Hudson nodded. "Yes, Fraser said you had a bit of a swoon earlier. He said you weren't eating properly. I've sent him to pick up some takeaway. We'll do a proper shopping trip in the morning."

Tessa closed her eyes again, some of the fog lifting. She could remember Fraser coming up behind her, whispering in her ear, and then placing something over her face, and then nothing.

Her eyes sprung open. The fucker had knocked her out and kidnapped her. And brought her to...his house?

"I'm sorry, I'm confused. What am I doing here?" Tessa asked.

"Oh, you must have hit your head hard. You're finally moving in!"

"Finally?"

"Yes! Fraser has been asking you for ages, and you've finally agreed to move into our house. I'm so glad you finally came to your senses. There's so much to do before the wedding."

"The wedding?"

"Why yes, it's coming up quickly."

While Tessa's head was clearing, she was feeling more and more befuddled. Why on earth would Mrs. Hudson think she was marrying Fraser?

"I'm sorry, Mrs. Hudson—"

"You should call me mum."

"Mrs. Hudson—"

Mrs. Hudson's friendly demeanor immediately dissipated, as she narrowed her eyes, and the edges of her mouth curved down. "I don't think you heard me," she used a slow, measured voice. "You. Should. Call. Me. Mum."

Tessa's blood ran cold. "I'm sorry. Mum."

And as if someone had flipped a switch, her sweet grandma appearance snapped back into place. "Yes, dear?"

"I'm not marrying Fraser. I'm with James, remember? You met him last week at the shop." Technically, she wasn't seeing him at the moment, but as soon as she got out of here, she would sit down with James, and apologize for doubting him and his abilities.

"No, you're not," Mrs. Hudson contradicted. "You broke up this afternoon."

Tessa frowned. "How on earth do you know that?"

"Fraser and I watched it."

Tessa's heart skipped a beat. "What do you mean you *watched* it?"

Mrs. Hudson picked up the remote sitting next to her and clicked on the telly.

Tessa watched in horror as video of her shop filled the screen in four separate squares. The front of the shop, the kitchen, the alley, and the door to her flat, all displayed in color.

She leapt from her seat on the couch. "What the fuck?!"

"Language. I will not tolerate a foul mouth in my house."

"I'm not staying here. I'm leaving. And I'm calling the police." Tessa took two steps away from the couch and froze.

With everything going on, she didn't realize she had a chain on her ankle. She followed the length to see they had chained it to the foot of the couch.

Mrs. Hudson smirked. "You will not be leaving, and you will not be calling the police. Now, *sit* down like a good little girl, and wait for Fraser to get home."

Tessa walked back to the couch and perched herself on the edge. She stared at Mrs. Hudson. Sweet, fragile, Mrs. Hudson. It was all a fucking act. How long had she and Fraser been playing her? When did they get the cameras in the shop?

The front door to the flat opened, and Fraser walked in carrying bags of food. The scent of frying oil that wafted through the air made her stomach churn.

Fraser smiled at her as he walked over to the table, setting the bags down in front of her. "Oh good, you're awake. I was a little worried I may have overdosed you with the arsenic. The internet wasn't very specific about how much would be too much."

Fraser shrugged off his coat, and bent to give his mum a kiss on her cheek.

"I'm going to take my food in my room." Mrs. Hudson stood easily from her chair, scooping up one bag from the table. "She has a mouth on her, Fraser. You'll need to fix that."

"Yes, Mum."

"And she likes to argue. We'll need to fix that, too."

"We will."

"I'll leave you two alone to talk about the wedding. We have lots to plan." Mrs. Hudson walked through the hall and entered what could only be her room before closing the door behind her.

Tessa turned to Fraser. "Is your mom even ill?"

"Of course she's ill," Fraser argued. "She's been ill for my entire life. I've had to give everything up to take care of her. I didn't lie about that."

Tessa pointed toward where Mrs. Hudson walked. "She doesn't look ill to me. She looks perfectly fine."

"She's having a good day," Fraser moved to the couch and taking a seat right next to Tessa.

She tried to move away, put distance between them, but Fraser wrapped his arm around her, pulling her close to his body.

He stuck his nose in her hair, pressing it firmly against her scalp, and sniffed.

Bile rose up in the back of her throat as he pressed a kiss to her temple.

"Don't. Touch. Me," she growled out through gritted teeth.

Fraser sat back, but didn't remove his arm, chuckling. "Oh Tessa, you'll need to get used to me touching you. I'm going to be your husband."

"You and your mum keep saying that, but I hate to tell you, I'm not marrying you."

Fraser laughed. "Of course you are."

Tessa decided convincing this man she wasn't marrying him was going to be fruitless. Neither he nor his mum seemed to operate in reality. Then it came to her.

"How long?" she asked instead.

"How long for what?"

"How long have you been watching me?" She gestured toward the telly.

"A few months now."

"A few *months*?"

"July, I think."

"But the letters didn't start arriving until October."

"Yes, I decided it was time to start properly wooing you around then."

Tessa was at a loss for words. "I'm not following. Wooing me? Through anonymous letters?"

"It was my idea. Mum wanted me to just bring you home right away. But I thought it would be more romantic if I were to write you love letters. Let you know how much I loved you before you moved in. Delightfully old-fashioned."

"Can we please go back and explain why me? Why did you choose me for your weird obsession?"

"Don't call me weird!" Fraser shouted, moving away from her and standing from the couch. "I'm not weird."

"I didn't say you were weird. I was calling your obsession with me weird. Because it is. It's weird. And I just want to know what brought it on."

Fraser stared at her his eyes wide. "You were kind to me. And my mum."

"That's it?"

"You have the most beautiful smile. And you're the most beautiful person I have ever seen. That first time I stopped in the shop to bring mum a treat last summer, you smiled at me and asked how my day was. And then you told me you hoped I would have a nice day. Being flirted with by a woman as stunning as you was an unfamiliar experience for me. I fell in love right then."

Tessa's stomach dropped. It was as James had said. Something so mundane as showing someone a bit of kindness caused them to become obsessed with her. And Fraser told his story with so much sincerity, it broke her heart to think of how deprived he was of affection he thought her plastered on smile and the same greeting she gave everyone who entered her shop was flirting.

"I brought mum in the next day, remember?" he continued. "She thought you were lovely and agreed you would be suitable as a wife. We started coming in every week after that."

"Fraser," Tessa whispered. "I want to say, I adore you and your mum. You're some of my favorite customers. However, I wasn't flirting with you."

Fraser's face crumpled. "You were. You flirt with me *every* time I come in!" he shouts, his voice filled with emotion. "You tell me you look forward to our visits each week. You ask my mum how she is. We lock eyes and share smiles. We're in love."

"We're not."

"We are!" Fraser screams, spittle flying out of his mouth. "We. Are."

"You're a stalker."

"I'm not. I'm not a stalker."

"Explain the cameras? Or the hovering in my alley."

"Once a week wasn't enough. I have a job, and mum needs me all the time. Your locks are really easy to pick, so I went in after you were closed and installed the cameras. The company I work for designs security software for companies, so I designed my own for you. Every couple of weeks I have to go in and take the cameras for charging, which makes it so I can't see you for a whole day. But it doesn't matter anymore, because you're here."

After she gets out of here, she needs to buy new locks, more secure locks for the shop. She looked at the feed on the telly of her empty shop. She should at least be thankful he never entered her flat and put cameras there. But why would he need to? Her fucking giant window she always kept open was enough for him to just lurk in the alley and watch her.

"And the alley?"

"To see you in person. To make sure you weren't doing anything you shouldn't be doing."

"James said you weren't lying to us. He could tell you were telling us the truth when you said you knew nothing."

Fraser smirked. "You can learn anything from the internet."

"I'm not staying here."

"You are."

"James, Freddie and Joe are going to notice I'm missing. They're going to come looking. And you're top of their suspect list. They'll come round and ask questions—"

"Lies!" Fraser yelled. "All. Lies. I've been watching. I know everything. I'm not a suspect. They're my *friends*. Joe and Freddie like me. And I watched earlier today. You and James fought. You told him you never wanted to see him again. He won't come searching for you, not after the cruel words you said. When Joe and Freddie ask, I'll be concerned. I'll help them look. They will never think to look here."

Less and Less Tessa was seeing the sensitive man who came to her shop every week, and more and more she was seeing the conniving arsehole who stalked her and kidnapped her. "What about my shop?"

"Freddie can run it, or it will close. Mum and I agree, once we're married, you don't need to work. You'll live here, and my job pays enough to support all three of us."

"You're mad!"

"I'm not mad!"

"You are. You're mad to think that I'm going to live here with you, let alone marry you. You've completely lost the plot if you think I'm going to give up my shop, my *dreams* for you. And you're daft for even thinking I love you. I don't. I don't love you."

Fraser shook his head. "You're going to change your mind. When you've been here long enough, you'll see how compatible we are. We are meant to be. We're soulmates."

Tessa let out a frustrated screech. "We are not soulmates."

"We are. We are. Don't you remember the night I went to the club with you? You touched my arm, and there was a spark. I know you felt it, too."

"It was you. You tried to kidnap me at the club!"

"Kidnap is such a harsh word. I prefer 'bring you home.'"

"Kidnap. You tried to kidnap me, just like you've kidnapped me now, and now you're holding me hostage."

"You're not a hostage."

"I'm chained to the fucking sofa. You're not allowing me to call anyone, and you just told me you're going to keep me here indefinitely and force me to marry you. I'm a fucking hostage, Fraser."

"Language," Fraser growled. "Ladies don't swear. And they especially don't swear in my mum's home."

A noise on the telly caused them both to look at it. The door to the shop opened and Freddie went rushing in, followed by Joe, James and...Bruno?!

Tessa watched as they ran through the kitchen and up to her flat. At the door, Freddie pulled out his key, opened the door, and the four men went inside.

They were inside for a long time. They must be looking for them.

Hope filled her chest.

The phone call to James.

He must have heard something on the line, which caused them to go to her flat.

They knew.

"Why is my boss with them?" Fraser asked.

"What?"

"My boss."

"Bruno is your boss?"

"Yeah, I work for his software company."

"He's one of my oldest friends."

Fraser shook his head and ran his hand through his hair. "Bollocks!" he yelled.

The door to Mrs. Hudson's room opened. She came storming out. "What's wrong?"

Fraser pointed at the telly. "Bruno is her friend. He's with them at her flat now."

Mrs. Hudson shook her head. "There's no way they know it was you. You were careful. We've heard them. They have no suspects. You're fine. We're fine."

Fraser's eyes widened. "I don't think we are. If they show him any of the footage, Bruno will probably recognize me."

"Impossible. We made sure you hid your face from all the cameras."

"Yes, but I wear the same hoodie in all my meetings."

Mrs. Hudson glared at her son. "Well, that's quite the pickle, isn't it? We need to move things up."

"The wedding?"

"Yes. I'll go and get the paperwork and the drug. We'll give her just enough to loosen her up so we can convince her to sign her name. And then we can file it in the morning. It will get the ball rolling. We need to find someone licensed willing to perform the wedding and forge the paperwork."

Tessa shook her head. She didn't understand why they thought if she married Fraser, everything was a done deal, unless...

All that talk about being old-fashioned. They still believed if she were to marry Fraser, she would be his property. Fucking idiots.

She looked around the room and settled her gaze to where Fraser had dropped the food. She frowned.

Keys.

Why hadn't she seen those before?

She looked at the key ring, and there was a small one. Looked like it would unlock the lock on her ankle.

Mrs. Hudson and Fraser moved quickly toward the bedroom.

Tessa quickly leaned forward and grabbed the keys off the table and brought them to her. She glanced up at the room and noticed they weren't coming back. She quickly undid the lock and threw the keys back on the table.

Mrs. Hudson and Fraser came back into the room. He was carrying a syringe of something. She didn't want to find out what sort of drug he had, or how he got it. And she definitely didn't want 'the internet didn't tell me the right dose' to inject her with anything.

She glanced up at the telly as more sound came out of it and her friends ran out of her flat and down the stairs out of the shop.

She had to have faith they knew where she was.

But she also had to be practical.

Her dad didn't raise a damsel in distress.

She waited until Fraser was close, leaning in with the syringe before jumping up and shoving him over.

He fell backward over the table, landing hard on the ground. The syringe falling from his hand and landing on the carpet.

Tessa put a foot on the table and hurdled herself over. She seized the syringe and held it out toward Mrs. Hudson.

Mrs. Hudson growled and drew a knife out from the pocket of her house dress. She came running toward her.

Tessa, shocked at how quickly the previously infirm lady could move, hesitated before turning and running toward the door and her escape.

Her hesitation cost her though, and the older woman bore down on her. Tessa's hand had just made purchase with the door handle when she felt the pain in her shoulder blade.

The bitch had stabbed her.

Tessa whirled around and, without thinking, stabbed the syringe into the woman and pressed the plunger.

She watched in horror as Mrs. Hudson collapsed to the ground.

"Mum!" Fraser screamed, scrambling to his feet.

This time, Tessa didn't hesitate. She ripped the door open, and she ran.

CHAPTER 31

JAMES

James looked around Tessa's flat. There were candles lit everywhere, and they looked like they had been burning for a while.

Freddie went into the bedroom to see if Tessa was there, but James knew she wasn't. This place was empty.

Joe looked around the flat and took out his phone. "Calling into Davies and reporting her missing."

"Tell him we know it was Fraser," James added.

Freddie came out of the bedroom. "Okay if I blow these out?"

"James, snap some pictures, and then yeah, blow them out. We don't want the flat to go up in flames."

James pulled out his phone and began taking pictures of the room.

He was taking pictures when he remembered something.

"Music," he muttered.

Freddie looked at him. "What?"

"Music. When I was on the phone with Tessa, there was music playing in the background."

Freddie frowned and looked around the room. "There's a speaker here," he walked into the kitchen and pointed at the corner where the counters meet, "this isn't hers."

"Fraser must've brought it and forgot it when he took her," James observed.

He looked around the room at all the candles. How long had he been waiting here for Tessa to come home? His eyes landed on Bruno, who was still standing in the doorway to the flat, but instead of looking in, he was looking out into the hallway.

"What d'you see?" James asked.

Bruno pointed into the hall, toward the stairs. "That's one of our cameras."

"What?"

"That's impossible. We don't have any cameras installed," Freddie stated. "Joe and I were buying one when James called to tell us to get over here."

Bruno shook his head. "I didn't say you installed it, did I?"

"You think..."

"I know." Bruno pulled out his phone and typed a few things into it. He frowned. "This isn't the only one in here."

"The computer software you sell to companies..." James started.

"Security," Bruno finished. "We have an entire line of cameras, and we customize the software for each company, and each of my software engineers manages the company's system."

"Can you see the footage from the cameras here?" Joe asked, coming up to them.

"Yeah, it's easy. Fraser didn't put any sort of security on them, probably because he didn't think anyone would even notice they were here. Showing you would be easier on a tablet."

Freddie walked into Tessa's room and walked back out, holding her tablet. "Already unlocked it for you."

Bruno got into it and typed. Within two minutes, he had the feed up. He moved over to the kitchen counter and set the tablet down so they could all see.

"This is the current feed."

"Fuck," Freddie muttered.

"Took the words right out of my mouth." James stared at the tablet. There were four cameras, and he could see the entire shop.

"So, it was really easy to hack into the recordings, because he's a complete berk and stored it all on his work account. I'm going to back up the footage until we can confirm Fraser is the one who took her. I'm going to guess he's just arrogant enough to think no one would notice the cameras, and he didn't hide his face."

James watched over Bruno's shoulder as he backed the footage up.

"Stop." James pointed at the screen.

Bruno froze the video.

Walking through the kitchen to the alley door was Fraser, and he was carrying Tessa, who was lying limp in his arms. And the fucker, the arrogant *wanker*, looked directly into the camera and fucking smirked.

"I'm gonna kill him," James growled.

"How long ago was this?" Joe asked, pointing to the screen.

Bruno looked at the timestamp. "About an hour."

"Where do you think he took her?" Freddie asked.

"His home," James replied.

"You think?"

"I know. He's delusional. His letters have all implied he had feelings for her. That he saw and wanted a future with her. Logic dictates he would take her home."

"He's right," Joe agreed. "At the very least, it will be the first place we look."

"Where does he live? Somewhere close, yeah?" Freddie asked. "He comes here every day with his mum, who can barely walk."

Bruno read out an address. Everyone turned to look at him.

"Employee records." Bruno held up his phone.

"That's two streets from here near the tube station."

"What are we waiting for?" James asked

Freddie ran around the room like a madman and extinguished all the candles while Joe called PC Davies and read him the address, telling him to meet them there, with backup.

The four men ran down the stairs and out of the shop, Freddie stopping briefly to lock the door.

They took off, running down the sidewalk toward Fraser's flat.

As James ran, many scenarios flashed through his head. In every single one of them, Fraser had violated Tessa.

Anger coursed through his body, causing him to run faster, dodging in and out of crowds on the street.

As they got closer, the crowds thinned, and it looked as if there was a figure running toward them.

It was really hard to tell in the dark, but as they got closer, James could see that, yes, someone was running towards them.

As the runner moved under a streetlamp, James' breath caught in his throat. Tessa.

She was running towards them, but he didn't think she knew they were there. She kept looking behind her as she ran. Her hair was down and flowed behind her in a chaotic stream, and he couldn't tell, but he thought she looked barefoot.

He didn't know it was possible for him to run faster, but he did.

As the gap narrowed between them, he could see the moment Tessa recognized him. Her eyes widened and her stride faltered. But not for long. She caught herself and she ran straight for him, no longer looking behind her.

When the two met in the middle, Tessa threw herself into James' arms, and he didn't hesitate to wrap his arms around her waist, tightly pulling her to his body.

"You're safe," he whispered repeatedly as she held on so tightly to him, she was almost cutting off his air, but it didn't bother him. His focus was on assuring the woman who was trembling in his arms that she was okay.

He felt more than saw when the other three men caught up to them. His focus was on the woman in his arms. Knowing she was safe.

"Tessa!"

James brought a hand up to push Tessa's hair out of his vision so he could see who was screaming her name.

Barreling toward them was Fraser.

"Tessa, you fucking bitch! I'm going to *kill* you for what you did to my mum!" Fraser screamed.

James reluctantly let go of Tessa, moving her behind him. She didn't argue. Bruno, Joe, and Freddie filled in around her, effectively putting her in a protective bubble.

"What happened to his mum?" James asked.

"I injected her with something they were going to inject me with," Tessa's voice was shaking. "She just sort of fell to the ground. I don't know what it was. They made it sound like it wasn't anything too terrible when they were going to pump it into my veins. But he also admitted he got everything off the internet and wasn't sure about dosage."

"They drugged you?" James growled, not taking his eyes off the large, angry man running toward them.

"He used arsenic to knock me out to take me to his house. Otherwise, no. I was able to find the keys and unchained myself from the couch before they could stab me with the needle."

"The fucking bastard," Freddie growled out. "I'm going to fucking chain him to the back of James' car and—"

"Get in line, mate," James snapped.

Joe got on the phone and was talking to someone, giving them directions to where they were, when Fraser made it to the group.

"What the fuck are you doing here?" Fraser growled when he was toe to toe with James. "You broke up with her. She's mine now. She's marrying *me*."

"I broke up with her five hours ago. I'm *pretty* sure she didn't just up and decide to marry you on a whim, so I'm going to go out on a limb and say you're full of shit."

"Kidnapping is a very serious offense, Fraser," Joe explained. "Much more serious than vandalism, but around the same level as installing cameras and spying on the shop."

"I didn't kidnap her," Fraser bit out. "She wanted to come with me."

"We watched the footage, mate. She didn't go with you willingly." James shook his head.

"How?"

Bruno poked his head around James. "Yeah, that would be my doing. By the way, I'm going to have to let you go."

Fraser stepped even closer to James, bringing his hand up and shoving his finger into James' chest. "This is all your fault."

"And how do you figure that?"

"Everything was fine until you turned up. I had a job, and Tessa was going to go out with me, and you came along and mucked it all up. Filled her head with lies."

"I dunno. Last I checked, you're the one who sent her creepy letters and installed cameras in her place of business. Oh yeah, and you kidnapped her. Can't force a person to do what you want against their will."

"She would have learned—"

"I'm going to stop you there, because I really have no interest in hearing whatever rubbish you have to say. We have the video of you taking her out of her flat, unconscious. And Tessa here'll testify about every little thing you've done to her. So, I don't really need to hear the whys of it, or listen to whatever delusions you have cooked."

The sounds of sirens filled the air, as the streets filled with police cars flying into the area.

"Oh, look, your ride has arrived."

The police cars stopped around them, and PC Davies stepped out of one car.

Fraser narrowed his eyes at James. "This is your fault. Your. Fault. Tessa! Tessa!" he shouted, trying to get a look at her from behind James. "I love you, and I know you love me," he babbled. "And I forgive you for what you did to Mum, you were acting rash. But tell them we're in love. Tell them I did nothing wrong."

Tessa didn't say a word. James felt her grab on to the back of his shirt with her fists, and press her head into his back.

PC Davies approached Fraser, handcuffs in hand.

Fraser, on his part, didn't put up a fight. He just stepped back, away from James.

"Can someone send an ambulance to mine and check up on mum? If she's not okay, we'll be pursuing charges against Tessa."

PC Davies ignored him. He walked up behind him and placed handcuffs on his wrists. "You do not have to say anything. But it may harm your defense if you do not mention when questioned something which you later rely on in court. Anything you do say may be given in evidence."

As PC Davies led him away, he didn't put up a fight. He just turned his head and looked back at Tessa.

"Once this is all over, you'll realize that we're meant to be. He can't bring you happiness like I can."

Davies put his hand on Fraser's head and helped him into the car. Once he was shut in, Davies turned back toward them.

"McCleary, will you be meeting us down at the station?"

"Yes."

"Bring the lot. We'll need to get everyone's statement on record."

"Will do."

Davies gave them a nod and got in the car and drove away. The other officers milled about, and Joe went to talk to them.

James turned around and looked at Tessa. Really looked at her. Well, as well as he could in the dark on the pavement.

She looked tired, and frazzled, but she mostly looked okay, which James thanked heaven for.

He smiled down at her.

She smiled up at him.

"Are you okay?" he asked.

"I'm okay. My head still feels fuzzy. But I think it's because he didn't know how to dose me when he knocked me out. I think it will clear up with some rest."

"I'm glad you're okay. When I watched you being carried—"

He cut off when he watched Tessa sort of sway on her feet.

"Tessa?"

"I'm fine." Her voice was weak, and as she said it like it was a question, he didn't quite believe her.

He reached out to steady her with a hand on her back and frowned when he felt something wet. He brought his hand back and held it so a streetlamp shone on it.

"Tessa, you're bleeding." He looked back up at her, meeting her eyes. "Why are you bleeding?"

She looked at him, confusion all over her face. "What?"

"Why are you bleeding?"

"I'm bleeding?" Her voice came out weaker than before.

"Medic!" James shouted. "We need a medic over here!"

Freddie came running from where he had been standing with Joe. "What's going on?"

"She's bleeding, and she's disoriented. Something's wrong."

Tessa narrowed her eyes at him. "I don't appreciate you talking about me as if I'm not here. I'm fine. I'm perfectly—"

She swayed as her eyes rolled back into her head. James wrapped his arms around her to stop her from hitting the ground.

"Help!" James shouted. "Someone, help us!"

"James?" Tessa whispered her eyes still closed. "I don't feel very good."

"You're going to be fine. Everything is going to be fine."

As Tessa went limp in his arms, James didn't believe his own words.

CHAPTER 32

TESSA

For the second time in twenty-four hours, Tessa woke without knowing where she was. Her head felt better than it did earlier, but not by much. Instead of feeling foggy, it ached.

She tried to open her eyes, but they felt heavy.

She was so tired.

She could hear machines beeping around her, and hushed conversations, but couldn't make out who was talking or what they were saying.

She tried to open her eyes again, but to no avail. They were not budging.

She gave up and relaxed, let the pull of sleep draw her under.

When she awoke again, her head didn't ache, and her eyes didn't feel as heavy.

She opened them and immediately shut them against the bright lights.

"Oh," a voice spoke up from next to her. "Let me fix that."

She heard James rustle around and footsteps walk across the room.

"There, try opening them again."

She opened her eyes, and the room was now dimly lit.

"Is that better?" James moved back to his chair next to her bed.

She nodded.

"How are you feeling?"

"My head hurts a little, and I'm tired."

"Yeah, you're going to be tired for a bit."

"What happened?"

"You lost a lot of blood."

"I lost a lot of blood? How—"

It suddenly hit her. Everything she couldn't remember. "Oh, my GTod, Mrs. Hudson stabbed me in the back! Literally and figuratively."

"Yeah, she did. At least someone stabbed you. Right near your shoulder blade area. Not deep, normally not a very serious wound. However, when you ran, your blood pressure rose, and caused your blood to pump faster. And it pumped out of your open wound at a much higher rate than if you'd been in a relaxed state."

Tessa closed her eyes. "So, I lost a lot of blood, and then I passed out in your arms."

"Pretty much. The doctors also think you still had some of that arsenic in your system, and that didn't help matters."

"I should have kicked Fraser in the bollocks rather than only giving him a good shove."

"Do you want to talk about it?"

Tessa sighed and opened her eyes. She looked over at James.

His red hair was a right mess, and he had dark circles under his eyes. His five o'clock shadow stubble he typically sported was heavier, and he was still in the clothes he was wearing when he had broken up with her for her own good.

"It can wait until you go home and get some rest. How long have I been here?"

"Since about eight last night. It's now round five. Shit, it gets dark so early." He rubbed his eyes.

"Go home and sleep."

"I pushed the chairs together and had a kip sometime around one. I'll be fine until Freddie gets here in an hour."

Tessa smiled. "You have shifts?"

"Of course. We didn't want you to wake up alone."

"I appreciate it."

James leaned forward and took her hand in his. "Do you feel up to talking?"

Tessa turned her hand in his until she could lace her fingers with his. "About the Hudsons and their creepy plot, or about us?"

Her question hung in the room's silence, the only sound being the beeping of the hospital equipment.

She kept her gaze on James, watching him chew on his bottom lip.

"Either," James finally answered. "Both."

Tessa turned onto her side, keeping hold of James' hand.

"I was going to be held hostage in their flat, and they would deny knowing my whereabouts if asked. They were *so* confident no one would suspect them. They had these antiquated ideas that if I were to sign marriage papers, it would force me to stay with Fraser. Nothing they said made any sense. But that could have been because my head was feeling fuzzy."

"Wait, so you're saying Mrs. Hudson was in on the whole thing?" James leaned forward.

"Yeah, I'm pretty sure she might have been the mastermind? She's not as feeble as they led us to believe. And I'm pretty sure she's been manipulating Fraser his whole life. They have a very fucked up dynamic."

James shook his head. "The old biddy has Joe and Davies believing she's a completely innocent victim. That you ambushed her while she was in her chair knitting and stabbed her with the sedative."

"What a liar! I can't wait to give my statement to Joe."

"He'll be back in the morning for it, with PC Davies. Because of his relationship with Freddie, he's transferred the lead on the case to Davies. But Davies's a good egg, so we have nothing to worry about."

Tessa gave him a weak smile.

"I'm glad you could escape." James returned her smile.

"Me, too. I wasn't going to let them inject me with whatever I shoved into Mrs. Hudson. I could see you on the telly, with Fraser's cameras. When I saw you running out of my flat, I knew you knew where I was. But I didn't know how far we were from the shop, or how long it would take you to get there. When I noticed the keys on the table, I thought I would take a shot and get out."

"You did the right thing. You looked out for yourself, and you got away. Luckily, Fraser was a shit criminal."

Tessa laughed. "He was pretty terrible. He left the keys to my lock within reach. I didn't even have to try."

"He stored all the footage of the shop on his work account. Bruno had absolutely no trouble turning the evidence over to the police. Didn't have to hack anything. Simply typed in Fraser's work credentials."

Tessa's mouth dropped open. "No."

James nodded, his smile wide. "Yes. Ridiculously easy. Speaking of Bruno, he wants to come see you, but doesn't know if he will be welcome. He wants to apologize for everything, build bridges, that sort of thing."

"Of course he can stop by. He bloody well saved my life. What are the odds that Fraser would work for Bruno?"

"Let me get a good eight hours of sleep, and I'll be able to tell you."

Tessa laughed. "Go home and get some sleep. I'll be fine here alone."

"I don't want to leave you here alone. I have so many regrets in my life, but I think the biggest one would have to be breaking up with you yesterday."

"James—"

"No, I have to say it. It was arrogant of me, and chauvinistic. I shouldn't have swooped in and tried to protect you. It was everything you said you hated, and I did it, anyway. I know I probably don't deserve it, but I hope you will find it in yourself to take me back. I love you. And I'm so, so sorry."

Tessa squeezed James' hand. "I'm glad you could see the error of your ways, but I also need to apologize. I should have heard the meaning of what you were saying, but my heart was so broken by the words and not the intent."

"We were together for two weeks and I fucked it up completely."

"Two weeks. Has it only been two weeks? I feel like we've been together for a lifetime."

"To be fair, a lot has happened in the last two weeks. More than most couples have to deal with in a lifetime."

Tessa smirked. "You mean not every couple deals with a kidnapping in their first two weeks?"

"Well, I mean, Patrick and Evie did, so I am thinking it must be a pretty standard thing most couples deal with."

"We'd better warn Freddie and Joe."

They both laughed.

Tessa smiled at him. "I forgive you. In fact, I forgave you when I woke up on the couch in the Hudson's flat. Because you were right. Us being together was causing Fraser to escalate. But to be fair, you breaking up with me escalated him further instead of having him cool down."

"Well, that was a misjudgment but who's to say he wouldn't have escalated to that point, anyway? He was waiting for the opportunity to get you alone. Staying at mine and Freddie's didn't give him that opportunity. I think he was waiting for you to move home."

"I wish I had thought to look for cameras. We could have used them to our advantage."

James chuckled. "Yeah, I've thought about that while waiting for you to wake up. We could have used our acting skills to really put on a show and set a trap."

Tessa laughed so hard her head ached again. "I'm really glad you have the confidence in your acting skills, because I'm pretty sure I would have given it all up with my poor ones."

"I'm sure you're an excellent actress."

"I hope you don't rely on those delusions for any future cases, because if you do, you're doomed."

James smiled at her. "Don't worry. We'll stay in our lanes. You can do the baking and I'll do the sleuthing."

"I mean," she drawled. "If you want to come and help at the shop if you're having a slow day, especially over the holidays, I certainly wouldn't say no."

"Oh, so, *now* I'm allowed to spend my day in the shop, now that you're not being stalked by a madman?"

"Yes, because the only heroic thing you'll be doing is stopping grannies from caning each other over sticky toffee pudding."

"You want me to be your bouncer?"

Tessa shrugged. "Maybe through Christmas?"

"What sort of pay does a bakery bouncer get?"

Tessa smiled coyly. "Well, I can think of a few benefits a bakery bouncer would get." She waggled her eyebrows.

James' face colored a delightful pink before he recovered and shot her a devastating half smile. "Oh, could you now? I'm thinking this gig would be right up my alley. My first order of business as security is going to be to upgrade all the locks on your shop and turn all the spy cameras to our good PC Davies."

"Mmmm," Tessa hummed. "Tell me more."

"And then, if the grannies get out of hand?"

"Yeah?"

"I'll walk over to them and flatter them with some flirty attention, so they forget they were even annoyed that the one in front of them purchased the last of the shortbread."

"You're going to earn every bit of your benefits."

"That's my aim."

Tessa leaned forward and captured James' lips with hers. They had only been apart for a couple of hours, but in that time, she had come to the conclusion that she needed him in her life.

He was it for her.

And she knew she was it for him.

EPILOGUE

JAMES

"T-Minus one hour until the shop is closed, and we're finished for the week-end." James set up the ropes that managed the queue in the shop for the fifteenth time that day.

"Thank goodness." Freddie wiped down the counters. "Hopefully, things will be slow, so we can close up a bit early."

"I hope we don't have to close up early." Tessa carried out another tray of strawberry tarts. "If we don't get our typical Saturday evening rush, I've over baked."

Evelyn followed her through the door carrying a tray of mini pavlovas. "Yeah, I finally mastered these impossible desserts, and I want to watch them fly off the shelves."

James smiled at the girls as they set the trays in the window cases.

As predicted, Evelyn jumped at the chance to help Tessa in the shop over Christmas. And then, surprising everyone, she opted to stay on and help Tessa permanently. She still taught at the University, but three mornings a week, she would go into the shop and help bake.

Having a second baker lifted a lot of pressure off of Tessa, whose business kept growing, and it was a perk to be working with another of her close friends.

Patrick walked out of the back of the kitchen carrying a beautifully decorated carrot cake. "If we don't sell this, it's coming with us on holiday, yeah?"

James perked up. "Yes. Please tell me we can take it with us."

"You two are impossible." Tessa placed her hands on her hips. "I'm pretty sure you eat more than your fair share of my products. But, yes. The cake will come with us."

James and Patrick simultaneously fist pumped, and the girls laughed.

James and Tessa had been dating for almost eight months, and he couldn't be happier.

After the stalker incident, they took some time to adjust to what a normal paced relationship would look like. She moved back into her flat, and they would see each other a few times a week, really slowing things down.

The whole slow down lasted a month, and Tessa moved into James' flat, opting to commute to the shop rather than live above it, since her flat held too many traumatic memories after the whole Fraser thing.

James was more than happy to have her move in, since he was feeling like a third wheel in his own flat. Freddie and Joe did the opposite of slow down, and Freddie had moved into the flat within weeks of the Fraser incident.

The flat was crowded with four of them, but they were happy, and not looking to change the arrangement soon.

In fact, having been feeling left out of the group living a mere ten minutes away, Evelyn and Patrick had moved into a flat two doors down from them.

The six friends were closer than ever.

"Do you think the pavlovas will travel well, too?" Evelyn bent down to gaze at them through the window.

"Maybe? But honestly, the rush will be here in twenty, and there will be no pavlovas left," Tessa joined Evelyn bending down to look at them. "They are your best batch, though. You're really improving."

"Thanks. These dang meringues, they're going to be the reason I go bald before I'm thirty."

"I thought we were the reason you were going to go bald before you're thirty?" James gestured between him and Patrick.

"Yeah, love, isn't that what you tell us every time we recount one of our cases?"

Evelyn stood up and glared at them. "You *and* the meringues are going to make me bald before I'm thirty. Is that better?"

"Yes, because now we're not left out." James smirked.

"You are being very cheeky today." Tessa observed.

"It's been a long week," James answered. "Gotta let it all out before you're trapped on a train with me for hours."

"Hours? You're acting like we're not simply hopping over to Paris to spend a long weekend."

"An hour and a half is a long time for me to sit still these days."

After people found out about the Fraser incident in the papers and the fact that Patrick and James had been involved in another high-profile case, this time involving one of London's top bakery owners, their business saw an increase in traffic. This time they were being called in to consult on cases with the police. Joe and PC Davies had a huge hand in that, which meant James and Patrick were often off on cases slightly more dangerous than cheating spouses and cats who've run away from home.

"This holiday will be good for you," Tessa replied. "For all of us. We've been so busy with our jobs, we haven't had time to sit and relax. Three days away will do us all a world of good. Especially with the case starting up next week."

The wheels of justice turn very slowly. The Hudson's trial was starting soon. James woke up to Tessa's fitful sleep more than once in the last week. The approaching trial was dredging up many memories for her.

She'd been in therapy to talk through a lot of the trauma of the stalking and kidnapping, but being prepped by Patrick's dad as the trial approached was giving her a lot of anxiety of having to actually face Fraser again.

The door to the shop flew open and Joe came sauntering in, singing a song emphatically in French. Behind him, Bruno walked in, shaking his head.

"Why is he like this?" Bruno asked, pointing at Joe. "He's been doing this since he got on the fucking train."

Joe kept singing, while giving the two-finger salute. He walked over to Freddie and gave him a large kiss, blissfully stopping the singing.

"You're a fucking stick in the mud," Joe stated after he pulled away from Freddie. "This weekend, we're going to help you loosen up a bit. Get you laid."

Evelyn wrinkled her nose. "Promise you won't have the same goal with my sister?"

Elizabeth, Evelyn's sister, was currently living in Paris finishing up a study abroad program, which was one of the main reasons the group decided to go there for a quick holiday.

Joe held up his hand to his chin and pretended to think. "You know, I didn't have that goal before, but now that you mention it...I think I shall try to match make Bruno and Lizzy!"

Everyone groaned at once, and Evelyn and Bruno began talking over each other while Patrick and Freddie tried to keep the peace.

James looked over at Tessa, who met his gaze. They shared a smile. This life was crazy, but it was their life.

James put his hand in his pocket and touched the small box sitting there, ready for when he could get Tessa alone on their trip.

This was a life he looked forward to living for the rest of his.

Stephanie R. Caffrey is a romantic suspense author who lives with her family in the Midwest. When she's not working on her books, she's a substitute teacher, and loves to write fanfiction. She is a proud marginalized voice in the Mexican-American community. Besides writing, she enjoys sewing, knitting, and cross stitching.

www.srcaffrey.com